UNTETHERED

DARK BRILLIANCE DUOLOGY BOOK ONE

GLORIA BOTTELMAN

First edition: December 2024

Published in the United States of America by Ravenwood Books. LCCN: 2024917577

ISBN: 979-8-9906910-0-1 (ebook)

ISBN: 979-8-9906910-1-8 (paperback)

BEFORE YOU BEGIN, THIS story contains elements that may be difficult for some readers, including:

-Body horror

-Death and murder

-Depictions of anxiety and panic attacks

-Implied sexual assault (not on page)

-Implied substance abuse

-Adult abduction

-Overdose

Chapter One

More saintforsaken rain.

It drowned the cobblestone street, casting a dreary gloom over an already dreary building. For being three stories and incredibly old, it only leaned a little and boasted a basement apartment shockingly impervious to filling with the town's most frequent, murky visitor. It was unfortunate the streetlamps held no such claim. Each flickered out with a hiss, and a hush settled over the town of Ghadra like a drawn-in breath as the world went dark.

Lux felt it moments before it came, that knock at her apartment door. Despite the late hour, she'd been awake when the streetlamps failed, and with the loss of the shoddy, free light, shadows sharpened inside her. Deep in her bones, she knew: Death stole across this night. How fast or slowly it would reach her, she wasn't always sure, but there was something about the way the rain pelted against her streaked windowpane that whispered *soon, soon, soon.*

The knock, therefore, was not so unexpected, and though it was late and her neighbors asleep, the door rattled and quaked beneath its uncaring ferocity.

Lux lounged in her favorite chair for a few seconds longer, swinging her legs back and forth and scribbling a final thought. Around a yawn, she said, "What a terrible night to die," and meant it. The streets had to be ankle-deep with water by now, and despite the summer month, the rain never warmed.

The frantic fist outside the door continued, relentless in its pounding, and Lux began to worry the old wood wouldn't withstand the assault. It would just be her luck for the door to completely give in to its age and crumble during a veritable downpour leaving her with no other option but to sleep on her kitchen table—or worse. She glanced at the dusty alcove where her precious books and loose-leaf pages lay stacked only a few inches off the floor. Maybe she should find them a new home after all. It wasn't like it'd been her idea to put them there in the first place.

A resounding *boom* rattled the wall.

Allowing her head to fall back over the armrest, Lux rolled her eyes to the peeled ceiling. "If you insist."

Swinging from the chair, she left the heavy book on her lap to claim her place and strolled up the few steps to her front door. It hung crooked, warped, and black, and when Lux felt particularly bad about herself, she sometimes thought it looked like her soul turned outward for all to see. Thankfully tonight was a night too busy for all that.

A click of the lock sent the door flinging wide. With only the fireplace from the room below casting any sort of light, it took her a moment to comprehend what she saw. Reeling, she clapped a hand to her mouth.

"What are you *doing* here?"

The young girl was soaked to the skin, light hair hanging stringy and limp, her pale cheeks awash in a cascading mixture of rain and tears. With eyes as frantic as her small fists had been, she bowed under the weight of another: a man, slumped, eyes closed, and a face drained of color. Despite her grumblings, Lux would have appreciated the sight—if this man were dead. Instead, every shallow breath pumped blood from the wounds decorating his chest, streaming all over her doorstep. Death in Ghadra meant money, but this? Lux curled her lip.

The girl sobbed, stumbling before righting herself. "I thought you'd help us."

"I'm a necromancer, not a surgeon, you dolt! Bring him back when he's dead!" Before the girl could protest further, she ground out, "And I mean *dead*, dead. Stiff, mottled, ashen, not...*bleeding?*" Lux slammed the door on those shocked eyes, her heartbeat a relentless whoosh somewhere about her ears.

Blood. She shuddered. "Disgusting."

Steadying herself against the railing, Lux stomped down the creaking steps. Rain continued to pelt the window beside the fireplace, as warped as everything else, and while it hadn't bothered her before, now each fat drop burrowed into her skull and stayed there. Soon, the pressure would grow—too much, too fast. Squeezing her eyes shut, her stockinged feet sunk into the plush rug. She tried to concentrate on the familiar sensation.

"Breathe, you ninny."

She climbed into the chair. *Breathe.* Clutching the book, she opened up its pages, inhaling its familiar scent as deeply as she could. It smelled of musty old parchment and herbs, and on the second inhale, the awful feel of a squeezed lemon eased, seconds ticking by. Her muscles relaxed as tension oozed from them. Rain became rain once more.

Ignoring her chipped cup of tea, Lux reached for the abandoned pen and paper on her side table, and though it hurt a bit to do so, she turned up the lamp. Without the streetlamp outside her window, she was forced to burn costly oil. No longer in a good mood, that annoyed her greatly. Why must everything this close to the wall, and subsequently the forest, be forgotten?

Spewing a few choice words for Ghadra's good-for-nothing mayor, Lux ran a finger down the yellowed parchment of the book's aged pages, finding where she'd left off. A dip into the inkwell continued her list. She'd been running low on too many ingredients for a while now, and it couldn't be put off any longer. Not if the rich of this town wanted to die and remain so.

With a jagged laugh, she scrawled:

Bat wings—BLACK
Wyvern claws—DEW only
Blue rattler venom
Moth powder
Howler teeth—CANINES

She frowned, tapping the pen along the paper's length. That last one would be tricky. Howlers didn't die often; their teeth were *expensive.*

Thunder boomed and the entire building shook, the fire sparking and spitting before settling into a relaxed flicker once more. Lux's pen paused mid-tap. Her unfashionably thick brows met, and she listened. Wheels. In the leftover silence, they rumbled over stone. Very few would brave Ghadra's streets on nights like this. Pure nosiness led her to peer through the gap in the curtains.

Ah, a reaper. Head down against the onslaught of rain, a world-weary brown horse hauled an open wagon behind it. Limp and blue, a hand fell from its cloth covering, bouncing along in rhythm with the cart's movements. A body. Two, in fact.

Lux wrinkled her nose.

Necromancy was costly: the exhaustion inflicted by reviving a soul was nothing in comparison to the overpriced items needed to perform the enchantment. Few of the poor could afford her services, and she couldn't afford to do it for *free.*

The lumbering cart continued on.

That only left one place for the dead to go.

A resounding knock pummeled her door again. "Devil's tits. Is the entire town dying off tonight?" With a forlorn glance at her now-cold tea, Lux strode up the steps.

Chapter Two

Rainwater ran in rivulets along the mottled body.

"Necromancer?" The disheveled man shifted the weight in his arms, his voice breathless with hope.

"The one and only." She beckoned him in. *Death sure is a greedy beast this evening.*

Through the kitchen, Lux lit a lamp in an adjoining room. A room where the dead kept her company and the living were only allowed for the time it took to deposit their coin. The flickering light danced off the body's unfortunate pallor before discovering the shelves. Spreading out like a scarce sunburst, the shelves slanted away from a single window, their angle just enough to notice but not so severe as to render them useless.

Arranged with an assortment of decanters sloshing with liquid, pots of powders both fine and coarse, and jars of talons, teeth, and wings, the display was unique to her profession and hers alone. A necromancer, just as a full glimpse of sunlight in Ghadra, was very, very rare. It remained one of the few things Lux was proud of.

The burnt smell rising from the snuffed match twined through the air. Below the window, several creeping plants shrank away from its path. Overly sensitive, their tendrils tentatively ventured toward the window from the worn countertop again once it dissipated. All these years spent in this apartment and she still hadn't found a use for them, but she kept them anyway.

Lux patted the bare table engulfing the room, dark wood gleaming after being thoroughly cleaned from the previous occupant. The man sniffed loudly, laying the body as if it were a newborn babe on the hard surface. He swiped at his nose, stepping back.

"Payment first, if you would." She kindly relayed the sum.

The man balked, eyes bulging. "So much?" When Lux only blinked like an expectant owl, he gave in, fishing within his dripping, long coat.

He made to drop the gold coins into her hand, but Lux shook her head, inclining it toward the stone jar perched on the counter. With several loud pings, the payment was made. She cracked her neck with the push of her palm.

"How long has he been—"

"Five, maybe six hours," he rushed in, interrupting her, giving Lux the feeling that hearing the word 'dead' would have been his undoing.

She stilled, her hands retracting to her sides. "Which is it? The timeframe is very important here."

His eyes darted around the dim room as he thought, fingers counting silently. "Six. Six."

She nodded. *Good.* Anything less and all her efforts would have been wasted. A handful more and—she twitched. She wouldn't, *couldn't,* think about it.

Undressing the body to the skin, she handed the items to the anxiously awaiting partner—for that's whom she'd decided he was—and shooed him into her living room. She didn't like people watching her work. In fact, she didn't like people looking at her at all. Invisibility, when she could manage it, had become her armor over the years.

As she covered the dead man with a thin white cloth, Lux scanned up his length. No obvious signs of trauma. He still appeared a healthy weight. "Bad heart, maybe." She shrugged. She wasn't a physician, merely guessing, as the cause of death outside of old age mattered little, after all.

Lux peeled back eyelids to reveal fixed pupils embedded within cerulean irises. "Pretty." The man's head remained positioned at an awkward angle, but it couldn't be helped now. Rigor mortis had thoroughly set in—as it must be. Languid bodies meant death was recent. Soft bodies meant warm, red blood.

Lux huffed through her nose.

Turning from the table, she quickly surveyed the assorted ingredients dotting the shelves. Six hours meant she didn't need the howler's teeth. Thank fate.

With a step stool, she pulled down two decanters, a jar, and several small pots before stepping down to haul a mortar and pestle to the forefront. Swatting at the weaving, green vines brushing against her in greeting, she set to work.

"You're lucky I don't toss you out," she told them. But just as with half the contents of the alcove, while they may be useless, they were precious to her. It was the sentimental ridiculousness of it all that ensured she would never follow through on her threats.

Grinding a wyvern claw took nearly as much effort as the dratted teeth, and soon Lux's body flushed with it. Down to a fine powder now, she added mashed marsh snapper eyes, a spoonful of snake venom, shredding the batwing into thin strings. A few more bits and pieces, liquids and powders, and the entire concoction was complete.

It looked like marsh mud, and it smelled even worse. Years had gone by, and Lux still hadn't gotten used to it. She crushed a sprig of mint beneath her nose. "Your man better not have been wrong about you," she told the body at her back. "These aren't any old healer's ingredients; I have to buy them special."

Carrying the paste, she placed it beside the man's fixed eyes. Dipping her fingers into the bowl, she painted in thick strokes beneath the lashes, swiping up into their corners. Pulling back the cloth covering, she drew the required array of intricate whorls from the center of the body's chest down to the navel. Symbols that were ingrained into her mind's eye and crucial to define. A final flourish embellished each hip.

She used it all as it didn't work to skimp. She'd tried that before.

The Rise enchantment, as it was so named, was intense. It sapped so much of her strength every time. Yet, she'd perfected it years ago, memorized it even before then. Still, she laid out the leather-bound book, the one that smelled of musty parchment and herbs, and ran an unsoiled finger over the words. Their familiarity always eased the twinge of nerves that threatened before she began.

Confidence had never been counted among her strengths.

She cupped the man's face gently with both hands, pressing her thumbs to his open eyes. She closed her own. *"Back from Death we beckon."* With the very first turn of phrase, Lux felt the congealed silver loosen, and with the second, begin to churn.

Lifeblood.

She'd seen it once. Confined to a vial deep within the town's Dark Market, the silver liquid shimmered even in the darkness. She didn't know how it was taken, didn't know why. But she did know it was blasphemy.

If the lifeblood were removed, there would never be any coming back.

Her woven will within the incantation's uttered words penetrated the body now, delving into the space once occupied by the departed soul, dragging the silvery substance with it. It called to the soul, urged it back from the Beyond. Feeding on the thick potion smeared on the man's face and body, the whorls flared bright as starlight before absorbing into his skin, glimmering as it grew in strength, and drained Lux's own. The final words:

"From untimely death, we bid you Rise."

Lux opened her eyes and one at a time, removed her fingers from the man's face. The grey skin flushed, again and again, molten waves of heat crashing and receding, only to crash once more. Until, finally, it didn't depart. The bloom remained in his skin, soft and warm.

Lux always felt there was such beauty to be found in the greys and blues of death, but she'd yet to find a person who felt likewise. The blush of life was all that anyone desired. Luckily for this man, it was his to claim once more.

The muscles of the body's neck released, and his head lolled to one side. Several heartbeats of Lux's own and the one beneath started to beat as well; weak at first, but quickly rising in tempo, until it bounded with such vigor, Lux heard the echo within her ears.

And finally—the gasping breath of revival.

"Where am I?"

"Don't move." Lux stepped into his vision, and the man recoiled, eyes wide. "I'll get your companion."

She strode to the doorway, calling out, and was nearly toppled by the man in his haste to reach his partner. Falling to the table's side, he sobbed heaving gulps into his chest. The resurrected man, in contrast, stayed silent. Lux might have wondered after it if it weren't for how he held him: vice-like beneath blanched fingers.

She backed away. These moments brought her a twinge of relief, but it mingled too heavily with sorrow. Nose wrinkling, she spun from the reunion and out of the room.

In his haste, the man had scattered clothing across the scuffed wooden floor, so she scooped them up with a lengthy sigh. They weren't high quality, she realized, taking in the patched trousers and frayed neckline. This family did not possess much.

The familiar stab of guilt met her insides, and the sensation continued to build as she passed the clothing to brown, work-worn hands shaking with gratitude. This gift of life wouldn't be long-lasting, she was fairly sure, and it soured her stomach.

Ruptured insides, broken bones, gaping wounds, a sweeping infection—those were easily remedied once Death inevitably called. But if the vessel, if a person's very makeup was irrevocably altered from birth, *that* Lux couldn't change.

She had an inkling this one fell into the latter category. Lux could stave it off for a time, but his insides would fail again. They were never meant to last this long. Another few years history would be sure to repeat itself.

She only hoped his husband would be able to procure funds a second time. If not, his beloved was destined for a lumbering wagon ride across the bridge, and into the twisted forest beyond.

The dead were forever silent there.

CHAPTER THREE

SHE DIDN'T TELL HIM.

She'd thought about it, but in the end, Lux held onto her silence. Her assumptions could be wrong, and the couple's thirst for life hovered so evidently as they thanked her that it would have been enough to stave off anyone from shattering it.

Or so she told herself.

Hugging the black cloak tighter about her shoulders, she kept her head low as she walked the cobblestone streets. She'd fallen asleep shortly after bolting the door, barely possessing the energy it required to cleanse the table of the now very-much-alive body. Waking to a grey morning, she'd eyed her nearly finished list. She couldn't put off visiting the Dark Market any longer. Especially if last evening's happenings were an omen of what was to come.

Death always claimed in clusters.

The shouts of energetic conversation, bartered deals, and thinly veiled threats assaulted Lux's ears. The Light Market was in full swing, the city's square luring the townsfolk until it seemed fit to burst. Rich perfumes and food smells vied for dominance among open storefronts and cafes; meanwhile, even richer bodies parted with their coins as easily as if they were nothing more than muddy creek pebbles. Lux curled her lip, allowing her hair to fall forward as an impenetrable, black shield against the outside world. How she loathed crowds. The incessant chatter, unidentifiable smells, and the never-ending curiosity directed toward an unfortunate girl like her.

She'd perfected invisibility. Oftentimes, she could slip throughout the town entirely unseen, utilizing Ghadra's engulfing shadows to her advantage. She'd realized, quite young, that such a skill was not only desired but necessary.

Here, when you're not understood, you are feared. And when you're feared, you are scorned.

Not that Lux was complaining...but sometimes it did get rather old.

Considering its seclusion, the town was expansive. True, many still didn't know who or what she was based on appearance alone, but those who did would either bless or curse the ground she walked upon. Her inability to bring all back from death, regardless of time passed and required payment, only added fuel to the already-smoldering fire of their beliefs in what she was. And what she was capable of.

She doesn't speak, they say. She doesn't sleep, they say. Why does she only wear black? Why is her hair unnaturally long? Why does she stand, still as a statue, upon the bridge at twilight?

Didn't you know? She murdered her parents.

"Morning, lovely!"

A hand shot toward her, and Lux dodged it in a fluid motion. Like moving through a wisp of smoke and shadow, the man was left dumbfounded and confused as to where the easy armful had disappeared to. Lux shook her head with a small smile and continued down the dank alley she'd slipped within.

Puddles of day-old rainwater splashed over ankle boots, sloshing up black hose. Appropriate dress called for long skirts and blouses. Lux didn't have a care for appropriate.

Long skirts dirtied easily. Long skirts required hemming over and over. Long skirts made it difficult to run.

Lux brushed the few stray drops that clung to her billowing, knee-length skirt before they could be swallowed into the fabric. With her lace blouse buttoned at her throat, cinched tightly beneath a corset, hose and boots, at least one rumor contained some merit: she did possess a fondness for the color black.

Though the brick-and-mortar buildings leaned toward her, shadowing her path and confining the smells of mildew and spoiled food beneath their looming presence, Lux couldn't bring herself to mind. Even as there were many hiding places for thieves and other miscreants, the real threats were masquerading as honest men and women in fine clothing and fake smiles. At least those she encountered in these alleyways didn't possess the time-consuming luxury of ulterior motives.

Aside from *them*.

The Shield. Ghadra's guards. Obeying all orders without question, they were ruthless lackeys who didn't require direct bidding from the mayor to take matters into their own hands. The townsfolk were spoon-fed promises of protection, a *shield* against the overrun mess that was the rest of the world, but she'd heard rumblings ever since she'd been cast out onto her own two feet that they did a better job at keeping people *in* than out.

Lux skipped over to another alley as two of the uniformed men tackled a figure she could hardly see. A long blade clattered to the ground amidst the scuffle before a knock to the head dropped the victim to his knees. *Foolish of him to put himself in their path*. She frowned and pushed it from her mind before she could think of helping him. She could hold her own for a short time if needed, but it certainly wasn't worth bringing their wrath upon herself. The ability to administer a well-placed kick to the ankles had always come second nature to her, helped by the fact she was already quite close to the ground. Any other claim to skill had been harvested from spying on groups of children play-fighting in company she hadn't been welcomed in.

No matter. She'd always learned best on her own.

Lux swiveled toward the abrupt arrival of hissed conversations, blood-sworn contracts, and open threats caressing her ears, any thoughts of the Shield vanishing on the choking breeze. The Dark Market. Exiting the alley, she surveyed the square and discovered it bleak—as always. Sagging roofs, hanging hinges, crumbled brick, rust, and termite-infested wood. Even the few struggling rays of sunlight skipped over the cobblestones here, seeking a more worthy venue. Muted grey clouds hung low in their stead. They pushed into every space that wasn't already filled with acrid smoke.

Lux sidled up to the first dilapidated booth, careful not to spend any more time than necessary in her perusal. It never served to appear eager when studying the Dark Market's wares. She dropped her shoulders.

She'd stumbled upon this place by accident as a child. Five years old and chasing Ghadra's mangiest, yellow cat, she'd abandoned the Light Market and her parents' sides in her quick pursuit. She never forgot the smells: toxic metals and burning hair. She'd breathed in deep as eyes widened with unrelenting awe. Aside from a few side-long glances, people had paid her little mind, too busy furtively going about their indelicate business to dismantle the puzzle of a child in their midst.

That was when she'd first seen it.

Lifeblood.

Like purest starlight, it had twinkled at her from the deep corner of a worn and blackened booth. And, as any curious child would, she'd stretched out her fingers.

"Lookie here! If it isn't Ghadra's little death-chaser."

The memory fled.

Lux tracked the voice to the side of a rickety table filled with tins of teeth. Smudged and messily written, the identification cards slapped on them were difficult to read: *Dog. Cat. Horse. Wolf. Howler.* Lux picked up the howler canine, pressing it between her fingers. "This is fake, Finias."

He actually possessed the gall to appear affronted. With a swipe of his hairy hand, he snatched the tooth from her fingers. "No, it isn't!"

She rolled her eyes, picking up another. With a little added effort, she crushed it in her palm. "Do you have any idea how long it takes to grind a real howler tooth?" His eyes betrayed that, indeed, he did not. "Where are they? I know you have them."

Finias's stare narrowed a fraction, the conman within warring with his conscience. He growled, defeated. "Fine." Bending at the knees, he fished beneath the table, bringing forth a worn black box. "It's all I got. I swear."

Four. *Four?* "This is all? When will you get more?" This wouldn't be enough to last the month. And at the extent the mayor's family imbibed in their clandestine activities...

"I don't see you out there laying traps for the beasts, so you can quit the temper. I'll get more when I get more."

"Let's hope you don't die before then."

Finias huffed a wheezing laugh, rattling his chest in wet rasps, the meaning behind her words not lost on him. "I don't have the gold for your services, Necromancer. I'll happily be swallowed by the trees when it's my time." She frowned until he added, "Twenty silvdans?"

"Ten, you conniving scoundrel!"

Twelve fewer silvdans later, Lux bid Finias farewell. His laugh had bothered her. A permanent entry into the nameless forest flanking Ghadra's western edge didn't seem far off. She wouldn't miss the man himself—he was a perfect cheat—but he was the only merchant who maintained her supply of howler teeth. Her brow furrowed over the impending obstacle.

One item down and many more than she'd like to go, a hushed conversation found her from two stalls down.

"Stabbed, they said. Both of them. Can you believe it? That's three now." The greasy-haired man's attempted whisper carried on the smoky breeze for all to hear.

"Saints above, devil below." The woman signed a cross over bony shoulders. Leaning over her booth, long nails clawed for more information. "What of the eyes?"

The man's gaze swept over her, absorbing the openly eager face before him. He grinned. "Slit. Just as before."

She clapped her hands with a delighted gasp. "How tragic! A serial murderer in our midst." With a hooded glance about the square, as if the assailant lurked within the shadows, she leaned in again. "Do they have a clue who it might be?"

With hands placed strategically on either side of the woman's own, he moved within an inch of her. "A bloodied dagger. And a trail of red. Whoever it is, they didn't walk away unscathed this time."

With a puffed exhale and a sweeping tongue across her teeth, the woman gripped the hands beside hers. Lux knew she wouldn't be getting further gossip from the pair any longer—at least not of a variety of any interest to her. When they abandoned the stall for a more private venue, she muttered an oath beneath her breath.

That woman sold the particular bat wings she needed.

With a glance around to ensure no one paid her any mind, she hurried to the booth, tucking several bags of wings within her purse. Concealing the coin from passerby, she placed a more than fair amount within eyesight of the seller should she return from the direction she exited. Lux turned to move on.

A hand clapped painfully upon her shoulder. "This isn't the Light here, girl. I'll cut off your thieving fingers before you can run."

Lux shut her eyes. How she hated the living. With a resigned sigh, she dug carefully sharpened nails into the hand clamping down on her. When he yelped, loosening his excruciating grip, she spun, landing a kick to his knee with her booted heel. The brusque man dropped with a thud onto the injured limb.

She leaned over him. "Cut off my fingers? Use some imagination, man. That vendor abandoned her booth, and what's on it is ripe for the picking as far as the rules go. Touch me again, I'll next dig my nails into your throat. And I'll gladly refuse to bring you back."

Lux observed the wheels of his mind grind through the statement. His lips parted. "You're the necromancer?" His eyes swept over her, absorbing the thin build and average stature, wild hair curling at her waist and green eyes snapping in irritation. "You don't look like much." He actually appeared disappointed.

"The horns and fangs emerge come nightfall."

She turned her back on the surprised guffaw. He didn't bother her again, and having had enough of talking, breathing people for one day, Lux hurriedly purchased the rest of her supplies without so much as an attempted haggle before taking to the alleys once more.

Slit eyes. The two bodies she'd observed in the wagon bed seemed to have been assigned new identities: victims. Lux's bloodied doorstep had been washed clean by the rain, allowing her to leave the night behind, but no longer.

Whoever it is, they didn't walk away unscathed this time.

"Who did you bring me, little girl?"

And would she bring him back?

Chapter Four

"You followed directions. Grand job."

The rain-soaked child from the evening prior sat upon Lux's rough stone step, her golden hair dried and shining. The building was narrow but tall, with a truly awful seamstress' shop above Lux's home, and an apothecary above that. Lux had no markings about her door to identify whom she was or what she did. If her services were required, she was found. If not, she enjoyed her life of solitude. All nine years of it.

The young girl's expression hardened at her tone. "Yes, I did. Now will you please bring my brother back?"

Lux pushed the hair from her face. "If you've the goldquins." The girl presented a frayed pouch that jingled and clanged. "Excellent. Where is he?"

She followed the child around the building's corner. Lux couldn't claim more than an average height, but this girl was positively tiny. She couldn't help but be impressed the girl had lugged her towering brother to her door, not once but twice.

Propped against the uneven brick was a body, head covered with a potato sack. Lux raised her eyebrow in a silent question.

"I can't look at him."

The derisive huff died before leaving her lips as the sudden memory of her own unavoidable response to a certain liquid she would-not-think-about pushed into her mind. She said nothing. Instead, she gripped the brown boots laying before her own feet—and pulled.

The girl bolted forward, probably not wishing for her brother's head to collide with the cobblestones as he was yanked unceremoniously from his upright position. Glowering at Lux, she gently lowered him to the ground.

"Don't glare at me, child. It's not like he can feel it."

"Child? I'm twelve!"

"Really?" Lux couldn't prevent the vein of incredulity from entering the question. She'd have guessed nine, and that would have been generous.

"Yes. And you don't look much older."

Lux wasn't. Not really. She'd just celebrated her seventeenth birthday with a small, frosted cake and a lone, drippy candle a month ago.

Another unhappy memory to add to the treasure trove. Lux's mouth pinched. "Enough of this. Take the feet, girl. I'll get his shoulders."

Huffing, arms aching, and much, much too warm, Lux heaved the stiff body onto the table. This usually wasn't a part of her job. She wiped her forehead.

"I'm Aline by the way." The girl leaned against the table, breathing heavily.

"Lovely." She whipped the sack from the body's head, inspecting the grey skin and fixed pupils. "When did he die?"

Aline had backed away, avoiding her brother's unseeing gaze. "Eleven hours ago."

Lux sucked in through her teeth. "Devil's tits. Why'd you wait so long?" She would have to work quickly. Without a care for Aline's sensitive disposition, she stripped the body, covering it immediately after. Spinning, she dumped her purse on the counter, thwacking at the greeting tendrils.

"Get *off*, you blasted plants!"

The howler's tooth felt like it took an age to grind, but she had the potion ready minutes later, swirling thickly in the bowl.

"That stinks something awful."

"The living stink worse."

Aline curled her lip at the comment, though her eyes hinted toward interest when Lux dipped her fingers into the bowl. "You paint...bodies?" Aline stepped closer and didn't back away even as the mutilated chest and abdomen were revealed.

Lux's heart began to pound at the extent of the stab wounds. She kept painting on the paste regardless. Dried blood didn't bother her so much. It wasn't wet. It wasn't warm, and she inspected the wounds as she worked, looking from them to Aline and back again.

"Yes, it's my favorite pastime. How did he get these?"

Aline had gone a sickly green. She covered her mouth with her hand, shaking her head. "I don't know. I heard a loud noise, and when I opened the door, he was lying there. Blood everywhere..." The girl stopped talking, focused now on steadying her breaths.

"Turn around." Aline obeyed and Lux swept the rest of the concoction onto his hips. "Did you hear about the two people who were murdered last night?"

Aline turned back, mouth a perfect circle. "No."

"Stabbed. Apparently, the assailant was as well..." She let the sentence hang.

Aline's face darkened, staring at her brother's mangled chest. "He would never! He's the kindest person I know." With snapping, deep brown eyes, she flung her defiant gaze to Lux's.

"If you say so. But if I'm bringing back a killer, don't think you won't be staying here until he answers my questions."

Aline squared her shoulders. "You aren't the Shield. You can't force us to do anything."

Lux stepped back, palms up. "Then dead he'll stay. I wonder how hungry the trees grow?"

The ultimatum had the desired effect. "Fine!"

"Good girl. Now go have a seat. This will take a bit, and I don't want you peering at me with those doe eyes."

Muttering beneath her breath, the girl abandoned Lux to her desired solitude. *Eleven hours.* One more and the soul brought back would be tortured beyond repair, a shell of what it once was, volatile and deadly.

She pressed her thumbs to the boy's fixed pupils, stilling her shaking hands. The fire poker suddenly seemed too far away.

The girl had better not be wrong.

EVERYTHING ABOUT HIM WAS SO *warm*. Warm brown hair above warmer tawny eyes, and golden skin.

He sat up slowly, turning to dangle long legs over the table. Staring at the wooden floor beneath, he breathed deep—once, twice—before lifting irises like liquid copper.

"Hello, Necromancer. I wondered how long until we would meet."

Even his voice was warm; it dripped over her like honey. His hand moved across his bare chest, but all evidence of death vanished with the incantation. Instead, intact muscles bunched and moved beneath the gesture, and Lux couldn't help but track the progress. He wasn't much older than her, she decided.

Her throat grew parched. She cleared it.

"Original introduction."

"Yes, well..." His fingers rubbed the line of his shoulder as he studied her. "I remember your voice."

She huffed at the reminder. "Your sister is persistent in her attempts at saving you. I turned her away the first time. You were bleeding out all over my doorstep."

"... You can't be serious. And you didn't think to offer a child help?"

"She's twelve. I don't see how it should become my problem that you chose her door to collapse in front of."

"Pardon me for not wishing to die alone." A tick worked its way into his jaw, his stare making ribbons of her skin, but Lux couldn't be bothered. Dealing with the dying was not—and never would be—in her job description.

His glower swept the room now, briefly assessing the stocked shelves and the crock in the corner, before landing on his bare knees. "Revival calls for this, does it?"

It's just skin, you imbecile. A paltry suit over a skeleton. That's all. Never mind that this particular suit was muscled and smooth and probably one of the more attractive sets she'd encountered. Lux shook herself. She'd never blushed before a revived body before; she wouldn't this time, either.

"Unfortunately," she said and meant it.

"Where are my clothes?"

At his question, she gestured to the stool near the door. He followed the movement, and then eyed her, waiting. She stared back.

"May I have them?" he asked.

"In a moment." His eyes widened, but she pushed on. "I have a few indelicate questions for you."

"Do you often interrogate your patients?"

"You aren't my patient. I'm not a physician. And yes, I do, if necessary." She didn't add that it had never been necessary before. Her paste-dried fingers tightened on her skirt. "What do you know of the two murders that occurred last night?"

His lips fused.

Shoving from the table, he stood and scanned her length with obvious disdain before stepping toward her. Lux didn't have anywhere to go with her back already pressed against the counter. She told herself later she wouldn't have stepped back anyway.

"Thank you for your services."

Turning, he swiped up his clothing, and Lux couldn't hold her incredulous laugh.

"You're not leaving until you answer me. I won't be responsible for releasing a murderer onto the streets."

He spun, clothes tucked under his arm, not the least bit self-conscious over his state. Lux didn't move. He may have towered over her, all chiseled parts and beautiful eyes, but she refused to be intimidated by a naked man.

When he smiled it was all edges, and she blinked her surprise. "I'm sure you'll be safe from any madman prowling the streets, love. The mayor would never tolerate the loss of a prized pet."

Her lip wasn't even allowed a sneer over the mocking endearment before her body flushed hot. *Pet?* A coil wound within her chest, ready to spring forth and devour the boy before her.

"I belong to *no one.*"

He scoffed. "Yes, as evidenced by the good people of this town all reaching the ripe age of two hundred years and counting. But wait a moment... It would seem only the mayor's immediate family possess that luxury."

Lux's lips compressed to a white line, seething. "You know nothing."

The boy laughed, low and cruel. "More than you it seems. I know a pair of rapists were brought to justice. An abuser before that. Tell me what good you've done for this world that didn't require gold to line your pockets?"

Lux flinched against his serrated words, at his hard eyes flashing with hidden emotion. Belting his trousers, he watched her, expectant, nearly *eager*, but she had nothing further to say. She feared if she were to open her mouth, a gut-wrenching scream would escape instead.

"Aline!" He seemed as though he would say more as he finished calling his sister but thought better of it. With a quick once-over of the plants swaying with agitation and a final glance at her, he strode from the room.

Lux didn't move until she heard her door scrape open and closed. All the while the pressure in her chest grew, tight and heavy until she was sure her ribs would cleave in two.

He knew *nothing.*

The crock of gold erupted into a hundred sharp shards as it collided with the floor.

Chapter Five

Lux stood, unmoving, upon the stone bridge.

The sun had begun its hidden descent beyond the town's buildings, folding the world around her in deepening greys. The air was damp with a mist that never fully abandoned Ghadra's borders, what with the endless marshes on one side and the dark forest on the other. That mist clung to her hair, curling it further. It weighed upon her shoulders.

Without tearing her eyes away, she wrapped a long tendril about her fingers. She hadn't cut it for years and now it grew almost unmanageable in its length. She let it fall.

The forest mocked her. It knew she held no power there. It relied on the dead to sustain it even more than Lux herself did, and if it weren't for her, it would be more satisfied than it was. Every life she revived was one fewer for it to feed upon, and she knew it tracked her movements with an eerie, unyielding consciousness.

The dead were forever silent there. But at twilight, when the air thickened and the winds hushed, the grass damp with dew, Lux swore she could hear them.

Her parents.

Lucena. Lucenaaa.

She had been eight years old and only just beginning to learn the extent of her gift. Her parents were ordinary people. They didn't ask for a strange daughter capable of even stranger things, and they died for it.

Blood was everywhere. It coated the walls, stained the floors, and it had soaked into every pore of Lux's skin as she had attempted in vain to revive them. She'd mixed and painted and shakily read the words over and over through tear-muddled vision.

It hadn't mattered. She hadn't known what she was doing. She hadn't yet learned the tricks: sift the wyvern claw, stir three times clockwise, stir twice as many counterclockwise, and blend the lines but not *too* much. So many little things that made a world of difference. The difference between death and revival.

In the end, the hours drifted by. She had to stop; her time was up. Her lungs ached, pushing through the cracks of her ribs with every painful breath, and she was so, so tired. With red, swollen eyes, she'd surveyed the mounds of ingredients tossed and spilled and sticking to the shelves.

She'd enough for one more try.

Lux did indeed murder her parents, but the parents who had returned weren't hers anymore.

Along the setting sun, she'd watched the death-cart rumble across the bridge, through the worn, grass path and into the forest beyond. And when it had returned, her body shook with the grief, the guilt, and the complete *emptiness* of her new reality. She could not handle the sight of blood since that night, not the warm, clinging touch or the rich, copper scent. And from that day on, at twilight, she walked to the bridge. Still as a statue, she stared back at the unflinching, veiled eyes of the forest and listened to her name-calling through the twisted, black branches.

Lux released the memory from her grasp, sending in plummeting into the abyss. Until tomorrow. Shooing the crow perched curiously beside her hand, she turned to stride back across the stone, cracked and overgrown with thick, green moss. Her gaze swept over Ghadra.

Ugly, cold and grey, it melded into the bleak countryside like a wet, dead thing sinking into the marshes as it decayed. Lux hated this town. She hated the forest.

She hated the rain. She hated the sun for only gracing their dreary walls for one day out of seven.

If she looked too hard, she could see the toxic darkness rooted in her soul. Mostly, she hated that.

Her mind whirred anew with images of stacked, dusty books and crinkling potions' excerpts. They'd been untouched for years, resting in a hidden alcove. Transforming to a conjured likeness of murky-grey eyes and strange, slit pupils, her mind replayed what the prowler had said. Over and over, it rolled around in her head. Why did she care?

Two hundred years.

The mayor wasn't a good man. And he'd laid claim to the mayorship for as long as she'd known, but the chosen age growled by the boy confused her, because it was impossible. People would have noticed. Gossip would have spread. Hell, surely someone more important than an arrogant boy of the Dark would have discovered the truth ages ago.

Which meant it *was* impossible.

Wasn't it?

PERCHED AT HER KITCHEN table, on a rickety stool that squeaked in protest with every slight adjustment, Lux rubbed her hands across her face. Beneath the lamplight, she studied the aged pages. One after another—and another after that.

Misdeeds were undeniably rising in Ghadra, and the Shield was to blame. They turned a blind eye to anyone capable of supplying a worthy bribe, be it coin, flesh, or privilege, and she wasn't overly surprised someone had finally taken it upon themselves to do what they would not.

Shame seeped through her core as she admitted she hadn't ever thought about it. As long as it didn't affect her, secluded and cut off from the world as she was, she hadn't truly cared.

Lux shoved more pages aside, her jaw hardening.

It was true she'd revived more of the city's affluents than any other. Once, twice even. The mayor himself suffered from fast-spreading tumors—he'd been revived four times. They were rich, they were selfish, and the entire family sought out only what would allow them to climb higher. They possessed the money, so why wouldn't they acquire her services?

But how old were they, really? Lux couldn't extend a body past a normal lifespan. It wouldn't work. A moment or two and the lifeblood would congeal again, the soul abandon its vessel again. It'd be unnatural to sustain it further.

Not only unnatural. Impossible.

One sentence spoke heatedly in anger by a boy she didn't know, and now an entire new world of doubt and possibilities opened within her mind. It could have been an exaggeration of course, but if it hadn't been, Lux feared there was something far more sinister at work in this town, and there wasn't a soul she trusted enough to begin an inquiry involving such questions. Even her small standing with the elite could only get her so far. Which wasn't far at all if certain members of the mayor's family caught whisperings of Lux's name.

Which was why, with continued fiery fury, she dug through the pages before her. She'd remembered reading about lifeblood long ago, acknowledging it should never be drained—an abominable sin—and certainly should never be consumed. But there had been something else, too, and it gnawed at her.

Lux groaned as she flung another useless healer's book aside. She'd never possessed the gift. Her aunt had, before having disappeared without a trace. In fact, all these pages lining the table in further disarray had once belonged to her. Along with those bothersome plants.

Lux sifted through more books on curing common illnesses.

Her parents, upon realizing Lux seemed especially drawn to the dead and dying, immediately ushered the woman to her side. They had been so proud. A rare-brillianced family member. As well as they should have been. After all, Lux's aunt had been held in the highest regard.

Healing required fewer obscure ingredients, less energy and thus less coin. Riselda rose to become a very prominent member of the community, and it was told that the mayor himself relied on her more than his own personal physicians. Until one day, as it seemed to her child self, Riselda was there, tutoring her, encouraging her, and in the next, she'd gone.

Weeks later, upon realizing she wouldn't be returning, Lux dove into Riselda's abandoned books and pages of notes. Deep within an alcove of her aunt's home, she'd found it: *The Risen*. The book called to her like nothing else had. Heavy within her small hands, Lux had known with ever-strengthening certainty that this was what she'd been searching for inside herself.

She knew every word in that book now, and it didn't have the information she sought this time. Where had she seen it? When had she read it?

"Aha."

A loose-leaf piece of parchment. Odd. She'd remembered there being more to it than that. She shrugged the memory away; she'd been a child when she'd come across it, after all. Holding it to the lamplight, she studied the drawing first.

An uncorked vial tipped upon its side with liquid pooling thick and dripping onto the branch beneath it. Where it met, a winding, decayed hand reached forth. Lux's eyes widened, hurriedly moving on to the text.

Lifeblood: the essential element. Not akin to that of red blood cells, the lifeblood does not travel the body but rather remains contained, well protected by several layers of matter. However, much akin to that of blood, if the lifeblood slows and grows stagnant, death is inevitable.

A metaphorical anchor of the soul to the body, Revival is rendered impossible if the lifeblood is drained from its carrier, for a soul cannot remain in a vessel without it. Another lesser-known aspect of the substance, aside from its silver appearance, is the consequence of ingesting it. For should a vessel, even weakened to the point of near-death, drink another's lifeblood, not only is health restored, but another lifetime granted.

To harvest—

Lux flipped the page, back and forth, searching for the continuation of the instruction. It was useless. It was missing. Even knowing full-well she'd gone through every piece of parchment upon the table, she did so again.

If the mayor had truly discovered how to harvest lifeblood—

Lux's heart bounded in her chest as she shuffled the pages. Just as she'd suspected, this was all the information she had now. It was enough to cause her anxiety to rise to crippling, but not enough to give her answers on how to stop it.

That boy had known something. Lux pinched the bridge of her nose, shuttering her eyes against the lamp and the flickering firelight dancing across the walls. She blew out a breath.

She had no friends. She had no family. Her closest acquaintances were those from whom she purchased supplies every month, and those people were despicable. The longest conversation she'd carried with another living person aside from vendors had been with Aline, and only recently. Tiny Aline...and her murderous brother.

Perhaps there was a way to needle what information she could from them. Imagined or real. Either way, she felt she needed to know their theories. Or, at least, *his* theories. Especially as they seemed to cast a very dismal light upon her.

Lux still wasn't sure why she'd allowed herself to be so bothered by what the prowler said. Maybe, deep down, she'd begun to feel it herself. Feel that she could do more, should be doing more, rather than watching silently as the town further decayed in its rot. Though he clearly didn't understand how necromancy *worked,* and she certainly was no *pet.* Anyone could see from her small home and even smaller pantry that she only charged what allowed her to live comfortably. She never accepted anything more—even when the mayor had offered.

He'd stopped long ago though; she'd refused him enough times. Ghadra's mayor was short, nearly eye-level with Lux herself, with watering eyes and a stubbed nose, beneath which rested a curling, white mustache above an ever-present leer. A mocking smile that often led a person to believe the mayor knew something they did not.

Which was undoubtedly true.

Following her parents' deaths, the mayor had been the first to offer refuge. Of course, at eight years old, she had much to learn. He had immediately sought to move her into his mansion, dumping lavish gifts upon her, and boasted to all who would listen of his necromancer.

Lux was naïve and lonely, and she went for a time. But living within the mansion was like another world, separate entirely from Ghadra. The air was cleaner, the rooms lavish; the food was decadent, unlike anything she'd eaten before or since.

The people, however, were too much to bear. Every sentence held a double meaning, every compliment a hidden barb. They couldn't be openly cruel to her—what if they required her very particular services one day? Instead, they had counted on her innocent child's mind and limited experiences to shield her from understanding the rules of their wicked games.

But it was the repetition of subtle cruelties that left the deepest wounds, and when it had grown to where Lux felt the stinging even while alone, she'd known she had to leave. She'd packed her things that very night, and without a word to anyone, she'd climbed inside a carriage and left. The thought of going back to her home, however, had left her panic-stricken. Images of blood-splattered walls shrouded her mind though those walls had long been wiped clean.

She'd arrived on her aunt's darkened, abandoned stoop. She had managed to muscle her way inside, left nursing a scraped, sore shoulder and eyeing a door that would forever possess a grating creak. Riselda had been gone less than a year, and already dust and cobwebs had graced every nook and corner, but it'd been familiar. It had possessed good memories, and it felt like home. Or at least, it had held potential for what a home could be.

Over the years, Lux had stayed out of the mayor's business, and he stayed out of hers—so long as she was readily available should he or his family have need of her. Though, even then, she'd placed boundaries.

She'd perform her craft as many times as requested, but they must come to her. To lie upon the table just as every other lifeless body before it, because she refused to ever step foot into that mansion again. It came as little surprise they'd agreed to her terms so readily.

With a puffed breath through her cheeks, Lux rose from the stool. Moonlight embraced the streets outside in shifts as ever-present clouds roamed the night sky. She couldn't remember the last time she saw pure, unobstructed starlight. Maybe never. The hour grew late, but the table's contents were too precious to leave in the state they were currently. Even though the only thing she longed for was to nestle deep within a mound of blankets, she forced herself to stack them neatly away first.

A grinding scrape upended the quiet.

Lux halted mid-step, listening. She couldn't tell where the sound had come from. Her eyes skittered across the dimly lit walls.

The scrape came again. Louder.

She tossed the last couple books into the corner, eyeing the floorboards of her living room with widening eyes and growing confusion. This didn't sound like any mouse she'd ever met. The rug jumped, and she yelped.

Something *moved* beneath it.

"Enough of this nonsense." With clenched teeth, she tentatively reached forward, clutched the farthest bit of hem on the thick rug—and yanked.

A set of eyes blinked up at her.

A trapdoor. Its seams melded along the floorboards so flawlessly, she'd never noticed it. Not that she'd ever thought to look. Now, here it was, raised the barest fraction, as an interloper studied her as curiously as if *she* were the one trespassing upon its domain.

She stumbled back on a cry.

"Lucena?"

Her heart skittered and skipped. She knew that voice. She *knew* that name. But no, it couldn't be. Lux bent awkwardly, peering in the inadequate light. "Riselda?"

It couldn't be, and yet the trapdoor flung wide, revealing a cloaked, hooded figure as she climbed from within the impenetrable gloom surrounding her.

Before Lux could absorb the familiar wintry beauty of her aunt, she'd been wrapped within arms that encircled her so completely, she nearly sagged beneath the intense sensations it sent bounding through her. When a kiss was pressed to her brow, she had to bite her lip. Riselda's soft arms tightened about her in a reassuring pulse before stepping back.

"How is this possible?" Her aunt's musical voice doused the room before dropping to a whisper, "Are you alone?"

Long-fingered hands rubbed the length of Lux's forearms sending goose-bumps rippling up their length.

Her mind rattled in shock, her face gone numb. She lifted a hand to ensure her nose remained where it should. "I'm alone. I've been alone."

Riselda's expression dimmed. "Your parents?"

"Dead. Shortly after you disappeared."

Riselda scanned her face. If she heard the unintended accusation in Lux's tone, however, she ignored it, dragging her close once again. "Oh, Lucena. I'm so sorry. That sister of mine... She was always too trusting." She craned her neck back, a head taller than Lux, eyes bright. "You're living here? In my home?"

Well, to be fair, she hadn't thought Riselda would ever return. "I couldn't go back. Not after they died there."

"I understand." Riselda surveyed the cozy room, its bright furnishings and crackling fire. "You have kept it up well, I must say. It's much better than what I had expected to return to."

Lux found the opening she was looking for. "Returning from where, Riselda? What happened to you? Where did you go?" She squinted into the beckoning darkness at her aunt's back.

Eyes once flooded with emotion, shuttered. "So far away, Lucena, it may as well have been another world." Dropping her arms to her sides, she ignored Lux's parted lips and walked about her long-abandoned home. Wrapping her fingers around the lamp perched on the kitchen table, she entered the workroom.

Lux followed close behind, questions spilling from her mouth like seeds. If even *one* would root and be answered— "You've been outside Ghadra all this time? But Malgorm is in ruin. Has it improved? How did you survive? How did you *leave?* Will that tunnel take me beneath the marshes?"

Or beneath the trees?

An extended perusal of the walls, and Riselda spun toward her. "You're Ghadra's Healer now?"

It was almost a physical blow. Not a *sprout.* "I—no. I never did have the gift for it as you thought." She paused, but Riselda's expression urged her to continue. "I'm Ghadra's Necromancer."

Lux was sure her aunt's eyes would pop like little liquid-filled balloons. "A *necromancer?* I cannot... Lucena." Riselda scanned her length. "This is astonishing. I've never met another with this brilliance. Are you adept?"

"Yes. It requires a lot of my strength, but yes, I think I've mastered it over the years."

"Years," Riselda breathed. "I cannot believe it." Her eyes left hers and studied the swaying plants along the counter—and *The Risen* propped before them. "I'd forgotten about this." Riselda walked toward the book now, and Lux held back from acting upon the possessive shock bolting through her. It did belong to Riselda, after all. With careful fingers, her aunt thumbed through its pages, pausing now and then with a secretive smirk.

"Did you know I attempted this? Several times. Never on a human body of course." Riselda's smile faded to a grimace of regret as she let the book fall closed. "It didn't call to me, not the way healing did. You should be proud to possess such a gift, Lucena. But I find myself wondering, what does Ghadra's sweet mayor think of your ability? I'd have assumed you to be whisked away to a seat permanently at his side."

"He tried, but I couldn't endure the sort of people he surrounds himself with. I managed a handful of months before I snuck away. And I *refuse* to set foot in that festering nest ever again."

Riselda found amusement in her words and laughed deeply, the beautiful sound echoing about the room. Lux regarded her, how lovely she was, and how she appeared just as Lux had remembered. "Oh, what a sharp tongue you've grown. I adore it." Riselda rested one generous hip upon the smooth table, running her fingers along the surface. "I've a few things to drag up from the tunnel. Would you mind helping me much?"

Chapter Six

The newly discovered trapdoor, as well as the carefully crafted tunnel beneath, were hidden once again. Lux straightened upon releasing the rug.

Her aunt stood busy at the table, laying out the bags of belongings and sacks of goods she'd dragged with her. Lux wondered how far she'd carried it all. Her curiosity as to where and what her aunt had been doing all these years rose with every item drawn out, but Riselda was an iron lockbox. By this point, Lux wasn't sure there *was* a key.

Riselda caught her eye on more than one occasion, but she'd only smiled. Food, coins, and clothing gave way to corked vials and pots with fused lids. A long, bone knife was drawn next, followed by a coal-black axe Lux couldn't believe hadn't torn the worn bag to bits.

"Saints above, Riselda. Were you lost to the wilderness for a time?" Lux threaded the words with good-natured humor, curating her language, but truly, she wanted to know what need for an *axe* could her aunt have had.

Riselda smiled, patting the weapon fondly. "You'd be surprised." Then flicking her gaze to Lux, she frowned. "You look exhausted, with the biggest purple circles under your eyes. I've kept you up. Take the bedroom, I'll sleep in the chair tonight. We will figure everything else out in the morning."

"If you're sure..."

"Of course, Lucena. Good night."

Turning her back on Lux, Riselda inspected a vial beneath the lamplight. It was a polite dismissal as far as dismissals went, and it left Lux feeling her true age for the first time in years. She wasn't sure she liked it.

An intense guilt clawed at her. Had she not fallen asleep to this exact wish now materialized before her? Dreamt of family? Of anyone to care for her at all? She should be sobbing with joy, relieved to no longer trudge through this life alone.

Lux worked away the frown shadowing her face. With a final sweeping glance over her aunt's bent form, she left the room. Her bones ached, and she yawned. She *was* exhausted.

Swinging the door to her bedroom inward, she turned up the lamp on the bedside table, sending the darkness skittering from her side. The room was small. Enough for a bed, a small writing desk, and her wardrobe.

She shucked her skirt, thinking on how two people would live in such a cramped space. Unless Riselda expected her to leave? She couldn't necessarily blame her. Though it didn't stop the sharpness from entering her chest at the thought of never waking again in the place she'd called home for nearly a decade. Sharp despair—and grinding frustration. The vague responses she'd received from her aunt bothered her endlessly. Did Lux, as her niece and only living family, not deserve answers? Riselda might be resourceful, but she was not Ghadra's Navigator. She could never have managed the marshes and come out its other side alive without that brilliance; it was a warning made fact by the bodies lost and rarely found. Not to mention the dire consequences of entering the forest on its opposite end—those bodies were never recovered.

Ghadra was sequestered from the remainder of Malgorm. A land of chaos and crime her parents always said. *Be grateful you were born to be where you are.* And she had been. Until they'd left her here alone.

Lux glanced to the now-closed door, watching the shadows of her aunt's movements play across the floor through the space beneath. She'd not been touched in years; she'd not allowed it. Yet, here Riselda came, wrapping her up, and all Lux had felt was cold. Could she be any more damaged? She stepped before her wardrobe, swinging it open to stare at her clothing. Nothing but black. She stood on her toes and tentatively reached to the furthest corner. Her fingers collided with the little velvet bag, and she dragged it forth.

Glancing again to the door, Lux dumped the contents into her hand. She wasn't sure why she felt the need to look upon it tonight of all nights, what with her aunt being in the very next room, but she ignored the jab of warning. Instead, she watched the lifeblood glimmer against her skin.

She hadn't hesitated that day in the Dark Market, cradling the mesmerizing liquid within her small palms. It was unlike anything she'd ever seen, and she always loved shimmery things. Her mother had known this, dressing her in only the brightest colors.

She had twirled in her favorite sunshine-yellow dress, excited in her find, when a hand rested on her bobbed head of loose curls. Shocked at the touch, she'd looked up into indigo eyes regarding her sternly.

"How did you get here, Lucena?"

The tale of chasing the mangy cat hadn't seemed worthy. Lux had shrugged her shoulders, slipping the vial in her pocket, and Riselda's eyes had softened at the gesture. "Let's go find your parents."

Lux let the memory fade, rolling the glass between her fingers. How easy it would be to unstop it, let it coat her tongue, and live another lifetime. She brought it closer, and watched as it twinkled like starlight.

Whose body were you stolen from?

The thought jarred her from a dangerous frame of mind. Lives were not meant to be used this way, and this drained lifeblood before her was an abomination. She should dump it through the cracks of the old wooden floor, not fantasize over what it tasted like.

She did neither. Tossing it back into the velvet bag, she pushed it far into the depths of the wardrobe. And, because she was no longer alone, she shoved a pile of underthings in front of it for good measure.

She wasn't ready to part with it yet.

Stripping from her clothing, Lux burrowed into the mound of blankets atop her bed. Instantaneous, the weight of sleep pressed upon her, and she eagerly sank beneath it.

To Death, she begged, *Have mercy on me tonight.*

Chapter Seven

"A death-cart wandered by at dawn, waking me." Lux's eyes lifted from her breakfast in response to her aunt. "Two bodies and it left me wondering. Why didn't they seek out your services?"

Lux swallowed a bite of egg, and it slid, jagged, down her throat. "Perhaps they couldn't afford it." She hated the shame the words invoked. Riselda raised a perfectly arched brow, and she hurried on, "The ingredients cost a fortune. The wyvern claws, the howler teeth? And now those are getting hard to come by..." She trailed off at her aunt's expression.

"I didn't mean to cause you discomfort, Lucena. I haven't sought out those particular ingredients in some time, but I can well imagine the expenses you incur." She reached out a hand to grasp Lux's in reassurance. "Curiosity, nothing more." Riselda smiled, baring all her teeth.

Lux could focus on nothing but that hand on hers. Hidden strength pulsed from Riselda, to be sure. A confidence Lux could only dream of, and so she tried to siphon it. "Speaking of curiosity, Aunt... Would you tell me about your adventures these years? How you discovered this tunnel? Could it, say, be used by another?"

Riselda *tsk*ed at her, her silken hair flowing across one shoulder as she shook her head. "Absolutely not. You are never to go down there."

Lux's lips parted, sure she heard incorrectly. "But why?"

"These questions!" snapped Riselda, but rather than pulling away, she gripped Lux's hand harder. "You are *never* to enter that tunnel, girl. You'll meet fears you've never known you possessed, dangers you've neither knowledge of nor the skill to defeat. Ghadra, Malgorm, the very *world* takes and takes, and I will not stand by as it drains you dry. Have faith, darling, and stay put. I'm here, and all will be as it should now."

Lux's brow furrowed. She wanted to argue. To remind her aunt just how long the town had been taking from her without anyone to care a whit. But her hand was beginning to ache, and instead she said, "Speaking of Ghadra—"

"Oh, for pity's *sake*, Lucena."

"No, I wasn't—"

"I don't remember you being so impulsive. It is not an admirable trait." Riselda tossed her hand. "*Now.* How do we rearrange this room so it doesn't feel like we're in one another's way?"

Lux reeled at the change in direction. "You'll allow me to live with you?"

"Of course! Whatever would make you think otherwise? We are family. Above all else. We simply need to rethink a few things." Riselda studied the kitchen table beneath their plates. "Like this table, for example. It has always been much too large for this place." She wiggled it side to side. "Would you like to visit the shops with me today?"

"Oh. I—"

"Never mind, I'm sure you have much more exciting plans. Don't cancel them on my account. I'll meet you back here. At home." With a wink, Riselda rose from the table, and hips swaying, left the room.

"Why yes, I do," Lux mumbled to the empty space.

Very specific plans. Beginning with calling on the boy whose life she'd regrettably revived. Unfortunately, she didn't have much to go on as to where she might find him. Judging from his obvious disdain for her request of goldquins before all service, he didn't possess much of it, and while that used to narrow the range, now, more and more families fell into poverty. This left her with roughly half the town to scour, asking incessantly for a twelve-year-old girl named Aline.

What a nightmare.

Lux grimaced as she pushed back from the table. Her purse exceptionally heavy today, she shouldered through the door.

THE MARKETS DIVIDED GHADRA into jagged halves. On one half, the Light gave way to bricked shops, eateries and modest homes. Not to be outdone, the stone gardens and grand townhomes of the rich converged, hovering tall above them. Of course, then the mayor's hulking mansion rose, paces beyond those, looming over them all.

Lux's home, or now more so Riselda's, ran along the seam's outer edge, steps away from the wall, the forest's path and the Dark. The Dark, with all its taverns, dank alleyways, and homes that more resembled unevenly stacked blocks of crumbling gingerbread than true stone and brick any longer.

Lux kept her head low as she turned down a street directing her toward the latter. This side of town always breathed quietly in the morning, casting a pulsing silence about the walls that often left her feeling watched. Which she likely was.

All those years ago, darkness had already nestled its claws within the edges of her soul by the time she'd grown hungry and desperate enough to leave her newfound home. She'd avoided the living, as their frigid stares burned her, but when the final bits of food were pulled from the shelves and the tin of coins rattled no more, Lux had finally come to terms with reality.

She had nothing, and she would starve if she didn't muster the courage to do something about it.

She had experienced those invisible watchers of the Dark for the first time that day, a creased piece of parchment on which she'd scrawled a list of ingredients clutched in one hand, and a threadbare wrapping of trade-worthy goods in the other.

Irritation swept over Lux at the memory; fighting against the suspicion today would be quite similar to that one so long ago. Much less bartering, more so begging. She only hoped she'd turn out more successful this time.

Surveying the shuttered windows, crooked on their hinges, her ears picked up the soft creak of an idly swinging door, and just beyond it, the first echoes of voices. The Brewer's Bog: one of the larger, more frequented taverns. They served breakfast, though no one ever ordered it, and now its seeping existence greeted her as she rounded the corner. The thought of going in sent a shudder through her core—so many eyes—but she knew it would be the likeliest place to glean information on the whereabouts of Aline and her pretentious brother.

The door tucked within the crumpling porch was nowhere near large enough for the frame it'd been meant to encompass. Raucous laughter pelted her ears through its wide gaps. Lux curled her lip. It was much too early in the morning for this, but gossipmongers abounded this place, and any information could be traded for a pint of the Bog's signature brew. With a resigned sigh and leveled shoulders, she grasped the rusted handle and pulled.

She resisted raising a sleeve to her nose against the onslaught of puffed cigar smoke—mostly homemade marsh grass and much more potent than any that could be purchased in Ghadra. Clouds of it escaped out the door only to be replaced with the next breaths of conversation, arguments and laughter, and she couldn't hold back a cough. It was soft, but it was also vastly out of place, and as her eyes adjusted to the dim haze of the room, she regarded the probing stares of the patrons attracted by her disruptive entrance.

Mostly men, a few women, and one head of hair, the back of which held a touch of familiarity as its owner leaned over the bar in a faded blue shirt. She marched straight toward it.

He sat slouched, broad shoulders slumped, absentmindedly spinning a worn copton beside the pint before him. Lux ignored everyone else.

"It's a little early to be drinking ale, isn't it?" She plopped upon the vacant stool beside him.

Tired eyes met hers from beneath a wool cap only to widen. The rest of him didn't move. He spun the coin again. "Not for me." To prove his point, he swallowed another mouthful. "In fact, it's almost my bedtime."

The prowler smirked into his cup, knowingly, hinting toward what she'd already guessed upon discovering two more bodies bound for the forest at dawn. Her jaw tightened in her fight to keep the scowl from her face. That tactic wouldn't work on him.

"You don't sleep at night?"

"Neither do you if the gossip can be trusted." His eyes roamed over her face, and though their color appeared warm as ever, his gaze was decidedly not.

"If that were the case, go on and end my suffering now. I hate the moon."

A breath of a laugh escaped him, and Lux loathed the way he looked at her afterward: like she was ridiculous. Ridiculous and *insignificant*. She considered ordering a pint solely to pour it over his head.

"Who hates the moon?"

The question, for all its haughtiness, caught her by surprise. By all rights, she shouldn't hate the moon. It was cold and pale and distant—like the dead. But for some foolish reason, a part of her still sought an unattainable warmth. A warmth that abandoned her long ago, and the moon mocked her for wanting its return. The few minutes of sunlight on her skin, however, were almost enough.

"It taunts me."

The boy stared at her for a time, his brow furrowed. "Saints above." He turned back to his drink. "What I wouldn't give for a pretty girl open to a flirt. I'm too tired for this."

Your own doing, imbecile, Lux thought. Meanwhile, she soaked her voice in polite innocence and asked, "What's your name?"

"Why?" Palms pressed to his eyes. He didn't look up.

"I'm Lux Thorn."

Lucenaaa.

Lux twitched involuntarily in her seat. She gasped a quick breath and hoped the boy would be too tired to notice. Because for a moment she'd heard it—the devouring forest—although this time it was different, more melodic. Another voice harmonized with the ghostly sigh of its own. She shuddered.

"I cannot begin to tell you how little I care."

So help me, I will kill him. "Excuse me?"

In a sudden movement, his hands dropped from his eyes, and the fierceness of his attention startled her. Did she really deserve the animosity she saw there?

"For what purpose? Thinking of turning my name into the Shield? Or toss it up to the mayor himself?"

Lux dropped her voice, nettled. "Believe it or not, Prowler, I hate the mayor and his precious guards even more than you." It came across a touch more menacing than she intended, but what could she do? He grated at every nerve.

His lips parted in disgust. "What did you call me?"

"It's my nickname for you. Until you decide to tell me your real name."

"That is by far the worst—"

"Is it?" Her lips quirked. The truth was she'd come up with far more intriguing ones since they'd last met. None of which would garner his assistance, however. If anything, he might stab her, too.

His gaze dipped to her mouth. "I'm a man, Necromancer. Not some dimwitted boy playing in the dark."

Lux ran a finger down the bar's sticky length, immediately regretting the decision as she eyed the result in disgust. "Pity the reminder, but your dead self did get dragged through the streets by your waif of a sister...and required a girl younger than yourself to revive you. A man? I'm afraid you must convince me."

His eyes narrowed, and Lux grew very happy they were in a public place. "Shaw."

"Shaw...?"

"Roser."

"Okay, Shaw Roser. Why do you believe the mayor is some everlasting creature?"

He made a show of returning his ale to the ring it'd left on the bar top. "I would think you'd know better than anyone."

"Why?" It was less a snarl than a growl. A commendable effort, she thought.

"Devil's tits," he grumbled.

Lux opened her mouth to demand he answer, when without warning, he leaned forward, mercilessly crowding her in. His voice cut between them, unforgiving and brutal, "Maybe it's that you've revived him time and time again. Or maybe, *perhaps*, it's because you've lived in his mansion. *Maybe* it's because we would have been rid of the lot of them several times over if it weren't for *you*. Tell me how it feels, *Necromancer*. Tell me first how your conscience has dealt with your subscribing to this terror before you come for mine."

Those final words knocked her like a fist to the gut. Lux took quick note of the number of people now intently focused on their conversation. Her whisper fell into a strangled hiss. "You know a lot of details about my life."

"Don't flatter yourself, love. I know a lot of details about *his* life."

He leaned away, and she shuddered a breath outside his line of sight. She couldn't allow him to see her undone. "Necromancy can't extend a lifetime. I would think someone as all-knowing as you would understand that."

Though he'd be far from the first who hadn't. The fear of her own brilliance grew crippling following her parents' deaths, made all the worse by the continued rumors and misunderstandings surrounding it. The darkness had burrowed deeper and still, she couldn't ignore her gift. *The Risen* whispered to her in the night, and her heart had yearned to answer.

Shaw's chair scraped over worn wood. "Have a nice day, Necromancer." The way he said it sounded as if he sincerely hoped she would not.

She wouldn't allow him to escape a second time. Scrambling from her stool, she stepped in his path. He stood anyway, the barest breadth between them, and she vaguely registered she only reached his chest as she lifted her eyes.

"I need to *know*."

"I'm tired. Please go away."

"This girl bothering you, Shaw?" With a hearty laugh, the brew-spattered barkeep scooped the empty pint from its perch.

"No."

"Yes."

"Where do I know you from?" The middle-aged man rested rolled-up sleeves on the counter as he leaned in, studying her. She opened her mouth only to close it when he snapped his fingers in her face. "That's it! The Dark Market. You're always buying up all sorts of weird things." His expression drifted into one of intrigue. "I heard a little rumor you're the necromancer."

"That's true. Though I don't waste my energy on those who annoy me."

Hazel eyes creased at their corners as the man smiled. "Let this one go." He inclined his head toward Shaw. "He's always brooding. Have a seat, I'll buy you a drink." He patted the bar top before her vacated space.

"I don't drink alcohol."

"Breakfast?"

"I've already eaten, thanks." Not that she'd ever touch a bite of food that came from this place.

The barkeep laughed. "Fine. I guess I've got nothing to keep you here."

Lux made to reply, something like "You certainly don't," when she noticed the absence of warmth at her side. Whipping her gaze through the Bog's expanse, she glimpsed a flash of blue as it disappeared out the front door.

"Damn it all." Ignoring the barkeep's calls, she weaved through the growing crowd.

The following lungful of clean air did little to ease the ache in her chest. Shaw had vanished. Cracked cobblestones branched off into foul-smelling alleyways, and he could have gone any number of ways. She puffed a breath through her cheeks, kicking out and missing a rock as she stepped down from the tavern's entryway. She was irritated with herself for allowing him to slip away so easily.

That blathering barkeep. Seeing no help for it, she chose to continue following the street. Maybe she'd get lucky again.

Midmorning approached and thin clouds coated the sky, hinting of sunshine once midday ascended. Even the promise of it brought a smile to her lips despite her annoyance over what occurred in the Brewing Bog. Face upturned to still-hidden sunlight, she startled at the sound of rocks skittering over stone. When midnight skirts swished in the corner of her eye, she spun. Ebony hair disappeared around the bend.

Riselda?

Shops on this side of town would offer nothing she'd ever want to lay her head upon. Surely Riselda must know that? Before she could think otherwise, her feet changed direction, following her aunt.

Skulking through the alley, spying on Riselda, left Lux feeling like the worst sort of miscreant. Head held high, shoulders back, her aunt's blue skirts sashayed as her hips swayed with every step. She certainly appeared as if she meant to be here rather than refurbishing their home as she'd led Lux to believe.

A mound of trash offered a perfect, if not odorous, hiding place when Riselda suddenly stopped before a descending basement door. Lux dove behind it as her aunt's head swiveled, scraping her knee and landing her palm in something that squelched. She barely suppressed the gag. She readjusted as best she could, neck screaming in protest, her heartbeat loud in her ears.

A fist upon wood echoed against the crumbling mortar around them only to be followed by a screech as rusted hinges ground open. Lux breathed as softly as she could, hoping to pick up conversation, but was met with only silence. She didn't trust herself to measure time correctly with her pulse so wild; she counted out several minutes before peeking around the piled garbage.

The alley had emptied.

Riselda must have gone inside.

Lux bit at her lip, indecision drawn in every line of her crouch. Self-preservation warred with curiosity. What could her aunt possibly desire in the Dark after spending so long away from home? That question, along with how easily she'd maneuvered away from Lux over breakfast, led her to believe it to be something unsavory.

Before the cautious half of her head could overrule, she crept forward, keeping close to the wall. Muscles tense, she discovered slime-coated stone steps leading toward a basement entrance. But the door was closed. Lux's heart plummeted with disappointment, though it battled a little with the relief over not finding her aunt's angry gaze glaring up at her. She wasn't sure how she'd talk herself around why she'd followed Riselda here.

Lux pivoted only to pause partway. A glimmer snagged her eyes.

A window? Very few of these buildings possessed functional ones, and those that did overlook the street. This window not only faced the dim alley, but it rested just inches off the stone path. Shoddily shuttered, Lux caught the glimmer again as it leaked through the cracked wood.

She crept forward, intrigued.

Candlelight. Through the shutters, she could see they lined the planked walls in dripping sconces, and the resulting shadows danced over a large desk and even larger worktable. An old, bent woman, a wart her only adornment, dug carefully through a chest in the corner of the room. Riselda watched on, fingers drumming a silent tempo beside a bubbling red liquid puffing fumes from its beaker.

It wasn't the only one.

The entire workspace was a mess of transparent tubing, glass beakers and flickering flames. The old crone was some form of alchemist. She must be. Riselda sighed, voicing a question Lux couldn't hear. Judging from the eye roll at the answer received, her aunt wasn't pleased. She appeared in a hurry to be done with this particular errand and the old woman's snail-pace wasn't helping.

Finally, the alchemist straightened. Or rather, she unbent herself slightly, with a small item tucked carefully within her hand that Lux couldn't see no matter how she strained her eyes through the cracks. Riselda lit with a palpable eagerness and reached greedily toward the woman, gripping the small vial deposited in her palm as if it were a pound of purest gold.

Though a staggering pound of gold is what it appeared to cost, as her aunt proceeded to count the mass of goldquins into the alchemist's awaiting purse. How could such a tiny vial be worth so much? What did it do?

Lux burned with curiosity, gaze fixed on the bubbling, steaming liquids with ever-increasing interest. How she'd love to sneak inside and explore...

A door's old hinges screeched.

Lux lurched, scrambling back, her aunt nowhere to be seen in the basement room. Which meant—

With a panicked whine, Lux scanned the nearest buildings, her pile of trash mocking from far away. She would be caught. Absolutely. What could be her excuse? Her legs pedaled backward all their own; maybe she should run? But no. *Wait.* A narrow doorway materialized. One tucked within the shadows along the building abutting the alchemist's. Thank fate. Lux hurtled forward, praying to find it unlocked.

She shoved against it once. It didn't give. Not a bit.

This is it. What lie will you spin now? But her mind had thickened to sludge.

When her sweat-drenched hands grasped the handle a second time, she closed her eyes. *Please!* she begged.

And toppled headlong into the gloom.

The latch snicked closed beneath her palms, her forehead finding the worn door a heartbeat later. Against it, her breath huffed in relief until a strangled laugh replaced it. *This is why you stay out of what doesn't concern you.*

She pushed from the door.

There wasn't even a moment to react before her chest collided with the rough wood. Instead of her brow, her cheek scraped along the grain. Lux scrabbled rather than shouted, her nails coming round her shoulder, searching for vulnerable skin, but the forearm shoved against her neck was covered and unyielding.

A hand gripping a knife encircled her wrist. Before she could continue her attempts, it flattened her palm beside her cheek. A knee met the back of her thigh. Lux was losing, and badly, but before she could decide if she should scream, breath brushed her ear.

"You are *psychotic.*"

Shaw Roser. Lux's eyes widened at the glimmer of his blade beside her head. It couldn't be possible for so much ill luck. She wasn't religious, but clearly, she'd angered *something.* She pushed back against him, one last test, but his forearm sent her neck pulsing, his knee driving a hot ache into her thigh.

"Get *off* me, you lout!"

His response was to lean in closer. Lux could hardly breathe between his body and the door; she was so angry she thought flame would lick across her skin.

"Explanations first, Necromancer. Though I think I shouldn't believe anything out of that mouth."

A headache brewed behind her eyes, her thigh and wrist gone numb. She wanted to rake her nails along his face and see what he thought of *that* explanation. Instead, she gritted her teeth and said, "I didn't follow you. I'm hiding, you blasted idiot. Maybe you should utilize that lock if you wish to keep out the world."

His answering scoff blew across her cheek. "Hiding from who?"

"My aunt."

"I thought you didn't have family."

Didn't know the details of her life, indeed. With renewed fury, she struggled against him, her free hand searching for any revealed part. But all that earned was the freedom of her neck as her other palm met the door. Lux's teeth ached from the grit. "I didn't think I did either."

There it was—the force against her wrists alleviating by the barest fraction. She used it, wrenching her hands down. Spinning in his arms, she made to duck, and it might even have worked—if the chilled flat of a blade hadn't frozen her in place. Shaw tipped her chin upward with a careful pressure.

Lux's gaze lifted along with the knife, defiant. She glared up at him, noting his cheekbones tinged with color and how his eyes snapped with pent fire. It appeared she'd caught him in the process of undressing, and her attention dipped to his unbuttoned throat. Heat sang along her skin, and with her back pressed to the door as it was, she couldn't prevent the look of bewilderment from washing across her features.

"Lie to me, Necromancer, and I will never forget."

I should have left you for the trees. "It is no lie."

His eyes searched hers, and she let him find his truth there. Abruptly, the chill disappeared from her jaw. The knife returned to his side. "Get out of my apartment."

"Wait—"

"Damn it *all*." The blade moved, and Lux flinched, but he only sheathed it. "I will pick you up and toss you out, *Lux Thorn*."

Eyes narrowing over that idea, she unwound the purse from her wrist and held the bag toward him. His gaze flicked from it to her and back again. His fingers twitched at his side.

"It's what Aline paid me. Increased threefold. I want your information. All of it. And then I want you to stop murdering people."

Shaw burst into laughter.

Lux frowned, dropping her hand.

"Do you think I'm so easily bought? I don't need your money." He strode to the door, unlatching it and throwing it open. "Now *go*."

"Fine. I will." Lux looped the purse around her arm. "*After* you tell me what you think you know."

Exasperated, Shaw ran his fingers through his hair, leaving it tousled to one side. "Think? I have record of it."

"You do? May I see it?"

"No, you may not."

"Why are you so difficult? I've already explained my limitations. If he has lived this long, it's not merely because of me."

"Not merely, maybe. Though he should have stayed dead several times over now."

"So should you."

Shaw's lips thinned, his jaw hardening until he spun on his heel and strode down the dark hall. Lux debated for a second more before she ran after him.

His apartment seemed comprised of nothing but crumbling brick and warped wood. Lux eyed the bowed ceiling with unease. But it was clean, and it smelled of cinnamon and tea leaves; two things she'd always thought of as warm. Turning up the lamp on his bedside table, he caught sight of her trailing in his wake.

"Turn around."

She huffed but did as commanded. His bedroom was smaller than hers and even less decorated. Odd splotches of color marked the old wood; she frowned over their possible purpose. The scrape and slide of something being unearthed went on behind her for some time until Lux again felt warmth at her back. She braved to turn without his order and was rewarded.

He handed her a limp journal, frayed along its edges.

"My great-great grandfather's. He worked for the mayor for a time, and when that old cretin's ambitions delved into the unnatural, he started taking note. According to this," Shaw tapped his finger against the scarred cover, "he will be celebrating his two hundred and twenty-seventh birthday this year."

Lux's jaw dropped. "How?"

"My guess? Lifeblood. Whatever else could it be?"

"You know of its uses?" A stone dropped in her stomach. "How could anyone do something so despicable? Draining another's lifeblood is sick, inhumane, and *unforgivable*."

Shaw visibly twitched before his eyes shuttered. Prying the book from her fingers, his opposite hand gripped her wrist. From there, he led her from his bedroom with sure, silent steps. Lux stumbled, too flabbergasted that he'd the audacity to touch her again and unsure what she'd said now to upset him. If anything, she'd *agreed* with him.

Before he could push her out of his home entirely, she spun. "Why do you slit their eyes?"

Shaw blinked his own. "Because they don't deserve to see the afterlife. Even if it is Hell."

And just like that Lux was left standing in the alley, a worn door an inch from her nose.

CHAPTER EIGHT

Her stomach rumbled and Lux pressed a hand to it, the heavy purse still dangling from her wrist. She felt like a fool for her overconfidence in Shaw's wish for money. Maybe she'd become jaded after all, following her experiences with the elite sprawled out like fat cats within Ghadra's walls.

Crossing over into the wealthier side of town, Lux decided to brave an eatery and its crowd. She needed more time. More time to deliberate over her aunt's mysterious whereabouts in addition to the mayor's guzzling of drained lifeblood, and she didn't feel she could do that in Riselda's presence.

She scanned the streets. It was midweek. The Markets slowed, and it appeared if she must eat a meal surrounded by people, today was a good day for it. A carriage ambled past, and Lux moved further against the cold buildings, her eyes locked on the least threatening café that came to mind: The Blooming Begonia.

The painted sign swung in the breeze, an aged bell tinkling with enthusiastic peals. Though the sound grated, she still moved to claim one of the few outside tables. The sunlight peeking through clouds every few minutes was worth the risk of worsening her headache. Sliding onto the iron chair, she eased back, allowing the rays to bathe her cheeks.

"Afternoon! Need a menu?"

Lux opened her eyes as the sun ducked behind another grey cloud. "Yes, thank you." Outstretched fingers met, and Lux held the handwritten menu to eye level as the flower-splashed pattern of the woman's skirt hovered for a minute more.

Lux glanced up from the list of soups.

"I'm sorry. I only just realized who you were." A palm rested over her heart. "My daughter drowned in the marshes. We didn't find her body until much too late, but your compassion, I've never forgotten it. And you, being only a child yourself." The proprietor leaned in and would have grasped Lux's hand if she hadn't pulled it into her lap. The woman's brow furrowed for a breath before it smoothed. "Your meal is on me. Whatever you like." With a sad smile and a swipe of wet cheeks, she hurried into the Begonia's inside.

A man's shout distracted Lux before she could attempt to place the memory of the woman's dead child. Down the street from the café sat a shop, though she fought to remember what it sold. The commotion coming from it, however, told her whatever it had been, was surely destroyed. Glass continued to shatter, mingling with shouted curses and grunted oaths.

Struggling to peer above the heads that continued to materialize, Lux finally stood on her uneven chair. A risky move, that. She tightened her core against its attempts at removing her from her perch and hissed.

The Shield. Their white uniforms were completed with sleek, brown batons, though she knew the simple garb concealed much more. They currently wielded their weapons without mercy against an aging man whom they'd dragged onto the street.

How strange. They didn't often cause this sort of public display on the Light side of town. They were growing bolder—and more vicious. The man fell to his knees when the blow to his back found its mark, his spectacles skittering across the cobblestones. Another kick to the gut and he rolled to his side with a pitiful groan. An arm raised with brutal intent.

They would kill him.

Lux sprinted down the street before she realized she'd given her legs permission to move. She hated how her heart bounded as curious eyes followed her. She hated how cold sweat trickled down her neck as the looming guards turned to take her measure. She *hated* blood.

What am I doing? But the thought came too late.

The elderly man laid gasping and bent at her feet, a red stream trickling from his mouth and ear, puddling beneath him. Lux wrinkled her nose but surprised herself in that she didn't step away. The stupefied Shield was enough to steal her attention from it.

"Can we help you, sweetheart?" The one nearest her swung his baton in lazy circles.

Lux curled her lip before pitching her words loud and lofty, like a true member of the Light. "*Can* you? Perhaps if you've a time-turning tonic in those uniforms of yours. My afternoon is ruined because of this barbaric assault on my ears! A pleasant lunch—ruined! How do you suppose you can remedy that, hmm? I say, *this is the Light!*"

The three guards glanced between each other, at a loss. Apparently, it was easier to destroy a glassware shop and murder the proprietor in the street than attempt to explain themselves to a hysterical girl.

Resisting, they said. They were always resisting. And Lux was never offered the option to revive them.

"What did the criminal do?" Lux appeared to calm enough to toe at the old man, whose attempt to sit only led to another ungracious collapse.

The middle Shield spoke this time. "He's delinquent on his taxes." He spat a brown stream onto the stones. "And the mayor has been very generous in his patience."

"I see. How horribly distraught the mayor must be over his loss of funds." As if he needed it. She nearly snorted. "Go ahead, continue to beat him. I apologize over my outburst, for he certainly deserves it."

By now Lux had wasted enough time that the streets filled with interested onlookers, with more than a few darkening in anger. Even if it were only for selfish reasons that they were bothered at all by the scene before them, the guards gauged the crowd, glanced to the bleeding man before them, and finally back to Lux.

"You've a dark mind for a woman." The Shield nearest Lux, the one who had spoken first, licked his chapped lips with approval. Lux almost vomited.

"We'll be back for you. Once the mayor hears how you've failed—yet again—to meet fair demands, you'll be thrown into prison." Lashing out one last time, the middle Shield kicked the proprietor brutally.

Lux buried a wince, and the old man retched onto the cobblestones.

Laughing between them now, they turned back the way they'd come. Back toward the shelter of their master. Though Lux couldn't help but catch the eye once more of the lumbering Shield who had regarded her like a dark prize.

She waited until they rounded the corner before falling to her knees. Lux assessed the man quickly. Blackening eyes, bruised limbs. Maybe a few broken ribs. With some help, he'd live. She sighed in relief.

"Did I make things worse for you?"

The shopkeeper's eyes were startlingly young in so worn a face. "Not likely, my dear. I think you may have saved my life." The man coughed a mess of blood to the side, and she twitched away. He struggled to draw breath. "It isn't my fault no one wants trinkets anymore."

She had planned to part with it anyway. That's what she told herself as she handed the heavy purse upon her wrist to the broken man at her feet. "For your shop. Or if you should die." Lux stood before he could protest—or worse—thank her profusely and pushed her way through the dispersing crowd to enter another alleyway.

Her stomach rumbled. They really had disrupted her lunch.

TUCKING HER HANDS INTO the pockets of her skirt, Lux trudged through the streets, dejected. She couldn't help but feel the day had been a thorough waste of time. And aside from pulling very little information from the one person who appeared capable of providing it, she had now caught the attention of the Shield. There wasn't a soul in Ghadra that wished to reap their scrutiny.

Buried in drawing up plans for her next attempt at winning Shaw over, and consequently getting her hands on his ancestor's journal, Lux didn't hear the rumble of wood on stone. She didn't hear the crack of a whip through the air. But she did hear the manic shouts.

"Out of the street! Oy, crazy girl! Out! MOVE!"

Lux dove to the safety of a random building's front as a death-cart passed over the exact space she'd been a moment before. Barreling away, the driver, a reaper, waved his crop in the air at her in irritation before shifting in his seat, hunching forward. The old horse picked up its pace.

And she watched as a foot bounced along in its new rhythm. Blue, stiff, and covered with monstrous black boils, it fell further from beneath its covering. One by one, the pustules burst. Dark fluid spread like ink upon parchment. Lux had never seen anything like it. Just as she had never seen a death-cart move so fast, or a driver so panicked.

She returned to the street, glancing back the way it'd come, and then toward its destination.

She broke into a sprint.

Slumped over the bridge's joined stones, Lux heaved gulping breaths. The wagon had slowed at last, navigating the narrow path with care before reaching the grassy stretch on its opposite side. With another crack through the air, the reaper pushed the horse faster than it had likely gone in years, disappearing into the hovering tree line.

Lux swore she heard them groan in anticipation.

She had never crossed the bridge. Not even when it was her own parents entering the looming darkness. The trees tracked her movements, she was sure of it, and she didn't know what they would do to her should she enter their domain.

And so, she waited.

She waited until the reaper's eyes widened above his simple black mask, taking her in upon his return. He slowed the horse to a stop, and the poor beast was too tired to even blow out a breath of greeting as it lowered its head in appreciation of the reprieve.

"Well, well. The little girl that almost hitched a ride to the trees." His eyes creased at their corners as he jabbed a thumb at the wagon behind him. Clearly having been relieved of his cargo had elevated his spirits.

"I never knew death-carts could move so fast." Lux sniffed at his flippant disregard in nearly trampling her. "And I've never seen a body covered in black, festering boils before. Do you know what caused the death?"

The man shrugged. "I don't get paid enough to care. All I know is the building he came from stunk of jasmine and rotten flesh. Bad mix." He shuddered, his mask slipping from his hooked nose. "I wanted that body out of my wagon as fast as could be."

"Which side of town?"

The man studied her like she'd gone addled before his mouth twisted beneath the fabric stretched across it. "Which do you think?"

Chapter Nine

Twilight found her propped against the bridge, staring into the trees with a fiercer expression than was her norm. Though, for once, it wasn't directed at the wood itself, or even in remembrance of her parents. Tonight, Lux focused on the mayor.

Waves of grey crawled toward her, rolling from the impassable marshes and across Ghadra's bleak walls to greet the forest beyond. The trees swallowed it greedily, but Lux barely registered the damp clinging to her.

Two hundred and twenty-seven. The mayor celebrated each and every birthday with a fanfare second only to the Festival of Light at high summer. Of course, only the wealthy were invited, those above Ghadra's invisible line. And Lux herself, though she'd yet to attend.

Self-centered clod. He spent more on those parties than would be required to feed the poor of his city for months—and Lux had never truly cared what he did. Until now. Because it had been one thing to count on her attempts at his revival being rendered useless someday soon, an end to the mayor's reign in sight, a decade or two out of reach. But now... Now Ghadra sank beneath a man seeking immortality, who clearly didn't care how he achieved it.

"What have I done?"

The trees bent and sighed, lapping at her horror like parasites. Maybe she would have noticed it sooner had she not been so absorbed in her own misery. If she'd not purposefully dulled her senses, her emotions, her mind. Maybe—

Lux pressed the heels of her palms to her eyes and forced the guilt back. She couldn't change the past version of herself. The version that had crawled within, folded about her insides, shutting out the world even as it clawed for air that was always *just* out of reach. And light... Light so unreachable, it may as well have been lost to the stars.

A little of that air finally seeped in now, and she relaxed her gritted teeth, breathing deeply. Her nostrils flared, her mind tricking her into believing she could smell jasmine on the wind. Her thoughts abandoned the mayor as it reached her.

Lucena. Lucenaaa.

The driver had scoffed at her question. Of course, the body had come from the Dark. If it hadn't, his family would have sought Lux out, seeking her brilliance, dumping goldquins into her pasted-together crock.

What could cause such a terrifying symptom? Lux pinched the bridge of her nose. It wasn't as if she knew all the diseases of the world. She dealt with death, not the sickness that led to it. Her breath lodged tight. No, she didn't often have a care for sickness.

She shoved away from the slick stone beneath her fingertips.

But healers did.

RISELDA'S EYES WIDENED ALMOST imperceptibly over her disheveled state. Lux knew her hair had to be a wild mass, but she didn't bother to smooth it. Instead, she rocked on her heels.

"A body was taken to the forest today. His limbs oozed: some watery, dark substance bursting from black boils. Have you ever seen such a thing?"

Riselda studied her as she repositioned a stool beneath the new kitchen table. She scrunched her forehead in thought. "I cannot say I have. Was there anything else of note?"

Lux thought over how the foot had bounced along and pictured the pustules bursting. "Oh! The reaper. He said the home smelt of jasmine and...rotting flesh." She wrinkled her nose.

"I would have to research. Jasmine, you say? How interesting." Riselda tapped her chin a moment more before focusing on Lux with a satisfied smile. "How do you like our home?"

Lux frowned at the abrupt change, scanning the room briefly from the edge of her vision. Taken aback, she whirled toward the space.

Her favorite chair was gone. So was the plush rug, where she'd always buried her toes. The floor of her living room had become engulfed by a thinner brown rug, which now rested beneath a small bed pushed to one side. Two hard-backed rocking chairs pressed close to the fireplace—a matching set that looked hideously uncomfortable and impossible to curl up in. Lux wasn't sure why her heart hurt suddenly. She rested her hands upon the table before her.

"I know it's a big change, but it wasn't as if there was another option."

Lux glanced at her aunt, who, for all her smiles, appeared ready to move to the defensive. "I'm not upset, Riselda." *Am I?* She couldn't pinpoint what she felt. "I'll move my things from the bedroom."

She took two steps before her aunt stopped her with a cool hand on her forearm. "No. You keep the bedroom. I don't require near as much sleep as you." With a caressing hand, she cupped Lux's chin.

Lux allowed her surprise to show, and Riselda laughed. "It's as if you're not used to anyone looking out for your needs."

"How could I be?" She hated the weak pitch of her voice over the words.

"Oh, Lucena." Riselda pulled her in, wrapping her arms tightly about her shoulders. "I will ensure you *never* feel that way again. Believe me."

The fierceness in her aunt's voice startled her. She believed Riselda completely. And yet, she couldn't keep the tension from arcing across her shoulders even as she returned the soft embrace.

Chapter Ten

Lux's strides were purposeful as she raced against the rising sun toward Shaw's apartment.

When another cart had woken her already-troubled slumber an hour earlier, she'd thrown aside her blankets in fury. His murdering was growing out of control. There was no possible way there could be this many people deserving of death in Ghadra.

Though, even if there were, he was going about it all wrong, picking off those the Shield ignored. Because if the corrupted source wasn't stopped, it would forever continue to trickle downward and into the worst of souls. Besides, he couldn't go on killing indefinitely. He'd only die again, and next time she'd refuse to revive him.

She planned on telling him exactly that, too.

Shaw's home wasn't hard to find, as she'd learned the route while following Riselda that day. Lux turned down the vaguely familiar alley, sweeping her gaze across the windowless buildings, and stifled a scream. The largest black rat she'd ever seen darted from the shadows. It studied her with beady eyes, annoyed by her disruptive presence before skulking back to the darkness with slow, purposeful steps.

She shuddered. "Nasty varmint." As if in defense of the whispered insult, a whiskered nose poked forth once more. With a squeal of protest, she ran.

Rounding the corner, she nearly collided with a reaper. Other than to frown at her from beneath large eyebrows and a masked face, he continued to shoulder the body through a doorway. A sobbing man trailed at its feet. Even wrapped tightly in white fabric, Lux could clearly see the perfect black circles as they seeped into the material, staining it with its putrid, sweet scent.

Jasmine. And rotting flesh.

Lux gagged into her bent elbow, covering her nose and mouth. Another body. Another fallen to this same, mysterious sickness—and so soon. She stumbled away as the scent rolled from the home, filling the air so thickly, she felt she could see the noxious cloud.

Her back bumped into something solid, and she mumbled an apology. Glancing up, her cheeks heated at the familiar eyes glaring into hers.

"Returned with more money, have you?"

Lux ignored him, observing the dead being tossed onto the cart instead. She wondered if the body she'd seen the afternoon prior had lived near here.

She could feel Shaw's eyes on her, absorbing her interest. "That's the third one. That I've heard of, at any rate."

"Third?" She hadn't been aware of the second. Unless—

"Another fell. Shortly before dawn."

Lux felt a fierce blush forming on her cheeks. It would appear Shaw wasn't to blame after all. She shifted her feet, trying to think up a new reason for being so close to his home as her practiced lecture crumbled, useless.

"Are you feverish?" Shaw eyed her with distaste, stepping back.

"No!"

His stare narrowed, not entirely convinced. "What are you doing here? I thought I made myself clear the last time you tried to sneak through my door."

"*Sneak?* I hardly—"

"Hello, Lux." Aline's abrupt appearance sported a stare nearly as icy as her brother's.

"Aline." She couldn't recall having ever told the girl her name, which meant her criminal brother must have informed her all about Lux's visit, and, she was sure, embellished it greatly. Suddenly, Lux didn't have the energy to deal with the pair of them. Her sleep had been riddled with nightmares.

"You're far from home, aren't you, Necromancer? I'm not sure you'll get your money so easily with that one." Aline nodded to the body tucked within the wagon.

Flames began to eat at her veins. Tempting as it was to throttle Aline, she decided she didn't owe these two anything, not even her words. When the death-cart began to rumble away, Lux moved to follow.

A hand gripped her elbow, strong and sure. The third time now he'd touched her, and his third mistake.

"Don't go anywhere near that body. This disease is likely contagious. All three deaths have been on this street."

"How kind you are to be concerned for my well-being." She jerked her arm from his grasp.

His voice darkened alongside his words. "I'm not. I'd just rather you didn't spread the sickness further. Besides, who would remain to scar little girls and revive our poor mayor should he die? Again."

His sarcastic blade of a smile was her undoing.

Whipping around, she shoved against his chest. The unanticipated retaliation took him aback, and he stumbled. Eyes widened in wonder as she bore down on him.

"I'm *trying* to determine its cause! Not even my aunt has seen the likes of it, and she's the best healer Ghadra's ever known." Her glare having turned murderous, she tossed, "And I would watch your back, Prowler. Because my services are forever closed to you."

With a mocking bow, she left them.

Rounding the corner at a near-sprint to catch up with the cart, Lux abruptly slowed. The mourning man. He had followed the body only to collapse upon the street's edge, head buried in his hands. Quiet surrounded him. No sobs wracked his body any longer, but instead, his chest rose and fell in drawn, deep breaths.

She approached tentatively, unsure what to do. She wanted whatever clues this man may have as to this strange illness's origin, but comforting others was a skill she'd never honed. She stepped closer.

"Hello. I'm sorry for your loss."

The man's head snapped up in surprise, hands retreating to his knees. He didn't speak. She stepped forward again and patted him on the worn shoulder of his shirt. It looked awkward. It probably felt even worse.

"Your wife?"

The man began to shake, lips thinning as he fought to hold his emotions from spilling across the stones. Until he couldn't any longer.

The laugh that echoed across the street sent Lux stumbling back with wide eyes. She glanced around in a darting panic. Was he mad?

"*My wife!*" He wheezed, sucking in whistling breaths. "Saints no, girl. That was my mother." His loud guffaws drew onlookers, and Lux seriously considered running into the shadows. "Blasted woman. I never thought she'd die. She often told me that too. *You'll go before me, Ned. Mark my words.*" Ned waved a bony finger in the air.

"Oh. Well. I saw you crying..."

"With happiness!" Ned grinned from behind too-stretched lips.

Lux was at a loss. "I see. Congratulations?"

"Thank you!" Standing now, the tall man clapped her on the shoulder. "Have a blessed day." He spun, meandering down the street, a carefree tilt to his shoulders.

"Ned!" The man slowed, glancing back. Lux jogged to reach him. "Do you have any idea what may have led to her illness? Was it slow? Quick? Did she eat something odd?"

Ned pondered the questions, eyeing the dreary sky. "Quick. The last I spoke to her she was complaining about her bed, as always. It makes her itch. And she was demanding her third cup of tea. Woke up this morning, and—" Ned drew a finger across his throat. At her expression, he hurried on, "It was peaceful though! Her eyes were closed in sleep and everything." With a soft pat on the top of her head, he dismissed her, whistling out of sight.

"Bizarre man," Lux muttered into the gloomy morning.

It didn't appear there would be even a brush of sunlight today. With a final glance about the grim neighborhood, now the location of three inexplicable deaths, she slipped within the alley.

Lux perched like a bird upon the back of a faded bench and chewed a buttery pastry in thought. The Light Market was odious, a true testament to everything she loathed about people in their entirety, but the baker's booth was worth the torture.

The poor in Ghadra were growing poorer, the line forging deep, separating the town by an unbridgeable chasm. And now death claimed them by new means. Lux finished the last of her sweet roll. Maybe she was reading too much into it. Perhaps it was spread through the water, soon to find its way into the mayor's morning tea mixed with just a spot of liquor. Perhaps it would infect the entire malevolent lot of them.

Perhaps it would infect Lux herself.

She brushed sticky fingertips across the bench, wincing as a splinter embedded itself into her thumb. She sucked on the offended finger, eyes now trained on members of the Shield winding languidly through the market. A thin-lipped man caught her eye, and running tongue over teeth, he curved toward her.

Lovely.

The uniformed brute sidled up to her, completely undeterred by the fire burning behind her eyes. He rested a gloved hand beside her own leaving Lux no other choice than to draw hers immediately away. The wait for him to speak stretched abysmally long.

"I was wondering when I would see you again."

He'd pitched his voice low, all syrup and smothering, and Lux didn't bother hiding her grimace when she replied. "I'm not interested."

He scoffed, disbelieving. "Not interested in a prestigious member of the Shield?" His hand crept closer.

"Oh! You didn't mention the *prestige*."

Lux thought she had slathered on the sarcasm thick enough, only to realize her mistake when he preened.

Men with brains this dim and egos this large never allowed ridicule to sink so far.

"Very prestigious. I expect to be proclaimed Captain by year's end. Would you like to see my weapons?"

"No, tha—"

The guard pulled his jacket aside, and Lux couldn't escape the expanse of knives decorating his chest in hidden sheaths, or the row of corked vials, tiny enough they would only allow one swallow. She stifled the huff of laughter in her throat. He mistook it for a gurgle of awe.

"Yes, impressive, isn't it? These sleeping draughts work wonders. They go into effect immediately, just needing to pass over the lips." A carriage ambled over stone behind them as the guard's eyes latched onto her mouth.

She snorted. *I dare you to try...*

"If it isn't my elusive necromancer!"

Lux's body stiffened at that voice, though nowhere near as impressively as the Shield's. Muscles as rigid as a board, he sprung to attention, arms flush along his sides. If her stomach hadn't been twisting over the newcomer, she would have laughed.

The mayor stepped from the carriage.

She had effectively avoided him since his last revival, but there was nowhere to run now. Dressed in a maroon coat too short and striped trousers too tight, the rouge decorating his cheeks was much too red to mimic good health. With arms outstretched, the mayor greeted her like a long-lost daughter. She backed away lest he touch her.

"Mayor Tamish." She inclined her head.

The squat man chuckled. "Oh, none of that formal nonsense. Call me Mayor." Lux fought to keep her eyes from rolling upward. "Have you received my invitation?" Apparently mistaking her look of confusion for one of chagrin, he frowned in annoyance. "It is to be a masquerade this year. The most beautiful masquerade. And you have avoided them long enough. I *expect* to see you there."

Devil's tits. The mayor's birthday party.

No, she hadn't seen the invitation. Having been focused on more pressing matters, it'd been forgotten entirely.

Lux was about to concoct the most elaborate lie to excuse her from such a loathsome event when it died on her lips. The mansion was full of secrets. She knew that from her time there, of course, but now, she sought the answer to one particular question.

She smoothed her smug grin and said, "I'll be there."

"Doubtless." Finally, that knowing leer she despised so much appeared on his face. "Now, onto the rest of my adoring citizens." The mayor shuffled away, only to turn back. "I have heard a rumor," his watery eyes watched hers closely, "that my favorite healer has returned from her adventure. She must come as well. We have *much* to discuss."

Lux frowned after his retreating form.

"Necromancer?" An incredulous voice wafted over her. The stiffened guard, relaxing at last.

Lux sauntered up to him. "Yes." With bold fingers zigzagging down the length of his coat, she watched the man's eyes darken—and roll back in his head as the stolen vial of unstopped liquid passed his lips.

Like a marionette with severed strings, he crumpled at her feet.

"Saints above. You weren't lying."

Chapter Eleven

The invitation was a garish thing. Lux held the sparkling, sweet-smelling parchment by the barest edge lest her fingers become permanently tarnished at the contact. She shifted in the hard-backed rocker with a scowl.

Her mind surrendered to the saddened wonder of just whose dirty bottom rested contentedly upon her favorite chair's cushions, or worse—if it was moldering within the marshes. Jaw tightening, she studied the flowery script again:

Please join us in a
Masquerade Celebration
Of our most illustrious Mayor
On the Eve of his Birth:
The evening of the fifth Noxday
Of the month of Mortema

Two days' time. Her eyes traveled over the bold illustrations:

Gifts, though not required, are greatly anticipated

She nearly choked on her biscuit. Greedy, odious man. He had *everything*. What did he expect? A slew of guests lined up with wrapped parcels of lifeblood, harvested just for him?

"Doubtless." Lux's imitation of the mayor left much to be desired.

The creaking of the front door caused her to sink further into the uncomfortable chair. As much as she appreciated having someone in this life to look out for her well-being, this home was much too small. Especially when expected to encompass one such as Riselda. She filled up the space, and Lux couldn't help but feel eclipsed in the shadows.

"Lucena?"

She drew a long breath before conceding. "Here, Riselda."

Her aunt floated down the stairs. "Oh, there you are."

Lux battled to keep her expression neutral at Riselda's appearance: clothing askew, tangles in her hair, a smudge of dirt along her jaw. Riselda pushed a few wayward strands from her eyes before washing at the basin resting on a corner pedestal.

Lux peered at her aunt from the edge of her teacup as Riselda gazed into the mirror, rubbing her chin clean.

When Riselda's piercing stare met hers through the glass, Lux flinched. "Plucking about my old solarium. A mundane task." Before Lux could question her, she added, "Not all of a healer's necessities can be bought." She laughed darkly, pulling a dried leaf from her hair. Twirling the dead thing between her fingers, she tossed it to the floor. "Or maybe they can..."

Lux's brow furrowed, wondering at the meaning—until she remembered the mayor's message. "The mayor requests your presence." She waved the invitation in the air, and Riselda was there in a breath, snatching it from her outstretched fingers.

"Oh, my sweet Bartleby." Spinning on her heel, a grin stretching her cheeks, she strode to the kitchen, plopping onto a stool. It groaned beneath her. "Hush, or I'll replace you too." Frightened into silence, the rickety piece of furniture obeyed.

Riselda traced the elaborate sketches with curling strokes of her long finger, and Lux wondered aloud, "I can't believe he still requests gifts. What could that man possibly need?"

Her aunt turned toward her, eyes softening. "Oh, it is never about needs with these men. Wants, my dear." She turned back to the parchment. "What do you have...that he wants?"

Lux glanced around the small room, taking in the bright furnishings in too cramped a space, knick-knacks and a lone painting. "I don't—"

Riselda tutted. "Not so hard. It's quite a lot easier than you think." She glanced at Lux's shifting form. "Services. Promises. Secrets." She laughed without humor. "Our mayor certainly knows how to enjoy his parties."

Lux was severely reconsidering her assent in attending such an event. "Will you go?"

Riselda inhaled the paper, filling her lungs with its scent. "I haven't decided." Her eyes sought Lux's again. "Will you? I assume from your questions that you haven't attended before."

Lux shook her head, draining her teacup. "I've never had the desire to step within that house again. But now, I wonder—" Cut off as if of their own volition, the words grew heavy, and she couldn't pull them out. Lux swallowed against her tight throat.

Where did this bout of anxiety rear from? Why couldn't she tell Riselda her concerns, her frightening theories? Her aunt had been closer to him at one time than his own family if rumor could be believed. She may have heard something or noticed peculiar happenings.

Lux tried again. The words bit into her tongue.

"But now you wish to experience it?" Riselda finished for her. "I can't imagine it's much changed. The mayor only lays out the most beautiful banquet, dozens of wines and barrel-aged ciders. The music is lovely, and the dancing..." Riselda grinned devilishly. "With the right clothing and your eyes, you would never be without a partner."

Lux scoffed. "That's hardly my priority."

"Oh, but it should be, Lucena." Riselda's stare darkened. "It should be."

Lux pulled her gaze away. There would be no dancing for her. Her muddled plan was to greet the mayor with one breath, place a ludicrous gift upon the table with the next, and sneak quietly into the shadows.

She couldn't very well hunt for the mayor's secrets while *dancing*. With a muffled laugh, she stretched as she stood, then strode to the door.

"Where are you off to?"

Lux paused. "A walk."

Riselda's eyes roved over her face before she smiled. "Fresh air is important. Tell the crow I say hello."

Lux opened her mouth, then closed it. What could she say anyway? Turning with eyes uncomfortably wide and feeling uncomfortably seen, she ascended the steps.

THE CROW PERCHED UPON the bridge, its interest revealed in the haughty tilt of its head. Twilight neared, and the bird expected her. Lux's fingers brushed against the familiar stones.

"Riselda says hello, crow."

The bird cocked its sleek dark head further, studying her. She shook her head. Absurd animal. It hopped closer.

The air thickened, the wind hushed, and Lux drew in a deep breath full of damp grass, old stone and a lone, brave wildflower. Her gaze found that of the forest as feathers brushed her arm. She ran a finger absently along the bird's head. *Twilight.*

Tall, dark, and crooked, the trees spiraled up and forward, leaning toward Ghadra as if they could smell the scent of its occupants, and longed for much, much more. Blackened leaves hung still, unmoving, stuck fast to ink-dark branches that twisted in whichever direction they chose. Sometimes, when the fog shifted, Lux could trick herself into seeing a thin branch curl inward. Inward and out again.

Lucena. Lucenaaa.

Lux glowered at the forest, and the crow cawed. Something was changing. Or had changed? So small, she couldn't understand it, yet so large—

One hand trailed the length of the bridge until the stone fell away to nothing. Until Lux stepped amongst the grass on its opposite side for the first time in her life. Startled, she didn't remember ever having moved. The air was so still she could feel every breath stretch and unravel around her. Yet leaves rustled through the deepening grey. She blinked against branches curling inward.

A trick of the fog.

A trick.

Lucena.

Tears pricked her eyes. Lux crouched, letting her fingers brush wet blades of grass—grass she'd never touched. It didn't *feel* any different, but...shouldn't it? She pushed to her feet. She stared into the darkness, and that darkness beckoned.

This time, she would see what it had to say.

A FRIGID BREEZE GUSTED from the wood like an exhale, enveloping Lux, piercing exposed skin. Crossing one black sleeve over the other, she stood still, craning her neck. Up and up.

The forest edge. She could touch it if she wanted. Her fingertips dug further into her forearms instead, leaving half-moon imprints along their lengths.

Why was she doing this? What did she hope to find? She didn't know. But she knew she would enter the wood anyway. A surge of reckless adrenaline warmed her, a torch to her fear, and Lux's lips twitched into an awful sort of smile, a fragmented chuckle up her throat. Because surely its darkness wasn't any deeper than that having rooted within her soul so long ago?

No. Surely not.

Dampened by soft moss, Lux stepped, noiseless and imperceptible, through the forest's edge. The wood breathed around her. The wood breathed her *in*. Boughs high above appeared to shift toward her scent only to shudder back at her quick glance.

She blew out a silent breath, watched it puff into the gloom.

"You can't have me, trees. My heart beats still."

Her admonishment was met with a hiccup in the air. A hidden smile.

Silly girl.

Lux fought against the trickle of fear down her spine. A trickle that threatened to crash over her in debilitating waves. *Hunger. Want. Desire.* It pulsed from the forest's center, coating her skin, enticing her further inward, even as her insides turned to ice. Adrenaline's welcomed flame snuffed out.

A rhythmic creaking met her ears. Soft at first, but only growing in intensity, and Lux swung around to the grassy plain she'd strode across.

A death-cart.

She lunged behind the nearest tree, careful to avoid the barest brush of skin against its rough bark. There, she waited.

The reaper flickered in and out of her vision as he neared. Cloaked and masked, he drove the horse fast across the wood's edge, into a natural clearing covered in that same thick moss. Yanking back on the reins, the horse tossed its head in irritation as the driver jumped down, pulling the dead by limp arms and dangling legs. He didn't have a care for them, tossing four bodies into a heaped pile before leaping again into the wagon and forcing the horse to retreat. Back and back, until they hurtled toward Ghadra once more.

Lux clutched at the breath longing to escape her chest, for she didn't dare allow it. Not now.

Black boils burst and oozed, coating the forest floor, and the wood released another cold exhale filled with a new scent now. Jasmine. Lux stepped away from the tree, craning her neck, peering into the shadows. Any moment now, and—

She stilled.

There, amongst the trees. Something had formed from where there'd been nothing before. It was grey, this something, silent and unmoving, and the wood caught its own icy breath before it. Lux sensed her heart bounding in her chest; she was sure she could hear it too. And if she could hear its beat, what else might?

The figure stood rigid and cloaked, a deep hood hiding the face beneath. Lux whispered a silent plea that it would pass her by.

Another exhale from the living darkness around her, and the wraith glided forward. Did this phantom play a part in the wood's devouring? Lux shook so badly her teeth rattled. She clenched her jaw tight. If this being were anything like its towering companions, it could sense her presence on much less. But it didn't turn toward her.

The flash of a long blade winked in the waning light, held tight by pale fingers. The figure crouched among the bodies. Lux couldn't see what it did, but it worked quickly, and when the knife retreated, she expected it bloodied.

It wasn't.

The figure rose, and as silent as it came, faded into the darkness.

Lux peered into the treacherous shadows for so long, her eyes threatened to send tears down her cheeks. When the wraith didn't reappear, she swung her gaze to the bodies. They'd been moved, but only just. Aside from that she could discern little difference.

Yet, there must be. What had been done?

Lux strode forward only to stumble, a protruded root she hadn't noticed earlier humped and warped at her feet. Her booted foot was wedged tight. She growled at its refusal to budge and, forgetting for only a second, braced a hand upon the tree to free it.

The cold.

It stole the breath from her lungs.

And when frigid fingers wrapped themselves around her own in an unbreakable grip, Lux could only gasp—for her voice was gone. She clawed at the invisible binding. The fingers ignored her and brushed along her wrist, caressing, so cold it burned. Her tears grew rigid on her cheeks.

A trick.

She dragged in a frozen breath; her lips cracked, raw, and with every-thing in her, she whispered, "It isn't real. It isn't real. There's nothing there. *There's...nothing...there!*" She pulled, wrenching her arm at the shoulder.

The fingers. They slid to her forearm.

A silent fissure crept downward along the black trunk. Roots shivered, crawl-ing like monstrous snakes. The soil shifted beneath her stuck-fast feet.

Only a trick.

"No." A sobbed hitched in her chest, weak and useless. Lux kicked out at the root reaching for her unbound foot. Her boot hardly moved.

The icy grip held her by the upper arm now, her entire limb gone numb in its embrace. The fissure widened with a horrid crack, frost and darkness spilling out in puffed breaths. The root triumphantly gripped her ankle, winding to the knee. Unable to move any longer, Lux stared into the yawning abyss before her.

Lucena.

Her name wafted over her like the scent of rot.

Lucenaaa.

Something broke inside her. Interesting really, as she didn't think there had been anything left inside to break. *Foolish.* Foolish to believe it'd been her par-ents' soothing voices from the Beyond, floating upon the breeze. Because it was *them.* All along, it had been death's own coaxing call.

Darkness curled around her face, cool tendrils stroking her cheeks. Lux glared back, defiant, her blood hot, then cold and dripping into her boots. And though it sounded too alive, too warm, for this place, a warbled shriek filled the air.

Crow—

Dark wings dove from above and into the chasm. Unwavering, a heart met its end.

The fissure snapped closed. Icy fingers retracted. Roots released. And a satisfied shiver swept through the dark leaves that never fell to the forest floor. Lux collapsed, her knees aching and bruised, her head bowed before the tree, and with the shocked eyes of a person embracing death only to be cast back to the living, she finally found the strength to lift her chin. She scanned the wood.

The bodies.

They were gone.

Chapter Twelve

Riselda wasn't home when Lux stumbled down the stairs, reaching for the stool to rest her head in her hands.

She took several steady breaths before lowering quivering fingers to her lap.

"So stupid. So, so stupid…"

Her vision faded to unfocused colors and shapes, the lone lamp flickering weakly. Night had fallen and she had missed dinner, but the thought of food now only sent her stomach roiling.

A quiet tap, and the room sharpened.

A gentle knock came again upon the door. She wasn't used to the type, and especially not at night. Warily, she rose. Her knees buckled, and she steadied herself on the table only for the wood beneath to send her reeling back over the forest's memory. Lux shook herself.

"Quit it, you ninny," she chided, climbing the steps.

The door creaked open against her hand.

Honey-colored hair tumbled into Shaw's eyes as he stood on her doorstep. Eyes that widened in shock at her state and then at the door being slammed in his face.

Lux strode back down the steps.

"Necromancer! I need to speak with you."

His muffled voice reached her ears, and she rolled her eyes. Now he wanted a conversation? She huffed a humorless laugh, stoking the fire. He could yell through the night for all she cared.

A fist pounded on the wood. She ignored it.

Until it creaked.

Her jaw dropped, the poker falling to meet hungry, meager flames. "How dare you!" She charged around the corner, glaring up the stairs at Shaw closing the door behind him.

"How dare *I*? At least I had the consideration to knock first." He quirked his lips as she stomped up the steps.

The landing was nowhere near big enough for two people, but Lux wasn't going to give him the benefit of towering higher above her than he already did. He backed away, but there wasn't anywhere for him to go but out. Bodies nearly touching, she flushed with rage.

"Get *out*."

His gaze roved over her face, the mockery of a smile vanishing from his mouth. "Are you all right?"

She jabbed a finger into his chest. "No, and I have nothing more to say to you. You want to ruin your life, blacken your soul? Fine. Fall to the darkness for all I care. But don't think I won't be keeping track of your *excursions*. I'll discover the mayor's secrets on my own, and I may even report you to the Shield in the process."

Lux didn't think she would actually give them his name. Not unless his murderous tendencies shifted toward the innocent as well. She noted on an afterthought that perhaps he would kill her for the threat she posed. She smirked.

He could try.

"You look dreadful." His brow furrowed as he glanced down the cramped space between them, her threats seemingly ignored.

"As well I should! I was almost swallowed by a tree, *alive,* saved only by the bravest crow." A pang of guilt leaked into her chest at her unfortunate treatment of the bird. She should have been kinder. "There is a phantom in the wood doing *something* to the dead before the trees claim them. And I *hate* that I hate my aunt's returned!"

A look of doubtful speculation crept over Shaw's face, and Lux pressed sharp nails into her palms to keep from slapping it away. Finally, he shook his head, wiping it clean from his features on his own, and strode down the steps.

She sputtered at his retreating back. "Where do you think you're going?"

"I need time with this."

She dashed after him.

Around the kitchen table, he settled into the rocking chair, running his fingers along the armrest with a thoughtful turn of his brow. "Do you like this chair?"

"Obviously not. Riselda threw mine out. As I'm about to call someone to do for *you*."

He shifted in the hard seat, unperturbed. "I see now why you hate her."

"I never said that."

Shaw shrugged, his attention drifting over her in a lazy manner. "Your stockings are ruined. And I think you're bleeding. For sure, you've *bled*." She crossed her arms, and his features shadowed. "Why would you enter the forest? A death wish?"

She ground her teeth. Whirling, she strode to her bedroom. He could stay there all night for all she cared. He and his infuriating questions and irritating observations would make for good company well enough without her.

"Lux." She stopped in the doorway, though she didn't know why she had. Maybe the vein of hope threading through her name on his lips. The possibility pricked her skin. "I need your help."

She laughed. Not a chuckle, but long, loud and deep. She crossed her arms over her middle until her muscles ached. Finally, her laugh diminishing to hiccupped giggles, she turned. He stood just feet away, one eyebrow raised. His expression almost sent her laughing anew, him being so hopelessly bewildered by her outburst. She bit it back.

"Only if you have gold with which to line my pockets." She gestured to her ruined skirt, one pocket torn and gaping, a still-fresh wound oozing somewhere beneath.

An unexpected flash of regret swept across his face. "I'm sorry I spoke so harshly that day." The words grated on his tongue. It would seem the prowler didn't apologize often.

She didn't bother with a reply, and he studied her a moment more. "Are you invited to the mayor's birthday party?" If she expected anything to come from his mouth, this wasn't it. And it certainly wouldn't have been followed by, "Will you bring me with you?"

"You—" She paused, her mind attempting to right itself. "You want to go to the masquerade? As my escort?"

"If you must call it that. I can't very well go on my own. Those of the Dark are rarely remembered, let alone invited to such things." Lux allowed him to finish his lamenting without comment. He blew out a breath. "I want to know what the mansion hides."

Ah, there it is. "I'd thought of the same. But, alas, I prefer to work alone."

"Take me. I can help."

"No, I—" But a sudden idea pushed all others aside, and gleefully, she changed her mind right then and there. "Will you let me borrow your grandfather's journal?"

Shaw's lips thinned, and Lux straightened her spine. She'd go alone. It didn't bother her any. But his gaze turned calculating as if reading the turn of her thoughts, and, at last, he nodded.

"Excellent. We should hire a carriage, though. I'll have the driver take me to your apartment, and we can ride the rest of the way together."

He exhaled through his nose. "I should be retrieving you."

"Oh, I think this route will do just fine."

Shaw rolled his shoulders, and she grinned, feeling sure she could manage the sacrifice of this victory. Before he could scowl much more, likely unsure now if what he promised was worth the cost, frantic pounding interrupted the silence.

Skirting around him, Lux jogged up the steps.

Now this knock she knew quite well.

A DRIPPING BUNDLE LAY wrapped in a ragged blanket. The sobbing woman held it tight and clutched close to her chest, while a man stood behind her. Tears ran down his bearded cheeks as he lowered a hand a second away from rapping on Lux's nose.

"Come in." Lux backed from the sense of heartbreak that billowed around her. Always so much heartbreak—and always laced with a threadbare shred of hope. She glanced at Shaw, urging him to say nothing. With hooded eyes, he obeyed.

Lux entered the workroom and turned up the lamp. Twisting back, she watched the parents, observed as they didn't even look at her, their hands laying the little body ever-so-gently upon the table. It looked so small.

"How long?"

The woman raised her eyes. A gaze filled with so much sorrow, Lux felt instantly sick. "Eight hours, nine at most." She bit her lip against a sob as the man fished through his coat. "We've been searching most of the day. We finally found her. In the marshes. She's only just reached her second year. She—"

Tears poured from her eyes, yet she didn't look away. Begging.

"How much?" the father asked, hoarse.

Lux relayed the sum, and the color drained from his face. He frantically searched again, turning up a button and a roll of string. Desolate eyes found hers.

"I don't have it." He laid the single goldquin on the table. Followed by a silvdan. Five coptons.

The woman's mouth opened and closed, staring at the child as if she could will the life back. Her skin paled to ash.

"We must. We must. We must." The mother rocked back and forth, holding her middle. She shook her head, unwilling to believe. "We must."

Lux stared at the unmoving bundle on the table. She should turn them away. *Would* turn them away. Exceptions were always a mistake: a rule in dark business.

She opened her mouth to tell them to go—but something else tumbled out. "My door creaks terribly. It's been years now." The man's eyes snapped to hers. "Perhaps you could fix it for me? I'd pay you well."

Understanding swept the despair from his features. "Of course, *oh*, of course. Of course, I could fix that."

She nodded and her attention left him. "Put the money in the crock."

Stepping toward the body, she carefully unwrapped it. The blanket gave way to rounded features: a soft face beneath a head full of dark curls, and a little body in a sodden, dirty dress. She was cold and wet and blue, her limbs rigid in death. Lux undressed her carefully.

She remembered that proprietor's daughter now. The one she couldn't save. They'd been nearly the same age. And she'd lain just like this. But it had been too long. Too wet, too blue, too *cold*. Lux couldn't have brought her back.

She wouldn't have been the same.

Lux draped the small body in a sheet much too big for it before turning back to the shelves, to *The Risen* propped just as she'd left it. She allowed a moment for the greeting plants to wrap their vines about her fingers in welcome.

"That's enough."

Normally, she would never allow family to watch, but she didn't know if Shaw had managed to sneak out her front door yet. She gestured them to the stool resting in the corner instead, handing the mother a dress that dripped. The woman snatched it to her, where she clutched it so tightly to her chest, Lux was sure her hands would be left aching long after their release.

Lux took one of the precious howler teeth from the jar. Grinding, measuring, stirring, she settled the paste beside the child's face. Then she painted.

"Back from Death we beckon,
A guide between Life and Fate.
Mend what has been broken:
Time
Mortality.
Through the veil between realms,
shall you follow this road.
May your eyes become mine
Until you return home.
Time of death, death in time.
From untimely death, we bid you Rise."

Waves of pink crashed and receded and crashed again. Until the bloom of life remained.

Lux removed her thumbs.

But, for some inexplicable reason, her hands remained still. They laid there, cupping the girl's face, as bright green eyes met another's. Tiny, pink lips trembled. A single tear ran from the corner of the child's eye, seeping into Lux's skin.

"Shh, you're all right."

The girl calmed at her voice, and Lux stiffened, taken aback she'd spoken at all.

She glanced to the parents. They needed nothing further. Rushing forward with deep cries, they scooped their daughter up together.

Lux watched on as plump, little arms encircled the mother's neck, before her gaze met the father's. With tears running down his face anew, he nodded a promise, and she turned away. Though what she feared he'd see, she didn't know.

Bundled in her softest blanket, Lux ushered the child and her parents out of her home on a threat to maintain their silence. She shut it after them, resting her back against the rough wood. Sure she'd never been so drained in every aspect, she pushed from its surface.

Shaw threw a log onto the fire, brushing his hands along his trousers when she stepped to his side. Exhaustion had stolen the heat from her skin; she wanted to be near something—some*one*—warm.

Even if that someone was him.

"I thought you'd left."

The family had seen him, sitting with his back unnaturally straight, fingers steepled, in the chair. But they'd been much too focused on their returned child to bother with a second glance.

Shaw stared at the fire, his expression distant. "I know I don't have a good reason for staying." He turned back to the chair, grabbing his coat. His thumb traced along its faded edge. "Curiosity, perhaps." His gaze flicked to hers, and Lux covered her mouth against a yawn, her eyelids fluttering.

She was too tired to truly care.

But when she focused on him next, his jaw had hardened, his eyes boring into the bloodied tear of her skirt. She snapped her fingers in his face, and he sneered.

"What?"

"Don't forget our bargain."

"I don't often forget what I dread most." Ignoring her own sneer now, he pulled on his cap. "Until the masquerade."

"No."

Shaw caught himself midstep, shadowed eyes sharpening and ready for battle. "*No?*"

"I want that journal beforehand."

She had errands in the Dark Market anyway. The image of three howler canines resting in their jar demanded her to try her luck at acquiring more. It had been *years* since she'd run this low.

"Suit yourself," he said. "You know the way easily by now, I should think."

She scowled at his retreating back.

A death-cart rumbled along the cobblestones, and he stiffened on the stairs, listening to its path. "How did the bodies appear? In the forest."

"Black boils." She stared at the break in Riselda's horrid curtains, thoroughly unwell. "Just as before."

Chapter Thirteen

The morning faded beneath dreams for the first time in so many days, Lux couldn't even drudge up another recollection.

It had been nearly noon when she'd finally stretched her sore muscles and aching joints. Cautiously adjusting the mussed rug of the living room floor, she'd taken the time to note her aunt's absence before leaving herself. Perhaps Riselda was out shopping for more extravagant potions.

Lux trailed gloved fingertips along the brick, crumbling mortar giving way beneath the black material. It was a cold morning for high summer. Then again, it was often cold around the mayor's birthday. A weird blip in the season that occurred with an unsettling regularity.

She wiped dusted fingers against her dress.

She rounded the street corner where the smells of the Dark Market greeted her first and a sea of masks second. She slowed, surveying the crowd. The furtive glances were magnified above the thin fabric, spread to even the vendors as they hardly bartered their prices, voices hushed and foreboding like the sickness could latch onto their words, coat their tongues and slip down their throats.

Lux scanned the sellers, searching for one in particular as she strode to his usual place. It was empty of its usual tins, the dark wood scratched and weathered. Her eyes traveled the market again swiftly, but she knew Finias wouldn't be found. Which wagon ride had been his?

And how would she replenish her supplies now?

Lux caught the stare of the old woman from whom she often purchased wyvern claws. Across the Dark Market, she hurried to stand before her squat booth, observing the jars of claws and talons without turning her lip up at the hideous jewelry the woman attempted to craft from them.

"When did Finias die?"

The old woman hacked, no mask in place, and Lux backed away. "I don't know. Yesterday. Maybe the day before."

"Was it the new sickness that took him?"

"How should I know!" Irritation dragged the woman's eyebrows down, and she swatted the air. "Why do you care?"

Lux glowered. "Howler canines."

The humped vendor clucked, jowls quivering. "Ah, guess you best set your own traps about the forest, girlie." She cackled, revealing toothless gums. "Are you going to buy claws from me today?"

Lux spun, ignoring her entirely.

"Rude, ungrateful chit!" A spew of hacking coughs followed.

Lux called over her shoulder, "You really should cease smoking those marsh-grass cigars or you're sure to join him soon, madam."

A massive talon grazed her cheek, but she kept walking. *Perhaps not.* The old crone did possess more strength than most.

STANDING BEFORE SHAW'S WORN door, Lux wondered at the flutter in the pit of her stomach before quickly deciding it must be indigestion. It couldn't be anything else. A glance over her shoulder at the alchemist's now-covered basement window made her huff in annoyance. Attempting to glimpse any further clues of its secrets would be a wasted effort. *Damn it all.*

She turned her back on the disappointment and knocked once. Then she shoved her hands deep into the pockets of her dress as she waited. She hoped he was actually at home. They should have discussed a time.

A mimicked screech sounded from behind her, and Lux whipped her head toward it. High above, a child dangled from a fourth story balcony, picking her teeth with a bone and grinning. A second screech left the little beast's mouth.

Don't leave me out here, Prowler.

She knocked again, harder.

Not a handful of heartbeats passed, and Shaw's bare chest filled the doorway, trousers low on his hips. He squinted up at the overcast sky. "It's afternoon."

Lux couldn't say a thing. The odd flutter in her belly had morphed into an unfamiliar flame that not only sent a flush of heat through her but burned every thought from her head. She had seen him in less once and hadn't even blinked. *Fine,* she'd blinked a bit. But this was something else entirely. What was the matter with her?

Shaw finally took notice of her silence. He stared at her now, bemused.

Why did he look at her like that? Could he see the flush against her skin? *Death take me.* "What of it?" she demanded, nose in the air.

"I assumed you'd have come by this morning."

"I slept through it."

Shaw yawned and she frowned at the implication, the heat fizzling. "Well, come in." He stepped back, ushering her through. She obliged, skirting wide of his bare skin.

She found its inside to be brighter than the time before. She'd not realized in being shoved against the door, and subsequently held at knife point, that he'd an entryway table perfectly sized for a lamp. One burned atop it now, and it lit the brick wall behind it, drawing her attention.

Lux felt the ground tilt.

She tripped forward, stretching out shaking fingers.

"They're—" But she couldn't finish.

They hung from nails bent and scuffed due to the force required to drive them into the mortar. She ran her forefinger along the first frame, the dark wood sleek and polished. She did the same to the second, and finally, the third. By then, she could sense what threatened, her throat thickening and begging for an escape, but she'd die before she allowed Shaw Roser to see her tears.

Majestic mountains. A crashing ocean. A vast, red forest.

The outside world.

Lux wiped at her eyes just to be sure.

"Necromancer…"

"Who did this?"

"Lux…"

"Who *saw* this?" Lux spun back toward him only to stumble. Her eyes were blurred and his were so…

Hands grabbed hold of her elbows. Heat poured from him—into her. She'd never been stabbed but she imagined it must feel something like this. She jerked from his grasp.

"I did."

"*You—*"

"In dreams."

Vulnerable. That's what his eyes were. Damn it *all*. "You painted them. I can *hear* them. I think I can even feel them."

Neither breathed for entirely different reasons. Lux didn't want it to end: the rhythmic fall of waves, the crisp mountain air, the rustle of green leaves. She looked back toward the scenes, and when she wiped her eyes next, her fingers came away wet.

Horrified, she spun away bodily.

What a gift he had. Common knowledge said every soul possessed their own. Gifts of arts, manipulations, healings—necromancy. But for many, at least in Ghadra, they seemed to remain undiscovered. Or, even if discovered, then uncultivated. To deny a part of yourself so completely? Lux had tried. Once, she had sworn to never open *The Risen* again, her spirit crushed and splintered by the festering hand the fates had dealt her. But the gaping hole it'd left behind…

"It's certainly no bringing back the dead," he murmured.

"How can you compare?" Forgetting her reddened eyes, she glared up at him. "The only thing you might say is that you've discovered your brilliance same as I've discovered mine. If it weren't for a book, I'd just be a girl uniquely obsessed with bodies, dressing them for a trip to the trees. Look at what you've made!"

At some point during her tirade, Shaw's lips had parted, his eyes grown wide. And it wasn't until its end that Lux realized how close she'd moved. A half step more and she'd be flush against his warmth.

Would it feel as good as she imagined?

A hoarse clearing of his throat brought her careening back to her cold reality. She was chained to Ghadra. She was a necromancer who preferred the dead for company. He was a murderer who despised her for her past.

Imagining only hurt.

"The journal is this way."

Shaw continued down the hall and rounded the corner without glancing back to see if she followed. Lux did, though slowly, and looked everywhere but his naked back. She'd *cried* in front of him. *What an idiot, you are.* She passed into his main room, where a small wood stove sat and an ancient kettle trilled a high whistle to greet her.

Since Shaw had already escaped to his bedroom, she swiped up the cloth on the counter and moved the kettle from the heat. Tea. She'd half-expected him to rise to a pint of ale. Lux studied the teacup set out for his use, delicately painted with woodland animals so real she saw them wriggle their noses back at her.

"Did you get lost?"

She startled, clattering the cup to the worn counter. She hadn't meant to pick it up. "No. Your water was hot." When he didn't speak, she glanced over her shoulder in time to catch his sardonic expression. She scowled, turning entirely. "And I was admiring your teacup."

His expression faded to smooth indifference as he strode toward her. His eyes refused to leave hers as he reached around her body, his newly donned sleeve brushing against hers, before returning to his side with the cup in hand. Her forearm tingled. She ignored it.

He pressed the book to her chest, and her hands reached to clasp it. "The journal. As promised." He backed away, pouring a cup of tea, the steam wafting upward in twining tendrils. "Would you like one?"

She'd planned to say no. "Yes."

With a tight-lipped smile, he gestured above her, and she followed it to the three remaining cups hanging from rusted hooks. They were really much too beautiful for such things. She chose one painted with various birds in flight, soaring beneath rays of yellows and oranges. Running a thumb over their fluttering wings, she turned toward him.

"Have a seat."

She sat, holding a beautiful, empty teacup across from Shaw, and for the life of her, unable to think of a thing to say. Stacks of small boxes rested between them, and he sifted through the lot.

"You have a lot of teas."

His eyes lifted. "Yes." Raising the lid of one, he held it out to her. "Black vesper?"

"Yes, please." He spooned aromatic leaves into an infuser, pouring the kettle immediately following. "Thank you."

"You're welcome."

Silence ensued, the weighted awkwardness of their forced politeness stretching without end in sight. Lux could hardly stand it. She watched him shrug suspenders over his shoulders, his lashes lowering as he drank from his cup. Her foot began to tap a disjointed rhythm, and she thought, *This boy? This boy paints dreams?*

She said the first thought that came to mind after that. "What must you do to bring them to life?" She tapped the teacup's edge, and Shaw followed the gesture.

"I drip my blood into the pigments while mixing. They remain this way only while I live."

Lux's mouth gaped, horrified. "You use *blood* for your brilliance?" The muscles in Shaw's jaw twitched at her expression, and only too late did she realize he'd lied. "I despise you."

"No blood. I only whisper sweet words to them, and they respond."

Knowing he probably lied again—*what sweet words could he even know?*—Lux seethed, her spine straightening in her chair. "Anyone die by your knife last night?"

Over a long sip of strong tea, she watched his eyes shadow, though not in the anger she expected from her goading. "No. Not last night."

She carefully replaced her cup on the table.

His eyes flicked down her face, finger tracing the rim of his own cup. "That child. The grief. How you allowed the father to work off his debt. I couldn't put it out of my head."

"You were eavesdropping?"

He scoffed. "It would have been impossible not to."

"Not if you'd left when you were supposed to."

His brows slashed downward. "I wished she weren't the exception. That all the poor of Ghadra could choose to utilize your services if they wanted. It was gut-wrenching to overhear."

Lux slowly placed her palms flat upon the table, fingertips blanched white. "Shaw, do you have the slightest idea what ingredients are required for the enchantment?" He opened his mouth, only to shake his head. No, of course he didn't. "I just discovered my only source of howler canines *died*. They're the most expensive, as they're the hardest to get. And if you're not brought to me before your eighth hour, they're *essential*. If I'm to be free to revive all of Ghadra, how do you suggest I procure the funds? Hunt and harvest them myself?"

He contemplated the question, but she knew he wouldn't find any answers. She couldn't find any answers, and it was her *job*. At last, he sighed, giving up. "Have you chosen a costume yet?"

Lux lifted her eyes from the first page of the journal, taken aback at the change. "Yes. Have you?"

He grinned, shadows giving way to reveal that rarely seen gold shattering the copper of his eyes. The flutter in her stomach returned, that traitorous thing. "I've an idea."

"Care to share?"

"Not at all."

Lux bit her cheek. If he turned out dressed as a barrow troll or a marsh creature, she'd be forced to abandon him. She knew her opinion had next to no weight, however, so with a final swallow, she stood.

"Thank you for the tea. I'll see you tomorrow." Clutching the journal to her chest, she slipped from the chair.

Shaw remained where he was. "Be careful with that." Lux waved a dismissive hand, her back already to him as she strode down the hall. "Necromancer! No one can find it."

"Yes, Prowler. I will guard it with my life!"

She allowed herself one last reprieve before the paintings, one last imagining, regardless of the hurt, before she opened the door and closed it tight. Against all the wishes that could never be.

CHAPTER FOURTEEN

"WHAT AN INTERESTING CHOICE, Lucena."

Riselda eyed the feathered wings with no small amount of uncertainty. For the second time, she reached out a hand to stroke the black tips. Lux only smiled.

It was perfect. Exactly as she'd pictured.

She studied her kohl-lined eyes and red lips, the rest of her face hidden beneath a feathered, black mask. Her hair would have become hopelessly entangled within her wings if she had left it long—instead she'd coiled and pinned it at her nape. Several tendrils brushed along her temple, trailing down behind the mask, but she didn't try to contain them again.

She stepped away from the mirror.

"Have you thought on a gift for the mayor?"

Lux wondered at the near-pained expression on her aunt's face. Yes. She had thought on a gift for some time. She'd been thinking on it ever since she'd read the journal cover to cover, stashing it deep within her wardrobe, resting alongside the stolen lifeblood.

The mayor's obsession with immortality, or as near as one could get, seemed to have begun long ago. Fifty years old, and reaching an age when one realizes life does, in fact, come to an end, his research dug into the unnatural.

Lifeblood, in particular.

Not much was known about it then, perhaps only slightly less than what was known currently, but that didn't stop the man from hauling in every physician, psychic and healer that could potentially offer him answers. None impressed him, according to the journal's notations. None, save for a young girl. A girl with a strong brilliance.

Sixty years old now and gravely ill, the girl brought him back from the brink. And from that night forward, she never left the mansion. Remaining at his side, he consulted her on all matters. Matters that a young girl couldn't possibly understand.

His family grew jealous. His wife attempted to have her killed. The wife died instead.

And the mayor appeared to stop aging. One by one, his family did as well. His favorite cousin, a niece, an uncle. But as for the young girl, she grew. Into a woman, bound and talented, with churning shadows in her eyes.

Shaw's great-great-grandfather dated his entries until his death, which ended in speculation rather than significant findings. Lux had glanced over them briefly, mind sifting through the information she'd learned. He had been eighty-six years old. The mayor should have been an ancient man—one hundred and one. He was not.

Lux didn't understand it. Didn't understand how the oldest of Ghadra were not concerned that their mayor looked as fresh as he ever did while they all aged and died. She'd become adept at listening in to conversation not meant for her ears, and still, she'd not heard a whisper.

Looking up to Riselda now, her aunt smiled, patting a masked cheek. "I'm sure you'll think of something worth his time."

"You're not coming then?" Lux surveyed Riselda's plain dress, dirt at its hem. She hadn't dressed in much more for several days now.

Riselda followed her gaze, a serene smile lighting her mouth as she studied her soiled skirt. "Perhaps. Perhaps not."

Her aunt was a puzzle Lux couldn't solve, growing more difficult with each passing day. So she gave up trying and attempted to appreciate having someone who cared for her well-being at her side instead. Lux forced a smile.

A carriage rumbled along the cobblestones, slowing to a stop. "That will be my ride."

"Have fun, Lucena. Don't drink too much wine." Riselda patted her hand. "You do look beautiful. Very much like your mother."

Lux's eyes blinked much too frequent behind her mask. "Thank you, Riselda."

She climbed the steps and opened the door, Riselda's sing-song voice trailing after her, "Secrets, my dear. He adores secrets."

LUX ADJUSTED THE BLACK silk of her gown again. It was long and flowing, tight through the plunging neckline and across the waist. It had been her mother's dress, and with a bit of tweaking, it fit every inch of her. She would have purchased more appropriate shoes, but sneaking about a den of predators required comfortable, trustworthy footwear.

Lux tucked her sturdy boots beneath her dress with a swish of dark skirts.

Her wings were delicate things, black feathers draped artfully down her back rather than spread wide. Shaw could sit beside her if he chose. Not that he would. No, never.

The carriage slowed. She adjusted her mask.

The door swung open with a click. At first, she could see nothing in the waning light as cool mist rolled through the opening, swirling about her knees. But as it settled, Lux caught a glimpse of black boots, a black coat, and a skeletal mask that caused her to bite back a scream as she pressed herself further against the seat.

Shaw's laugh filled the carriage with a warmth that sent the mist skittering away, returning to the night air. "Did I frighten you?" He swung in with ease, settling across from her.

Lux couldn't stop staring at the white mask, edged in silver, appearing so real it may as well have been made of— "Is that *bone*?"

Her hand quickly dropped to her lap at the smirk of his lips beneath it. "Too morbid?" He studied her then, their bodies jostling as the carriage ambled forward once more. In the dimness of the small space between them, his eyes appeared black as midnight. "You have feathers on your mask."

"And on my wings." At his continued scrutiny, she added, "A crow."

His head tilted, his lips unmoving, until at last, "I like it." She laughed, and it coaxed a ghost of a smile to his mouth. "What?"

"It nearly sounded genuine is all. What are you? The dead?"

His grin turned wicked. "Death, itself. I feel the mayor needs a reminder he cannot cheat the beast forever."

She scoffed. "Probably not the best choice for stealth and secrecy, however."

"You underestimate me, love."

Lux rolled her eyes, parting the curtains to stare out into the deepening shadows. Several heartbeats of silence passed, marred only by the crunch of carriage wheels.

"How did you find the journal?"

Her gaze swung back to his dark one. "Terrifying. I read it through. It certainly sounds as though he discovered how to harvest lifeblood. And offered it up to his family. Though I wonder how he's gotten away with it. Even more I wonder how he's gone about choosing his victims over the years."

"Well, if I were him, I would choose people I wished to be rid of. People unable to fight back. I'm sure there are many in the Dark that fit the description, and it isn't as if the Shield mind doing the work."

"I'm not sure those of the Light are much safer any longer." At his questioning stare, she recounted her encounter with the old shopkeeper. "They mentioned the prison, though I've not a clue where that might be."

Lux couldn't see much at all within the darkening space any longer, save for a glimmer of stark white now and then as the carriage ambled over loose stone, rocking their bodies. She shivered.

"I'm surprised you could have slept at all in that house. What with their screams."

"What are you talking about?" Spiders, real or imagined, skittered up her arms.

The skeletal mask shone, sudden and clear in the moonlight, and Lux nearly believed Death did hover beneath, watchful and biding. "Under our illustrious mayor's home lies the most uninhabitable prison you could imagine. A sentence to it may not need be for life, but it will claim it regardless. This is where the mayor harvests his precious lifeblood. I'm sure of it."

Lux allowed the horror to cascade over her. "How do you know this?"

"My father. Resisting the Shield has only one consequence, and when I failed to save him from that cell, when I discovered his death not many days ago, something in me broke." Lux twitched away the outlandish urge to reach for him. "There are so many innocents buried within those walls, begging for light, for life—for death. I killed an abuser that night. On his way to the tavern after beating his wife to unconsciousness, I stabbed him in the back and slit his throat. It was easy. Too easy. The dagger passed through like melted butter." She scrunched her eyes closed, but the images rose vivid anyway. "If the Shield won't defend Ghadra's people, if the mayor only selfishly seeks that which will make him immortal, who am I to do nothing?" The carriage slowed, and streetlamps peered through the curtains. Lux gazed at Shaw, forearms resting on his thighs, head hung low. "It should have been me in there, you know."

Pebbles crunched as the wheels stopped. "Why?"

His lips parted as the carriage door swung outward, bathing them in soft light. He smiled, straightening. It was an expression brimming with retribution.

"Never mind. Let's not keep the mayor waiting."

Chapter Fifteen

The mansion before them glowed like a beacon, every cross-barred window illuminated from within. Lux gazed up the expansive stone stairs, wide and gleaming from ornate lampposts, flanked by the Shield on either side. She worried her lip.

"Nervous?"

She felt Shaw's quiet question warm the frigid air between them, heard the carriage continuing on, another taking its place. She released her lip. "I'm not sure what I am." She studied the towering wooden doors flung wide, guests milling inside and around the pale stonework. "I don't have fond memories of this place."

She turned then, taking in Shaw's appearance in the light. Dark, mysterious—dangerous. She shook her head. Certainly no ideal disguise for remaining inconspicuous.

He studied her just as closely. Though what conclusion he came to, she would never know. He held out a black-clad arm.

Lux stared at it with all the confusion of an impossible puzzle.

"Ahem." He grabbed her hand, linking her arm with his. "Have you never been escorted anywhere before?"

The warmth of his touch crawled up her fingers, spreading outward and through her. She stepped forward, pulling him after. "No. It would only slow me down."

To make her point, she hurried up the stairs, forcing him to match her pace. He scoffed, his long strides meeting hers, then exceeding. "It can be nice to move slow sometimes."

The suggestive flicker of humor in his eyes caused Lux to curl her lip. "Don't be crude."

He only shook his head, a breath of laughter leaving his lips as he glanced over the Shield in their passing. "Spineless bastards."

"Did you know they carry sleeping potions? Potent ones, too. I tested it out on one of them the other day. He dropped like a sack of flour." Lux smiled at the memory, and when her gaze inadvertently found Shaw's, she was struck by his expression. What she could see of it. "What?"

They'd reached the landing and Shaw shrugged off his coat, revealing a crisp, black shirt lined with silver buttons matching that of his mask. He handed it off to a servant with an appreciative nod, causing the girl to offer up a befuddled blink in response. Appreciation was not often found here.

"Don't allow this to go to your head, Necromancer. But I think I could like you."

She laughed aloud, drawing several sets of eyes before stifling it. "Trust me, I never let *anything* get so far."

He grinned. "Me neither."

I SHOULD PROBABLY TELL you," Lux muttered beneath her breath as they entered the lustrous foyer. "The mayor expects a gift." At Shaw's quick glance of irritation, she hurried on, "A secret, a favor. Something of that sort."

"Of course, you only tell me this now." The arm beneath hers tightened.

"I forgot." She lifted her eyebrows at a puffed peacock of a woman.

So much color, so many sparkling jewels. The crowded room of Ghadra's elite preening one another was enough to make her head spin and her stomach knot. Lux noted that Shaw drew just as many stares, though most shifted from frightened shock to intrigued admiration as he led her into the ballroom. Her gaze swept over large urns spilling roses the color of blood.

"I think we made a mistake."

Shaw's voice darkened. "What now?"

In her effort to choose a costume that would allow her to slip easily through shadowed corridors, and to honor one very brave sacrifice, she had foolishly forgotten one thing:

Those of the Light never wore black.

"That suit. This dress..." His eyes traveled down at her words, and her skin heated.

"This can only be my Deceiver of Death!" The mayor's voice boomed louder than necessary, drawing the attention of those nearby. As he liked it. Lux stepped closer to Shaw—and turned.

Clad in a shocking pink waistcoat with a matching mask tilted up at the corners, his gaze swept over her. "I shouldn't have expected anything other than black, of course." He sighed dramatically, bringing a few feigned chuckles along with him. "But I must say it suits you. A raven?" He reached forward, gripping her hands before she could dodge.

"A crow."

He quirked his lips. "We will say raven." He forced her into a spin before his eyes. "Much more beautiful than a *crow*."

Lux stopped with a swish of fabric, tugging her hands from his icy grip. "And what of your costume, if I might ask?"

The mayor adjusted his mask with a grin before snatching a proffered goblet of wine. "A flamingo! Rare bird. I'm sure you've never heard of it. Few know of such things." Lux had indeed heard of it. She refrained from rolling her eyes upward. The mayor drew closer, the stink of too much wine coating the air between them. "Did you happen to bring me a present?"

His hand reached out to finger a feather at her back.

"Yes. A secret." She leaned in further. There were certainly many secrets she could have divulged to the mayor, but there was only one that wanted for revealing tonight. "There's a phantom in the forest."

Strange, she thought, *how the words come easily now.*

His eyes gave away nothing. "A phantom? You've entered the wood?"

"Once."

"How very brave." He studied her. "Or very foolish. You never were the best at following tradition, and now I'm sure you've disturbed a grumbling ghost." He winked. "Intriguing all the same. Where is your aunt?"

"We came separate." At Lux's statement, the mayor finally took notice of Shaw at her back. He squinted up. "What's this? A corpse?" His abrupt guffaws sent wine sloshing from its crystal dwelling onto the patterned tiles.

Shaw's voice cut through, scraping. "Something like that."

The mayor sobered. "What's your name?"

"Shaw."

"Have I met you before?"

"One other. Perhaps you don't remember." His eyes blazed and Lux contemplated stomping on his foot.

"Of course I remember. I've the best memory." The mayor finished off the last of the wine before staring forlornly at the puddle on the floor. "If only all could have as great a mind as mine..."

Lux coughed against the derisive laugh bubbling from her lips. "We have been monopolizing you, Mayor. We should allow you to greet the remainder of your guests."

"Yes, yes." The look he directed at her turned leering. "Save me a dance."

Lux considered knocking the goblet from the mayor's grip until she felt the reassuring pressure of Shaw's hand against her back. "Of course."

She stepped away, more than ready for something to coat her suddenly parched throat.

"Wait. Doesn't Shaw have a gift for me, as well?" The mayor eyed her escort with renewed interest, and the taller man stepped forward, his hand never leaving her.

"Death is like the mist that coats this town every twilight. Hungry and inevitable."

If the mayor weren't so happily intoxicated, Lux was sure Shaw would have been thrown into the mysterious prison for such a statement. Instead, the mayor fixed his well-honed grin upon his wide lips.

"Some would say."

Reaching around to her lower back, Lux dug nails into Shaw's hand, gripping it within her own. Dragging him from the mayor's presence, they approached a covered table laden with goblets of wines and mugs of cider.

"What were you thinking?" she whispered heatedly, pushing a glass of wine into his hand. "Water?"

At the servant's shake of his head, she frowned. Cider it would have to be. She picked up the nearest cup, sniffing its contents. A tentative sip later, the pleasant taste of orange swept over her tongue.

Shaw eyed his gloves with interest. "That buffoon's so drunk he won't even remember what I said by hour's end."

"We can hope." She steered them toward the nearest sculpted column, their backs to the wide windows and faces to the sparkling sea. She eyed the decorated balustrade above them, thick ribbons tumbling from its height. "Where is your murder weapon, Prowler? Please tell me you've left it at home."

"Who needs mine when you've brought yours." The pull of his glove revealed scarlet marks on his skin. "Fiend."

She choked on a second swallow. "I saved you from yourself! You should hope it will scar and forever remind you that not all your thoughts need voicing."

His narrowed gaze lifted to find hers. He raised his hand and instinct told her to retreat. Instead, her back met the cool column, pinning her in place. Clad in achingly soft leather, his thumb drew along her mouth, coming away wet. All the while, a roguish glint lit his eyes.

Lux tossed her head to the side. "What was that for?"

His lips met the edge of the bone mask. "Not all my thoughts require voicing, I'm told. Relax, Necromancer. You look poised to attack someone."

"Perhaps I am. Leave me be."

"Suit yourself. Though your body must ache every night, being kept so rigid."

"Please, don't overtax yourself with thoughts on my body." Glowering, she slid around his side. "I'm starved. We can discuss what to do from here afterward. If you'll excuse me." She didn't bother inviting him along.

Most gave her a wide berth as she wove toward the tables tumbling with food. Those that didn't, she needed only to bare her teeth to send them stumbling. Lux smiled. She wasn't here to make friends. Not with these people. Not with anyone.

She surveyed the rising confections, stacked on crystal and arranged in towers of delectable scents. She selected a meat-filled pastry and wondered how she should go about scrubbing the feel of Shaw's thumb on her mouth from her mind.

"No napkin? How barbaric."

Lux froze at the dripping voice, her chest stinging.

Morana, the mayor's daughter, and the source of nearly all the invisible wounds Lux had received while trapped within her domain. She apparently took after her mother in all ways but one: of a height like her father, she and Lux were nose-to-nose now.

Lux took in the elaborate leather costume before her, ample curves on near-full display.

"Outlandish choice, that." Morana gestured to Lux's gown. "It's just as well, for color always did give your skin a jaundiced look." The mayor's daughter smoothed back a loose tendril of golden hair, blue eyes made brilliant beneath the row of garish chandeliers.

"Pleasant to see you as well, Morana. Interesting costume."

"Isn't it? A wyvern-rider."

Lux nodded, already bored and suddenly tired.

"And here comes my wyvern now."

Lux couldn't prevent the huffed breath of laughter as Morana's husband weaved through the crowd, an elaborate headdress rising above them all, complete with spiked horns. Tall, weak-shouldered, with black hair and even blacker eyes, he stopped at his wife's side—after taking the time to observe every other young woman along his journey, of course.

"Lux." His eyes traveled down and up her costume. "You've certainly grown."

Morana's lips tightened.

"Yes, I have. Though nine long years haven't appeared to have aged you both in the slightest."

The mayor's daughter flashed her teeth in a semblance of a smile. "True. My darling Colden is as handsome as the day we married." An arm snaked around his waist.

He didn't reciprocate. "Likewise, my dear."

The two of them were going to give her a headache. Drenched in sarcasm, Lux said, "As lovely as this has been, I must get back."

Morana's hand clamped on her arm, icy tendrils winding upward so like that of the tree's, she flinched. Morana felt it, and grinned. "Get back to whom?"

Lux glanced at Shaw from across the room, and Morana laughed. A thick sound that oozed over her, bringing back memories she wished to forget. "He doesn't appear to mind your absence, you poor thing."

It was true. As the crowd moved about, dancing to the music or swaying unnaturally with drink, Shaw stood surrounded by no fewer than three bright and sparkling creatures. His lips even appeared upturned in a smile.

"One must drop a few crumbs for the chickens every now and then."

Morana's brow furrowed in confusion at her words, and Colden's lips quirked. Lux abandoned them before she was made to suffer more. Striding back through the crowd, her sole focus rested on Shaw. Shaw and his deep laugh that, strangely, sounded genuine to her ears. When his eyes finally lifted from that of the girl's before him, his grin lessened, and then faded away entirely.

"Excuse us," Lux purred, red lips stretching over her teeth.

The girls stumbled back in unison, eyeing her with a mixture of annoyance and unease. Not willing to confront her, however, they allowed a forlorn glance at the man behind her before slowly disappearing into the crowd of bodies. Lux bit into her pastry. She hated how delicious it was and wiped away the crumbs from her lips before glancing upward—to discover Shaw's gaze intent on her progress.

At her attention, he cleared his throat. "I say we start with the mayor's study."

She paused, the pastry partway to her mouth. "You know of his study?"

"He must have one. He's the mayor."

"It's far from here."

"Good thing you wore your boots then."

She glared.

"Finish that. I can't stand here rocking on my heels any longer."

"Spare me. You were perfectly content to flirt your way into a Light match a moment ago." Lux popped in the final mouthful, followed by a swallow of cider.

Shaw took the empty mug from her hand before she could protest, his gaze flicking down briefly before returning to hers. "Death is never content, Necromancer. Now, let's get this evening over with."

Chapter Sixteen

With guests coming to and from the lavatory with increasing frequency, it was almost too simple to dart off to an unoccupied hall. The lamplight diminished the further they ventured, and soon only one lone flicker could be seen from its end.

Lux walked alongside Shaw, their footsteps silent on the plush runner extending the length. Yet another bust of the mayor passed them by with eerie, empty eyes, and she fought the urge to knock it from its mighty perch. She settled for curling her lip at the likeness instead.

A sudden shadow descended from the hall's end, and Lux flattened against the wall the same moment as Shaw. The Shield continued in another direction, and she exhaled in relief. Peeling herself from the polished stone at her back, she peered around a statue.

Shaw's breath wafted warm over her ear. "Is it much farther?"

She refused to allow her face to turn into it. What in the *world*? It must be that thrice-damned cider's doing. "Yes." The end of this hall would branch into three. They would need to take the center route, following it to a lacquered door with a stamped handle.

Instead of confiding any of that information in him, she stepped around the statue, hurrying along the corridor. She moved fast, but her legs were far from long. Shaw's strides sent her into a jog only to keep up.

Far sooner than she was ready for it, the lone lamp hung above them, highlighting their forked path. Shaw glanced down, expectant.

"We can't be caught." She forced her imagination to cease bombarding her with images of their capture as she angled her face toward his.

The small flame had turned Shaw's eyes a molten gold beneath his mask. Lux's blood warmed, and she immediately pulled her gaze away before it could travel much further.

"I hadn't realized. Any further advice?"

She fixed him with a glare only to feel it fade. He played with her, the edge of his lips hitched up in a half-smile. That traitorous flush returned, crashing through her veins.

"Only one: I think it best if you didn't speak any longer."

THE HALL WAS DARK, though nowhere near as dark as the door now looming tall before them. Lux's hand hovered over the gold handle, a forked tongue protruding from a gaping mouth and stamped with the letter *T*. She'd been here once before. She never thought she'd return.

Shaw grew impatient. She could feel him, stiff at her back. His arm brushed hers when he reached around her, but she didn't move, allowing him to turn the knob and push the door inward.

A cascade of yellow light and the stink of old cigar smoke welcomed them in. The circular room possessed no windows; a decision made by the mayor no one could question. Lux glanced over the walls lined with flickering lamps until her gaze found the sprawling desk. She strode toward it, Shaw moving to investigate the glass-encased shelving about the room. It was neat. Too neat. She worried any item slightly moved out of place would alert the mayor of their trespassing. Wrinkling her nose against the lingering scent of the mayor's cologne, she slid open the first drawer anyway.

Reports. Stacks of them. Her fingers slid over the first page's edge: a description of the sickness sweeping through the Dark. The mayor had signed it: *Bartleby Tamish*. A sentence-long note following:

Contamination—will investigate further if it crosses.

Crosses. If it crosses to the Light. Her blood boiled even as she wasn't the least bit surprised. How convenient for him that it hadn't. How very convenient—

Her gaze flicked to Shaw's broad back as he reached behind a stack of leather-bound books.

"Shaw." He turned, softly closing the glass. "Does it strike you as odd that with the number of casualties of this sickness, it hasn't yet crossed to the other side of the city?"

He navigated around the furniture. "What did you find?" She handed the page to him, and he shook his head. "It may be a matter of luck. Or time."

She raised an eyebrow. "Maybe. But something tells me different. What if he's growing desperate for more lifeblood? What if he's allowing the poor of Ghadra to die for it?"

Shaw's jaw clenched; his eyes bore into the page.

Click.

In tandem, their attention swung to the door. Shaw shoved the paper back onto the stack, pushing the drawer closed. Lux knocked a pen out of place and fumbled to right it. The handle began to turn.

His gaze narrowed on her. "Don't hit me."

"Why—"

Strong hands gripped her waist, pulling her in, and before Lux could question him further, his lips came down onto her own.

Warmth.

It dragged her under.

She gasped a drowning breath; it was his air she pulled. Unfurling and lengthening, heat spread throughout every inch of her skin, pulsing, relentless, with every feverish beat of her heart. Lux's lashes fluttered against her cheeks, her body curling into the sensation as if it couldn't get enough.

And she couldn't. She couldn't get *enough.*

She wanted to burn with it.

Shaw's lips moved and hers followed. They were so soft when compared to the scrape of his chin, and even though he tasted of wine, she didn't mind. Not even a little. Her hand moved to grip the back of his neck. His fingers tightened against her, releasing bolts of fire in their wake. Lux sighed into his open mouth. To speak of bliss would be to describe this kiss, and she would surely—

"INTRUDERS!"

The two of them sprang apart, cheeks flushed, bodies tight. Lux tore her eyes from Shaw's smoldering gaze to take in the white uniform of the Shield in the doorway.

She dropped her hip. She bit her lip. "Oops. May we not be here?"

The man sputtered, "In the mayor's personal office? Of course not!"

Shaw turned with a suggestive grin that Lux would never have thought him capable of. "We were looking for the lavatory."

A hand then ran the length of her, making her frantic heart bound and cheeks heat further. She licked her lips as he pulled her flush against him. "Right. The *lavatory.*"

The Shield's jaw tightened. "Get out."

Lux released the breathiest giggle, making her own stomach churn in the process. "Our apologies, good sir."

Shaw saluted with a wave of his hand, and the Shield curled his lip as they swayed past. She could hear him muttering long after.

"Drunks. I loathe these frivolous parties."

Chapter Seventeen

Lux refused to look at the boy next to her. *No, not a boy.* With the taste of him still tormenting her, she was certain she would never think the same way again. Just as she'd once told him to, he'd convinced her with that kiss. Only, she hadn't—could *never* have—expected his methods.

Silent, they rounded the corner, the doors leading to the ballroom flung wide before them. She wasn't sure with whom she was more furious: Shaw or herself. Though she also wasn't sure she had cause to be mad at all. His quick thinking was potentially all that saved them from being tossed into prison. She knew her brilliance could only allow so much indiscretion.

Shaw's hand gripped her elbow, and she pulled away. His touch burned her insides, quicker now that the scorching paths had already been forged with that absurd kiss. It made her feel alive.

She didn't *want* it.

"Should I apologize? Trust me, Lux, it's not as if I'd planned it."

Shaw's irritation sent her into the glittering room two steps ahead of him.

She adjusted her mask as she surveyed the mass of bodies. The music was lively, the crowd pairing off in an intricate dance that sent several stumbling in their drunken haze. Lux smirked as the haughty peacock's skirts were sloshed with drink, her screech a respectable imitation.

How she yearned to leave. She couldn't do any further investigating this night, not with the Shield having noticed her, but it would also seem much too suspicious to disappear immediately following what occurred in the office. She reached to her lips. They must be swollen; the only explanation she could think of as to why her mind could focus on no other part of her. She made to wipe away the sensation.

A vulgar creature weaved forward, stilling her hand. "May I have this dance, my delectable raven?" Colden bowed, nearly losing his lofty headdress. His too-dilated pupils studied her figure as he straightened, and she shook her head, prepared to administer a scathing rebuke.

"She's spoken for."

The wyvern puffed his chest, ready to fight this new adversary until his gaze landed on his leather-clad wife weaving her way toward him. He ground his teeth, focusing on Lux once again.

"I always knew you would amount to nothing. This only further proves my thinking." He gestured to Shaw, a sneer on his lips, transforming his face into less of a fearsome beast and more an oily serpent.

Lux scoffed. Because she knew Colden, and a man like him? He deserved none of her attention.

But Shaw did not know him. When his hand encircled the other man's throat, she could only offer a half-hearted protest. Shaw leaned in close, his mask scraping grooves of red along Colden's smooth cheek. "Say it again."

The man flailed, but Death's grip was unyielding. He stood nearly a head taller than Morana's husband, his shoulders twice as broad. "I said she would amount—" A choked sound cut off the remainder. Colden's eyes bulged, his gloved fingers clawing for purchase.

"Say. It. Again."

He could not. They all knew it. And it was only the level of drunken obliviousness swirling around them that prevented Shaw from being beaten by a force of guards. Yet, Colden's face was purpling, and Morana weaved closer. That was a mess she wished to avoid.

"If you murder him, you'll ruin my night and yours. Mine because I'll have to boil my eyes after seeing him unclothed again. Yours because you'll be in prison."

Shaw tossed him off.

Colden stumbled backward where he hacked and wheezed. "You *dare—*"

"Listen to me, you winged weasel." Lux stepped close until his blown pupils found hers. "*You* dare mention anything, and I will purposefully botch your inevitable revival. Decide your course." When he continued to only stare and seethe, she hissed, "*Now.*"

Morana was upon them, and the decision was made. The wyvern flew away entirely. The mayor's daughter stared at his vacated place, her eyes giving away little even as her shoulders drooped. When her gaze flicked to Lux, however, they rose, stiff and proud, daring her to say something. Anything.

Lux remained silent.

"We should dance."

She lifted her attention from Morana's retreating form to huff at Shaw, but he didn't look at her. Rather, he frowned at the Shield who had discovered them in the mayor's office, searching the crowd until he spied them.

Wonderful. This night can officially be stamped a disaster.

Without another thought, Lux rolled her body into his, sending them stumbling sideways. An uproarious laugh left her lips, partly in her pretend drunken stupor, but partly at the look of utter shock on Shaw's face. He righted them both, his hands gripping her upper arms before grinning himself.

He really was quite good at acting, and her eyes were drawn to the creases at the corners of his, barely visible beneath his skeletal mask. She held out her hand. He took it within his warm one, and with a sweeping bow, led her onto the floor. Just in time for the beginning of a new dance.

Lux took her position across from him, curtsying when the other partners did. She smiled at Shaw's exaggerated bow again, the line opposite her own bending forward as one. She wasn't sure she knew the dance, but she doubted it really mattered. The more real stumbling she did, the less she would have to feign her missteps.

When Shaw stepped forward in perfect sync with those who flanked him, she nearly missed the turn, into his arms. Her open mouth snapped closed as he brought her hands to his shoulders before dropping his own to her waist—and lifting.

For once their eyes were at level, and Lux felt...exposed. He could see too much of what made her, and she hated it. At her release, she staggered back into line, weaving around a fairy with wings that threatened to send her crashing to the floor if she hadn't given them an exceptionally wide berth. Shaw returned before her.

"Careful, Necromancer. Your admiration is showing."

She released her lip to scowl at him. "You know this dance."

"As I've said: you underestimate me."

He lifted her again, and in an attempt to avoid his eyes, she found his mouth. Never had she ever been so grateful for a masked face. Her cheeks burned at his release of her waist.

She circled some green-clad creature. Thankfully, wing-less.

"I don't think we should stay."

His hands gripped her again, and the heat grew almost overpowering. It had her thinking of what might have happened had they not been interrupted. Of what his lips felt like.

Oh, they should definitely go.

"Bored, love?" Her boots hovered above the ground as he brought her chest against his, his breath skimming her mouth.

He held her too long. The couples were moving again. Nevertheless, Lux couldn't pull her eyes from the dark, wanting depths of his. He bent his head.

The hush over the crowd fell, sudden and complete.

Lux felt her feet touch the floor, a trickle of ice traveling along her spine as a trailing silver dress parted the crowd. Sparkling bodies stumbled away from the fanged smile, the unmasked face, and the sheer magnetism of the woman before them.

Indigo eyes met Lux's.

"Riselda?" The mayor tottered forward as if in a trance. Though perhaps he was. He certainly wouldn't be the only one. His pink waistcoat was splotched with spilled wine, and he rubbed over the spots self-consciously.

"Bartleby."

"You—" His gaze raked over her costume. "You're breathtaking. What are you?"

Riselda smiled again, revealing pointed teeth. "A simple bat, my good mayor."

The mayor's brow furrowed beneath his mask. "But you wear silver."

"So it would seem." Riselda scanned the crowd with a predatory smile as the mayor fought to dispel the fog from his mind. "Would you like your birthday present?"

Nauseated, Lux watched the unabashed greed swarm into the mayor's eyes. "As if you need to ask, Riselda."

Her aunt ran tongue over pointed teeth, steering the mayor into a more private location, and Lux's stomach churned, the glittering dress vanishing from view.

"I need to leave."

Without waiting for Shaw, she twined her way through the crowd, many of whom were still whispering and pointing. They ignored her. The bodies grew thick, and she felt her chest constrict.

She needed air. Badly.

Weak as she was, those who didn't move readily, did so at her hiss. At last, she staggered onto the landing, the expansive stairs widening before her. She breathed in a cleansing breath, feeling her head clear with each pulse of her heart.

Warmth radiated from somewhere at her back.

"Are you going to faint?"

Lux rolled her eyes, studying the moon as it smirked down at her. Shaw stepped to her side, following her stare. Together, they watched the cool moonlight play over the courtyard walls, highlighting the spired gates.

She shivered, then stilled when black fabric draped over her shoulders. Shaw's coat. She stared at it, her mind blank. "Would you have done it?"

She could sense the exact moment his attention fixed on her, felt it lap at her profile like flame.

"No. Not over words."

Lux sniffed. "He was wrong. To imply that about you."

She startled at Shaw's laugh, deep and incredulous. "You think—"

His thought broke abruptly, and it was her turn now to stare. His strong jaw was unfashionably rough as it upturned once more to the moon, his mask aglow beneath the cold light. She noticed his hair mussed from dancing—or perhaps she'd done that, burying her fingers in the thickness of it. She fidgeted against the ache building inside her. *Devil's own tits but am I a mess.*

She burrowed further into his coat. "What sort of *secret* do you think my aunt is sharing with the mayor at the moment?"

"Well... Power does draw people."

"Not me." She scoffed in disgust. "Never me."

CHAPTER EIGHTEEN

Lux didn't want to go home. Riselda's inevitable presence later that night or the following morning only solidified her decision. She didn't tell Shaw this plan, however.

They didn't speak much on the carriage ride to his apartment, each occupied by their own worries, own theories, and own schemes. But when the door opened, when he descended the step, when he turned his gaze back to her, she watched the shadows in his eyes fade beneath the moonlight. She never thought she would see him without them, and yet the emotion staring back at her puzzled her, for his clearly whirled with confusion.

"Will you be all right?"

She laughed mildly, shaking her head. "I don't have a choice." When the conflicting emotions in his eyes only deepened, she continued, "Thank you for your help tonight."

He sighed. "I only wish we'd had more time." She nodded her agreement. "And I truly am sorry. For the kiss."

Shoulders stiffening, she retreated against the cushioned seat. "It was nothing. No need to apologize."

He mimicked her earlier laugh. "Right. Well, goodnight."

"Goodnight."

The door clicked closed, and she sagged into the seat. It was so far from nothing, she couldn't believe the lie had managed to leave her lips without wounding her. Her eyes fluttered closed, her breaths returning to normal. The carriage jerked forward. She couldn't recall the last time she felt even a semblance of what Shaw sent bounding through her as his lips touched hers. Lux twitched, her brow furrowing.

She couldn't recall. She couldn't remember.

Because she had forced herself to forget.

THE BOARDS NAILED TO the windows protruded at odd angles, faded and warped. The ones covering the door were much the same, aside from the jagged bits—a reminder that more than one unwelcome visitor had forced their entry. Lux's blood chilled, her heart skipping and irregular, spots dancing in her vision.

She needed to unlock her knees. She needed to step forward.

But her body wouldn't obey.

Her breath puffed cool clouds into the surrounding air, her skin prickling with cold, and yet she still stared at the scratched and faded door.

Her door. Her parents' door. Go in.

Go in. Go in. Go in.

She hadn't. Not since that night. Not since she'd found them lying in warm, wet pools of blood, their hands entwined as tightly in death as their hearts had been in life. How she had loved them. How she missed them still.

Tears pricked at her eyes only to be whisked away by the wind. And finally, *finally*, her knees released. Lux stepped forward, arm outstretched, panic rising in her chest and threatening to carve out her consciousness entirely. She forced it back.

The doorknob was cold; it burned her palm. She turned it quickly before she could think better of it, and with a push, the door creaked inward. More darkness.

She really should have chosen to do this in the daylight.

Ducking beneath the lone intact board running slanted across the top of the frame, Lux stepped into her home—and into her memories.

The door had been unmarked that night; closed without sign of forced entry. She had opened it softly. She had been so tired. The other children knew of her bizarre fascination with death. As a child, herself, she hadn't thought to keep it secret. She was thrilled over her newly discovered brilliance, having only been realized the day of her aunt's sudden disappearance. When she'd first touched *The Risen*.

Her parents were so proud of her. Why couldn't anyone else be? Why did people suddenly shy away from her? Whisper behind age-lined hands?

Such thoughts had occupied her mind, until nothing occupied it at all.

The world had muted and faded behind that door. No sounds, no smells, no colors. Save for the sound of shrieking cries, the smell of tangy iron, and the color of deepest red.

The first of her footfalls sent dust swirling about her ankles, and the memory faded.

There were no stairs in this house. Lux stepped through the shadows of the entryway, shoving the walls away from her on either side. They ceased their collapse around her mind and straightened, replacing their looming presence instead with her father's laugh and her mother's touch. She choked.

She knew if she were to keep going, if she were to turn the corner, the glimpse of the now-bare kitchen would give way to a rectangular room. One that once held a sofa just large enough for the three of them. One that held their bodies in death.

"First the forest. Now this house." Lux rubbed clammy hands over her face, pushing hair from her eyes. "I must be some sort of masochist."

The darkest part of her soul whispered, sickly sweet: *You deserve it.*

Hands shaking, she tried to shove them into the nonexistent pockets of her skirt. She frowned, wrapping them around her middle instead. Moonlight shone through the few cracks of the window ahead, highlighting her path in derisive, pale shimmers, and Lux had little choice but to obey it. She refused to let herself run away now.

The kitchen met her first, the cupboards open and hanging at odd angles, displaying bare shelves. The table and chairs must have been stolen long ago, as dust coated the floor without any sign of disturbance. Lux's lips parted against the pulling sensation flooding her body, digging into her feet, turning her.

That room.

That sofa.

Her body, her mind—they were no longer under her control. She tipped forward, staggering before it. Why must it still be here? Why must she still be? Surely, she should have been taken along with them.

Lux fell to her knees.

The walls, the floors, they had long been washed clean, but the dried stains, splashed across the fabric, glittered with a silver sheen in the darkness. A cruel trick of the moon itself, never wishing to spare her from a moment's truth.

Her mother's voice rose from memories. Forgotten words uttered softly into her ear every night. The days spun faster and faster, her mother aging before her eyes over the short eight years she was at her side. Lux braced her hands on the fabric, and that became her undoing. Her fingers dug deep, scrabbling for air. For warmth. For light.

Shine bright, Lucena.

The sobs wracking her body, the cries echoing around her, didn't sound like her own. The tears streaming down her cheeks felt foreign. They burned like acid. An old window cracked against the cold, and then shattered entirely.

The frigid, night air whipped in, triumphant, clawing at her skin. The clouds descended. They blocked even the moonlight from her now, but she could still feel it, watchful behind the veil.

"I'm so *cold*." She could see it: her soul, blackened and shriveled, a pit from spoiled fruit. Lux collapsed, her fingers slipping. What a horrible thing: to discover yourself rotted. "I should have known better. I should have *been* better."

Panic. It returned with renewed ferocity. It knew it would win this time, and it shrieked with a terrible pleasure. Lux couldn't breathe any longer, her cries choking her, her tears drowning her.

"I. Can't. Remember."

And when it seized her consciousness with a clawed, shadowed grip, her lashes fluttered closed in aching relief.

Chapter Nineteen

Rain tapped against a window in its redundant dreary call for her to open her eyes. Lux didn't want to obey. Her head pulsed and her face felt gritty. The stiffness in her joints let her know, quite irritated, that they didn't appreciate being left on rough, creaking floorboards for an entire night, either.

Lux propped an elbow underneath her with a groan, her lashes pressed tight against her cheeks. If she didn't open them maybe it wouldn't be real.

The rain drummed louder.

She squinted open her eyes. They burned. Her eyelids felt swollen, and for once, she felt thankful for the gloom rather than bright sunlight searing her pupils. With a final moan, she pushed herself to sitting and stretched her neck.

How different it all looked now.

She picked her mask off the floor, she took off her wings, and once shedding her feathers, she stood.

The sofa's dark stains waited to catch her notice once more, and Lux didn't want to avoid them any longer. She didn't want this place to hold power over her at all. She stepped toward it.

Her eyes burned with a vengeance, but she didn't look away. Not when the stains turned to red, and the cushions sank beneath the weight of her parents' bodies. Not even when the walls splattered with blood, the floor pooling with it at her feet.

She stared until it faded again. The floral wallpaper peeled, the floor covered in dust around the imprint of her prone body, the sofa unmarred but for several brown patches soaked into its old fabric. Her chest released like an unbound spring. She stepped back only to trip over the edge of the worn rug, nearly toppling headlong into the fireplace.

She tumbled forward and into the mantle, gripping it tight as she waited for her heart to calm. Then, without a backward glance, she entered her old bedroom. She had taken all her belongings when she'd left, along with a trunk of her parents' things she couldn't bear to part with. She'd forgotten what she'd left behind.

Empty vials and overturned pots lay strewn about the floor. Another jarring reminder of her last night in this house. Only just beginning to study her brilliance, her parents had generously purchased the ingredients for her to learn. Lux bent to pick up a small vial, the scent of venom barely clinging to its insides. She had used it all. She'd sapped every ounce of strength she possessed from her body, and she could never forget the look in their eyes as they rose to stand before her.

Lux dropped the vial, and it shattered across the floor. Backing from the room, she would have fled, confronting her fears be damned, but something else caught her eye. The rug. The overturned corner. She tilted her head, brow furrowing, and stepped toward it.

A near-invisible seam. But a seam, nonetheless. She gripped the edge of the rug, tugging it away.

A trapdoor. A mirror image of that in her current home. Tucking her fingers into the deceptive handle, she pulled upward. Remarkably noiseless, the door lifted. Darkness spilled out. Outside, the rain drummed harder, and in it, she heard her own words echoed:

Decide your course.

Lux grinned a terrible smile—and pulled on her wings.

THE SPUTTERING LANTERN PROTESTED its use; it'd not been lit in nearly a decade and had grown accustomed to the idea. Its random acts of fading and flaring were about to stop Lux's heart.

When she'd first climbed down, she'd not allowed the tiniest intake of air, awaiting some summoned monster. But after an extended period of standing still, in which she'd grown lightheaded from lack of breath, she'd finally given up and began to walk. Next, she'd been worried about touching the walls. Would they tumble in? But no, they were constructed of soil so hard-packed they mimicked stone. It smelled of dirt and earth, and it was dark and terribly cold. All things she would expect to experience below ground.

But the lantern—the ancient lantern her parents had never replaced because they'd never replaced anything unless it was irrevocably broken—would be her undoing.

The flame flared brightly as day only to gutter so weak it nearly went out. The resulting shadows crawled around her, pushing her heart out of rhythm.

You'll meet fears you've never known you possessed. Her aunt's voice rang in her head. But Riselda didn't know Lux had met her greatest fear last night and survived. There wasn't anything else in existence that could be worse.

"I *fear* you should have been honest with me, Aunt."

Still, time seemed impossible to mark down here, and that was bothersome. She'd guessed the tunnel must lead to her and Riselda's home. Far more likely that it was a network, too, one her aunt knew the way of—and hopefully nothing else.

Lux gave the lantern a hearty shake, same as she'd done the last time it threw such a fit, and with a pulse of light, it brightened and steadied. "Finally, you obey. You wasted bit of iron."

And just like that, it went out.

"Devil's tits!" Lux shook the lantern again, but to no avail. The flame was fully and surely gone.

Pressure built in her chest, a telltale squeeze. "Breathe. You're not dead...yet." She reminded herself that the heaviness of the earth was not growing. That nothing skulked behind her in the pitch. Of course, it would have been easier were she Riselda with her bag of weapons and oddities. Lux only had her wings.

Certainly, she should turn back. She knew what awaited her at that end. She could run, even, if she wanted. There would be no one but her own contemptuous inner thoughts to judge. Except...the idea of it. Of going backward when all she'd ever yearned for was to forge ahead. Surely, this moment shouldn't define anything to do with her future—but then, why did it feel like it did?

She'd once cast off wishes in exchange for survival. It had kept her alive for nine entire years. But what if a shriveled pit from a rotted fruit could still be planted and urged to grow? Would it hurt to maybe try?

Probably. A good thing, then, that she'd grown accustomed to pain.

With the lantern clutched to her chest for protection, she muttered as she walked. "The walls are not narrowing. The ceiling isn't shorter. The dark is like any other. You are alone."

She repeated the lines until she lost count, and then repeated them countless times more. Until the lantern met a wall and pressed into her front, and there wasn't a way forward anymore but only right or left. A damned-all fork.

It'd been impossible to keep track of each bend in the tunnel. She hadn't any idea where she might be, if she was even beneath the town any longer or meandering contentedly beneath the wicked trees. She loathed the sensation of indecision, it felt like a not-so-distant relative to fear. She turned to her right.

Half odds were against her, but what did it matter if it meant half odds were with her, too? Lux stepped forward, brave and sure—and screamed.

It was the shock of it that yanked it out of her, she thought later. The cloud of frost drifting in that portion of the tunnel like the yawning abyss of a devouring tree. An actual assailant, she could muster courage for, but an invisible one? Not today.

Left. She would go left.

She dashed through the tunnel now. The lantern bumped against her hip every few steps, the result would surely be a purple bruise, yet she couldn't keep from glancing over her shoulder. Something watched her in the blackness of the direction she'd run from. She'd bet her life on it.

Fine, maybe not her life. But she'd bet Shaw's.

Why was there a trapdoor beneath her parents' home to begin with? Had they used it? Like Riselda used hers? She couldn't fathom her parents doing anything of the sort. They were content in this town. Content to do as was bid, to make the most of their small life and small family. It was Riselda. Riselda who'd always been larger than them all.

A gust of frigid air met the back of Lux's neck. Though she felt fairly certain it was only her brain playing its tricks, she had to check to be sure. For the hundredth time, she glanced over her shoulder—

And smacked headlong into a ladder.

The lantern fell from her hands.

Once the echo of its shattering faded, all her senses allowed for was the stinging on her left side and the feel of rough wood beneath her fingers. Fine enough with her.

It meant she'd made it home.

THE LIVING ROOM RUG became a problem to push aside, what with Lux's attempted effort at stealth. But move it, she did, until she peered from the crack in the floorboards, surveying the closest item in her line of sight:

Riselda's bed.

It clearly hadn't been slept in.

Pushing the trapdoor higher, Lux climbed out, hauling the remains of the lantern up behind her. Even with the fire entirely banked, the room felt like sinking into a hot bath, and she closed her eyes, indulging a moment.

But a moment was all she allowed. Who knew when Riselda would tire of her night with the mayor and return to her? Lux lowered the door, pushing the rug over it so as not even a corner was overturned.

On a relieved breath over making it home alive, she threw some kindling on the fire, her body chilling as it adjusted to the new temperature and greedily found it wanting. As the wood caught, beginning to crackle and spark, she stood.

Clothes. She needed real ones.

Striding to her bedroom, she stripped out of her dress, tossing it across her bed as she shivered. Pulling the doors of her wardrobe wide, she grabbed for anything and everything, wanting her skin covered from neck to toe. The usual ensemble would be enough, and she yanked up the hose so quickly she tore a hole down the length of the seam.

"Dratted, worthless…fabric!"

She hauled another pair from the back, pulling them on instead while glaring daggers at the ruined ones as if they'd torn themselves. A silver shimmer flickered in the corner of her eye, and it stilled her hands. The lifeblood.

"Lucena? Are you here?"

Lux toppled sideways at Riselda's call. Tossing the destroyed hose in front of the tempting gleam, she pulled on a skirt, tightened her corset, and smoothed back knotted strands of hair.

"Yes." Standing in her doorway, Lux watched her aunt circle the kitchen table. She still wore her silver dress, though the hem dripped, muddied and wet. The fangs were gone.

Riselda's smile widened.

"Good. I'd nearly come to the assumption that you'd spent the night elsewhere." Lux's abdomen tightened. Riselda laughed. "But that would have been absurd. Even with that young man draped around you like a second skin."

Her aunt's true meaning settled over her, pricking her skin. Lux's spine straightened. "I would never."

Riselda's lips pressed together, a smirk pulling at them. "All right, Lucena."

Lux's teeth sank into her inner lip, trying in vain to snag at the words pushing from them. "And what of you? The last I saw you were disappearing with our honored mayor. Was it secrets? Or *service?*"

Useless. Her teeth were useless.

Riselda's smile vanished, and her eyes hardened into crystal. Her aunt trailed fingertips along the wall as she followed the bones of the house toward her.

Lux didn't move. And she told herself she wouldn't even flinch should Riselda slap her for her questions.

Riselda glided before her. Though instead of reddening her cheek, she placed calloused palms on either side of Lux's face, sending cool wisps flitting over her skin. Soft lips pressed to her brow.

"My dear." Riselda pulled back, eyes brimming with mirth. "Secrets. I have *endless* secrets." And with a jarring laugh, her aunt released her, pulling the plunging gown from her shoulders as she strode to her small bed.

Riselda's body must be what dreams were made of. Lux glanced from the curves as they were displayed before her. It was unsurprising why the mayor had maintained his infatuation for these nine years; Riselda radiated power. But it was equally surprising that her aunt had encouraged it.

"I've errands today, Lucena, but I want to have dinner together. If you've no other plans?" Riselda stood in a murky, grey gown. An extension of Ghadra.

Lux stuttered, taken aback. "That's...fine, Riselda. I'll be here."

Combing through black waves, Riselda nodded. "Excellent."

Lux pulled her gaze away and strode to the basin, washing her face, allowing the water to scour away grit and the memory of tears. When she glanced into the mirror, she met Riselda's eyes behind her, boring into her own.

"You're so lovely. And your spirit reminds me of my own." Riselda's long-fingered hand caressed her shoulder. "If that boy hurts you in any way, do not hesitate." Nails bit into her skin, and Lux flinched. "Rip out his heart and feed it to the trees."

Chapter Twenty

Black pustules burst and oozed, coating the doorstep in jasmine-scented drops. Lux stepped back, coming to the stunning realization she may have found something she despised more than blood.

The middle-aged woman adjusted her footing, propping the man up further.

Ned. The bizarre, laughing man. It would appear his mother had left behind her contagion in lieu of an inheritance. How unfortunate.

The thick fluid pooled and dripped onto the woman's forearm. Even covered against the cold, Lux doubted it would be enough to stop the spread.

"I've the coin, if that is what's preventing you from opening that door further."

Lux peeled her eyes from the puddle forming at her feet to meet ones narrowed at her in frustration. She studied the deep lines at their corners. "Are you aware of how easily this disease spreads? I wouldn't have touched him if I were you."

Ned collapsed to the rain-soaked ground as hands pulled back from his mottled body.

The woman studied the black substance slipping along her fingers, her cheeks losing their reddened hue. "I'm going to be next?"

Lux stepped back further. "Probably."

Shaking hands fumbled for a purse, dragging it from a pocket close to her body. "Revive me! When I die, find me. Swear it!"

Wild eyes clawed at Lux's features. "What about him?" Lux nodded toward Ned's array of awkward angles.

"Ned? He always was a selfish imbecile. In bed and outside it. Always running home to his wretched mother. I deserve this!"

Lux shook her head. "As unsatisfying as that must have been, I don't do house calls. Please arrange for someone to bring you, should you die."

"Who will risk touching me? You must!" The woman was growing louder, and Lux winced at the assault upon her ears.

"I'm sorry. I can't."

The woman sneered, stepping forward with a pointed finger. Her color having returned, her face darkened in anger. Anger and fear. "That is the most insincere apology I've ever heard, you little wench." Her eyes spun, the white's blood-shot. "Do you enjoy it? All this death? Maybe you began it. Nasty, filthy *murderer*."

Lux slammed her door, spinning to hold it in place even as the bolt slid home. The woman flung her body against its length. Once, twice. Until silence hung, thick, in the air. Then a sing-song voice.

"*Murderer. Murderer. Murderer.* We know what you are, Necromancer. You're a little *monster*." She cackled, and Lux clamped her hands over her ears, her eyes pressed closed.

She would ignore her. Shut it out.

The voice whispered like frost through the cracks. "*Murderer.*"

A sudden cry from the street caused Lux to jump. The presence disappeared from the wood at her back. Still, she wasn't about to risk opening it. She darted down the steps and around the corner and yanking back the curtains, she peered through the window.

A man's broad back blocked her view. A knife flashed in the light. It waved at the woman, and in response, she growled with a feral snarl, circling it, taunting him.

Finally, spitting onto the cobblestones, she straightened. With exaggerated strokes, she painted her face in jagged, black streaks. A mark of the contagion. The walking dead.

Her lips moved into a sweet smile. Lux couldn't make out what she said. Leaving Ned behind to adorn her stoop, the woman swayed down the street, baring her teeth at any who glanced her way.

The man tucked the knife away.

A soft knock sounded against her door.

Lux reluctantly strode back up the steps, straightening shoulders that kept fighting to droop. "Who is it?"

"It's Shaw. Let me in. Are you hurt?"

To her horror, tears pooled in her eyes. She swiped at them furiously, should they fall.

You don't deserve to cry. "I'm fine."

"Open the door."

"I need to call for the death-carts."

"You'll still need to open the door to accomplish that."

She scrunched her eyes closed, breathing deeply. The door creaked open, and Shaw immediately filled its frame. His cheekbones were pink against the cold, a cap low on his brow.

"Did she hurt you?" He scanned her body, and her muscles grew languid rather than stiffen. "Nothing on your skin?"

She shook her head. "No. Nothing on my skin."

He nodded, satisfied. "If I send off a message for a reaper, will you let me back in when I return?"

It was a fair question. One that she contemplated for only a heartbeat. "Yes."

She watched him until he disappeared from view. Then she stepped out to Ned's side. No one else came near them, the scent of rotting flesh and the view of a disfigured body being enough to sate any gossiping appetite.

It wasn't enough to sate her curiosity, however. She hadn't seen a contaminated body this close, and she refused to pass up the opportunity to learn more of it. She even found herself wishing for Riselda, as she could discern more than Lux ever could. Unfortunately, Riselda wasn't here, and she wasn't about to let the body sit here in its filth until her return.

Holding a sleeve to her nose, she bent at his side. Most of the boils appeared intact but for the few oozing their contents from beneath his arms. Likely burst open from the pressure of being held against a well-meaning woman.

Lux surveyed the rest of him, but aside from a few splotches of red clusters on his limbs, she found nothing else that hinted as to how this disease came to be. And why it seemed to be focused on Ghadra's poor.

"Why do you smell of jasmine of all things?"

"It's strange, isn't it?"

Lux tipped her head over her shoulder to find Shaw standing behind her. "That was fast." She stood, brushing debris from her skirt.

"Reapers are everywhere these days. Did the three carts last night wake you?"

They might have, being as how she lived on the only street that led to the forest. Except she'd slept the night elsewhere.

"I wasn't home. I visited my parents last night." Before he could question her further, she turned and strode through the door. "Would you like some tea?"

It annoyed her that his tea had been better, but she wouldn't admit it aloud. Instead, Lux stared at their feet, hers and Shaw's side by side, in contemplation. Their eyes bore into the brown rug beneath them, toward what lay below even that.

"The tunnel connects this house and your parents'? What would be the purpose in that?" His confusion only mirrored her own.

"I've no idea. And I've even less of what may be at the end of the other."

He lowered the cup from his lips, and she tracked its progress much too closely. "There's another?"

She nodded, her gaze now unfocused upon the floor, recalling the cold air and darkness that wrapped around her. "I don't feel good about it. And I can't discuss it with Riselda; she'd skin me for disobeying."

"I've wanted to talk with you about her. She visited the old woman who lives near me today. I believe the same one you spied on?" He quirked an eyebrow at her, and Lux glowered at him. "I left as she did, and she approached me."

The warning Riselda offered now crashed to her mind's forefront. "What did she say?"

"That she cares about few things in this world, and next to none of them are within Ghadra's walls. Aside from you. I'll admit I was taken aback she recognized me, what with the masquerade and all, but I wondered what she believes our relationship is? Have you told her anything?"

"I think she may have misunderstood our association following the party, but I assured her that wasn't the case." Though whether she believed her... "But about our theories involving the mayor and this disease? About the forest and the phantom? She's ignorant."

"Why?"

"Why what?" Lux finished her tea and entered the kitchen.

"Why have you kept it from her?" He followed, placing both his empty cup and hers in the basin, washing them clean.

She hung them to dry. "I tried to tell her once. But now, I suppose it's her behavior. She's rarely here, and when she is, I feel smothered and small. Her secrets outweigh ours, I'm certain, and there's also the little problem of her relationship with the mayor. She didn't return home until late morning. How can I trust her with our information when she may run to his bed with it?"

Shaw rested his hips against the counter, hands braced along its edge. He appeared relaxed. Much altered from their first encounters.

"Fair enough. Though after her veiled threat toward me today, I'm not sure you need to worry."

Lux snorted, mimicking Shaw's pose. "I'm sorry. Should I discuss our relationship with her again?"

Shaw's eyes creased, attention on his boots. "Let her believe what she wants."

The blush threatening her cheeks startled her, and she turned her face until it dissipated.

"Can I ask a personal question?"

She hesitated. "I may not answer it."

"I figured you'd say something of the same." He huffed a laugh before sobering, leaning toward her. "What made you decide to visit your old home?"

"Your kiss."

He reeled back. "What? How?"

She only shook her head. The air grew heavy with what she refused to say, the sound of quiet breaths blanketing it further.

"Lux." She looked up. His copper eyes delved into hers, but she shied away from it, glancing toward the workroom instead. "What that woman said... What she did to you..."

Her laugh was a sad thing, and he quieted. "I am a murderer, Shaw. She only spoke the truth." Lux pushed from the countertop. "Now, I have a question for you."

"I don't like that look. What is it?"

She grinned. "Have you ever trapped a howler?"

Chapter Twenty-One

Shaw fingered the black rope, coiled and wound tight. "This should work."

Lux copied him before glancing up at the merchant behind the stained booth. The Dark Market's usual rabble was scarce, with those who remained exposing eyes brimming with fear and lack of a good night's rest. The merchant's were no better. Deep blue circles edged into the top of his mask. He probably wouldn't even fight her if she offered him half the cost.

She slid seven coptons across the expanse. The asked-for price. He nodded his grey head and with their business concluded, gazed out across the cloud-covered square.

Lux grabbed for the rope at the same moment as Shaw, their hands meeting. She yanked hers back, her veins inflamed, at the same moment he stilled.

"Shaw! There you are. I've been waiting at your apartment for hours!"

Lux rubbed her hand down the length of her skirt before shoving it into her pocket. Then she turned to watch a blonde head bobbing toward them, too bright for this place.

As if a wall erupted before her, Aline halted. Glancing between the two of them, her mouth dropped wide, and Lux widened her stance on instinct. Ever observant, Aline's lips met one another once more, thinning.

"I didn't know you would be coming by." Shaw stepped toward her, his embrace quick.

"And I didn't know I needed to give you fair warning now." Dark eyes snapped with irritation, and she lowered her voice, "What are you doing with *her*?"

Lux laughed, harsh and threatening. "I can hear you, girl."

"I know." Aline's glare held no hint of fear. "Mind your business while I speak with my brother."

"Don't talk to her like that."

At the admonishment, Aline pulled back, spine straightening. "Excuse me?" Rising onto the tips of her toes, she poked Shaw in the chest. "Since when do you defend her? We hate her, remember?"

"I don't—" He glanced to Lux, his gaze revealing the same bewildered expression as the previous evening.

"Oh hell, enough already. Aline, your brother needed my help, and I'm asking him for a favor in return. When it's finished, we will happily go back to never speaking to one another. Satisfied?" Lux didn't look at Shaw as she spoke, sure she wouldn't see anything worthwhile there anyway.

Aline's eyes narrowed. "Good." She sniffed, apparently believing she'd won at whatever match they'd fought. "What's that for?" She pointed to the rope clutched in her brother's hand, his fingertips blanched white around it.

"Trapping."

"Trapping what?"

"Howlers," Lux interjected.

Aline's mouth fell open once more. Lux wished something would fly into it. "You'll be eaten! You can't do this for her!"

Shaw gripped Aline's shoulders, pushing her back to her heels. "Calm down. It's laying a few traps around the forest edge. It'll be done before nightfall."

"And what happens when you catch one?" Her glower tracked between the two of them.

Lux grinned, tongue pressed between her teeth. "Both your brother and me are familiar with the unsavory uses for a blade."

"You *witch*. You'll get him killed and laugh about it afterward!" Aline lunged for Lux, who did laugh then. Shaw hauled his sister backward by one ensnared wrist.

"Stop baiting her, Lux." His glare turned her laugh into a smirk, but she humored him, not speaking further.

He released his sister. "I'm tired of the both of you. Aline, I'll see you at dinner. Necromancer?" Turning his back on them, he marched off in the opposite direction.

Lux stared after him for a moment before she felt Aline's eyes fixed on her like a branding iron. "If he doesn't come back, I will personally pierce your heart."

Lux laughed inwardly, pulling the hood of her cloak up against the icy drizzle from the overcast sky. Her face eclipsed in shadow, her gaze found Aline's, meeting the challenge with one of her own. A last parting smile, a mocking bow, and she strode after Shaw.

THE STINK OF RAW meat enveloped them, and Lux struggled to remember to breathe through her mouth. What she wouldn't do for a sprig of mint.

Shaw had barely spoken to her, aside from discussing the best cuts of meat from the butcher to lure the elusive beasts, and who would be stuck with carrying the odorous load. He was adamant she should be saddled with it given it was her idea, but Lux knew it had more to do with her treatment of Aline.

Of course, one look at her pale face and sweat-slicked palms, and he had given in. Swinging the blood-splotched sack over his shoulder, he'd turned from her. They were steps before the bridge, and he still hadn't spoken since.

Shaw strode across the stones at the same moment Lux stilled.

A crow. A crow sat perched at its edge.

"Stop."

A sudden gust of wind whipped Shaw's coat about him. "What now?"

Lux studied the crow. The familiar tilt to its head. "I recognize this bird." With slow steps, she passed by an incredulous Shaw until she paused before the black-winged creature. "Hello, crow."

The sleek head tipped further, and she smiled at the acknowledgment. Except—the eyes. There was something unusual. Not quite right. Rather than familiar obsidian, they were murky and grey.

"Why—"

The bird lunged for her face.

Lux shrieked, batting it away, but the crow only continued its attack. Talons raked her cheek. She felt its beak pierce the skin at the corner of her eye, felt blood trickle hot from the wound. She screamed. The animal would not relent; it came for her, again and again. Until, abruptly, it ceased.

Lux stumbled back against the bridge, feeling the familiar cool stone beneath her fingers. She sought Shaw and watched him lower his spotless blade. Bloodied, her knife clattered to the moss at her feet.

Murderer.

Her back scraped down the stone as she fell.

"Saints." Shaw's arm reached beneath hers, his opposite thumb pressed to the edge of her eye. "It's over, Lux. The cut is shallow; I'll fix it up, so you won't even notice."

She shook her head against her parents' eyes, lit with life before they transformed into a sinister grey and back again in her mind.

"I killed it. I killed them. I killed them, again." Panic clenched her lungs, ripping out their air, and she clawed at her chest. "I'm a monster."

Shaw dropped to her side, but his warmth couldn't reach her. Her body shivered with cold. "You're not a monster. Listen to me. *Lux.* Look at me."

But she couldn't *breathe.*

Rough hands gripped either side of her face, turning her toward him. A furrowed brow pressed to her own. Warmth. A little, at last.

"Inhale with me."

"I—can't—"

A hand left her cheek to push beneath her chin, extending her throat. The other grabbed her palm, pressing it flush to his chest. "You will. Do as I do."

Lux couldn't hardly hear his words anymore, but his touch...

His chest expanded beneath her hand. Warm breath grazed her face. And the more she focused on the rhythmic pattern of those two things, the less she focused on anything else. Her eyes desperately sought his. Near as they were, she scarcely managed to make out their familiar shape, but it was enough.

Her lungs ceased their frantic cry.

The pressure on her brow increased for a heartbeat before lessening; her breaths matched his pace.

His next exhale seemed to come from the depths of him. "You may act as if you're sculpted of ice, Necromancer, but a true monster? I've met those before. I've shaken their hands, stared into their eyes." His hands left to trail the lengths of her arms before gripping her frozen fingers. "You are not one of them."

Chapter Twenty-Two

It took the complete rigging of one trap on the outskirts of the forest for Shaw to finally ask the question Lux could see lingering in his eyes.

"Will you be able to kill a howler should you catch one?"

Her earlier panic having ebbed to a low-frequency hum in her veins, she huffed. "I wasn't upset because I killed a crow if that's what you're thinking."

"It isn't that, no. I heard what you said."

She straightened, eyeing the dripping meat with distaste. Inside, however, where no one but her could see, she withered. "A body that's been revived past its time comes back twisted and unnatural. Its soul is warped and hungry for things it should never hunger for. Eyes are dulled, the color faded like fog. The crow had those eyes. And so did my parents."

"Your—"

"I did do it. But they were murdered by someone else first."

Cool rain drizzled from clouds so thick, Lux felt compressed beneath them. Drops fell from Shaw's lashes, where he'd pushed his cap back to better see her.

"Saints above," he breathed.

"More like the devil below, I should think. But I've never been a worshipping sort."

She watched him swallow. "You think that crow was revived? I thought you were the only one capable of that."

"I watched the bird swallowed into the heart of the tree. And I watched it today, perched on the bridge. I can't explain any more than that." She touched the thin scratches stretched along her cheek and decidedly avoided the deeper one by her eye.

"I'm sorry about your parents." Shaw moved to her side, and though his hands reached between them, where she struggled to handle the remaining bait, his gaze wouldn't release hers. It brimmed with understanding.

"It was a long time ago."

"All the same, I didn't know. Or didn't understand. The rumors... You could say they paint a different portrait."

Lux snorted. "I've heard them all by now, I think." Her expression turned thoughtful as she walked alongside Shaw, farther from Ghadra. She was stunned to discover she wished it wouldn't end. That they could keep walking endlessly, far away from here. What might it be like? To stay beside someone who understood her.

She wiped rain from her nose. "Do I truly act like I'm sculpted of ice?"

"In the dead of winter."

She laughed, and Shaw smiled down at her. "Thank you."

His smile faded to a quizzical frown. "For what? If anything I should apologize for not getting to you sooner."

"No. Don't." She swallowed, unsure how to go on. But he'd asked, and she found that her heart ached to answer. "Since the night of their deaths, I struggle to control my thoughts sometimes, and when they spiral out of control as they did... I can't always find air. My mind is this irrational, uncontrolled nightmare without an escape. But you pulled me back from falling to it entirely this time. I've never had someone do that for me before."

His smile returned, exceptionally brittle. "Knowing my father was down in that prison, witnessing the conditions they kept, and learning of his death, I experienced something of the same. Horrific paintings came into existence during the worst episodes. Art no one should ever experience. But I think it helped me cope." He cleared his throat. "Lux, if you ever find yourself in that place again, know to find me."

For the second time that afternoon, and for an entirely different reason, Lux struggled to draw breath. When she wiped her nose again, it was less for the rain, than the tears.

"I'm sorry for the loss of your father."

Shaw pulled the rope from his shoulder, preparing to craft another snare. His soft "thank you," floated between them before it was swept greedily into the wood.

THEY HAD WALKED AS much of the forest's edge as they'd dared, and now the foul-smelling bag lay empty at Shaw's feet. Six snares. Lux hoped it would be enough.

Twilight neared, but it no longer brought the same urgency to look out across the bridge, studying the watchful trees. Dread filled her instead. Beginning in her soul, its roots crept throughout her body, and she motioned for Shaw to hurry.

They had used up nearly all the supplies, and so it was with light arms that they turned their backs on the wood, the bridge a distant outline they strode toward. She quickened her pace.

"Lux—"

Lucena.

She broke into a jog.

Lucenaaa.

She ran outright.

"Lux!"

Fog swirled about her boots, and she slipped on the rain-soaked grass. A hand grabbed at her arm, but if it had meant to steady her, it had the opposite effect. She faltered, and then fell, bringing Shaw along with her.

She gaped at him in the tangled aftermath.

In his attempt to break her fall, he'd pulled her partway atop him, and now she was stuck staring into his eyes. Nose to nose. Again. Grey waves brushed and curled her hair. Dark grass pressed against his. The wood silenced.

"Why did you grab me, you halfwit?" Her words were whispered. Where she'd expected invisible, icy fingers, were very real warm ones. He had scared her. But the pounding of her chest against his wasn't anything to do with fear now.

"I didn't want you to fall."

Lux's brow furrowed, speechless at the absurdity, but when he shrugged beneath her, sweetly apologetic, she felt it bubble up her throat.

She couldn't help the laugh. "You're ridiculous." And she kept laughing, even as his eyes darkened.

Perfect. I've upset him. Hurt his sensitive feelings.

His lips against hers felt entirely different this time.

She could have pulled back and leapt from him, but she didn't. His hands stilled. He barely breathed. This kiss was a question, the answer uncertain. Yet, the fire climbed anyway, twining between them. Lux was sure it poured from her, sure there would be no excuses when it ended. So she gave the only answer she could—and pressed her mouth harder against his.

His hand left her forearm to caress her cheek, his opposite settling on her hip, and it was at that moment, dangerously close to the edge of something, that a crow screeched. The sound startled her back to reality. Her lips left his as she pushed up on her arms. Dew soaked through her sleeves.

His hand dropped from her face.

"What are we doing?" Breathless, chest heaving, her words barely reached her ears.

He watched her closely, his eyes so dark. "I have no idea."

His voice had roughened, and Lux groaned over the ache it caused. But his words... "I thought as much."

Sitting in the grass, she shoved the hair from her eyes, the fog so thick she could hardly discern Ghadra. She sighed, climbing to her feet.

"That's not what I... I'm sorry, I could have phrased that better."

"Probably. But then you wouldn't be you." Lux grabbed at a pack stuffed with rope ends, a long knife, a ball of twine. "Thank you for your help today."

Shaw rose slowly. "Lux. Let me try to explain."

"Another time. Riselda will be waiting for me, and Aline for you. I'd rather not have my heart pierced just yet." *In more ways than one.*

Lux turned her back on him and his blank stare. On his dark eyes clearing of their confusion. She didn't linger to observe what pooled in its stead.

Chapter Twenty-Three

Riselda was smoothing back waves of hair in the mirror when Lux stepped through the door. Their eyes met through the glass before her aunt turned toward her.

"There you are, Lucena! You look frozen. Been wandering the marshes?" Riselda chuckled, swinging back to her reflection in a swish of burgundy skirts to fix a sparkling drop into her lobe.

Lux didn't answer. Shucking her cloak instead, she skirted wide of her aunt, moving toward her bedroom. She felt a cool gaze at her back but shut it out with the click of her door.

Dirtied clothing was tossed to the floor, and Lux pulled a dress from her wardrobe. Black, with a rounded neckline, a beaded bodice to catch the dim light and a bow at the back. She couldn't remember the last time she'd worn it, but if her aunt wanted to dine out dressed as she was, Lux figured she would at least make a little effort.

The small looking glass adhered to the ornate door offered her a well-enough view to wind her wild hair into a chignon at her nape, and with neck and ears free of adornment, she stepped out to greet Riselda.

"Ready?"

Lux studied her aunt and her expanse of creamy, pale skin that would surely protest exposure to the cold night air. Her face was smooth and perfect. Youthful.

And, for the first time, a new doubt crept in.

"Yes."

Riselda swished toward her so fast, Lux couldn't dodge. Fingers gripped her chin. "What marked your beautiful face, Lucena?" Releasing her, a fingertip wiped at the ointment Shaw had applied to the deeper wound. Riselda sniffed at it before licking it clean. "What is this amateur work?"

Endless secrets. Lux had them, too. "The Dark Market. I tripped and scraped my temple against one of the stalls. The crone gave me some paste."

"You accepted treatment from that old decrepit? You'll be lucky if you're not poisoned! I thought you'd better sense, girl. You are to always come to me, do you understand?"

"Yes, Riselda."

A carriage rumbled across the cobblestones at her words. Riselda extended a hand. "What timing. Come along, darling." Lux stepped toward those outstretched fingers, watching them wind around her forearm. "We have much to discuss."

Riselda may as well have had her fangs still in place as deep as Lux felt the words bite into her flesh.

THE CARRIAGE RIDE SITTING across from Riselda had reached an uncomfortable silence. Lux stared out into the evening's fading light, aware of her aunt's continued scrutiny. A death-cart shadowed her face, passing their sleek carriage within the narrow street. She sucked in a breath at the mound of bodies.

Riselda's eyes followed hers.

"This plague is rampant. I would stay far from that side of town, my dear."

"That's not possible. The Dark Market supplies most of what lines my workroom." She didn't add that Riselda, herself, wasn't bothering to heed her own advice, and when her aunt said nothing further, she continued, "Speaking of, will you return to the role of Ghadra's Healer now that you've returned?"

Riselda laughed, deep and musical. Goosebumps erupted on Lux's arms at the sound.

"No. That part of my life is thankfully dead."

"But the mayor—"

"The *mayor*," Riselda leaned forward, eyes raking her face, "cannot touch me."

Lux eased back, watching her aunt drop her shoulders once more from beneath a hooded gaze. It would appear she'd been wrong to assume the mayor would demand Riselda's return to the role which he'd appointed her so long ago. Or perhaps he had. And Riselda had refused him.

Though Lux puzzled at why she would. She was Ghadra's Necromancer. It didn't make her the mayor's puppet to be named so.

It didn't.

"I was welcomed home by a most disturbing site on my doorstep this afternoon. Did you attempt to revive someone with the contagion?"

Lux shook her head. "No. The woman that brought him left without payment. I called for the death-carts, but they must have been delayed."

"I would strongly suggest you do not attempt such a thing. Even should payment be presented."

"What? Why not?"

"It isn't safe. If you should come into contact with the fluids bursting from those boils, you will succumb just the same."

"I am more than capable of making that decision on my own, Riselda."

"Not in my home you will not, Lucena." Lux's jaw ticked around clenched teeth as the shadows deepened between them. Riselda sighed. "Enough of this dreary subject."

The carriage slowed to a stop.

"At last. You will simply love the wine here."

"I don't—"

The door opened and Riselda exited with a flourish. The vacated space left Lux to wonder just how much more disappointment her aunt would tolerate from her.

Superfluous was the best word that came to mind whenever Lux passed this establishment, and now, here she stood, on the threshold, absorbing the out-of-sight violin's sweet melody.

Riselda smiled, surveying polished tables, thick candlesticks, crisp uniforms—an abrasive reminder of just how far they were from the Dark. Lux had never possessed the desire to enter this place. She felt like an interloper and fervently wished she had worn a necklace at the very least.

Did Riselda not know her at all?

No. Of course she didn't. Lux changed much from the little girl who thrived on color, music and joy. She must be unrecognizable.

Lux squared her shoulders and pasted a smirk on her lips. More and more eyes found her: her hair, her dress, her body. Never focusing on her face. She could not vanish here and so must do the next best thing.

Confidence. She oozed it. Rather, she faked it. Lux learned long ago that the more superficial the person, the less likely they were to see past her mask. Unable to read deeper and discover the truth.

"This way, madams." The vested server led them through the center of the foray.

Lux's gaze landed on one man in particular as he unabashedly stared at Riselda, the woman at his side looking on with scarlet cheeks. His dramatic squeal reminded her of a chased piglet as his drink tipped onto his lap by her clumsy fingers.

She tucked them demurely in front of her once more, never pausing. But inside she sparked with flame. She longed to kick the chair from beneath him and press a booted heel to his face, forcing him to apologize to both Riselda and his companion in order to secure his release.

She breathed it away.

Riselda was seated first, followed by herself. The round table was lit by a single candlestick flickering with white flame, at a vantage perfect for observing the entire room. Though Lux was keenly aware this meant she would also be so easily inspected. Riselda ordered wine for them both before she could protest the drink, and, with an unapologetic lift to her lips, gazed at her from across the sleek wood.

"That was a nice trick with the glass. I hardly saw your fingers move." Riselda's eyes flicked across the room. "He's still confused as to what happened." She chuckled, reaching for the napkin.

"People like that disgust me."

"Oh, so your male friend is not of the same?"

Lux bit her cheek to keep her harsh words from bursting forth. Unfortunately, the pause allowed Shaw's face to enter her mind instead. Beneath her. She felt the sear of his lips against hers and heated at the mere memory.

"Oh my. Apparently you don't believe so." Riselda turned her wicked smile upon the server, accepting the outstretched glass. "I am going to give you some advice, Lucena. Did you see that woman beside the man you deposited wine upon? Her power was drained long ago. Her gaze holds no fire, her words weigh nothing. She can no longer speak because she doesn't remember how."

Riselda took a scandalously large sip of the crimson liquid.

"Do you want to know a secret?" Her eyes were a storm. Lux felt sure she could see the lightning striking within. "I almost became her. And when the last of my flame flickered and sputtered, I made my decision. I disappeared—and rose from the ashes." She eased back into her seat with eyes that slowly shifted back to familiar indigo. "My power is unfathomable now."

Lux assumed it to be a metaphor, but a small voice deep down rocked back and forth, terrified it was not.

"I'm sorry about all you've been through, Aunt, but you don't know her story." Though the scene Riselda had painted left her anxious—a situation she would never near. She meant what she had said to Aline. She fully planned to cease contact with Shaw when this was over.

She frowned. When exactly had they become allies?

"I know enough." Riselda swirled a final swallow in the glass, studying her. "You haven't tried your wine."

"I don't enjoy alcohol."

Riselda's mouth tightened, her gaze chilling. "You remind me so much of your mother." She sniffed, draining her glass. "Your father too, in fact." She reached across the table, her fingers enclosing greedily over Lux's wine. The candle's flame sought her skin, and either she did not feel it, or she didn't care.

The server returned.

"The chef here is brilliant." Riselda's mouth relaxed around the words. Turning back to the server, she added, "Please tell her we would like something new. Something unique." The server's lips parted, but her words vanished under the pressure of Riselda's fingers on her forearm. "Thank you."

"Tedious." Her aunt's eyes found hers again. "Your face is much improved; you're welcome. Now, tell me how you have been. I feel as if we haven't spoken much since my return."

Lux blinked, the demand unexpected. "I have been worried, Riselda. As we all should be."

"Oh yes. The plague again." Lux's eyes bulged against the dismissive tone. "Follow my advice, and you've nothing to worry about."

"I'm not only worried for myself. While I've no love for this town, there are still some good people within its walls."

Riselda snickered into her glass. "There is nothing good left in Ghadra."

"What do you mean?"

A breadbasket was set between them, and Riselda ripped a roll down its center. "Just as I said. This town is rotting. First the wildlife, the flowers, the walls, and finally, the people." Riselda bit into the thick crust. "It is rotting. And soon the forest will lay claim to what remains."

Lux's appetite was a nonexistent thing. "Is there no stopping it?"

Riselda studied her from the rim of her glass. "Not in the slightest."

Shadowed tendrils crept through her mind, bringing nightmarish images in their wake. "What will happen to us?"

"I've spent many years perfecting my craft. As have you. I've little doubt that we will be standing long after these walls fall."

The answer might have satisfied her once upon a time. Not anymore.

Their plates arrived. Mounds of buttery potatoes had been carved into bird-like shapes, a breast of some roasted fowl dripping and fragrant resting atop each. The aromatic scents nearly brought her hunger back, which was no easy feat considering how nauseated she felt over Riselda's words. Wings fluttered in the steam as it twined through the air.

Riselda lifted a laden fork to plump lips, her crystal eyes assessing the ones across from her. "You have braved the forest at last, I see." Lux choked against the bite of food she'd attempted to appease her aunt. Surely, she couldn't know about her venture. "I happened to notice your departure this afternoon. Don't worry, I wasn't spying." Riselda laughed then, finishing Lux's wine.

Lux's constricted chest uncoiled, just a little, thankful Riselda hadn't been aware of her true encounter with the forbidden wood. She swallowed quickly, wincing. "I had no other choice. The vendor who supplied me with howler canines died. And Shaw has a little knowledge in trapping, so I enlisted his help." Lux shrugged, unapologetic. "It won't be possible to revive most without them."

"You've laid traps around the forest edge?"

She nodded.

"I wish you would have consulted with me first."

Lux fought back a lengthy sigh. "Why is that?"

"Because, darling, I can get you the teeth you need. Quite easily, in fact, and it won't even require the deaths of the poor animals. Though it may irritate them, that is for certain." Riselda brought another bite to her full lips.

"How is that possible?" Disbelief coated her words. Howlers were exceptionally quick, vicious, and deadly. The possibility of killing a trapped one set her heart to hammering; she couldn't fathom coaxing the teeth from the mouth of a very-much-alive beast.

"Every soul yearns for something, Lucena. Give it what it wants, and it becomes a much more amiable being."

"Fine, what does a howler yearn for?" Her flesh, surely.

Riselda smiled, guessing her thoughts with startling accuracy. "Not your assumption, that's for certain. Dismantle your traps. I will procure them for you."

"Well...Thank you, Riselda." Lux couldn't hold back her sigh of relief; she'd been dreading an encounter with the creature, half hoping it would fail.

"You're welcome." Her aunt's hand reached across the table, gripping her wrist, her thumb stroking the bare skin. "Now enjoy your meal. Who knows when this, too, will crumble?"

Lux rested back into her chair, eyeing Riselda as she promptly followed her own advice. Beneath the table, she rubbed her wrist, sure it had been worn to the bone.

Chapter Twenty-Four

Very few ventured to the bridge past twilight, let alone crossed it. Midnight dragged the moon to the highest point in the sky, and there it sat, watchful over a cloaked girl slipping through the wet grass like a wraith. She walked alone, clutching tight to a borrowed, bone-handled knife.

A shriek pierced the air. Fury and fear melded into a cry that tore at Lux's ears and sent cold sweat trickling down her back.

A successful trap. She had hoped to find them empty. She didn't have a choice now, and, with a quick glance at the glimmering blade, the flicker of resolve grew to a steady weight within her.

She neared the wood's edge, the trees silent and unmoving, the darkness within complete. With a slash of the knife, the rope suspending the first trap fell.

The cry filled the air again.

Lux crept along the outskirts of the forest, eyes trained on its insides. Another empty trap fell beneath her blade. Three. Four. Five.

She destroyed them all. Save one.

She stared across the moonlit grass, watched it writhe. Howling, the creature fought to free itself from the binds. Fingers blanched even as sweat slipped along the knife's handle. Lux only gripped it harder, squeezing her fear away.

The beast stilled.

It smelled her, and yellowed eyes tracked her scent as she stood tall, the gleam of her weapon shining beneath the moon's light. A low howl sounded again, but it was no longer one of fear.

Rage.

How it longed to tear at her throat.

She swallowed. "Your sacrifice is appreciated, beast."

But the eyes left hers. They sought the trees. Lux dropped to a crouch as a shadow moved within the copse.

Cloaked in grey, it floated from beneath the boughs toward the restrained howler. Yellowed eyes closed. The animal fell to its dark, cat-like haunches, the rope buried deep into the skin of its thick neck. With pale, dirt-encrusted fingers, the phantom reached forward, wrapped them around the rope, and released the beast.

Lux's body was stone. She didn't move. She didn't breathe. She simply waited.

And when the phantom disappeared into the trees, the howler stalking at its side, she allowed the bone handle to slip through her fingers. She understood something now, and it made her all the more frightened for the knowledge. For the figure was an extension of the wood itself—an ally of all within. And anything that allied itself with such evil could only be an enemy.

It must never find her.

Lux allowed another heartbeat to stutter before she tore from the forest's edge. Back to Ghadra. Returning to a different sort of darkness, and a very real terror, but one she understood.

The whole while, she felt the trees grin at her back, watching her go.

LUX STRIPPED DAMP CLOTHES from her body.

She had kept her gaze from traveling to Riselda's small bed as she crept silently across the floor, not wishing to meet her aunt's questioning eyes should she awaken. Lux's skill at moving unseen had proved ever useful, however. Riselda hadn't stirred.

Lux piled blankets atop her, extinguishing the lamp. Then wished she hadn't. The encompassing darkness brought the phantom to her side, and soon, a heartbeat filled the air.

Her own.

Why was she so frightened? Yet, she knew. Deep within. The phantom drifted through the wood like the very soul of the trees given form. It was a friend to howlers, unaffected by the dead, and in league with the night.

She shut her eyes and pulled the blankets higher when a swish of fabric against wood stilled her thoughts. Outside the door.

Her breath took root in her lungs, and she listened with parted lips, but the sound didn't reoccur. In its place, rose the heavy presence of another, unmoving, against the wooden frame.

The swish of fabric again, and the presence was gone. Lux exhaled.

Only Riselda coming to snoop.

With an irritated huff, Lux rolled to her side, and promptly fell asleep.

CHAPTER TWENTY-FIVE

"Not only do you want to go for a stroll through the forest, but at *night*?" Shaw laughed, bringing the pint of ale to his lips.

Lux watched him swallow before turning her head, eyeing the startlingly empty room. The Brewing Bog's regular crowd had dwindled to a few glassy-eyed patrons focused on their drink rather than their companions. The barkeep had been arrested, as rumor told. Dragged to prison for crimes no one knew. He may very well have done whatever they accused him of, but the Shield, and certainly the mayor, were deeply involved in much, much worse. Her imagination spun with the image of his laughing eyes clouding over, and, finally, descending into dust.

Shaw's coat bulged, the faintest outline of the returned journal beneath it. Lux hadn't meant to stay longer than a moment, but the warmth drew her in again. Why couldn't she ignore it?

She made to pull back now. Her body leaned in further, instead. "Why is that so ridiculous to you? This phantom clearly resides in the wood, amongst the trees, with howlers as companions and who knows what else. Aren't you curious?"

"Certainly not curious enough to die."

"You didn't enjoy it the first time?"

Shaw quirked his lips at her. "Take my advice. Don't do it."

"Hmm. No, I think I'm going to. Riselda would have me knitting in front of the fire, waiting for Ghadra's collapse. There is something I'm missing. I feel it, and I can't sit here and wait for the plague to take me. To take everyone." She clutched at the black fabric covering her lap, abruptly puzzled.

Saints above. Who have I become?

But no, that wasn't quite right. Her hands overturned on her thighs so that she stared at her palms, the lines she found there. Her gaze narrowed. Perhaps it was more like: *When did I return?*

"Ghadra's own vigilante." Shaw's eyes creased above the rim of his mug.

She scoffed. "I thought you had already claimed that title?"

Smile fading, he rubbed his thumb over the handle of his drink. "It's getting worse. It's as if they're feeding upon the fear already blanketing this town." He touched a bandage as it peeked from beneath his sleeve.

"We have to put a stop to this."

He nodded. "I want to go to the prison."

"*What?* And you tell me venturing into the forest is mad…"

"That *is* mad. If the mayor is harvesting lifeblood, if he's behind this sickness sweeping through Ghadra, I think we'll find the evidence of it there."

"In the prison?"

"In the prison."

Lux observed a drunk woman stumble through the doors, pulling her mask into place. A mask that served no purpose. "I'll come with you."

Shaw returned his mug to the bar top. "You don't have to."

"As if I don't know that."

His eyes darkened, and she narrowed her own. There was something there. Something that hadn't been before. "I thought we were finished. Happily never speaking to one another?"

That bothered you?

She could hardly believe it. An airy giddiness suffused her chest: a remarkable sensation she refused to analyze.

"Perhaps we could work together a little longer." Frowning then, she added, "Only don't kiss me again."

He twitched, taken aback. "I won't."

"Oh, and one more thing." Tawny eyes flicked to her as she rose from the stool. "You're coming into the forest with me."

LUX WALKED ALONG THE street for a time before slinking into an alley, an alley that would bring her to the invisible crossover to the Light. She skirted wide of another large rat pilfering the trash left along leaning walls. She sneered at it, disgusted, when a shadow fell across her.

"We meet again, Necromancer." Scorn dripped from the word, and Lux spun from the rat, cursing the Shield's sudden appearance. One man quickly turned into three.

The sack of flour. He certainly didn't appear as pleased to see her as the previous encounter.

"Sorry, are you sure we've met?"

Heavy-lidded eyes sharpened on her. "I've been looking for you. You really believe your title of *mayor's pet* allows you to assault the Shield? You must be thick as marsh mud."

She bristled at the familiar assumption. "I think you have much more experience petting the mayor's ego than I do." A lovely shade of purple entered his skin. "But semantics aside, I never assaulted you. Please move. I've a mountain of things to accomplish today."

"You dumped my own sleeping potion down my throat! You're about to be arrested!"

Spittle flew from his mouth. Lux tracked its descent, happy to be out of range. "Now doesn't *that* seem far-fetched. I doubt the mayor will be pleased when Ghadra's only necromancer dies inside his prison only because a man's ego was bruised."

The two uniformed men behind him shifted their feet.

"The mayor doesn't know half of what happens down there, girl. You won't die. But you will wish you had." A manic gleam had entered his eyes now, and he stepped toward her. "I have a few techniques in particular that I enjoy, and maybe, upon your release, you'll understand the price of disrespecting someone of my station."

Her hands twitched, longing to throttle him, but she stifled their movements. "You're not taking me *anywhere*."

The heavy-eyed man grinned, tipping his head back to his comrades. "I love it when they say that to me."

He lunged, only to reel back when Lux's perfectly pointed nails raked along his face. With a roar, he brought his hands to the dripping mess. "You clawed out my eye!"

"As I said." She crossed her arms to hide their shake. The men behind him had yet to offer assistance, their gazes traveling from her to the blood splattering the ground and back again.

A guttural growl spewed from his lips. "If you don't help me in this, I'll throw you both behind bars myself."

His uninjured eye hadn't left hers, but Lux knew whom he'd addressed.

She ran.

She had barely made it partway back the way she'd come before the air was knocked from her lungs. Lux collapsed to her knees and then her stomach, feeling as if her back were cracked in two. She tracked the iron ball as it rolled from her side, the chain clanging against stone, another trailing in its wake. She couldn't breathe. It hurt too much.

With a cry escaping her lips, she was hauled into unfamiliar arms, her own trapped behind her back. The pain sent spots raining down from the skies. Hazy features moved before her then, a blood-soaked smile stretching his face.

Lux gagged as the taste of iron swept across her tongue, dirtied fingers prying her lips apart. She felt them crack. Lashing out with her boots, she connected with a shin. Whose it belonged to, she wasn't sure, but a hiss resounded from somewhere.

"Goodnight, Necromancer."

Bitter liquid rolled down her throat, pitching her into darkness.

Chapter Twenty-Six

Stone scraped. Chains clanged. A rasping cry filled the mildewed air.

Darkness.

Lux pushed herself to her elbows, a hammer relentlessly pounding against her skull. Had that Shield felt like this, a side effect of the potion? Or had they beaten her for the scratched eye and bruised shin?

Her throat was parched, her back sent painful spasms of molten heat through her core with every breath, yet she forced herself to sit, resting gingerly against the crumbling stone.

She couldn't see anything. Perhaps a faint outline of her hand in front of her face? She wasn't sure. It hurt to open her eyes anyway and she let them slide closed as she focused on the rest of her body instead.

Aside from her back and head, the only thing that irritated her now were her cracked and swollen lips. Lux fantasized of a cool drink of water, imagined it sliding past them, down her aching throat.

What was he thinking? Doing this to her? She glared beneath closed lids. She would demand to speak with the mayor. Pound on the door until they obeyed. Though first, she would have to find the door. No—first she would have to convince her muscles to support her. They didn't appear in a very amiable mood right now.

Lux unclenched her fists, her chest tightening instead with a familiar ache. "Help me." The whisper didn't leave her side, blanketed by stagnant air.

A key scraped and clicked within a lock from somewhere in the distance, and she opened one eye as yellow light crawled through the widening crack. It flooded the space, the door pushed wide, only to be shuttered behind the form of a man.

"Sleep well?"

The familiar voice sent ice skittering over her skin. She shut him out, retreating once more into the dark. She couldn't fight him. She could barely move.

"I didn't take you for the type to give up so easily. I'm disappointed. I like the ones that fight the best." The voice was closer now and her eyelids twitched. A rough hand cupped her cheek, a cold finger running across her bloodied lip. "Pity."

His hands moved beneath her arms as he hauled her up. Her legs buckled, but when he held fast, she felt her muscles begin to obey. At last, they ceased their spasms and supported her weight.

"If you can't walk, I'll throw you over my shoulder. Your choice." The voice slid into her ear, and she staggered forward. His oily laugh echoed against stone walls, and he let her go.

Lux squinted against the lantern shining through the narrow doorway, but she didn't look away. One. Two. Three. She counted her steps. Just one more. Just one more after that. Her back screamed at her to fall to the filthy ground and cease these repetitive, worthless movements, but she couldn't heed it.

Not when she could feel the beast's breath against her neck.

Triumphant light caressed her skin at the same moment a gloved hand clamped down on her arm, forcing her to follow its ascent to hardened features, reddened gouges along one cheek. He smiled beneath a bandaged eye.

"This way, girl."

The brick tunnel loomed. The shadows created from the lantern-light twisted the length of it, making it bend and warp. Or perhaps that was simply a lasting effect of the potion. She allowed the uniformed man to lead her forward, taking shallow breaths against the pain.

"You're awful quiet. Head hurt? I've been there myself." His hand came up to squeeze behind her ears, and she gasped. He laughed again. "You know, you probably deserve this more than anyone I've done this to. For some time anyway." He shrugged, enjoying the sound of his own voice. "The mayor won't mind. If fact, he'll thank me. He'll thank me for breaking you, just a bit."

Lux trudged on.

She questioned what Shaw had said. She didn't hear any—

Screams. They ricocheted through the air, pummeling into her, and her heart flew into a wild pattern. Guttural. Agonized. *Tortured.* Then, light. It beckoned ahead, calling to her with a false sense of hope.

For once, she yearned for the darkness instead.

The Shield pushed through double doors where the resulting brightness blinded her. Her head pounded harder. Vomit threatened its way up her throat.

Though it wasn't her pain this time that caused it.

A bone-chilling scream filled her ears again, and Lux couldn't look away from him. The man strapped to the table. So much white: the table, the sheet, the surgeon's coat, the linens he used to sop away pooling blood.

"The body has always intrigued the mayor. He used to use cadavers, but we've found a better method. It loosens most tongues. If they survive, that is." A low chuckle filled the air between them, and when an exceptionally large clot of crimson fell to the stone with a splat, Lux emptied her stomach along with it until she wheezed. Tears tumbled down her cheeks.

The surgeon glanced up from behind a blood-splattered white mask, only to resume his work as if she didn't exist. The prisoner appeared to have passed out. Either that or he'd died from shock. With blurred eyes, Lux watched a scalpel slice deeper into his insides.

Her feet grew roots as the guard at her side rocked on his heels. Eager. The surgeon crudely stitched the man's abdomen closed, a thick needle and even thicker suture. Once complete, he reached forward. Felt for a pulse at the neck.

He didn't find it. But his eyes did find Lux's. They creased at their corners.

Tossing off blood-soaked gloves, the surgeon strode to a table, selecting a vial. Moving back to the body, he procured a new scalpel. Longer, but thinner. It flashed beneath rows of lamplight.

Peeled back eyelids revealed fixed pupils, staring forever upward. Lux gasped, horrified, as the scalpel sliced deep into one then the other. Thin, watery liquid trickled from the wound. The surgeon waited for it to slow and then pressed a vial to the incision.

The Shield dragged her around, hauling her into another room. One much darker, but much less terrifying. For Lux knew she didn't imagine the gleam of silver as a thick substance oozed from the body.

The mayor had, indeed, learned to harvest lifeblood.

And so had Shaw.

Chapter Twenty-Seven

Slit pupils.

Rapists. Abusers. Murderers. That's what he had said. *They don't deserve to see the afterlife. Even if it is Hell.*

Liar.

Lux didn't flinch as the man before her shoved her into a hard-backed chair. Didn't move as her wrists and ankles were shackled to it with thick, leather straps. The buckles clicked closed.

Her parents' deaths had shattered her. Broken, the pieces remaining were then scattered to the wind beneath the treatment of the mayor's family. And as much as she wanted to, she didn't trust Riselda. She couldn't. Something held her back.

But, against her better judgment, she had begun to trust Shaw.

Fool.

Ghadra was rotting.

Let it.

Lux rested her head back.

The Shield lit a lone candle, its flame pulsing hungrily against the dark. With quick fingers, he sifted through the wall of vials. Each clink of glass knocked against her skull.

Offering a wide grin, he jabbed the needled point of a syringe into a narrow glass. "I bet you have all sorts of nightmares. Do you meet them often?" Lux bared her teeth, splitting her lip further. A drop of blood formed and dripped down her chin. He wiped it clean. "Answer me, girl."

She watched him through hooded eyes. "I am the nightmare."

The man chuckled, bringing his face within a mere breadth of hers. "No, you're not." He pressed the needle to her skin. "You're just a pathetic, broken doll. I don't know what the mayor is afraid of."

Lux fought back a cry as the metal punctured her jugular, but not hard enough. She screamed as it burned through her veins.

A satisfied murmur in her ear. "Let's meet them, shall we?"

The Shield retreated into the shadows as did the burning in her body; she couldn't see him any longer. Instead, she watched the flame. Flickering, flickering, tendrils of smoke winding from its tip.

The smoke grew. It puffed from the candle in clouds. Clouds that twisted and warped and began to take form.

The darkness quaked around her. It beat in tempo with her heart, and Lux couldn't help herself. She gripped the chair beneath her, her bruised back pressed tight against it.

Murky-grey eyes materialized, staring into her own. A shape. A shadow. The form of her mother floated toward her. Lux's feet pushed uselessly against the stone floor.

"*No.* Stop."

A second form shuddered into view. Her father.

You have forgotten us, Lucena.

Rasping voices filled the room. It filled her head. Their mouths didn't move, and yet they spoke to her, and her alone.

A tear tracked down Lux's cheek. "I haven't."

Dark blood ran from their throats—from where they had been murdered the first time. It ran from their hearts. Where they had been murdered the second time.

Lux stared at the site. At the knives resting in their chests. The knives she had placed there. *Pierced.*

As one, the shadows of her parents pulled them forth, leaving gaping black holes in their wake. Smoke and darkness poured from the openings.

How could you?

They moved closer. They raised their blades high.

We loved you. We trusted you. You betrayed us. You failed us. It should have been you.

It should have been you.

And Lux screamed as the blades tore through skin, muscle and bone. She screamed as they pierced her heart.

All she could see were the eyes. The distorted, unnatural eyes of those that should be dead, but were granted another life. Their faces warped, their lips pulled up in scorn, twisting into unrecognizable shapes, until they dissipated into nothing. Lux was certain their blades had remained. Her chest hurt with every heaving breath.

The smoke hovered, unmoving.

Until, slowly, it churned anew.

The mayor. And another. Morana.

Lux's breaths picked up speed. The shadow of Morana noticed, and smiled, but it was the mayor's form that spoke first.

Little Necromancer. You will always be second best. But if I cannot have the healer, I will gladly take you in exchange.

A grey finger brushed across her cheek, and she flinched.

Such a gift. With me, I can make you the most powerful woman in Ghadra.

"Get away from me!" Lux growled at him, but her words were less than nothing.

You'll not so much as breathe without my permission. You cannot escape me.

The shadowed form drifted aside to watch her beneath an expectant gaze. Only for Morana to take his place. The sneer she directed toward her cut her as sharply as ever, casting her back to her eight-year-old body.

Just look at you. Pale, bruised, bleeding and ugly. The shadow sniffed in disdain. *You always were useless. Worthless. It suits you—being strapped to this chair.*

Lux glared defiantly.

Don't think I don't notice how my family looks at you. And for that alone, I will destroy you.

The stinging slap across her cheek opened every crack in her lips and jarred her back so painfully she cried out. Morana's laugh echoed through the small chamber, before they, too, dissipated.

Stupid girl.

Shaw crossed his arms in the corner of her vision, his usually warm brown eyes darkened to black. Lux closed her own, the betrayal too fresh. She heard him anyway.

A menacing chuckle filled her head. *Lifeblood is all I've ever sought. All I have ever cared for. Eternal life. Do you think I'll stop with the dregs of Ghadra?*

She swore she could smell his scent, his honeyed breath against her lips.

You're next. And when I slit your eyes, drain them entirely, and drink the silver that resides within you, know that I will personally toss your body to the darkness of the trees.

You will never see the light.

The candle snuffed, pitching her into an abyss. Lux pulled against her bonds, felt them dig into her flesh as the pain clutched her with an unyielding grip.

A disembodied voice filled the room.

Oh, Lucenaaa.

Didn't you know?

I murdered your parents.

"Who said that?" Lux's eyes snapped open at the unfamiliar voice. They roved frantically about the impenetrable room.

A wild laugh raked at her ears. It echoed in thunderous waves.

"WHO ARE YOU?" Tears dropped from her lashes and blood dripped from her fingertips. Both trickled down her raw throat.

That laugh. It wouldn't stop. She couldn't take it. The darkness pulsed in rapid tempo, mimicking the pace of her heart. Lux felt her consciousness slip.

Secrets, secrets, secrets.

He'd broken her—just as he promised he would.

Her head lolled, her voice a ragged sob. "Tell me. Please. Tell me…"

THE SPLASH OF COLD water on her face jolted Lux from her stiff, bent position. She groaned.

"Wake up, girl."

Her attempt to roll from the voice proved futile. Something held her still, and she squinted open her eyes.

The chair, the straps, the candle. They all came into focus at once, and she lurched back, cracking her head against the wood behind her.

The Shield grinned. "Did you enjoy that? I certainly enjoyed watching you squirm. Who came to you, I wonder?"

He hadn't seen what she'd seen. It had all been within her own mind. But it had felt so *real.* Lux glanced at her chest, the fabric intact.

No knives extended from her.

"Such a mess you've made, though." The guard sniffed at the puddles of blood on the stone, directly below her hands. Turning, he reached for the vials once more. "What will we try next?"

A very real knife found its home this time.

The man slumped into the wall, sending potions raining from their perch to shatter against the floor. Puffs of mist and smoke melded in their midst.

Lux didn't spare a second glance for him, craning her neck instead to the doorway. To a seething Riselda, eyes snapping with flame. A second knife flashed in her hand. With quick movements she stepped over the body, slitting his throat.

Blood spurted across the chamber, and she shoved him down. "You think you can take her from me? *Never.*" Riselda spun toward Lux, hands miraculously clean. "Lucena. Are you all right?"

Lux nodded once, and Riselda retuned the gesture, striding over to her and unbuckling the restraints. "Who else was involved in this?"

Lux regretted every foul thought that had ever entered her mind regarding her aunt. "Two others." She described them quickly.

"Can you walk?"

"Yes."

"Good. I will see you home. Then I plan to have a nice, long conversation with our mayor. Despicable. He should count himself lucky if he makes it through alive."

With a careful hold on her arm, Riselda hauled her to standing. Lux swayed on her feet. Her aunt's grip tightened, and she steadied herself at last. "Thank you, Riselda. I think I can stand on my own now."

Riselda released her one finger at a time. "Have you had anything to drink since your capture?"

She shook her head, once again acutely aware of just how parched her throat had become. "How much time has passed?"

Riselda's lips thinned. "When you didn't return home last night, I began my search. It wasn't until I found a drunken woman this evening who remembered your leaving the Brewing Bog and encountering several members of the Shield, that I finally realized where you had been taken."

An entire night and day had come and gone. No wonder she felt so miserable. A wave of dizziness descended, and she stumbled. Riselda frowned, gripping her around the waist.

Walking alongside her, Lux entered the adjoining room. The dead body was gone. The surgeon as well. In its place was a cleaned table, though she was sure she could see stains marring its surface.

She made for the doors, but Riselda's grip around her tightened. "Not yet, Lucena." Releasing her slowly, her aunt left her side, striding to the shelves filled with decanters, vials and powders.

Pulling a fresh beaker toward her, Riselda opened several of them to sniff and slosh their contents. Without another glance at Lux, she began to pour, sift and mix until the mixture changed from coarse opaque to a clear, light blue.

Riselda inhaled the newly crafted potion. With a satisfied smile, she held it out to Lux. "Drink up."

"What is it?" She was too tired to keep the distrust from seeping into her voice.

"As much as I value your self-preservation, if I wanted to poison you, darling, I would have done so by now. Drink it. It will help."

Lux took the lightly smoking beaker and tipped the contents into her mouth. It tasted refreshing, like the air on a rare, sunshine-filled spring day. Almost instantaneously, her head cleared. She hadn't realized there had been a low, pulsing ache at its base until it was gone, and she sighed in relief, her shoulders dropping in exhaustion.

"Feel better?"

"Much. Thank you."

"It's a simple tonic. I remember it being one of the first things I attempted to teach you, though I believe the resulting potion actually *gave* me a headache." Riselda laughed, low and quiet in memory, and Lux forced a smile to her lips, though she couldn't recall the same.

It died, however, as she glanced about the room. "The mayor is harvesting lifeblood, Riselda."

"I know, Lucena."

Lux's eyes sprang wide. "How long have you known?"

"I was once his most prized possession, my dear. I have prepared countless tonics, endless potions, and uttered the incantations so many times, I can recall them in an instant. All for him. And believe me, I noticed when he failed to age. I also knew there was only one substance that could cause such an outcome."

"So you've known how it's harvested as well?"

Riselda stared down at her. "No. That knowledge is his guarded secret. Why? What did you see here?" Lux shifted her feet as a moaning cry echoed from somewhere down the tunnel. It jolted Riselda. "Let's get you out. Forget what you've seen." As Lux's mouth opened in protest, Riselda held up a hand. "Not even a necromancer is worth so much. You will have disappeared by morning."

"But I—"

"Lucena. Trust me in this. If nothing else…trust this."

Her aunt's gaze implored her to swear it. Swear she would put it all behind her. To trust her.

But Lux trusted no one.

"As you wish."

Chapter Twenty-Eight

RISELDA NAVIGATED THE UNDERGROUND labyrinth with ease. Soon Lux was beneath the evening's somber sky, across the manicured courtyard, climbing within a carriage.

"Sleep, darling." Riselda pushed a vial into her hands. "It's mild. Nothing like the Shield utilizes. But it will help you rest without nightmares."

Nightmares.

She mumbled her thanks, the door clicking closed to seal her within. She watched Riselda's eyes harden as the horse jerked forward, watched her spin in a swish of dark skirts. Toward the mansion. Toward the mayor.

Lux shoved the curtains aside, throwing the potion with every ounce of strength she could muster, and listened with satisfaction to its shatter against an obscene townhome. She rested against the cushions.

She would never allow a fog to descend upon her mind again. Not of any kind.

Staring across the carriage summoned the image of Shaw's smoldering eyes and a mask of bone. Lux kicked out with a heel, tearing a rip through the seam of the fabric and effectively destroying the mocking memory. What had he truly been after? The mayor's likely stores of lifeblood? To avenge his long-dead grandfather and become mayor in his stead? Lux scoffed. He was probably working alongside the mayor. He probably had no family.

Aside from Aline...

Lux licked her dry, cracked lips and winced. The little wretch was likely his accomplice. They didn't look much alike, after all.

The carriage ambled over the cobblestone street, and she lost herself in dark thoughts, spinning deep in sweet imaginings of revenge. She didn't realize she had arrived home until the door was opened, and the night greeted her.

Lux managed to climb from the carriage with a quiet murmur of gratitude before her body went rigid. She didn't register the horse moving on or the crunch of carriage wheels, as her eyes were focused solely on who paced in front of her door.

A sudden wind swept through the street, sending her hair streaming along with it and her skirt pulling against her legs. His gaze found her own then, and Shaw tugged on his cap as he stepped from beneath the streetlamp and into the darkness. Toward her.

"I'll have you know I've been asking after you for hours," he said. "Where have you been?"

Lux's mind buzzed, numb. She didn't move, and she didn't speak.

He moved closer. Close enough to see her proper. And from somewhere outside her body, she registered his jagged intake of breath before hands gripped her arms, hauling her forward and into the light. "Saints! What's happened?"

Her eyes tracked his. Concern, fury, terror. His emotions were unveiled. What a fool he was.

His rough hands continued to travel upward, his thumb brushing along the tender point of her neck, and she flinched. "Lux." His voice cut on her name. "Tell me who did this to you."

She had never heard him this way. Like he would scorch the earth.

But darkness, not fire, was all she knew.

You did.

"Why do you slit their eyes?"

Shaw blinked. "What?"

The wind whipped harder. Lux fisted her hands only to release them. Shaw dropped his own to his sides.

He stepped back. And she watched on as he filled with shadow.

"Why do you *slit* their eyes?"

"So you've taken your discovery and formed an entirely new opinion of me, have you?"

"A question for a question." The chasm inside her widened, cold and dark and gaping. "I never want to see you again."

He actually laughed, low and severe, and the sound felt every bit like the blades to her heart. Though it was stifled quickly when her boot connected with his hip, sending him staggering.

"What the hell!" He gripped the offended area, righting himself.

"I haven't trusted a single soul in this town for nine years." She used his shock against him and kicked the ankle directly beneath his injured hip, hobbling him. "You power-mad, conniving—"

He growled before he lunged. She was fast, but his legs were longer. When he snagged her wrist and pulled her bruised back against his chest, securing her hands in his own, an animalistic rage clawed through her skin.

She hissed, "I trusted you. I trusted you in everything you have ever told me. But it was all a lie." She could feel his breath against her neck, bending low to reply, to calm her. "Including that I am no monster."

She knew she couldn't bear to hear his voice.

Lux flung her head back, reveling in the satisfactory shout from behind her. Shaw's arms went slack to attend to his injury, and she sprinted for the door. Flinging it wide, she dove within the welcoming darkness, shutting out the insidious warmth trailing in her wake. Forever.

CHAPTER TWENTY-NINE

LUX PERCHED UPON A stool, enveloped by the night. A sliver of moonlight attempted to penetrate the small window of her workroom, only to be cut short by the vining plants as they slumbered.

She rested her back against the far wall, studying the faint glimmers of her short life's work, the outline of *The Risen*, resting closed before them, and the rolling vial of lifeblood between her fingers. Over and over, the silver liquid turned, shimmering across her hands.

Her theories did the same within her mind.

The mayor clearly was harvesting lifeblood, that much was certain. And Ghadra's poor continued to die from some unknown, incurable plague. That was also certain.

What remained less so, however, was whether the two were connected. How much lifeblood did one family need?

And where, for goodness sake, was Riselda?

She wasn't particularly worried for her aunt's safety even with the Shield's murder beneath her feet. Rather, she itched with interest over what slew of excuses the mayor had offered up for his minions' behavior, and what promises he had made in exchange for secrecy.

Perhaps she waited for nothing. He was clearly untouchable. More likely, he would laugh in Riselda's face, deny all, and see her through the doors.

A sudden shadow obscured the window, casting Lux in one in turn. On instinct, she hid the lifeblood within the pocket of her skirt, but the figure moved on, simply passing through. Though in the dead of night, that wasn't reassuring either. Nothing good happened at this hour.

A scuffle outside sent her standing. Grunting and groans and finally a shout that was abruptly cut off, and Lux found herself kneeling on the counter as vines sighed in irritation at being awakened. She squinted through the clouded glass.

A blurred outline of a body lay draped partway across the street as another knelt beside it. A thief. The figure hurried through pockets, nimble fingers disappearing within his coat with possessions never meant to be his. With a darting glance about darkened windows, he swept away.

Lux watched on for a moment longer, but when the body didn't move, she landed back on her feet. She walked across her workroom, toward the door.

There absolutely would *not* be another body decaying on her doorstep.

Mellow night air brushed across her skin as Lux stepped through the doorway and rounded the corner. Without the hazy glass to mar her view, the distinct form of a man greeted her, his head lolled to one side as if in sleep.

Surely he must be dead. She stepped to his side, avoiding the trickling stream of thick liquid following the grooves of stone beneath it. Not a man, in fact, but a boy—much too young to be out at this hour. Several years younger than herself, his face appeared almost angelic, as if he rested contentedly, his mind filled with pleasant dreams.

Sad business. She made to turn when a shuddered breath left his chest. With a quick glance down at the boy's still form, she frowned. Well, now she definitely didn't know what to do with him.

Lux tipped her head to the side, observing his chest rise and fall with shallow breaths. He would probably still die. But judging from his clothing, his family could likely afford to bring him back. Once the appropriate amount of time had passed.

"You idiot boy." She shook her head at his folly. The rich thought themselves invincible. The youngest of them, even more so. This boy was probably gracing the Light's gambling dens as they turned a blind eye to his smooth chin due to the coin in his pockets. That coin was certainly no more.

Lux shifted her feet against her bed's call. She really didn't feel like slipping through Ghadra's streets to find a physician in an attempt to save a child that may be dead by the time they arrived.

She huffed a sarcastic laugh as she turned. The few physicians she knew were likely deep in the dens themselves, their minds clouded with drink and whatever else. They would be of no help to her. She told herself she would simply revive him when the family discovered his unfortunate death. She rounded the building's corner again.

Her breath caught, and she leapt back as a hooded figure, their face obscured in shadow, stood silent before her door.

"Gah! What are you doing perched outside my door like that? Unless you come on business, away with you!"

Her heart returned to its normal rhythm as the figure lowered the hood in response to her demand for answers.

"I should be asking you the same question, Lucena. I would have thought you sleeping after your trying ordeal." Riselda's eyes glinted in the moonlight. They shimmered like lifeblood, and Lux flung her hand to her pocket at the reminder.

Still there. Thank fate.

Riselda tracked the movement before her gaze met Lux's once more. Her eyebrow retreated beneath tendrils of dark hair as she raised it in question.

"There is a boy dying around the corner. Mugged. The shouts woke me."

Riselda said nothing more, skirting around her instead to validate such claims herself. Lux groaned. Exhaustion had sunk its teeth into her, refusing to let go. She didn't want to deal with the boy tonight. Covering a yawn, she followed Riselda to the body.

Bending low, Riselda turned his head toward her own with two slender fingers. She tutted. "Nasty head injury. A club or the like. Wretched." She released him, and his head fell back to its resting place. "Help me get him inside, Lucena."

Lux's blood slowed, ice hardening her veins. "I'd rather not."

"Excuse me?"

Lux bit into sore lips and immediately regretted the action as sharp pain sliced into her. *You may as well tell her.* "Warm blood, Riselda. It bothers me."

Her aunt scrutinized her a moment more before she chuckled to herself. "And to think I spent so much time attempting to make you into Ghadra's next Healer. How wrong I was." She sighed in resignation. "Grab his feet at the least. That should be a safe distance for you."

Riselda didn't wait for her to comply, but instead, grabbed beneath the boy's arms, lifting his upper body against her own. Not a sound left her lips, even though he would never be described as small. Reluctantly, Lux gripped his boots. They were much nicer than her own, and she scowled. If he had died, maybe she could have afforded a new pair.

With one arm around the boy's chest, Riselda used the other to open the door, and Lux held back a grunt of protest as she carted his legs in after her. Down the stairs, and onto the smooth worktable he went. Riselda lit several dust-coated candlesticks tucked away in a corner before eyeing the shelves in contemplation. Why she didn't use a lamp was beyond Lux.

"If you don't need me—"

"Are wyvern claws not hard to come by? I would have thought them more difficult to procure than howlers." Riselda studied the jar with interest, her finger sifting through them.

A rattled breath wheezed from the body at their backs.

"The north has a population problem, I'm told. They grow docile and fat, spending more time lounging on mountain peaks than taking to the skies and terrorizing villages. Also, they apparently mate like rabbits." Though that could have been the marsh-grass cigar speaking for the woman from whom the tale came. And it certainly hadn't brought the price down any.

Riselda huffed a laugh, replacing the lid, and then the jar, back on the shelf. The decanter she selected next had its top removed. "Witch hazel." She pulled down several jars of various mushrooms and a vase of dried petals Lux had never paid much attention to. With her selection of ingredients displayed before her now, Riselda took to measuring.

"I thought you were no longer healing, Riselda?" Lux watched a drop of blood ooze from within the boy's ear, splattering onto her table. She grimaced.

The pestle continued to grind petals against the mortar in a rhythmic pattern beneath her aunt's hand. "I'm no longer Ghadra's Healer, Lucena. That doesn't prevent me from using my brilliance when I choose to do so. Besides, he's just a child. There's still hope for him. Hope that he won't turn into a despicable man."

It must be the exhaustion clouding her mind, allowing Lux's lips to move so freely. "Did something happen between you and the mayor?"

Her aunt didn't pause, instead dumping the contents into a small wooden bowl before pouring a generous amount of the witch hazel into the mixture. She laughed, low in her throat, and counted out a handful of mushrooms.

"You believe my view on men to be tainted? Perhaps it is." She shrugged unapologetically before bending to inhale the concoction. The flowery scent wafted toward Lux, stinging her nose. "Or perhaps, darling girl, you are naïve."

Indigo eyes seared her own, but Lux didn't look away. Her aunt's gaze churned, retreating to a past Lux could only guess at. Riselda broke away first, smearing the lumpy paste onto the wound extending from the boy's temple to his left ear. Red dripped from her fingers, and Lux fought back a gag.

She could never have been a healer.

"The mayor denied knowledge of the torture occurring within his prison. As I knew he would. But he did seem genuinely upset about your abduction. He denied its authorization and appeared shocked that the captain had handed out the punishment. Though he became quite irritated when I informed him of the death. All it took was a reminder of your skill. And mine as well. He plans to bring the entire Shield forward to dole out a forced recollection that he is the sole authorizer of such things. Of course, I suggested the other two men be found and dealt with. A quick death, I think, would be much too generous, but it's ultimately not my decision."

Riselda observed her work, and Lux absentmindedly noted that the boy's breaths were becoming fewer as the minutes ticked by. "Power like that cannot be bought, Lucena. The brilliance in your veins alone holds enough to sway Bartleby Tamish, and that is no small thing."

Lux knew she should be paying attention to what her aunt said, but she yawned instead. "I think he's very nearly dead, Riselda. Do you need your books? I've kept them in the alcove."

Riselda's responding smile was a touch condescending. "I've those words seared in my mind, darling. Thank you, but I haven't had a need for them in a very long time."

And to further prove her point, Riselda began:

> *"Within mists, beneath rays, we summon from sleep.*
> *To lessen weight.*
> *To mend all aches.*
> *Peace in whispers, strength that saves.*
> *Stitches and binds.*
> *This cycle rewinds."*

Riselda's words sent Lux back to her childhood, listening to the statuesque woman at her side as she healed an old woman who had fallen, breaking her hip in two places. It had amazed her then, sending shivers down her spine. It did the same now, as all witnessed works of brilliance around her did, and she couldn't help but lean forward, studying the wound as it shot through with wisps and whorls of gold, stitching itself closed before her eyes.

"Stay with him. I'll fetch some rags."

Riselda left her alone to monitor the boy as his chest rose and fell deeply. As the blood dried beneath him. Lux slouched onto a stool. His eyes fluttered open, and she allowed him to survey the room before flinging himself to sitting.

"Calm down, boy. You're safe." She was not in the mood to deal with a frantic child.

Hurry up, Riselda.

"Where am I? What happened to me? Is that...my blood?" The boy leapt further down the table, away from the puddle at his fingertips. His frenzied eyes roved over her face, her clothing, before studying the room. "No... You're the—"

"She is the necromancer, yes. But you didn't die. It was I, who healed you." Riselda swept in with glittering eyes and long skirts trailing behind her.

The boy's eyes rounded. First with fear, then in pink admiration. "I was taking a moonlight stroll, lost in contemplation of the wonders of life, when I was accosted. I remember nothing else. Thank you, madam. I am indebted to you."

Lux rubbed her temples.

"No need, young man. Though perhaps you should save your contemplations for mornings or dinner time from now on."

"Wise words. Yes, I believe I will. Thank you. May I..." The boy pushed from the table, stretching to his full height, his heels leaving the floor in an attempt to match that of Riselda's. "May I inquire as to your name?"

Her aunt smiled. "Riselda."

"Magnificent. Are you named after a flower? It must be a flower."

"No. Nothing of the sort. Will you be able to make it home safely?"

He puffed out his chest. "Certainly."

Riselda nodded. "Be on your way then. The gambling dens have terrible people hidden within. Be mindful as you pass them by."

Pink cheeks deepened to red. "Yes ma'am."

Riselda handed him a cloth to wipe his face lest his mother faint at the sight of him, and with persistent thanks and fervent compliments, the boy finally stepped through their door to be swallowed by the darkness.

A snort of laughter left Lux at his departure. "You've gained an admirer."

"Admiration is more effective than fear...in the long run." With a pointed stare at Lux, Riselda returned to the workroom, mopping up the remaining blood. "Though anything that delves deeper should be promptly smothered at the source."

She wasn't about to argue with her aunt, though her experience thus far had been quite the opposite. Fear of her brilliance had allowed her solace from many who would have hurt her otherwise. Admiration only invited them in.

But Lux wasn't sure she disagreed with Riselda on the latter. The image of Shaw's eyes narrowed in anger sent her own flaring again, and she began shoving jars back onto the shelves. The plants swayed in admonishment for her disregard of the noise she made.

Riselda paused, studying her progress. When a vial shattered at last, she intervened.

"I can clean up, Lucena. Get some rest."

LUX HAD OBEYED AT first. Though now, instead of sleep, she pressed against twin bruises formed over her chest, naked in the night. They hurt. Purple and blue, they shone starkly against her pale skin. It would seem that even shadow blades could mark a lingering reminder of the previous day's nightmare. Lux covered them quickly. She could feel her mind drudging up memories she was too tired to wrestle back to the recesses and turned her gaze onto her own reflection instead.

A much fainter bruise decorated her cheekbone. Morana's parting gift. She had never struck Lux before, but rather chose to sneer in passing instead.

Look at her hair. I wonder if her parents had wished for a boy. Is that why they kept it so short?

Goodness! That unhealthy, pale skin. It's almost translucent. Don't flit about in the night, child, or someone will take you for a ghost and chase you back to the forest, surely.

Some days I wish I could murder my family, too. I would never of course. I love them, after all.

Lux glanced to the opposite side of her wardrobe, but the lifeblood was tucked safely away once again. She closed the doors with a snap and climbed into bed.

Shaw had wanted to venture into the prison. She had asked him to accompany her to the forest first. Lux sighed, extinguishing the lamp at her side.

No matter.

She had been alone for nine years. She had grown up, faced the worst of Ghadra, and made them fear her. She could handle a few trees, a phantom and a howler or two on her own.

But she would buy a new knife first.

CHAPTER THIRTY

Lux's headache was a furious thing that Riselda had thankfully anticipated. Having awoken after too little sleep, sweating and shaking with a lingering sense of nightmares, Lux had found the blue liquid stoppered alongside a note on the kitchen table.

A tonic for your head, should you need it.

No mention of where she was or when she would return. It had suited Lux just fine. Downing the liquid, her pulsing head finally released her captive body.

And now, she found herself in a deserted Dark Market.

The air had finally grown warmer. High summer approached, and the Festival of Light along with it. It was absurdly close to the mayor's birthday, but at least everyone was invited to attend this particular celebration.

Lux had always avoided the entire affair when she could. Especially as it was the busiest time of year for her. The town line blurred for one day and one night, and when the people of Ghadra mingled as one, with entirely too much to drink, it often led to more than a body or two carried through her door. Though that might be lessened somewhat if Riselda utilized her gift.

Her aunt would likely be their only hope; at the last festival, Lux had revived their best physician.

A muffled blanket of fear and dread covered the square, but as she had suspected, the crooked, old crone continued to hack and wheeze behind her booth, the sole vendor remaining within the entire market. Lux walked toward her, a faint smell of rotted jasmine in the air and little else.

Dark, knotted fingers were busy creating yet another gnarled necklace. "You had better buy something today, girl. I haven't had any business in days."

Lux paused before the booth, eyeing the stacks of claws and talons. It appeared the old woman had added to her collection in hopes of drumming up more customers. An array of feathers, frogs' eyes and snake skins were pushed ahead of the display of homemade jewelry. A stack of red apples drenched in green poison consumed the remaining space.

Lux didn't waste her breath in telling her that no soul worthy of living would be tricked by such fruit. The crone certainly wouldn't listen.

"I'm in need of a new knife. Nothing else." She glanced around the quiet square. "Everyone die off from the plague then?"

A string of hacking. "That or hiding like the cowards they are. Just as likely to die tucked in your bed than out here, braving the world."

Lux snorted, already turning. "Nice apples."

"Wait! A knife you say? I have just the thing, Necromancer." With quicker movements than Lux thought her capable of, the crone whipped a shockingly long, serpentine blade from her side. The handle was comprised of black, polished wood, and Lux's eyes widened at the weight of it as it was pressed into her palm.

"A dagger. Made from the wood of those devouring trees." The old woman raised untamed eyebrows.

"That's not possible." The trees never died. Their branches never fell. And you clearly couldn't touch their surface lest you be swallowed whole.

"Not for you, it isn't. Not for me, either. But for someone, a very long time ago, it was." The ominous ring to her voice could have swayed Lux to believing if it weren't for those conspiratorial eyebrows waggling at her.

Lux snorted. "If you say so." She adjusted it in her hand. It did fit rather nicely.

"If you don't believe me, so be it. Either way, it's a quality blade. You can't argue that. And you won't find better. Those with weapons are sure to be hoarding them now."

"Why?"

"Why! Child, the Shield is imprisoning anyone who looks the wrong way at the moon. And no one who enters that prison comes out. I don't know why those pebble-brained white-coats bother. The mayor is already purging us well enough."

"Purging?" Lux's face remained impassive, but her heart hammered against her ribs.

"Why else hasn't it crossed to the rich? No invisible line keeps a plague at bay. Mark my words, that mayor is behind this as sure as I can make the loveliest raccoon claw necklace." To further prove her point, the completed piece of jewelry dangled from her arthritic fingers, a full, dried raccoon paw swinging at its center.

"Indeed." Lux batted it away as it crept closer to her head.

"Some poison cooked up by those slimy potion-masters he calls his personal physicians, no doubt. Though, I certainly wouldn't turn down one of those anti-aging creams he's using." She ran her hand over matted, grey hair, her smile wistful. Then she laughed again, a harsh, barking sound that rattled her chest.

Lux frowned. "How do you know if he's aged well or not?" The woman had been blind for as long as Lux could recall.

"Just because my eyes are broken doesn't mean my ears are!" The crone tossed the necklace in irritation, smothering the paw's fur in poison as it came to rest on the pile of apples. "People are always whispering on how he's hardly aged since they were children themselves. I'll bet he drinks some nasty concoction every morning, noon and bedtime. Too late for me, that. I'd need to start over, peel a fresh face off a youngster. Now, cough up some gold for that blade."

A hand waved beneath Lux's nose, expectant. She fished within her purse. It was growing light, what with the majority of deaths lately being poor and plague-ridden. Perhaps the approaching festival wasn't all that terrible after all.

"How much?"

"Five goldquins."

"Never!" She charged the same for a revival. It wasn't possible for a dagger to be worth so much.

"It's not a simple blade, girl. If you're going to cross that bridge again, you're going to need it."

Lux bit her cheek, shaking her head. What other gossip had this woman turned sensitive ears to? More likely she was guessing, utilizing a well-honed skill in marketing her wares. Either way, the vendor was right. She did need it, and she wasn't about to begin knocking on doors to inquire about purchasing one. She certainly wouldn't be asking Riselda to lend hers.

"This is outrageous." Lux dumped the coins into her weathered palm. The purse hung, sad and limp, at her side.

"You won't regret it, child. Take good care of it."

Lux huffed, tucking it through her corset where it winked its curved edges across the empty market. "I can't afford not to."

The crone smiled, and Lux walked away, only glancing back once to witness the biggest, most foul-smelling, marsh-grass cigar whipped forth and placed between the old woman's lips.

As she puffed away happily, Lux pitied the tree that would inevitably swallow her down.

Chapter Thirty-One

Cold, fat drops of rain splattered across moss and stone, creating a treacherously slick surface on the bridge, and forming a curtain between herself and the trees. It was afternoon, but night may as well have fallen.

Lux adjusted the dagger within her cloak. She didn't want to confront the phantom any more than she wanted to face a howler, but if it became inevitable, she felt better about her decision knowing she wasn't entirely defenseless. The wrongness of it all gnawed at her nerves. No soul, dead or living, should be wandering amongst a devouring wood as if they were companions. The wraith was tied to Ghadra in some way. It was tied to them all.

With a hand outstretched for balance, Lux stepped over the stones. The downpour had come out of nothing, as it often did, and now she was soaked through to the skin. She shivered as it seeped through her hood, wetting her hair and dripping along her spine. The cold coupled with the gloom should have sent her back to try again another day, but there wasn't time.

The death-carts weren't slowing, and Lux had an inkling that when the Festival of Light allowed the line to be crossed, the previously saved rich would be saved no more. How long before she was next?

Her thick boots kept her feet dry, but nothing else was by the time she stood beneath the canopy of the trees. The leaves were wet, black, and dripping onto her upturned face. Rainwater stung her eyes as she slid her gaze deep within the boughs.

It was silent. The wood didn't whisper. Their branches didn't beckon. The trees were asleep.

Or they waited.

The death-carts dumped their cargo within the clearing once every day now. One large wagon, loaded with the dead, as the horses and their drivers had been run ragged keeping up with them before. Lux knew all she required was patience and the phantom would come to her. Unfortunately, she wasn't a patient person.

With a tight grasp on the handle of her dagger, its hue an exact match to the surrounding trunks, Lux crept deeper amongst the trees. A stray drop found the fabric draped over her body now and then, but otherwise the rain never met the forest floor. Twigs didn't snap beneath her feet and leaves didn't crunch. For there were none. Instead, Lux's boots sank into thick black moss that sponged and oozed dark liquid across them. There wasn't any avoiding it—it coated the entire floor.

The clearing fell away from her vision; it was the farthest she had ever gone. The farthest any of the living had gone, save one. Her mind whispered it wasn't possible. The cloaked figure couldn't live and remain here, but if it wasn't, that only left one alternative. Because Lux didn't believe in ghosts.

Her breaths sent puffs of white billowing from her mouth and nose, and her fingers numbed around her blade. She'd had the foresight to pull gloves on, having learned at least one thing upon entering the frigid forest the first time. Well, that and never to touch the treacherous trunks. Her remaining hand was kept securely within the pocket of her skirt for exactly that reason. If she were to stumble and fall, she would rather collapse face-first amongst the oozing moss than feel the icy fingers of a tree's soul enclose her again.

No one knew how far this perilous forest extended because no one who ever left to investigate it returned. Lux knew Finias had never ventured further than the outskirts in order to ensnare his prey, and why would he? She had certainly never planned to. Yet, here she was, traipsing about the wood as if it didn't pose an imminent threat to her life with every beat of her heart.

A slope in the earth rose before her, sudden and deceptively gentle. Lux strained her eyes in each direction, but from what she could see, it extended indefinitely. So she climbed. The moss was slippery, and every step made it slicker by the inky-black substance released around her footprints. And finally, the trees grew tired of the game. They offered their assistance. Branches bent and curled toward her, coaxing, extending.

Let us help you.

She couldn't touch them. She couldn't let them touch her. She climbed faster, but her boots slipped from beneath her, and the dagger plunged into soft moss until it reached hard soil deep below. Lux clutched it like a lifeline, refusing to use her other hand to steady herself. For a moment she didn't move. The branches didn't either. She felt the wood breathe.

And then she fell.

The blade pulled free, and Lux collapsed to her front, her hands clawing for any hold. There were none, and when she came to rest at the base of the hill once more, she pulled herself onto her knees to stare down her body.

Dark liquid dripped from her. It coated her clothing, her boots, and the blade. She could feel it dripping from her chin, and she wiped it away with quick, furious strokes that only smeared it further. She gagged at the putrid scent. Her gloves were soaked through.

She did manage to catch a drop before it fell into her eyes, having no idea if the mess was harmful or not. She certainly wasn't about to risk it. She wouldn't even sniff a rare wildflower if it grew, beautiful and sweet, in a place like this. Nothing could ever be trusted here.

Lux walked along the base of the slope, avoiding the shimmering wet place her body had created as she slid. The wood was darkening. Too much time passed in this place. Resolved, she studied the blade in the waning light, dripping black droplets onto the floor beneath it. Then she drove it into the moss of the hillside. Liquid pooled around the shaft but, as with the blade, it rolled off without so much as a stain. Impenetrable.

Her gloved fingers dug into the soft substance next: she winced against the feel of it soaking through to her skin, puddling in her sleeves. Steadily, she began to climb anew. Using the dagger as an anchor, and with steady, slow steps, she ignored the curving boughs this time and reached the crest at last.

Saints above, devil below.

The forest stretched on and on in every direction she looked, fading beneath a setting sun she could sense but not see. Her breaths grew rapid. She'd expected it, but it didn't make the fear any less palpable. Everything changed at twilight.

A shadow fell across her.

Lucena.

Lux slipped down the opposite side of the slope. More dark droplets peppered her face.

Lucenaaa.

Something moved beneath her fingers, and Lux jerked them back. Using the blade, she pushed off the ground, climbing to her feet. She wiped at her eyes. Then wiped them again.

A soft, silver glow emanated from the tree before her. Another tree lit the same at her right. Though many of the trunks remained dark and eclipsed in shadow, more and more shone with a steady, eerie light that extended up through their branches, highlighting even the veins of the leaves. She'd never seen anything like it.

"What is this?"

Her words were less than a whisper, but still they were snatched, drawn up and through the boughs.

And from far away, a faint flicker answered.

Chapter Thirty-Two

A stuttering, yellow light shifted toward the window of the antiquated cottage, yearning for air.

It wasn't possible.

This can't be possible.

Yet here it sat.

The stacked stones were overrun with black moss rather than green, the thatched roof intact from lack of exposure. No trees had been felled to make room but instead been built around them. Lux stared slack jawed at the three towering black trunks pushed through the cottage's middle, glowing silver. *Wrong, wrong, wrong.*

The air weighed heavy on her body. Heavy and stagnant and hatefully cold.

She crept toward a window's murky glass. *This is the phantom's domain,* she reminded herself. *Don't do anything foolish.* Like she hadn't done ten foolish things already. Like she hadn't stepped beyond the forest's edge to start.

She held her breath, lifting to the tips of her toes. Enough to raise her eyes over the lip of the sill and nothing else. She could make out little inside. Nothing except a stump of a candlestick burning away atop what might be a mantle. She didn't think anything was at home...

The candle snuffed.

And howls broke through the quiet. One by one.

The harmony chilled her blood more than any icy breeze ever could. Her skin pricked, every tiny hair standing on end, and she crouched against the cottage wall, her back scraping against the rough stone. She scoured the shadows, focusing on those pushed aside by the illuminated trees.

There wasn't a thought to spare on what moved within the walls as shining eyes peered from around one wide trunk after another. And when those eyes gave way to foaming, dripping snouts and gnashing teeth, Lux's mind went entirely blank—save for her focus on the blade brandished at her side, and how it could possibly find its home in a howler's heart before its fangs found her throat.

Either way, it wouldn't happen with her back pressed low against a wall, so she peeled off her gloves. The low growls were deep, coarse, almost unnatural, and the beasts moved forward, already reveling in her death. Pointed ears, short horns, thick chests—the creatures were more aggressive than wolves and stealthier than panthers. The odds were bleak, but Lux rose anyway, tossing the dagger from one hand to another, her gloves falling to the mossy floor. She bared her teeth right back.

When the first howler lunged, she slashed its throat.

She had told Shaw the truth that day. Death didn't bother her. Not when necessary. Not like this.

Dark blood spurted from the next howler's chest, its teeth leaving behind deep marks as it tore through the fabric of her forearm. Yellow eyes faded as it sunk to the ground, and Lux furiously wiped the blood onto her cloak.

"Ignore it. Ignore it." But her thoughts went fuzzy as a single, hot droplet traveled the length of her finger and dripped onto the frozen soil at her feet.

You can do this, she thought. *It's only a few more.* But her quick glance counted ten.

The creak of aged wood wrenched her attention. It forced her mind away from blood-coated fingertips and stinging pain.

The phantom stepped from around the cottage.

Lux lurched, slipping in her haste to press herself flat against the wall. The wraith shifted. It sniffed at the air, bare feet tucked into the moss and arms hung limp. Lux slunk into the deeper shadows. Away from the bodies, she crouched at the cottage's back.

You witless idiot! She was about to be caught and fed to howlers if she stayed put. She knew it.

The snarling growls grew quiet, and Lux stared on in mystified horror as the phantom paid them little mind, as if they were simple strays, and turned its back on their fangs. Long fingers crawled from beneath the grey cloak to examine the fallen at its feet. They felt along the thick coats, pressing at their sides, until they found the mortal wounds delivered by a peculiar blade. The hooded face lifted, its gaze traveling to the exact place she'd hidden.

It wouldn't find her there.

Lux's pulse beat loud in her ears as she eased back from the window's inside, and the figure swept away, set out to hunt for her amongst the trees.

Lux BREATHED IN LUNGFULS of the cottage's musty scent. Of moldering walls and a generous helping of dust. If it weren't for the trunks of three monstrous trees glowing pale at its center, she would have been completely lost when she'd first tumbled in, giving away her hiding place by stumbling into the furniture. Even though the *wrongness* continued to pry at her, she was thankful for that at least.

The candle she'd glimpsed through the window had puddled wax atop a black mantle at her right. Both sat above a fractured fireplace, its insides long gone to ash, and Lux knew then, that the phantom could not feel the cold. How could it and live here? Her breaths continued to cloud as she treaded carefully across the warped floor, toward a second window, a cluttered table and chair, her arms crossed all the while lest she brush a tree.

She bit back a yelp when she tripped over something that squeaked and skittered away before she could determine exactly what she'd injured. Naturally, her mind conjured up all sorts of nasty creatures that would enjoy such an oasis hidden amongst a devouring forest. Her lip curled, and she shook herself, only for her next steps to deliver her to the rear of the cottage—and shelves upon shelves of books. Books intermixed with decanters, vials, and jars with fused lids. Her mouth relaxed in surprise.

She reached for a tiny vial as it called to her, familiar. Where had she seen it?

The window nearest her darkened for only a moment, the outside glimmer of silver light returning in a breath.

Her borrowed time had ended.

Lux dropped to yet another crouch, thighs burning as she crept along the opposite side of the trees. She passed by a rumpled bed with an unexpectedly bright quilt and a washstand before arriving once more at the door. It creaked open on ancient hinges.

The cloaked phantom floated in with soft footsteps—and Lux slipped out on silent ones.

Illuminated trees were soon lost to the deep wood, her eyes straining as one black trunk after another appeared in her path. Lux rushed, knowing that if she slowed, the next time she looked over her shoulder a howler would be staring back at her. A howler or a cloaked figure with a deadly long blade.

A jut on the forest floor appeared from nothing, catching the toe of her boot and sending her stumbling headlong into a looming tree. Lux gasped and spun, narrowly avoiding it, only for a second knot to catch her opposite foot. Her shoulder slammed into rough wood and her ankle twisted, searing hot.

Icy fingers clamped around it. Unseen nails dug into the skin of her shoulder, encircling her ankle, and Lux didn't care any longer if she drew everything to her. She screamed.

There wouldn't be a crow to save her now, and the sound of splintering wood echoed against the night as the tree yawned wide. The scent of rot, of death, wafted up from the darkness, so thick she could taste it, and the tree greedily sucked back what escaped. Lux flailed, her hand brushing against the blade tucked into her corset.

She drew it forth as black roots spiraled up her legs. But she didn't use it against them. Instead, Lux sliced at the invisible fingers holding her hostage. The ones that sent streaking cold through her.

She didn't know what she expected. Nothing, perhaps. But the five dark twigs that fell at her side were certainly not it.

The tree shuddered with fury. She could feel it as the roots loosened, and she pushed from them, falling backward into the oozing moss. Though, when that too, began to roil and shift, she shoved herself to standing and ran.

Her ankle screamed in agony. It wanted her to slow, to stop, but she couldn't give into it. If she did, she would die. Her fingers held tight to the miraculous dagger in her hand, swiping at anything that neared.

Could the trees speak to one another? Did they know what she had done? It would certainly seem so.

The air around her trembled with a deep, pulsing anger.

Lux dodged branches and pivoted around roots, their sole intent to bury her amongst them. To punish her for the injury she'd caused. To feed on her body for eternity.

The bones of her ankle sent hot surges up her leg with every step, but it wasn't until she saw a faint glimmer of moonlight that they gave way entirely. She screamed anew as something inside snapped. She didn't fall but stumbled, trembling and broken from the trees and into the wet, fog-brushed grass.

Only then did she allow herself to collapse, sobbing beneath the bleak light of the moon. The pain came in massive waves, and she emptied her stomach because of it.

She rolled to her back when she was done, exhausted, her chest feeling as if it were splintering with every drawn breath. She was too tired to cry anymore. Hurting too much to crawl.

Had it been worth it? To discover the strange, glowing trees, the residence of the phantom, and the trick of her dagger? She didn't think so.

Hot tears fell from the corners of her closed eyes as the moon fell behind shadows. She didn't move. It was a cloud, nothing more.

Yet, this cloud was warm.

This cloud could speak.

"What the devil are you doing out here?"

Her eyes sprang open to make out Shaw's dark gaze, his brow furrowed in either irritation or worry. She could never tell which.

"My ankle is broken. I didn't feel like crawling." She closed her eyes again. Let him send somebody else for her. Let him send no one at all. She would figure it out in the morning.

"Of all your ludicrous ideas, this is by far your worst. I should leave you here."

She cried out as he lifted her, one arm at her back, another beneath her knees. Tears streamed down her face, falling against him. "I hate you." But she let her eyelids fall, her face pressed against his warmth. She hadn't realized she'd grown so cold.

Pressure against her ribs, there and gone.

"As if I don't know that."

He held her tight, keeping her legs from jostling as much as possible. Her fingers tingled, sending shooting sparks up her arms, and she burrowed closer, wrapping her hands in the thickness of his coat.

When his steady heartbeat pulsed against her ear, she suddenly had to fight to stay awake. "Where are you taking me?"

"Home. Wherever else?"

Lux didn't move. She was too warm, her ankle a dull throb. "I can't go home. I can't tell Riselda what happened to me."

She could feel him turning over what she said, thinking.

"A physician, then."

She breathed a laugh. "If you can find one."

Lux squinted against the lamplight, her ankle swollen to twice its natural size, blackening and bare upon the table.

The physician peered at her, glancing at her foot and back again. "You fell into a sinkhole? Near the marshes? I guess it would explain why you are covered head to toe in *this*."

He gestured to her person with a distasteful flourish before dark hands, callused and sure, lifted her ankle. Lux hissed. She'd never met this physician, but Shaw apparently trusted him. Though that didn't mean much to her anymore, either.

She glared up at him, though she knew somewhere deep down, he treated her as gently as possible. "How bad is it?"

"Broken. More than once. Like you took a midnight stroll after your injury." Deep, clever eyes studied her above half-moon spectacles, and she fought the sudden urge to shrink away.

She stared back instead, unflinching. "Wouldn't that be absurd?"

"Indeed." His face dipped to her arm, but when she turned it outward so he couldn't see, a tired sigh left him. His attention returned to her ankle. He prodded a particularly sensitive spot, and she cried out, biting her lip against a sob. "I'll have to set this before it's bound. It will hurt plenty. I have sedatives?"

The question surprised her. He'd already deduced something about her, though Lux wasn't sure what it was.

"No sedatives." *Never again.*

"Suit yourself. You'll want this though." She stared at the thick strip of leather. "And don't move."

Chapter Thirty-Three

No person would ever venture near the physician's home again after that—Lux felt sure of it. Her throat ached, raw from guttural screams, just as every muscle was now sore from keeping them locked in place. It had been one of the hardest things she'd ever done—going against instinct shouting at her to kick the physician in the nose with every twist and pull.

She hadn't expected Shaw to be waiting for her when she shuffled into the street on her new-to-her crutches. The bulky and difficult to maneuver contraptions were certainly something she planned to toss at the first opportunity. She caught Shaw smother what looked suspiciously like concern as she wobbled past him.

Her chest burned over it, anger pooling before seeping through every part of her. She hated that she was indebted to him. Again. She hated that he'd deceived her. She *hated* him.

"Do you need a carriage called?"

She stared at him like he'd sprouted a third eye. "At this hour?"

He shifted his feet, flummoxed. "Right. I'd forgotten." His attention left her to study the falling moon.

It was late. So late, it was nearly morning, and she didn't want Riselda awake when she arrived home. Lux pitched forward, righting herself awkwardly before continuing down the street. Two long strides and Shaw was alongside her.

"What are you doing?"

His gaze didn't leave the buildings. "Delivering you home. You're injured, and the streets aren't safe."

She scoffed. "You're the most dangerous person on these streets. I don't need your help."

He didn't even acknowledge that she'd spoken, which somehow irked her more. She seethed silently as the click of her crutches over stone resounded against darkened buildings. She couldn't fight him off as she had done the night before. She was helpless.

Physically helpless. "Does the mayor employ you? A hired assassin thriving on violence, coin and a promise in a share of lifeblood?" Lux didn't actually believe that theory. More likely he was a greedy man who happened to possess a little skill with a blade, though what he did upon draining all those bodies he'd murdered was beyond her. His sister likely had a vial or two.

Shaw snorted. Still, he didn't speak, but continued to match his pace to her much slower one. *Like I am not even worth his energy.* Her teeth ground against one another until an idea formed, bringing a wicked grin to her lips, hidden by the night.

She stuck out a crutch. And Shaw's tall frame was his undoing as he tripped, sent sprawling against the stones.

He growled through gritted teeth. "What in the saint-forsaken *hell*." By slow, menacing measures, he pushed himself from the ground.

Lux passed him by, ignoring him as he had her. When he pulled on her crutch, she whipped it from his grasp. He barely dodged the aim she made for his groin. "Don't *touch* me."

He scowled after her. "I didn't touch you. Just your wooden attachment. Though, you didn't seem all that bothered by it when I saved you from becoming a howler's meal."

Her embarrassment in just how much she *wasn't* bothered by it twined inside her until it took a new form. One that was easier for her to accept. Anger. Always more anger. "I don't need to be *saved* by you. Not then, not now."

"What were you doing out there, anyway?"

Oh, now you want to talk?

"Your memory is abysmal. But I'm unsurprised." When her glance revealed his bewildered expression, she huffed. "You told me you wanted to investigate the prison. I told you I wanted the same for the forest. For the phantom. Now I have done both without you. And survived both. Without you."

His sudden grip on her arm was unyielding yet gentle. She supposed he didn't want to send her stumbling after going through all the effort to get her fixed. "You snuck into the prison? How?"

"*Snuck* is probably the wrong word. I'd use thrown, personally."

If she didn't hate him so much, she would have laughed at his shocked face. Until it darkened. "It was *them* who hurt you? Which Shield? *Why?* How did you get out?"

No questions about what she'd found. The idea of it gave her pause for all of a heartbeat before she shook herself free. "Quit pretending you care about my well-being, Shaw. You've been using me since the day you asked me to bring you to the mayor's masquerade."

"You have been using me too. That doesn't mean I don't care about what happens to you."

Her laugh was harsh. "What you've kept hidden is unforgivable."

"You won't even be bothered to know why?"

"No!" Lux reigned her voice back. As much as she didn't want to admit it, the streets really weren't safe for anyone anymore, let alone a broken girl. "Nobody has the right to drain another of their very *essence*. Be they criminals or innocent. How *could you*?"

Shaw's voice heated with passion. "Criminals deserve retribution, and they don't deserve for you to bring them back simply to do it all again. Need I remind you, the people I've killed are not petty thieves. They are the worst Ghadra has to offer. Ones the Shield turn a blind eye to as they imprison those who oppose the mayor in any small way."

Lux blocked the surfacing image of a tortured man upon a table, a menacing figure in white slicing deep behind his eyes. *No.* She could never condone what Shaw did, what he still continued to do, and her heart seemed hellbent on breaking all over again at the reminder.

Her street. At last. Her ankle throbbed with searing pain, and all she wanted was her bed.

They walked in silence the rest of the short distance, but Lux paused outside her door.

"How did you find me?"

Shaw opened his mouth only to close it again. She watched the war rage in his eyes by the lightening sky before they shuttered. "Chance, I suppose." His gaze traveled her length, lingering on her wrapped ankle, and then her eyes. "Goodbye, Necromancer."

She didn't say anything as she watched him go, and he didn't look back. As soon as he was out of sight, she tossed her crutches in the nearest alley before pulling open her freshly repaired, and thus silent, door to hobble down the steps.

RISELDA WAS ASLEEP, SOFT breaths puffing from the bed beside the coal-lit fireplace. Lux struggled against waking her, her good foot creaking down the stairs with its awkward added weight.

She crossed the floor, seriously contemplating entering her workroom to try her hand at Riselda's potions for something to dull the pain, but in the end, she passed it by. She'd likely end up poisoning herself instead.

She winced, holding back a hissed oath as the rug brushed across her bandaged foot. Rumpled again. Her old one never had this problem. Lux glared down at the offending material.

She needed a bath badly, but it would have to wait until morning. As would the tale she needed to spin regarding how she obtained her injury. Her mind was sluggish with pain and exhaustion. The best she could think of right now was that she'd tripped.

At least the pitcher atop the washstand was filled. Lux scrubbed her face, neck, and hands as quickly and quietly as she could.

Stripping out of her clothes was tedious once entering her room, what with her new sense of balance fighting against the old. She'd nearly toppled more than once, but she couldn't sleep covered in the black grime of the wood. The longest nightgown she owned just brushed the thick covering over her ankle and, victorious, Lux pulled back the pile of blankets.

A violent knock reverberated through the walls.

She shut her eyes. *No, not tonight.*

It pounded again, harder this time, insistent that she not even glance toward her welcoming pillow.

Lux tossed the blanket back onto the bed in fury, grabbing for her robe instead. Cinching it tight around her middle, she limped through her door to see Riselda opening another. Morana waltzed through, not a hair out of place, and two Shields bearing a collapsed body. Colden. Lux's irritation swelled. *This* was her reason for not sleeping? Let him rot.

"I'm terribly sorry to wake you both. Something's happened to dear Colden. Something horrible!"

Lux had an inkling it was the same *horrible* something that had claimed him last time.

She shuffled after the party into the workroom, watching as the body was laid out on the table. She hadn't revived him in some time, but this must be at least the third. She'd been a child at his first, when such habits were unbeknownst to her.

Lux moved to the table as the rest of them stepped back. She sensed Riselda's presence peering over them all from the corner of the room, but she didn't look at her aunt. Instead, she pushed back the tip of Colden's mottled nose.

White powder.

"Something horrible, indeed."

She could feel Morana's rage directed toward her. Lux didn't care. Her cheek remembered the sting of her shadow's strike. Instead, Lux gestured toward the crock at her back. Morana stomped forward with a scowl, tossing the coins within.

"Time since death?"

"Six hours, five minutes."

Lux smiled to herself. Maybe Morana did care for someone other than the reflection in her mirror. "As you remember, I don't permit anyone to watch. Out." Her eyes met her aunt's. "Please."

Riselda gazed at her a moment longer than the rest before following in their wake. As soon as they disappeared from view, Lux got to work. The sooner this was over, the sooner she could sleep.

She yawned widely as she prepared the thick paste, distantly wishing she'd had the time to pull the canines from the dead howler's jaws before she'd fled. At least this revival wouldn't require one. She turned and, forgetting her injury, cried out as she put weight on her ankle. The bowl she carried fell to the table with a clatter, where she clutched the worn edges, breathing the pain away.

"Lucena?"

"Fine, Riselda." Lux pushed herself to standing lest her aunt make an unwelcome appearance.

She should have made Morana undress him for her. Pulling off his clothing while balancing on one foot caused a sheen of sweat to form across her brow. With a final grunt of frustration, she pulled the fabric free, covering his still body with a white sheet in its wake.

Faint, round bruises peppered his neck. Another on his chest looked to be the result of teeth. Lux curled her lip. It may have been Morana, but she doubted it. Colden was never a faithful sort.

Not that she cared about either of them.

She painted the concoction over his body with quick, practiced strokes. She'd forgotten to use something to guard against the smell, but it was too late now and wouldn't have been worth hobbling around on her ankle for anyway. She would just have to deal with it.

Lux breathed through her mouth the best she could, and pivoted, ready to turn back for *The Risen*. But as her hand reached, she thought of Riselda. Of her confidence in her brilliance. Lux's fingers retracted, curling inward. The words were etched in her mind. She could picture the entire script down to the flourishes adorning the page. Effortless.

She didn't need it.

Lux breathed in deep, her nose hardly wrinkling, and peeled back his eyelids, preparing to begin.

Her hands stilled.

Her stomach plummeted.

And her uninjured leg wobbled beneath her.

A perfect slit adorned each pupil, slicing through the iris, extending down to where the dark met light. Lux peered closer, and her shock gave way to intrigue. She had never seen it up close, and it was so slight. No wonder it took so long to drain such a small amount.

She told herself she'd planned on touching them anyway.

Lux pushed her finger against the precise incision, separating it, and sucked in through her teeth when the barest remnants of lifeblood shimmered on her fingertip. She brought it close, studying it in the flickering light.

It was smooth—like oil. Instead of absorbing into her skin, it spread, highlighting every groove in the pad of her finger. There it remained, silver and glimmering and impossible to replace.

"Morana!" Her call ricocheted back to her, hurting her own ears.

A blonde head flounced through the door a moment later. Her eyes, bright and ready to greet her departed husband, fell to shadow at his unmoved form.

She fixed a glare on Lux. "What?"

And as horrid as it might be, Lux decided to test a theory. She gestured Morana forward, to study her lost love from the opposite side of the table. The cry of rage that followed was all the evidence she needed.

Morana, too, knew the secret to harvesting lifeblood.

"*NO!* Who did this? Why!" Her gaze raked over Lux. "YOU! You always hated me, hated him. Hated that he chose me again and again even though you tried to lead him astray. Straight to your filthy bed!" Morana climbed atop the table, no longer caring for the body beneath her. Her eyes were roving wild, her hair frizzing at its edges.

And Lux was so focused on the strangeness of it all, especially on such little sleep, that she didn't react until much too late.

Her head cracked to the side as Morana's hand met her cheek.

She tasted blood and spat on instinct before tottering back on her good heel. Words of fury, hurt and *truth* cut their way up her throat, her cheek stinging in imitation of that haunting day in the prison, and yet, they died before they passed her lips.

For Morana sat perched beside Colden, tears tumbling down her cheeks from eyes stained red. And if Lux struck at a grieving girl, however old she may truly be, she would be no better than Morana. No better than Morana ever was to her.

"I did nothing to him, and you very well know it. I'll give you your privacy. Take him and leave."

Lux hobbled out the door as choking sobs filled the room at her retreat.

Thankfully, Morana and the Shield left with Colden's body sooner than anticipated. Though she watched them go, Morana never brought her eyes back up to meet Lux's own. It wouldn't have been a notable gesture, except that Lux had never seen them downcast before.

Even though it would have felt so good to air exactly what she thought of Morana and her treatment of her all those years ago, Lux had made the right choice in keeping silent. The mayor's daughter was more broken now than Lux could have ever made her. Maybe once Morana began to heal, a few veins of compassion would grow throughout her newly knitted heart.

A murderous gaze sliced toward her as the door swung closed.

Then again, maybe not.

"She struck you?" Riselda's stare rivaled that of Morana's as she sat in the hard-backed chair.

The early morning sun struggled through the curtains, already dimmed by an overcast sky, and Lux yawned wide. "Yes." She stepped toward her room, wincing against the pressure on her throbbing ankle.

Riselda's burning gaze watched her go. "Mind the blood."

Lux swiped at her mouth, wiping the sticky warmth on her robe without glancing at it. Riselda hadn't asked about her other obvious injury, even though she'd glanced at it pointedly more than once. And when Lux had informed her about Colden's irredeemable wounds, specifics withheld, she'd shrugged.

"I'm not sure why she was so shocked."

Well Lux had been shocked. She still was. She'd come to think of the entire family as indestructible. And when they'd shattered the illusion by dying, she'd simply rebuilt it by bringing them back.

Lux collapsed into her bed, the throbbing in her newly aligned bones vibrating in her ears. It hurt miserably. She shifted, her teeth gritting against it.

Seconds stretched on indefinitely, and she soon entertained thoughts of downing whatever alcohol Riselda kept within the house, when her aunt knocked, tentative and slow.

"Come in."

The door swung open, revealing Riselda and a small, smoking goblet. Lux's eyes trailed the twining red wisps.

"I've brought you something for the pain. It's been brewing for days and happened to cure tonight."

Lux's tongue ran over the cut of her lip, even as she knew it wasn't to what her aunt referred. She eased herself up. "Thank you."

Riselda smiled softly, pushing the goblet into her hands. "I've some things to see to."

The door clicked shut behind her, leaving Lux staring down into the cool mixture of deep red liquid. She should have asked exactly what it would do to her. Lux narrowed her eyes at it—until her ankle throbbed with an excruciating streak of heat up her calf.

She downed the contents in one swallow. Within so many heartbeats her bones began to tingle. Pins and needles prodded and poked, the sensation mounting in intensity as the pain remained unyielding.

"Ah! Devil's own—" Without a care for the meticulous wrapping, she tore the thick bandages extending from her foot to her knee. Her skin crawled, but with the final toss of white fabric, the sensation dissipated. The pain ceased.

Lux breathed a sigh of relief that was caught as she took in the fading bruises, the evaporating swelling, and the painless twitch of her toes. Riselda hadn't just taken away the pain. She'd healed the bones entirely.

Lux could only shake her head, staring at her foot as she moved the joint in a circular pattern. She huffed a laugh and fell back onto her pillows, then buried a wince as she remembered all she'd done to avoid Riselda's questioning. Her dried hair crunched with grime beneath her.

It likely helped that she hadn't been carried in, dripping an unknown black substance with a look of utter terror frozen upon her features in the dead of night. She couldn't imagine an unquestioning Riselda then.

Chapter Thirty-Four

LUX SOAKED IN AN unoccupied corner of the bathhouse. Though it wasn't so much unoccupied as she was avoided by most other women who entered. Furtive glances were followed by whispers and a quick swim to the opposite side of the warm pool as soon as the steam dissolved enough for Lux's uninviting stare to seep through.

Only Ghadra's elite had private baths, the mayor's mansion included. Lux's eyes had been so wide when she first sank within one as a child. It'd been huge, big enough for three grown people, and she had swum around like a fish for an hour.

Otherwise, usually in the early evening hours, the Light frequented this bathhouse. It was popular. A place for gossip and relaxation. And, for the first time, she wondered how the poor kept clean. For the Dark had no such luxury.

Lux studied the black strands of hair against one shoulder, thoroughly cleaned now with a floral-scented soap. Riselda's potion hadn't just healed her ankle; it'd lightened every bruise and cured every ache. She ran a finger over her intact lips before resting her head against the side of the bath, reveling in the warmth a little longer.

"Did you see her?"

A ghost of a smile crept across Lux's mouth. They never learned how easily sound traveled in places like this. They might as well have been speaking in her ear.

The group of three were about her age, maybe a little older, with bodies that hinted they'd never known hunger or pain. The mist blocked them from view again, and Lux closed her eyes.

"Morana's husband died. They say she wouldn't revive him. She *refused.* Even as Morana begged...on her knees."

A round of gasps followed.

"No! Not Colden! He was so handsome. So attentive, too."

A giggle erupted from the mist. "Yes. *Attentive.* I'd say he was a lot more than that with you!" More laughter followed, now amid splashes of water. The steam shifted again, and three pairs of eyes found her own.

"What a monster."

Lux didn't blink until they were blocked from view once more.

And when the steam moved the next time, three matching squeals filled the echoing chamber as a figure, cloaked in shadow, crouched at the pool's edge directly behind them.

Green eyes glittered beneath black strands dripping over bared teeth.

Lux purred, "You've no idea."

SHE'D LEFT HER HAIR long, curling wet down her back. Lux's cloak was a ruined mess that she'd discarded the night before, and so she possessed nothing to cover it with as she walked the winding streets leading away from the bathhouse.

The Festival of Light was in two days' time. Lux hoped Morana didn't think Colden's death so important that she pushed the celebration aside. The town would surely riot.

She could only recall one death within the mayor's family—one that remained so, anyway. She'd been a child, her brilliance but a pulsing hint of something in her chest, and the shops closed for days, shrouded in black in respect of the ancient aunt or some sort. At last, a wagon bedecked in flowers, ribbons, and bells, transported the swathed body into the awaiting trees.

Ghadra returned to normal after that, and it hadn't happened since.

Morana's reaction certainly wasn't promising; if anything, Colden's procession would be bigger, and Lux chuckled wickedly, wondering how many women would be left mourning the loss of his late-night visits as the death-cart ambled by. She bit her lip, but no trickle of remorse could find her. Rather, she stopped short. Her fists clenched, and she seethed over what played out before her.

Two boys. Two well-dressed boys of the Light. And one cornered child against a wall.

"You don't belong here. Go back to your hovel, you dirty Dark rat!" The taller of the two stepped forward, and she frowned at the shadow of a beard along his jaw. Older than she thought then.

When he shoved against the child before him, the body still blocked to her vision by their own, a muffled cry of rage rang out.

Disturbances in the Light drew attention, and Lux wasn't surprised when the Shield charged around the corner in quick response, baton drawn in a threatening wave. Lux's back, remembering its injury, throbbed. The party was oblivious, but rather than intervening, the guard slowed, observing. Then smiling. His eyes found Lux's, and his grin turned taunting.

Did he know who she was?

With a flourish, the baton was swallowed by his uniform once more and, following a mocking nod of respect toward her, he disappeared from view.

"Useless." Lux let the word ricochet against the brick walls and observed the boys' spines straighten only to curve again. A shout rang out from the squat one as a small boot stomped upon his own. The cornered rat was a fighter it would seem.

The taller boy, older than even Lux, turned toward her as the shorter wound his hand through a clump of thick, blonde waves.

Aline growled, punching him in the gut with as much force as she could muster while nearly bent in half.

"Can we help you?" No recognition showed on the taller boy's face.

"No. I won't be needing your help." Lux drew the winding blade from her corset. "Kind of you to ask, though."

His eyes widened, regarding the dagger's progress as she played with it. The shorter boy had Aline on her knees now, pushing her head down with all the strength he could gather while attempting to avoid her thrashing fists. She connected now and then, but other than a grunt or an oath, the boy refused to release her.

Lux pitched her voice so the one restraining Aline could hear. "It's rather embarrassing to admit, but I've not been practicing as I should. My aim is poor. I do know I won't hit the girl, but I'm not sure if the blade will sink into your thigh as I'd like. It's just as likely it'll bleed you out through your gut. Or stop your heart." She sighed dramatically, pulling back, raising the handle high. "I'll try my best not to kill you. My sincerest apologies if I do."

Aline came up swinging upon her release.

Her small fist just reached the jaw of the squat boy, and though he didn't stumble, his head rocked back with a jerk. She kicked him in the groin. She kicked him in the shin. She punched him square in the eye.

"Aline."

The older bully had already fled at Lux's threat, abandoning his friend. And judging from the whimper of the boy knocked to his bottom on the stones, he longed to run as well.

Brown eyes swung to her own, narrowed and searing, and it was enough time for the boy at her feet to rethink his prospects. Clutching a swollen eye, he took off down the street.

"What?" Aline straightened, smoothing her hair even as her knuckles bled into the light waves.

"Nothing. Only wanted to distract you from beating that boy to pulp on the street." Lux replaced the blade, tucking her hands in the pockets of her skirt.

"He deserved it."

"Probably. But then I'd be forced to revive him after his parents dumped his smelly body on my table." Lux wrinkled her nose. "I really did it to spare myself."

Aline snorted, trying, and failing, to coax her knuckle to clot.

Lux continued past her, the sun breaking through the clouds for a second to embrace her skin before retreating once more.

"Don't tell Shaw."

Lux smiled. A little thoughtful. A little annoyed.

A little sad.

"I don't tell Shaw anything."

Chapter Thirty-Five

"Lucena!"

Riselda's voice rang from the doorway of a shop that Lux had never possessed the desire to enter. From the displays alone, the floor to the ceiling must be compiled of the brightest, most expensive dresses and fabrics in existence. She recoiled from the mass bulging behind her aunt's form.

"Come inside. I've something to show you."

Lux stared after Riselda's retreating figure, angry with herself for having chosen this particular route home. She pondered feigning misunderstanding and scurrying away, but when her aunt's frown found her from above a puffed pile of orange tulle in the loosest form of a dress, she knew it wouldn't be worth the consequences of her ire.

And Riselda had healed her ankle...

Clenching her teeth, Lux climbed the steps, pushing the door aside. The inside of the shop smelled worse than it looked; the air thickened with perfumes that burned her nose and coated her throat.

"Riselda, I'm busy."

Riselda turned from the shopkeeper with a swish of plum skirts. "Aren't we all, but the festival is right around the corner. And this year will be especially spectacular." Lux studied the gleam in her eyes. "How is your ankle? All healed?"

Lux coughed. "Yes, thank you."

Riselda tilted her head, her eyes delving into Lux's own, searching for answers. She found none and shrugged, a laugh leaving her lips. "So secretive. No matter. You're welcome."

Riselda spun back to the slight woman she'd been speaking with. "Yes, yes. That one. A perfect match, I'm sure." The woman skipped away, likely ecstatic over Riselda's expensive purchase.

"You used to wear such lovely colors, Lucena." Riselda stepped forward to finger the red taffeta at Lux's back. "It's a pity you've lost your love of them." When the woman returned with a dress slung across her arms, she added, "But I do hope you'll at least consider this one."

Signaled, the shopkeeper released the skirt, holding the dress high. It was fitted through the waist with capped sleeves and a round neckline, silver leaves delicately stitched into the pale green silk from the bodice through the skirt. An exact match of Lux's eyes.

Eyes that burned.

"No, thank you."

The shopkeeper's face fell, the promise of profit falling through her fingers. "But it would look so lovely on you, dear! Your hair, your eyes. That skin. Yes, you must try it on."

Eager hands pushed the fabric toward her own.

"It's time to brighten up your wardrobe, Lucena. Ghadra's Necromancer doesn't always have to be dressed in shades of death."

The woman's eyes bulged.

Shine bright, Lucena. "Oh, but I adore death. How else could I afford my sweet rolls?"

The color left the shopkeeper's face entirely at Lux's words, and her hands began to shake.

"Be that as it may, I don't believe you need to dress the part of corpse if you're to accompany me to the festival."

This was new information. "You're attending? And you've decided I am too?" Nettled, irritation threaded her voice. She'd gone too long making her own choices, and this pushed too far.

Riselda's brow furrowed. "Yes. It's special to me. This one particularly so." Her eyes unfocused, and her gaze drew far away, when she rasped, "It's been a long time."

Lux blinked against the change overcoming the woman before her when Riselda suddenly lurched back to the present, staring down at her with a smile painfully wide.

"I don't ask much from you, darling. Please consider it?"

Without waiting for a response, Riselda paid the paled woman who then dumped the dress into Lux's arms before staggering back with a quick bow. She hadn't even offered to wrap it. Lux tucked her hands around the skirt to bring it further into her arms where the silver leaves glinted against her sleeve.

"Well then." Riselda patted her cheek, sending slivers of ice through the soft skin. Lux jerked away, and as if only now noticing her wet hair, Riselda inspected her. "You were at the bathhouse?"

"Enjoying the latest gossip." At Riselda's quirked brow, Lux humored her. "I've apparently begun refusing my services. Even as the mayor's daughter begs and pleads."

Riselda's mouth thinned, the skin whitening around her lips. "I see."

Lux had thought the whole encounter comical, a pathetic ploy of Morana's to further ruin her. Yet, Riselda was clearly and abruptly furious, and Lux frowned at the raging storm beneath the surface.

"I will find you later. Hang that up so it doesn't wrinkle." Riselda's clipped demands were followed by a sweep of skirts and a nearly collided hip as she strode through the door.

Lux tracked her progress down the street, but when Riselda faded into the distance, she turned into the shop's expanse. The shopkeeper caught her glance with a soft gasp and proceeded to pretend she didn't exist. Rolling her eyes, Lux balled up the beautiful dress in her arms and shouldered her way through the door.

Sleeping the day away meant twilight was upon her before Lux had managed to arrive home. And so, because she had done it many times in the past, her feet trekked the familiar path, past her home, through the archway and outside Ghadra's walls.

Lux watched the fog roll in, relaxing her harsh grip on the silk in her arms until it fell, loose and nearly to the stones beneath her. Movement caught her vision in the distance within the trees.

The death-cart. Making its way back to town.

"Thinking of offering your phantom a gift?"

Lux stifled a scream, spinning to connect her hand to the voice's jaw. Shaw caught it a fraction before it landed, his eyes wide.

Lux's were a mirror image. She ripped her fingers from his warm grasp. "What is *wrong* with you?"

"With me? What is wrong with you? I wasn't even walking quietly."

She glanced down at his heavy boots, the creeping fog caressing up and over them. "You followed me?"

"Only to ask how you're managing to not only walk without crutches but without a limp as well. Though, now I'm also wondering why you're headed into the trees again with a dress for a weapon. Call me curious." He crossed his arms.

Lux huffed, stepping off the bridge. "You distrust *me?* Go away, Shaw. My business has never been, nor will it ever be, yours."

His jaw clenched, a day's growth lining it. He looked older. Older, and tired.

She told herself she didn't care.

He opened his mouth, ready to fuel yet another argument between them, when the death-cart's wheels met stone. Shaw moved back, away from her and to the opposite side of the path.

Lux studied his gaze regarding hers as the wagon rolled between them, relieved of its cargo, driven by a man with bruises beneath his eyes and slumped shoulders. He didn't even glance their way.

Lucena.

Lux pressed her eyes closed briefly before giving in to the gathering grey. Shaw's tracked her movement.

Lucenaaa.

The boughs bent. The wood beckoned.

"What's happening?"

The branches curled inward. Inward and out again.

"The trees..."

But she didn't face him. Instead, she squinted into the clearing, her mind tricking her into believing she could see a faint figure, cloaked and hooded, hovering above a mound of bodies. She shook her head, the vision disappearing.

"I've got to go. Can't have this dress wrinkle." She crushed the fabric back into her arms, hopelessly creased, before turning on her heel.

"Did you know that lifeblood can bring back your health, even from the brink of death?"

She whirled with a glare. Was he implying she had drunk it to cure her broken ankle? Her lips parted, words of rage boiling, threatening to burn them both. But her fury went unnoticed.

Shaw was staring at the fog weaving between his boots, hands in his pockets, his shoulders curved inward. "Did you know there's a boy playing happily with his sisters at this moment when a week past, he was dying of fever? His family is so poor they couldn't even afford a physician...let alone a necromancer."

His eyes found hers then, and Lux almost stumbled back from them. "Did you know there's a girl your age who can continue to care for her young, orphaned siblings because rather than simply dying from the beating she'd sustained, leaving them behind and alone, she drank a murderer's *essence* instead?"

Something pricked at the corners of her eyes.

"Did you know, Lux, that every time a life left that of someone who purposefully hurt, mutilated, or killed innocents, I drained it, bottled it, and personally made sure it passed the lips of someone who deserved to *live*?"

Her soft exhale resonated loudly in the space between them.

"You can hate me for what I've done. For what I still do. But I will never repent to you."

A single tear fell from Lux's lashes to travel down her cheek. She didn't wipe it away. And Shaw didn't see it.

He was already gone.

CHAPTER THIRTY-SIX

THE WRINKLED DRESS GLIMMERED against the surrounding black fabrics, and Lux shut the door of her wardrobe against the brightness of it. She collapsed on the bed, her heart aching. A hand rubbed the throbbing area before falling back to her lap.

Her conscience hadn't left her alone since Shaw's words. He had spoken so quietly he may as well have shouted. She didn't think anything—*anything*—he could say would sway her beliefs. Yet, here she sat, questioning, as another aspect of her life that was once so black and white had fallen to grey.

She blew out a slow breath, catching herself before she completed her wish to return to a time where she was so sunken within herself, wallowing in darkness and sorrow, that she cared for no other living soul. Nobody could cause her pain because no one could ever reach her. But the loneliness...

It was tenfold.

A world where she'd begged to be invisible. To never be truly found or acknowledged or *seen*. They hadn't understood her then. How could they? *She* had been the one to do something unforgivable.

But now—

Lux raised a hand to her throat; she felt it thicken.

It was true she didn't care for many. But she cared for a few. She cared for Riselda, even as she was odd and secretive. She'd glorified her aunt as a child, and she still looked up to her for her meticulous sculpting of her healing brilliance and her fearlessness. She may even care for Shaw's ill-mannered sister. A watery smile tugged at the corner of her mouth, recalling Aline's fighting words and small fists against two boys twice her weight. She reminded Lux of herself.

And she cared for Shaw.

Undeniably.

Maybe even irreversibly.

Lux fell back into the pillows. She should change, her damp collar told her as much, but her muscles remained languid, stretched out upon the bed, unwilling to follow her demands. Yet, sleep wouldn't come. When she closed her eyes, she saw every person she'd given life back to, and every one she hadn't. Their faces flipped like pages inside her head.

Ghadra's history flipped like pages.

She was pulling the door closed behind her before she even knew where her feet led when it dawned on her at last: she would go to Shaw. She would…apologize. She couldn't say whether she agreed with his actions or not, but he didn't deserve her continued judgement any longer. And she must tell him exactly that.

Night descended, and the raucous street at her back faded to hushed silence as she entered the Dark. A gaunt man peered at her from a sagging stoop. A street over, and a woman's hollowed eyes stared down from a third-story balcony. Rats pilfered through trash, doorways and windows were boarded, and the ominous feel of Death lingered like a patient scavenger, knowing it would soon again be fed.

So many were dead. The Dark smelled of nothing but cloying jasmine and rot.

Lux stood before the familiar worn door in the familiar worn alley with her fist poised in the air. *Knock,* she told herself. *You've done it before.* Which was all well and good—but for the part that would come after.

She was *nervous.* How had it come to this?

Her fist met the wood, harsh and scraping her knuckles, and she dropped her hand afterward, pushing it into her pocket. *If he doesn't answer, you'll leave. He never needs to know.*

The door swung inward on her next breath. Tawny eyes, stunned then cold, stared back at her. *I—* Her lips parted, but no words tumbled out.

"What are you doing here?"

Lux fought against her shoulders, pushing them back. "I had something I wanted to tell you."

The door opened further, revealing Shaw's full height, his upper body shrouded with a dark coat and a bag slung over one shoulder. "Write a letter. I can't talk right now." He stepped out, practically into her, pulling the door closed behind him. The soft click ricocheted off ramshackle walls.

If he thought she would relinquish the barest distance then he didn't know her at all. Her eyes narrowed. "Why not?"

He bent, the heat of him enclosing her, and maybe Lux didn't even know herself, because she stumbled back and into the alley. Or she would have—if his hand hadn't reached out to grasp the damp collar of her dress, drawing her in.

His irritated sigh brushed against her mouth. "I'm breaking into the prison."

All her air abandoned her at once. *"Don't."*

"Don't? How kind you are to be concerned for my well-being." A rough laugh left him as he released her.

"The Shield will never let you escape."

Shaw stepped around her. "You managed it."

A shadow knife pushed through her breast. The memory made her flinch. "I had help." He looked back. "Riselda. And the mayor was furious about my capture. It helps when you have something he wants."

His dark eyes studied her closely before fingers raked through his hair. "I'm sure. Regardless, I have no other choice. But I do appreciate the warning." He seemed as if he wished to say more, but he turned instead, passing the darkened basement entrance of the alchemist's lair and continuing down the alley.

He pulled a cap further over his eyes and didn't glance back again until she neared his side.

"Then I'm going with you."

PEERING AROUND THE BACK garden's tallest, densest hedge, Lux crouched beside Shaw. The walk to the mansion had been long and uncomfortable, what with the endless silence stretching onward to infinity once Shaw finally agreed to her coming along. She had opened her mouth more than once to break the silence with her attempt at an apology, but the words still wouldn't come. Besides, she figured they would only end up in another argument anyway, and she didn't want to enter a place like the prison with her emotions in turmoil.

The garden was emptied of most of its occupants. If Lux squinted over Shaw's shoulder, as he insisted on going first, she could make out two guards in casual poses speaking in low voices. If there were more, she couldn't tell; rose bushes taller than any person blocked most of her view.

Her muscles began to burn, and she rested onto her knees in the damp grass.

"Stop shifting so much; we're going to be seen."

She rolled her eyes at his hissed reprimand. He had been the one that almost got them caught scaling the vine-wrought wall, groaning loud with effort as he hauled himself up and over. If she wanted to remain unseen, she would be. "Your poor excuse of a whisper is more likely to bring them down upon us than I am."

He shook his head without turning toward her, mumbling incoherently beneath his breath, and she fought back a smile.

I've missed you.

Her smile died as quick as it surfaced, a very real fear creeping through her chest unhindered. *No.* She shouldn't care *this* much. She couldn't. There was a colossal difference between opening the door to the idea and the enormity of actually letting him *in.*

Terror filled her as she traced his shadowed profile. It was familiar to her now. *He* was familiar to her. She knew how his arms felt around her waist. She knew what he tasted like. She knew his darkest secret; he knew hers.

She knew him.

And she felt absolutely sick.

"I'm going to create a diversion. We'll slip through easily enough. If we follow that gravel path, there's a passage leading down."

"It isn't barred?"

"It wasn't then. But even so," he said, jostling the bag on his arm, "I can pick the lock."

He'd been here before. She recalled his talk of his father and the discovery of his death. "Of course you can."

Shaw huffed, glancing down his shoulder. "Stay here."

Before she could inquire further or protest his abandonment, he left her to steal around the remaining outer hedges. Lux watched him go until the dark swallowed his form, then shifted the weight on her knees with a scowl.

"Tell me what to do one more time and see—"

She jumped, a hand clapped to her mouth, as the first explosion slammed into her ears. An array of crackling sparks and flares of light followed, a second explosion close behind. Shaw was at her side before she'd even realized the Shield had run to investigate.

"Go!"

The word hissed into her ear with searing heat. Lux leapt to her feet. The pair of them sprinted through the rose garden, her pace matching his. Moments later, they were through the archway, and Lux's legs would have continued to propel her forward in search of another door, any door, if Shaw's hand hadn't grasped her upper arm, hauling her toward him and into a shadowed alcove.

Booted heels thundered past. A small army's worth of guards.

They swept her fear along with them.

What did she have to lose? *Everything,* said her head.

Shaw's hands were splayed upon the stones at her back, enclosing her shoulders, his hard chest flush against hers. He bowed toward her, his breaths grazing her temple in warm pants. They hadn't run far; his shouldn't have been so ragged.

She knew hers shouldn't have been either.

"I didn't hurt you?"

She shook her head, and her nose brushed the hollow of his throat. His scent caused her eyes to flutter closed. *Everything!* her head reminded. But for the first time in her life, her heart protested the idea, and said, *But you don't have anything now.*

"Stupid on my part not to realize it'd bring so many. I'm sorry."

And saints above, how she wanted something. Even if it might hurt. Even if she couldn't keep it.

"I'm sorry," she whispered. "For judging so harshly, for not letting you explain, and for still being unsure if what you're doing is right."

Shaw's lungs filled, his body pressing harder against her. His slow exhale sent a lock of hair over her eye. "I judge too harshly, too." He straightened, one hand dropping to his side, and the other pausing partway in its descent.

It rose again to finger the wind-dried strands caressing her cheek and finally, to push them aside. She swallowed against the urge to lean her face into the sensation. When she lifted her eyes to his, his hand fell from her skin.

At once, an overwhelming anger came upon her. Over how badly she wanted his touch to continue. Over how *starved* for it she felt.

Over how she couldn't feed that want here.

She crossed her arms over her chest, dividing the space between them. "May I ask you something?"

His gaze lifted from her elbows jutting into his front. He raised an eyebrow in response.

"What the devil was that thing?"

Shaw grinned. "Aline's invention. She's brilliant. If you could see the sketches, the models she's thrown together, of the things she wishes to create. They're magnificent." Lux didn't try to hide her answering smile at the pride in his voice, and his faded as his gaze dropped to her mouth. "We should go. The entrance is near here."

She bit her lip, trepidation over entering the prison again dousing all other feeling. But he hadn't forced her to come along, she'd done it willingly. "What do you hope to do if it's found?"

Shaw peered down the length of the silent hall. "Steal what I can and destroy what's left." He stepped from the alcove, his hand outstretched. "Still desire to come?"

Lux didn't hesitate. She grasped it tight.

THE PASSAGE RISELDA HAD ushered Lux through upon saving her those few days ago had been lit with torches every few steps. There was no such light in this one.

The door hadn't been barred, just as Shaw had assumed, and it opened with a jarring creak that left them both stiff and breathless as they waited to be found out. But no one came. This entrance didn't appear to be utilized often—if at all.

She followed Shaw inside, faltering only when cobwebs clung to her face. Spiders didn't trouble her all that much, but that didn't mean she enjoyed them crawling through her hair. Shaw, on the other hand, appeared much more bothered. She was left to tug on the door, muscling it closed as he raked his hands over his face.

He shuddered, arms falling to his sides. "I *hate* spiders."

Lux smiled into the gloom, knowing he couldn't see it.

With a hand upon the wall and Shaw's body heat directly before her, she took her first step down. The musty air grew thicker with the coat of dust stirred by their boots, and she fought back a cough more than once. She hadn't any idea where this particular passage would spit them out, and she didn't want to take any chances on any small sound echoing ahead and alerting the Shield.

Shaw, for not being able to see even the barest shadow in front of his face, maintained a steady pace as they spiraled down. Until, at last, they were met with a forlorn, flickering torch. She squinted against its brightness, attempting to peer around his shoulder to get a glimpse of the tunnel beyond, when a gust of frigid air found her skin from the opposite side.

She spun with an inadvertent gasp, but only darkness greeted her. Tentatively, she stretched out her fingers.

"This way." Shaw motioned her forward, and her hand stilled.

Another torch further down the passage winked at them. No cells yet. Nothing, save stone and firelight, surrounded them both. Their footsteps were near silent as they crept.

Lux sucked a breath and braved a question. "Why should it have been you?"

Shaw paused for so long, she wasn't sure he'd heard her. She considered asking him again when he said, "I once had a bad habit of taking things that weren't mine."

"Like a pickpocket?"

She watched the shadows dance along the pale stones as he shook his head. "No." He paused, probably musing on exactly how much he wanted to disclose. "Do you know the houses closest to here? The tall ones with stone statues? I've been inside them all, and let me tell you, they're as overdone inside as they are out."

"You're a thief."

What next? An expert poisoner? A drug harvester?

"Not anymore. It started off as a test of skill. I simply wanted to see if I could. Young and senseless. But what I found, the excess, how it was just...strewn about. I grew so angry. It was unfathomable how little we had. How little we *all* had. We worked so hard, and still we went to bed hungry and woke the same. I stole jewelry that night. A couple of baubles I figured wouldn't be missed, and once I hawked them, I divvied up the coin with everyone I knew. The next time, I was able to give to those I didn't know. And the next, and the next. Years of it.

"But I misjudged the room one night, and I was found out. The Shield showed up at my family home hours later. Enough time for me to hide the coin, but not enough to concoct a believable alibi. My father—" He cleared his throat. "We looked alike: same build, similar hair. He took my place. He told me to take care of Aline. Six months I tried, but by the time I managed my way in—"

A cry reverberated against the walls, and Shaw fell silent.

The first prison cell. The occupant cried out again, visceral sobs that pulled at Lux's heart, simultaneously urging to run, saving herself, but also to plant her feet, never to rest until she'd set them all free. Neither would occur tonight, so she hurried by the door, trying—and failing—to block the cries that clung to her long after.

The next few they encountered were blessedly silent; either empty or their occupants' were unconscious or dead. Lux didn't know how often the surgeon made use of his torture chamber, but with every cell they passed, she fell further into vengeful imaginings of his scalpel in her own hand, doling cut after cut upon him until his sadistic grin grew fixed.

A sudden shriek bounded from the bars of the cell beside her. She spun out of her thoughts, the curved blade settled within her palm.

Shaw's hand enclosed over her wrist, softening her grip. "Hurry."

The labyrinth continued. It curled and twisted, enticing them forward with hints of decay and suggestions of filth. They curved around a row of locked doors, whimpering against far-traveled wind, where the loathsome scent grew foulest.

"This is a passage that leads upward and out. For the death-carts."

She'd no idea, even as it made sense that the bodies be removed as discreetly and efficiently as possible. A deep wooden crate filled the alcove at the opposite side, the fetid scent of death stifling. Shaw looked as if he might vomit, but Lux wondered if it was less the smell and more the thought of his father's body dumped within, as meaningless to the mayor and his Shield as the previous one.

She reached out her hand, all the while thinking of calling it back. But when her fingers connected with Shaw's, he entwined them like a lifeline and his breathing evened out, the pale hue leaving his face.

He didn't move for several heartbeats, staring at the crate with shadowed eyes. When he inclined his head to study their clasped hands, she started at the sheen of unshed tears beneath his lowering lashes. Suddenly, her hand in his seemed woefully inadequate.

But she couldn't do more for him. Not here. Not now.

His hand pulsed once around hers before releasing. "We need to keep following the tunnel. I've seen a place where prisoners are experimented on." He swallowed. "Where my father most likely—"

"I know the place," she said. "They brought me there."

"And you escaped their blades?" His eyes followed along the contours of her body, searching for signs of healing injury.

"There weren't any. Not for me." Her trailing whisper drew his brows together, but she wouldn't speak of it. Not here. Not so close. "You're sure the lifeblood is there?"

"Sure? In all honesty, no. But it's a good place to start."

Chapter Thirty-Seven

THE MAYOR AND, SUBSEQUENTLY, the Shield, must have been very confident in the ongoing absence of unwanted visitors. Aside from the wailings and occasional scream of those locked beneath the surface, Lux and Shaw didn't meet anyone.

When the narrow doors rose before them, Lux breathed a sigh of relief that only darkness pushed outward from behind it.

"I'll go first." Shaw stepped forward without waiting for a reply, and she cursed her cowardice as she offered no objection.

Her wrists and ankles throbbed in memory of their restraint. She followed at his back as they entered the cold room, and she shivered in the darkness, unable to see a thing. "How will—"

She startled at the flare of light illuminating Shaw's face.

"A thief, remember?" The small flame elongated his canines and sharpened his cheekbones, turning his grin into a wolfish sneer.

Her eyes dropped to the satchel slung across him. "What else do you have in there?"

Shaw strode to the surgeon's worktable, and said over his shoulder, "Lock picks. Rope. A set of knives. And a couple surprises I hope to go unneeded, courtesy of Aline." Her ears ached again just at the mention of them. "I don't know what half of these are."

She stepped around to his side as he stood, vial in hand.

"Then I wouldn't touch them. The concoctions created here are abhorrent."

He nestled the glass bottle very carefully back in its place, his gaze searching. "What did they do to you?"

Lux tried to fix her eyes in front of her, but the lone, narrow door pulled at her vision. She stared into its shadows. "I was bound, some toxin forced in my veins. And then...nightmares." She swallowed. "But before that, I watched a man gutted, and when his inevitable death arrived, witnessed just how exactly lifeblood is extracted. It was...enlightening. I vomited all over the Shield's boots."

She heard Shaw's breath catch behind her, but only too late did she realize he was likely imagining his father in the man's stead. She'd been tactless.

But when she turned toward him, the eyes mirroring the flame weren't filled with grief as she'd expected. Nor impenetrable shadow. Rather, her own widened at the compassion she saw there. And the immeasurable fury.

"I've changed my mind." His words were clipped, menacing.

"About what?"

"Our mission here, tonight. Don't look at me like that. I still plan on stealing every last remnant of lifeblood. But I'm burning this place down with it."

"You can't. You'll harm the prisoners."

"The flames won't get past these doors. It'll cause enough damage to prolong the fates of those down here until we can save them."

We. Lux bit at her cheek as she observed his determination. His faith in their alliance.

Irreversibly.

She cared for him irreversibly.

But she still had to ask. "What makes you so sure?"

"Another gift of Aline's."

She snorted. "Now I'm even less thrilled with this plan."

The room was empty. Empty of any substance that glimmered and glowed with a silvery sheen. Lux let Shaw investigate the small space she'd been held, tortured by her own mind. She had no desire to see it again. When he appeared through the doorway once more, his arms hanging in dejection, she felt only relief.

"Any other ideas?" Her nerves were getting the better of her. They'd been down here too long.

"Maybe his study—"

"We've looked there."

"Not long."

She clamped her eyes shut, shaking her mind free of the memory of a kiss she'd only ever thought of while alone. But when she opened them, something new occupied her attention. Behind them both, behind even a stacked set of stained, white sheets, stood a narrow cabinet with a curiously shaped padlock.

Lux plucked the wavering light from Shaw's hand and strode toward it.

The cabinet was dark wood and finely crafted, but other than keeping the flames from touching its surface, she didn't pay further mind to it. Her gaze roved over the lock instead. It was unusual, its ends coming to points instead of smoothly rounded, and, as far as she could see, it didn't have any place for a fitted key let alone a lock pick.

She tugged on it anyway. A bolt of cold swept up her arm, and she dropped it.

"I've never seen anything like that before." Shaw was beside her now examining the device with narrowed eyes. He didn't pull on it as she had done, but rather turned it over to study its back.

"Bastard."

"What?" Lux rubbed at her arm, still tingling as warmth worked back through her veins.

"*A pinprick of crimson, a droplet of warmth; so must be the Sacrifice.*" He stepped back. "Blood. How fitting for our mayor."

He reached for his knife at the same moment she pressed her fingertip over one of the lock points.

"Let me, Shaw."

"No. You don't know what else it might glean from you. I'm no one."

"Being no one is a very dangerous thing in this town." And she pricked the pad of her finger before he could protest further, glancing away from the drop as it pooled then splashed onto the lock's surface.

"You shouldn't have done that."

But Lux wasn't paying him any mind. Pressing her finger against her skirt, she knelt, eyeing the metal as it began to click and whir. The lock snapped free. With a triumphant grin, she swung the door outward.

The cabinet's insides glowed silver.

And still their faces fell in a mixture of confusion and disappointment, their brows drawn in an exact replica of the other. For there were only twenty vials stacked inside at most.

Where is the rest of it?

"This...is it?" Shaw's incredulity was plain. He snatched one of the vials from its resting place, fixing a glare upon the substance within.

Lux spoke the obvious, "He certainly isn't draining lifeblood from those dead of the plague."

Maybe it was a simple purge after all. She couldn't absolve him yet.

Shaw tipped the shimmering liquid into his cupped palm.

"What are you doing?" She backed away from him, his expression unreadable.

He smiled, almost animalistic, his eyes flicking up to hers. "What I do best, Necromancer." He dipped a finger into the silver pool as the vial shattered upon the floor. "Painting."

Hours later, once the fire was put out and the black smoke cleared, men would stare in horror upon Shaw's corrupt work. A gleaming, silver forest smeared across the walls in broad strokes, unmarred by flame. And the words:

Death is Inevitable

"Revive me if I'm burned to a crisp, won't you?" were Shaw's last words before he forced a hesitant Lux through the doors to listen to a begging cry from deep within the prison. He'd said he trusted Aline's skill. The fervor with which he scolded Lux into listening to him spoke otherwise.

He'd told her it was a mechanism with a slow-to-emit gas and a spark with which to ignite the flames. It had sounded simple enough, but when she swung the door inward to see what took him so long, she was sent stumbling back by his body propelling through.

"It took. Go!" Shaw gripped her hand, pulling her after him.

Already, she could smell the smoke trailing behind her. She only hoped those trapped behind stone walls and locked doors would have faith. They did this as much for them as for themselves.

They had stolen every last usable drop of lifeblood, cast a vial upon the walls, and left one very obvious message for their beloved mayor. This would be his final lifetime in this world. Even with her continued revival of his tumor-consumed insides, she doubted he would survive much longer without it.

Her thoughts were cut short, however, when a high-pitched sound screeched through the tunnel. She clapped hands to her ears with little improvement, the noise continuing in a rhythmic pattern she'd never heard before.

"An alarm!" The color fled Shaw's skin, draining Lux's own at the sight.

He yanked on her arm, her legs unable to keep up with his sprinting pace. They rounded a curved corner in the labyrinth of the mansion's underground. "What does it mean?" She'd never heard such a thing.

"It means we've been found out." The words were nearly lost to her. She'd almost hoped they had been. For they wouldn't live to see morning if the mayor discovered them, and with sweeping certainty, she knew their lifeblood would be the first vials in his refurbished collection.

The alarm rose, in both tempo and volume, almost eclipsing the pounding of boots upon stone beneath it. Shaw ground to a halt. Lux followed a few paces beyond him, breathing heavily. It was far more than exhaustion that screamed in her lungs and set her heart hammering, and even though her body was grateful for the reprieve, her mind was not.

"Why are you stopping? We can still make the old entrance!" She splayed her hand across her chest, trying and failing to ease her heart back to a steady rhythm. Shaw hung his head. "Shaw!"

The strike of boots drummed closer.

"Run, Lux."

He didn't raise his eyes, even as she was sure hers would pop from her skull. "What? No, come on, you imbecile!"

His eyes were twin storms, dark and thunderous when he lifted them. But his voice was sad. "Remember how I once said I could come to like you?" His quiet laugh was lost. "I think I have, after all, and I think it might be more than even that. I can hardly believe it." He shook his head, strands of gold highlighted and shimmering by the torchlight. She stumbled back beneath the weight of his bag as he tossed it to her.

"Use the last device in there. A switch on the bottom and then you run. Promise me."

"*Never*. I won't promise you anything."

Shouts lashed through the air.

He was before her in two long strides, cupping her face in his hands before bringing his lips down upon hers in a kiss that was unlike either of the ones prior. Fast and hard, it almost hurt. A goodbye. He broke from her. With unguarded eyes brimming with emotion, he shrugged off his coat. Settling it around her shoulders, he pulled the cap from his head. He fitted it over her hair.

"Be safe, love. Be happy."

A mass of tall, uniformed bodies barreled through the passage toward them. Shaw's hands dropped to his sides, and he squared his shoulders. Following a final, lingering look at her, he turned. Her eyes stung, but it couldn't be from tears. Wiping her cheeks, she stepped away from him. From his faded blue shirt.

This isn't real, she thought.

But the Shield kept coming.

It isn't real.

But he didn't look back.

CHAPTER THIRTY-EIGHT

THE PASSAGE HAD GIVEN way to quiet at last, the alarm a distant peal her ears strained to hear. Lux ignored her body's cries of protest, reveling in the physical pain that occupied her mind against every other form. It finally received its reprieve at the base of the darkened stone stairs spiraling upward. She'd found the entrance, and all that was required of her now was to climb.

She demanded her legs to obey, to step forward. But they only wanted to sink down and rest onto her knees. Lux hung her head, her breaths filling the air around her, loud and gasping, and she clutched Shaw's bag like it were Shaw himself, the scent of him wafting from his coat to torment her. She closed her eyes, pressing her nose into her shoulder, inhaling deeply.

A grunted oath floated down from the stairs. Followed by a shuffling gait and a steady thump as if something were being dragged.

Lux didn't give her limbs a choice as she shoved herself up from the floor, flattening against a shadowed wall.

The shuffling grew louder.

A swish of skirts followed.

Lux caught her lip between her teeth, forcing the air in her lungs to remain still. Her eyes squinted into the darkness to observe deep skirts of blue or plum. She'd only a moment to focus on them before they were hidden once more beneath the covering of a familiar grey cloak.

The hooded figure didn't look toward her.

Instead, long fingers reached back into the entrance alcove and dragged forth a body. A body in a blood-red gown and a mangy sack over its head.

The phantom hoisted it up and into its arms. Without a glance in either direction, as if it knew its path with comfortable surety, it continued to drag its captive. Down the hidden passage, Lux had felt but not seen, and into the icy beyond.

Shaw's long coat provided little comfort from the frigid gusts that assaulted her with reckless abandon. Lux wrapped her arms about her chest and attempted to keep her teeth from alerting the phantom to her presence with their incessant chattering. All the while, she followed.

The passage had sloped downward at first, but had since leveled out, making the pace easy if not terribly cold. At least the phantom had the exertion of towing another body along to keep it warm.

Lux knew she shouldn't complain—she'd chosen to give into the mystery. The phantom wore no rags or spectral skin but a very real gown. She doubted this event occurred often within the safety of the mansion, and right now, the being was an ideal distraction to keep her from running back to take on the Shield single-handed.

The tunnel eventually gave way to hard-packed soil. So much so, it was an almost imperceptible shift from the carved stone prior. She may not have noticed had she not felt something similar beneath the trap door of her apartment. And that of her parents.

At first, only the grating sound of booted heels upon stone, and then soil, alerted her to exactly where the figure walked ahead. But now the phantom's breaths were labored. It must not be accustomed to carrying bodies such long distances. It was little comfort.

A draft of warmer air brushed against Lux's cheek, and she turned into the darkness. She stretched out her fingers. Where rough soil had been beneath was now empty space. A connecting tunnel.

Her skin crawled.

She knew where this tunnel led. Which meant her growing suspicions about where her current path was taking her were also likely correct. Lux dropped her fingers back to her side, tucking them deep within the sleeves of Shaw's too-big coat. Another gust of frost-tipped air ran over her exposed skin in a gentle caress.

Welcome back, Lucena.

LUX PULLED BACK INTO the darkness of the tunnel when the first glimmer of silver fell through the trap door.

The phantom abandoned the body in a crumpled heap at the base of the ladder, rising to push along the seam, opening with ease against its hands. The silver glow emanating from the trees in the center of the cottage spread to the passage beneath it now, and with a grunt of effort, the cloaked figure hoisted the body up and through the narrow space. Red silks and finely made boots were the last things Lux glimpsed before they were swept from sight.

Tentatively, she reached for the rung at eye level.

When Lux first peered over the floorboards, her mind flashed with visions of her death, stabbed mercilessly by the phantom's narrow blade. When the attack didn't come, she braved a look around. A flourish of red and the body was gone—around the trees and to the opposite end of the cottage. Muttered whisperings and a choked cackle of feminine laughter followed. Her heart bounded.

A madwoman?

Pulling herself up and through the trap door, she reeled back from a snuffling snout pushing against a cage. A cage that had materialized at her side, shrouded in shadow, along with a rat. His companion laid asleep, curled in the corner.

What awful pets. Her lingering doubt over the cloaked being's sanity was no longer; it must certainly be unhinged.

Lux crept alongside the trunks of the silver-barked trees. She crouched, giving them as wide a berth as possible before peering around their glowing trunks.

The phantom finished tying its prisoner—either dead or unconscious—to a hard-backed chair with a coil of thick rope. The victim's soft hands rested limp and pale against the wood grain. The grey figure stood still, studying their charge for a moment. Then, with one quick movement, it flung the dirty sack from the prisoner's head.

Morana.

Her lips were blue with cold, and Lux thought she might be dead until she saw Morana's chest move with a shallow exhale. Her dress was askew, her hair a knotted mass about her head, and her skin much too pale. Lux could imagine how infuriated she would be to know someone saw her in such a state. Particularly, if that someone were her.

Morana moaned.

The sudden strike against her cheek rang out over the edges of the cottage, driving a gasp from Lux and ensuing silence from the mayor's daughter.

The phantom lowered its hand.

All Lux could discern was an unyielding shadow beneath the hood as it turned to her. As it took in her crouched position, her body hidden beneath a massive coat and her fingers clutching tight to a dead boy's things.

Lux bolted.

The phantom flew after her.

Down into the tunnel she dropped, no time for the ladder. Righting herself, she hurtled forward, her shoulder scraping painfully against the wall. The fabric shredded, the exposed skin stinging and hot, but she couldn't slow. For the phantom leaped down behind her.

She tore back a cry of panic.

The monster at her back knew these tunnels well; it didn't need light to guide its way, and Lux was going to die in the cold darkness because of it.

Even with the knowledge of her futile escape, adrenaline pushed her. Far beyond the normal boundaries of her capabilities. Her muscles bunched and stretched, heat tearing through them, sweat beading her brow, but she still didn't slow.

The phantom gained.

Lux could feel it, the long fingers enclosing around the narrow knife that had tended to so many bodies so diligently. Her exhaustion shifted into the realm of delirium. She wondered what appendage the phantom would choose from her. An eye, perhaps? She'd long been complimented on them. Her toes?

Maybe it would carve out her very heart.

A switch on the bottom and then you run.

Shaw's voice filled her head. So achingly real, it was as if he stood at her side calling her all sorts of foolish in her forgetfulness—which was exactly what she called herself in his honor as she attempted to maintain her pace, her hand diving within the bag.

A brush of warmth fluttered across her face, and Lux spun toward the welcoming air, racing down the connecting tunnel with everything in her. It wasn't much anymore, but the quick change of direction gave her the added time to enclose her fingers around Aline's device as the phantom regained the ground lost.

Hands fumbled in the dark until a small protrusion caught at the pad of her fingertip. She pushed against it and didn't hesitate.

She tossed it over her shoulder.

Blinding white light flooded the passage like the sun, and a cry sprang up at her back. But Lux didn't pause. The phantom's quick breaths were gone. The only footfalls were her own.

With the synthetic, fading sunlight, she came upon a ladder, and climbed.

The stains were ignored. Lux tugged and pushed the couch over the trap door within her parents' home, and when it was done, she collapsed upon shaking legs, resting her back against the rear of it. Morning had arrived, the grim glow of a new day creeping through the windows.

She wondered why she wasn't crying. Shouldn't she be? Part of her remained in denial, the rest of her too exhausted to argue the point. It couldn't be real. It wasn't possible that their plan had gone so awry. That Shaw was captured and now at the mercy of monsters, that the phantom had discovered her at last.

It isn't real. That's why.

Her eyes fluttered closed, a small, relieved smile on her lips, and with Shaw's scent cocooned around her and her head propped against his bag, she drifted into fitful sleep.

Chapter Thirty-Nine

The marching of booted feet faded from her dreams and grew louder once Lux blinked open her eyes. The crunch of debris over stone sailing through the shattered window forced her to stand and creep to the fragmented glass. Her legs ached with every step. Her heart ached even more. Denial wasn't a luxury afforded in the daylight. Lux peered through the window.

The Shield. They filed down the street.

An entire squad of them.

She kept to the shadows, but when they turned, their faces trained upon her parents' door, her breath caught.

They couldn't know. They couldn't know she'd accompanied Shaw, broken into the prison, drained the mayor's stores of lifeblood and set fire to its remains. They couldn't know she was here.

Could they?

She glanced to the dried blood marring the tip of her finger.

"Devil's tits."

Lux shoved the worn couch back to its place. The rug was rumpled, its edges pulled back from the trap door, and she wrenched it open. When no phantom flew out to run her through, she steeled herself, slipping onto the rungs of the ladder. She could hear them at the front door, prying off the final board attached to its frame as she reached around the edges of the floorboards, tugging the rug up and over. She only hoped they didn't look too closely, because she wouldn't be able to cover the seams entirely.

She sunk below, darkness clinging to her like chains, the weight of the bodies above sending dust raining onto her head. She stepped back.

Muffled voices drifted downward.

"The mayor wants her brought directly to him. Unhurt. For now."

A derisive snort. "As if she'll come quietly. Did you hear what she did to Blackwell? Clawed his eye!"

A new voice chimed, "And now he's dead."

"Orders are orders. I'd rather deal with one crazed girl than have the mayor after me. Check every corner of this shack."

Heavy footfalls sent more debris cascading down as they stomped over the trap door.

Lux released her breath at last, her body screaming for air. Clutching Shaw's bag tight to her chest, she turned, following the tunnel once more. She would go home. She would tell Riselda everything.

She was going to need her help.

LUX THREW OPEN THE floorboards of her home without a care if Riselda witnessed it. She'd planned to tell her all she knew—and all she'd guessed—and that hadn't changed in the time she'd spent below ground.

But Riselda wasn't there.

Lux smoothed out the rug, and with a quick sweep of the house to ensure no Shield had yet rifled through her things, she walked to her room. Shaw's bag and coat were the first items to go, shucked onto her unmade bed. Aside from digging inside to find the bizarre, but effective, invention of Aline's, she hadn't looked through it. Remedying that now, she let Shaw's coat fall from her shoulders before reaching for the bag once more, dumping the contents onto the mussed mound of blankets.

He hadn't lied to her. There lay the rope and the knives. The vials of lifeblood. But Lux's hand didn't reach for those. Instead, her fingers enclosed around a small, worn book.

His grandfather's journal.

She frowned. "Why would he bring you of all things?"

She flipped to the first page:

Keep it safe, Necromancer.

The cover fell closed. How had he known she would accompany him? Did he plan to give it to her all along? Or only if he were captured?

Her fingertips whitened over the fraying leather for seconds more before it fell from the bed as a door clicked closed.

Lux hauled Shaw's things to her, crouching to the floorboards to grasp the old book. She winced as the leather pulled further away, loose at the back, but when she took a moment to examine the damage, it was to find another page folded within. She didn't have time to read it, shoving everything inside her wardrobe with shaking fingers. The Shield could never find his things. It would damn her.

Footsteps descended the stairs at the same moment Lux materialized in the doorway.

"Lucena."

She sighed in relief. "Riselda. I—" And like once before, her lips ceased to obey. A twinge deep within, and a burst of ice bloomed in her chest. What was the matter with her? Riselda's arched brow, now raised in question, sent her stammering. "I...was curious how the rest of your errands went last evening." She blurted the first thing that popped into her head. It was a pathetic attempt.

Riselda's eyes narrowed before she laughed. It didn't sound the same. "Wonderful. My preparations for the festival are coming along as planned." Lux shoved her hands in the pockets of her skirt. "Though I am interested as to why the Shield is hell-bent on your arrest again, my dear."

"They were here?" Lux hurried toward her workroom, inspecting it closer. But as before, nothing appeared out of place, and she couldn't imagine the Shield to be gentle in their search. She turned back toward Riselda.

"They were. So was I, however, and unfortunate for them. I turned them away."

"And they obeyed?"

"Of course they did. But I cannot protect you forever." Riselda's gaze hardened. "Not yet anyway." She moved around Lux, studying her. "They did let slip a little something of interest, though. Apparently, a young man has been captured. And they've spent the morning torturing him for information. He must have done something terrible. I'm afraid they believe you may have done something terrible, as well. Have you, Lucena? Have you done something terrible?"

Her aunt's eyes didn't appear natural. Bile seared Lux's throat. "I've done many terrible things, Riselda."

She wasn't sure if she imagined the gleam fading away at her words or if it'd never been there to begin with.

Riselda smiled. "I know." Long fingers enclosed around Lux's forearm. "Ghadra's gossips have never been of the forgiving sort."

If the touch had been meant in comfort, it had the opposite effect. Lux shook off her hand. "I don't need your pity."

"And I offer none. But you must go into hiding, darling. Even I can only do so much. Your imprisonment prior wasn't your fault. This time... Well, I can tell from your face alone, you deserve the mayor's wrath. And if he deems what you've done unforgivable..."

Riselda stared upon her dirtied nails as the unsaid words pressed down above them, weighing on Lux's shoulders.

"He will die before he drains the lifeblood from me." Lux's voice was low, steady, and thrumming with an anger that pulsed and spat. She meant every word. She would carve his chest hollow, and there would be no one to bring him back.

A cackle filled the space between them. "I do adore your spirit, Lucena. I really do. Though that changes little now. Pack your things. I will purchase supplies, and you'll leave tonight." Riselda reached into the pocket of her blue cloak, pulling forth a small pouch. She placed it on the table. "As promised. Though you may not have much use for them anymore." She smiled, her teeth laid bare.

Lux stared after her for a long time. Even when the door closed between them, and the footsteps faded. Until, finally, she reached for the little pouch, dumping the contents onto the table. The howler teeth scattered across its surface.

"Oh, dear Aunt. You know nothing of my spirit."

CHAPTER FORTY

IF LUX COULD DESCRIBE Aline's face when she knocked upon her door, it would perhaps be *less than thrilled.* Perhaps even hostile. But also, maybe, there lay just a hint of curiosity.

That curiosity grew by a fraction at Lux's words: "I need your help."

Unfortunately, it didn't prevent the door from being slammed in her face.

Lux pounded on its worn surface again. But when another woman answered, she stepped back. A woman with Shaw's eyes in an age-lined face, its shape an exact replica of her daughter's.

"Can I help you?"

Lux absorbed the red-rimmed eyes and raw nose. This woman had clearly been crying, and for a long time, too. "I'm here to speak with your daughter, actually."

"She doesn't want visitors. And, quite frankly, neither do I."

Tears pooled once more, and Lux shoved Shaw's coat into the space between them. "You know he's missing, I suppose." The woman's eyes widened, her mouth slack. "I know where he is."

Lux sat in a decrepit kitchen at a rickety table as Shaw's mother listened with rapt attention. Aline, with her back slouched against the chair and her arms crossed, seemed not to listen at all. The space had been meticulously cleaned. Lux couldn't discern even a speck of dust marring any visible surface.

Shaw's mother pressed her hands flat against the table only to fold them. She did this again and again until Lux couldn't take it anymore and pressed her hand atop the one nearest her. It stilled, warm and callused beneath hers, and Lux bit back the urge to withdraw from the contact. She needed the woman to understand. For her and Aline both.

"They seek whatever information they can get from him now, and I don't believe he'll give it to them."

The hand beneath hers went limp in defeat. "No. No, no, no." Fresh tears spilled down her cheeks, following the grooves left there by hard work and a harder life. "This means..."

She couldn't force the word.

Death. Lux found most couldn't speak it.

"It means he's being tortured at this very enlightening moment, and they'll kill him when he proves himself no longer useful." Aline's eyes were twin daggers as she hurled the words at Lux. "And how did you escape without a scratch? You're not stronger. You're not faster. You're certainly not cleverer than my brother. *Tell me.*"

Lux wondered if her own eyes had been so hard at such a young age. She reined back her irritation. No, they hadn't. They had been worse.

"I abandoned him. He told me to; he gave me this." She swung his bag up and onto the table, packed with all except the journal. "I left him."

Aline's eyes couldn't part with the bag or the jacket beneath it. Her throat bobbed, and Lux looked away from her. She could handle Aline's anger. Lux wasn't sure if she could her tears.

She'd told them why he had gone. Why they both had. She told them of the destruction they'd wrought, and even praised Aline's innovations. She told them of their theories, of the one left in tatters upon discovering the limited supply of lifeblood, and Shaw's message painted upon the walls, meant to terrorize the mayor in the only way they could.

But in the end, it was this: Lux had abandoned him to his fate. His death. They knew it now, and they would hate her. She didn't care so long as they offered their help in saving him. So long as Aline had a stash of working proto-types hidden somewhere about their crumbling home.

"What do you need from me?" Aline's voice was quiet. She didn't glance up from the rows of lifeblood lined upon the table.

"A distraction. Whatever you can give me."

ALINE'S WORKROOM WAS MUCH different from Lux's. For one, it was much smaller. Though, she noticed that only second to the scorch marks, the missing chunks of wood, and the scratches decorating the floor.

"Don't touch anything."

Lux rolled her eyes.

"I mean it. Some of this stuff isn't all that stable. Not yet. Fine, maybe not ever." Aline pushed aside a stack of metal squares, their edges bent inward, from her worktable, and pulled a chest toward them. "Stand back."

Lux did as told. She didn't relish losing her eyebrows. Or her hearing.

Aline opened the latch with a click, searching the depths of the chest. At last, she pulled out a mechanism. It looked similar to the device eliciting the sunbeam, and Lux drew closer, intrigued.

"It has a switch at the body—here—that turns it on. But I haven't built in much of a delay yet. Whoever flips it will have to run. Fast."

Lux hadn't told either of them about her use of Aline's final creation. Her knowledge of the cottage, Morana's capture, and the phantom were her secret to bear. For now.

"Understood." She reached for the device, but Aline backed away, clutching it close to her chest.

"What is your plan, exactly?"

Lux dropped her hand with a huff. "I need to draw the Shield away from the mansion. I need to meet the mayor—alone. I have leverage that I feel can barter Shaw's release."

Aline's gaze was unusually penetrating for a child. "And if you fail?"

She wanted to say she wouldn't. But she decided on the truth, instead. "Then I will die, my lifeblood drained and drank by the mayor or one of his glowing family members. And you will use every explosive device in this disastrous room, bringing down the entire mansion and most of the surrounding buildings to set your brother free."

Aline's mouth twitched. "Good. I like that plan better anyway." She pushed the device into Lux's hands. "But, in case you don't fail and wind up dead...Thanks."

Lux bit her lip against a smile. "You're welcome."

Chapter Forty-One

The slew of curses over the soreness attacking every muscle of her body never left her mind, but Lux thought them furiously regardless. She'd never run so fast or far in her entire life as she had the night prior, and now here she sat, squatting amongst the blooming black roses, nursing yet another pricked finger as her thighs shrieked.

The Festival of Light took place in the Light Market square not far from the mayor's mansion. It would begin the following day with vendors of food, trinkets and drink, a parade of the mayor, his family, and his Shield, and continuing with dancing, more drink, and some show of a sort. The final event changed every year, and Lux would be hard-pressed to remember what any of them entailed. Only that it was meant to invoke envy in those who were not blessed with riches and favor while solidifying the privilege of those well-aware of their elevated status.

It didn't sound like an enjoyable way to spend her evening.

Though her current state wasn't much better. She pressed against a few of the loudest-protesting bones in her neck, sighing at the relieving crack of each as they slid into place. She sniffed. *Ugh.* She needed a bath, and the roses agreed as they clutched their sweet petals close, arcing away from her. She stuck out her tongue at them.

She wanted to plant Aline's device somewhere in the square. She figured it would cause the least damage while also providing the biggest space for the Shield to congregate once they were drawn from the mansion's walls. Lux contemplated the spindles protruding at odd angles from the metal cylinder in her hands.

She'd asked for a distraction. She counted on Aline to at least give her that.

Twilight descended, but she ignored the tug against her body. The forest would be left waiting today. A few stray members of the Shield meandered here and there, not nearly alert enough to be truly looking for her. Lux hoped that meant they were tired of the search for the evening. She observed the last few vendors pack their wares.

The fountain at the square's center always mesmerized her as a child. With a total of three towering tiers, the spindle atop the final one wound upwards and upwards, ending with a flourishing letter G. It was gaudy and expensive; a perfect fit for the mayor who'd commissioned it.

And the water to it was cut off every night.

Given the cover of darkness, Lux felt sure she could climb her way to the top tier and wedge the cylinder within. Hidden from view, she hoped it would confuse the townsfolk for a time. Enough for her to slip into the mayor's domain unwitnessed and unchecked. From there, she counted on her leverage being deemed worthy enough to free Shaw.

With her plan as solid as she could make it, and some time to waste until night fully cloaked the town, her thoughts turned to Riselda.

Riselda standing hunched, an unnatural gleam in her eye, with enough howler canines to last through months of revivals. And all following demands for Lux to abandon Ghadra to its fate. To flee as she'd always wanted. To save herself.

In the prison, strapped to a chair, Lux had plans to do just that. But, like the heaviest pendulum, she'd returned to her senses.

There were families just like hers here, and they had faces now. Aged and worried and kind—and young and vibrant and fierce. If she were to walk away now, she'd never overcome it. Her intuition had been right in preventing her from confiding in her aunt. Riselda would never understand and would probably never forgive her after tonight.

Lux forced her clenched fingers to relax against her new weapon. It would be just her luck to detonate the thing amongst the rose bushes, announcing her presence to the world. With a cleansing breath, and another readjustment that would have made Shaw groan, she continued to wait.

The final white uniform vanished into the din of a boisterous tavern, and Lux was already several paces into the point of no return.

She couldn't back away from this tossed-together plan because if she imagined the man tied to the table, his insides opened to the room, Shaw's face was in his place. She'd seen him dead once. She never wanted to again.

The first tier was easy to swing into.

The second required more effort, and her arms and legs shook from the strain. They held her though, and she climbed into the remaining pool of water before tipping her head back.

A shout cracked through the air.

Lux dropped like a stone to her knees, soaking through her skirts and splashing water across her chest. She shivered, goosebumps erupting over her skin, though it was from much more than the cool water. When several seconds ticked by, she peered over the fountain's edge.

A drunk and stumbling figure entered the square, leaving the tavern door wide and allowing light and an obscene amount of noise to tumble forth. He shouted again over his shoulder, whether in irritation or delight it was impossible to know. Either way, Lux breathed a sigh of relief she wasn't found out. An intoxicated man meant nothing to her so long as he wasn't the Shield.

When he disappeared down the street, likely in search of another establishment to grace with his coin, she reached for the final tier.

Even on the tips of her toes, her fingers could just cling to the carved stone above her. With a whispered prayer for strength, she pulled. Biting against the pain scorching through her arms and down her back, she stayed silent. Only when she hauled her knees over the brink did she finally allow herself a low, agonized groan. Her breaths came in pants and her arms hung limp, but she drew the device free with a smile.

She flipped the switch.

The resounding *boom* was so loud, it rocked the fountain to its core. Doors thumped open and windows banged wide. It drew people from every direction, wide-eyed and slack jawed. Already, rumors tumbled from them. Speculation, nothing more. Nobody truly knew its cause.

Though when the green gas twined from the topmost tier, billowing putrid clouds and bringing the rotten smell of eggs and filth along its path, those wagging mouths quickly became hysterical over the onslaught.

"Ack! What the devil?"

"Wake the mayor!"

"Gah! Right before the festival, too! I was so looking forward to it."

"Find the little demon responsible! It was probably my neighbor's evil child. Again!"

The relentless stayed and pointed fingers at every ill-behaved person they knew, which were many. The smartest scurried into their homes, sealing every opening closed and tight, speaking no more. The dimmest studied the gas as it neared, allowing it to caress their clothing, puffing around them. The odorous oil seeped into threads and soaked into pores, marking them as outcasts. Because, according to Aline, the oil would not leave, willingly or otherwise, for a month at the least.

Lux grinned, a wicked laugh almost escaping her. When the angered voices began to fade at her back and the Shield finished pouring from the iron gate to investigate, she slipped easily through the abandoned front doors.

Chapter Forty-Two

HER MEMORIES OF THE mayor's mansion as a child were few and faded, but Lux felt confident in that she couldn't recall it ever being so dark. Or so quiet. The loss of Colden, the loss of Morana, and, above all, the loss of lifeblood had apparently sent the mayor into confinement. Which meant she would only find him in one part of the house: his study.

Staying close to the walls of the foyer, she hurried around its expanse. She wasn't sure how long she could count on the Shield to investigate the cause of the nauseating scent currently enveloping the Light Market, so she didn't waste her time sneaking from alcove to alcove. With every step that landed, she imagined Shaw far beneath her, tied and bloodied, begging for a death that wouldn't come. At least not for some time. The images spurred her to move faster, even as her chest tightened over what must come next.

Lux had been alone with the mayor in his study only once, and now she was about to break the vow she'd made to herself long ago, to never do so again.

The lamplit halls were silent and empty, but only for so long. A glimmer of white caught her eye. The door to the study neared, a posted guard unmoving before it. She didn't have another of Aline's inventions to assist her, and because this guard probably wouldn't be open to bribery, she utilized the coin in her purse for another purpose.

The silvdan pinged against the far wall, and the Shield immediately hurried to investigate the source of the noise.

Lux waited until the shadows swallowed his frame before trying the gold handle. Locked. No party trick goes unpunished, she supposed. But she didn't think the Shield would stand guard over an unoccupied room, so she drew in a deep breath—and knocked.

"*What?*" shouted the muffled voice. "This is my private time! You are not to—"

The door swung in, and the mayor's watery eyes bulged from their sockets. "Necromancer!" The door swung wider, allowing lamplight to spill outward and bathe her. The guard must have been happily pocketing his coin; he did not reappear.

The mayor's surprise gave way to rage in the next breath. "Turning yourself in, are you?"

Lux allowed her body to remain lax as Bartleby Tamish dragged her into the room, his fingers clammy against her forearm. "Of a sort."

The mayor sputtered, moving around her to close the heavy door with a click. "To think I trusted you." Stalking around his desk, he piled his squat form into the chair. "Sit down."

Lux forced her legs to obey, and though the chair didn't swallow her up quite so much as when she was a child of eight, it diminished her spirit just the same. She straightened her spine against the smooth-as-butter leather and stretched her neck—only for a memory, grey at its edges, to flutter down upon her like a veil.

"Your parents were found murdered, child. You, with a knife in your hands. How do you think that appears?"

The mayor looked exactly the same. Lined face, wide, parted lips, eyes ever calculating. He rested his arms upon the gleaming desk.

Lucena was silent a bit longer, wringing scrubbed-clean hands above a blood-stained yellow dress, her little body swallowed by the chair in which she had been placed. "It appears that I've killed them."

She'd surprised the old man. He sat back. "Precisely. Do you have a particular reason why? You see, I don't enjoy locking children away. But I will if I must."

Her small frame began to shake. "I took too long. They told me they loved me, that they needed me. They told me they had missed me so much. Then they stabbed my heart." Quivering fingers brushed against the torn fabric of her dress. A shallow wound. One meant to extend much deeper. Though not even she knew how deep it really ran.

"It's all my fault. I shouldn't have done it. I shouldn't have brought them back after they were murdered the first time."

"I don't think I can permit you to live after this. After all, your blood was revealed to me from within the lock, and I can't allow this knowledge to be made public. Ghadra needs its mayor. It *needs* me." He sighed. "I'm the most important man in the world, and it's a shame, really, that it must be you or me. Your abilities were the height of useful."

"I thought you might say as much."

"Brought them back? What do you mean, child?" The mayor's hands blanched white, no effort to hide the eagerness from his face. "You can revive the dead?"

Lucena folded in on herself. "I never will again. Never."

"Where is your daughter, Mayor?" Lux smiled, teeth laid bare. A copy of Riselda.

"Taken to her bed, of course. What with Colden's death." A sudden shift and suspicion sharpened his eyes. "Why do you ask?"

"I wouldn't trust the source who led you toward that conclusion, is all. Servants can be easily bought."

The short man shoved himself to his feet, cheeks flushed crimson. "What do you know? Tell me, girl, before I order the Shield to make you speak for me."

Lux relaxed into the chair at last. "I know she isn't crying into her pillow over her departed beloved." She watched him seethe a moment more. "I *may* or may not know where she is. And torture me all you like, Mayor, but I think you know as well as me, that I will never make a sound."

The mayor held her eyes for an age, but when she didn't flinch away, he lowered himself into the chair once more. "You come to barter with her life? For what? Your own?"

"When the tumors clinging to your insides like great warts decide to claim you again, who will revive you? No amount of lifeblood is going to restore your health indefinitely; they're simply too quick. You've lived too long, and now you need me more than ever."

Labored breaths stained the quiet. "What is it you want, Lucena?"

"Oh no, no. Your gift needs to be cultivated! I had no idea, and right under my very nose, too." Lucena didn't recognize the greed for what it was. "A brilliance such as this is rare. Astounding, really. It's unfortunate what happened to your parents, but I will personally ensure your comfort and education from now on. You'll come to find that I'm a very generous man, my dear."

He was at her side, his hands like ice.

"How old are you, child?"

"Eight."

The hand left her thin shoulder to travel down her arm. "You'll be a young woman soon." His fingers left her to caress his curling mustache in thought. "I'll have arrangements made for you. You may live here. With me. And my family, of course. Do you see how generous I am? Everything you need will be at your fingertips, and someday, you may even stand at my side. As Ghadra's Necromancer."

"There's a man held within your prison as we speak. I seek his freedom."

The mayor chuckled darkly. "The man who, by all appearances, accompanied you? Who set fire to my infirmary—" Lux snorted, "—only after desecrating it first with a ghastly message? Never. He knows too much."

"Too much about lifeblood? About your harvesting of it from prisoners only after their torture and inevitable death? Or perhaps about your unnaturally long life? Twenty vials. That's a very small amount for the number of people I know have gone into that place never to come out again. What have you done with it all? Has it taken the place of your evening tea?" Lux tried to even her breaths, to tamp her temper, but *oh,* how she *hated* him. "You disgust me. You're a heinous, despicable, poor excuse of a man."

The mayor straightened, puffing his chest and prepared to fight. "Do you know where you would be without me, you foolish girl? Ghadra has no farmland, no livestock, no fruit trees. It is a blot between a seeping marsh and a wicked wood. Do you believe it would still exist if it weren't for me? I've built this city up. I've brought in the apples you eat and silks you wear. My secret path is the most secret and only disclosed to a dedicated few. Do you know how I've accomplished it?" A frenzied gleam entered his eyes. "By sacrificing the dregs of this town. Nobodies. The worthless poor that do nothing for me or these walls." His voiced dropped to a hoarse whisper. "The world outside pays very well for the gift of time."

What...? "You're selling your people's souls?" Like breaking glass, she felt her own shatter. This, she did not expect.

The mayor scoffed. "Not their souls. Don't be dramatic." He steepled his fingers. "So, you see, I cannot allow your friend, lover, what-have-you, to be freed. He would incite a riot, and with this obstinate plague still about, he may rouse enough to actually go through with it. And I'd rather enjoy the festival tomorrow, thank you very much."

"Obstinate plague? Do you not know its origin or how it can be stopped?"

He stared at her as if she were crazed. "Of course not! Quite frankly, I've been living in utter terror that it will infect the people of quality at any given turn. Perhaps even myself! Thankfully, it seems to be contained to the squalor for the time being."

Lux's heart hardened. She couldn't think on the implications of that statement yet. She had only one means of leverage left, and she'd use it to save a good man. "And if I agree to an eternity at your side? What would you say, then?"

His gaze meant to bore straight through her. "What are you proposing?"

"I remember a time when you wished for my presence. In your home. At your right hand. It's no secret you're attracted to power. And I am very powerful."

Lux pulled back her shoulders. "Let him go. As you said, he is no one. Should he even utter the word, you can murder him where he stands. Though people are unlikely to believe a nobody anyway. In his place, you will have me: my silence, my loyalty. And Morana's freedom of course."

His eyes were slits. "I could have you anyway, you know."

"I will take a knife to my own eyes should you even attempt." For good measure, she drew the black-handled blade, its curved edge glowing beneath the lamplight.

She could try to kill the mayor. Right now. But that wouldn't save Shaw. And it certainly wouldn't save Ghadra from the revenge his family would wreak upon it.

His gaze traveled from the dagger to her eyes and back again. "My darling girl. I do believe we have a bargain."

Chapter Forty-Three

The agreement was struck. Lux would see Shaw freed once Morana was brought before the mayor in exchange. Then she was to gather her things, say her goodbyes, and move within the mansion, giving her brilliance over to the mayor to use at his will.

She never had any intention of following through on that final promise, of course.

Rescuing Morana, planting her before the mayor, and seeing Shaw walk from those poisoned walls, she would do. But she would never truly consent to becoming another's plaything. Unfortunately, that left the problem of her likely murder once the mayor discovered he'd been cheated.

She'd think on that later.

Right now, she had to focus on escaping Ghadra's walls without being seen.

She couldn't go home. Riselda would demand to know where she'd been and why she didn't heed her warning. And she couldn't go through the tunnels. For one, she wasn't entirely sure she wouldn't end up lost, and for the other, she hadn't any desire to face the phantom in the dark again. Better to brave the trees.

A rotten hint still clung to the air as Lux passed through Ghadra, leaving it to rise behind her. A quick glance over her shoulder, toward the grey walls, and the mayor's threat entered her head: *Bring her back unharmed and whole, or my end is forfeit. The boy dies.*

She only hoped now that the phantom had indeed left Morana's body intact and that the bruise surely gracing her cheek would fade before the time of her father's inspection. She yawned beneath the cool moonlight. These late-night excursions may be the death of her yet, long before the mayor ever got to her.

It wasn't lost on her that several weeks ago she wouldn't have dreamed of entering the wood, and now here she stood, for the third time, beneath their black boughs. Desperate times. It only irritated her further that her reason for venturing amongst the trees again was to rescue an ageless girl whom she didn't even like, and maybe even hated.

For Shaw. He didn't deserve his fate, and the quick reminder propelled her first steps into the dark soil.

A swift swirl of cold welcomed her return, and Lux cursed her loss of gloves and ruined cloak. She shouldn't have returned Shaw's coat. If she could do it all again, she would have kept her mouth shut about Morana and left her to the phantom. She could be happily plotting her escape from a lush bedroom right now while Shaw walked free. Maybe, someday, she would learn to think things through.

Something niggled at her insides. *No.* She couldn't possibly feel *sorry* for Morana. Could she? Lux huffed, rubbing her hands along her sides. It returned the feeling to them somewhat but did nothing in drawing away the empathetic sensation.

Benevolence was not her nature. "Damn it all." She didn't even recognize herself any longer.

The moss squelched beneath her boots, and she curled her lip at the sound as it brought back memories of being doused head to heel. She hurried through the trees, and when she came to the slope that had made a fool of her once, she dug her dagger in deep and climbed. The wood didn't speak to her, and as she clambered down the opposite side, no roots greeted her descent.

All in all, it was already going infinitely better than last time.

The eerie glow of the forest beckoned her forward, and if her fingers hadn't felt as though they would fall off at any moment, she knew they'd be slick with sweat. For the cottage was near.

No light suffused the window, nothing but the pale glow of the trees. But Lux knew that nothing so simple meant the phantom wasn't at home. Slipping from shadow to shadow, she drew near and hunched over, her body well beneath the window as she followed along the exterior. Perhaps the mayor's daughter was already dead. At the least, she was drugged. The Morana of her childhood would have never made for a silent prisoner.

A spine-tingling howl rose up through the wood.

Though she would certainly take a dead body's discovery as opposed to *that*. Risking a quick glance through the windows, she picked out nothing of note. Another howl joined in horrifying harmony with its mate, and in that, the decision was made for her. Phantom or no, Lux opened the door and slipped inside.

Every muscle of her body tensed with the snicking of the door at her back. Her eyes roved the room, coming to rest upon the trap door. The rug lay askew across it, and a small seed of hope took root in that perhaps the phantom was gone and not hiding in the shadows after all. She stepped forward.

The floorboard creaked.

Lux jumped even as the sound came from her own two feet. She cursed her clumsiness. She didn't often make such mistakes.

Still, the hooded wraith didn't come.

With a relieved breath, Lux hurried toward the back of the cottage, where the bookshelf rose up first. She slowed. She hadn't gotten a proper chance to comb through it for clues to the phantom's identity, and now that she knew she was alone, aside from a sedated Morana somewhere, it drew her in.

Most were ancient. Most were thick. Most were covered in dust.

There was one that was none of these.

Lux pulled it from its perch and flipped open the cover. The subject was some variant of botany, but the topic didn't hold her attention long. A yellowed piece of parchment, folded several times over, fluttered to the floor.

Setting the book down, she snatched it as it landed. Drawing as close to the glow of the trees as she dared, she unfolded the old paper with swift fingers.

Lifeblood, one must make an incision directly over the iris, extending through the pupil and to its opposite side. The pocket located deep behind the eye is best drained by gravity, and thus repeated on the subsequent pupil when emptied.

WARNING: Harvested lifeblood must never be administered to the deceased. For should it pass a body's lips, regardless of time passed, Life will be granted. It is not human life. It is an abomination, and should the vessel awaken, it will yearn for the lifeblood of the living, and it will take it by any means necessary.

Lux couldn't concentrate on the dark images of gnarled hands crawling across the page, or of the anatomical eye, labeled and slit, an ink-black substance pouring forth. Her own hands shook too much.

The missing page of her book.

The missing page of *Riselda's* book.

When the soft exhale reached her, her heart nearly shattered. She shoved the page into the pocket of her skirt and rounded the corner. The chair she'd last witnessed Morana in sat empty, the ropes in a pool around its legs. She frowned.

But when another exhale broke the quiet, she spun toward it. To the figure on the bed. Lux backed away, sure it couldn't possibly be Morana. She had to have been wrong. The phantom was here. And asleep, no less.

She only made it several steps when the silver sheen emanating from the trees highlighted the thick chain traveling from the mattress toward an anchor hidden from sight.

Morana wasn't dead.

Morana was here, in the wraith's very bed. Napping.

"Don't touch me!" Morana's sleep-tousled head snapped up from the pillow following Lux's less-than-gentle shake of her body.

"Be quiet," Lux hissed back at her. "That's all we need is the phantom here to witness our endearing reunion." When Morana only stared at her with a blank expression, she added, "You're not dead. I'm surprised."

The mayor's daughter blinked her owlish blue eyes so many times that Lux finally grumbled in annoyance, kneeling to discover where the chain led. It appeared to be twisted around the far leg of the bed several times, but aside from that, she couldn't make out much more.

"Get up. I need you to help me lift this bed." Morana said nothing, and she didn't move. "Are you drugged? Can you not hear me? *Get. Up. Now!*" The heated words scraped against her throat, her voice a strained whisper. "Finally."

Morana had moved to standing, the manacle surrounding her ankle clanging loudly against the floorboards. She copied Lux's position without a word, and together, they lifted the frame. It was much heavier than it appeared.

The sharp ringing of the chain uncoiling felt loud as thunderclaps, and with panting breaths from Morana and grunted oaths from herself, they moved it back into position. She pulled the cool metal from beneath the bed and blew out a breath of relief that it came easily. The phantom hadn't thought her charge able to move the frame on her own, and she likely couldn't have.

"Are you real?"

Lux shoved to her feet at the tug of her hair. "Ow! Yes! What's the matter with you?"

Morana moved back with a clanging step. "I've had dreams similar to this." She shuddered. "And then they turn into very real nightmares." With a furtive glance, her eyes found the glowing trees.

"This still might become one of those. We need to leave. Can you walk?"

"Yes, I'm fine. It's my pride that's suffering more than anything. And my skin! I haven't been allowed to wash my face since I've been brought here! Can you imagine?"

Even in the scant light, Lux could see the blotches of color entering Morana's cheeks. "No, I can't. The atrocities committed here clearly knew no bounds. I don't have a key to that shackle either so hold onto the chain. And if the howlers are still outside, we're going to have to run."

Lux was already at the door, and with a quick scan of the wood, found no eyes staring back at her. She swung it open further. The forest's glow highlighted the cages she'd been met with on her last visit. The very ones that housed the largest rats she'd ever beheld.

They were empty.

"Where did the rats go?"

"Rats! Where?"

Lux shook her head. Clearly, they'd been gone long before Morana awakened. Perhaps they weren't pets after all but a light snack for the phantom's fanged companions.

"I don't have a cloak. It's freezing out there!" Morana shivered dramatically.

"Oh, I'm sorry, would you like mine?" Lux held her arms wide, coat-less, cloak-less, and thoroughly irritated.

Morana's eyes narrowed. "Sarcasm is a fool's humor. Lead the way then."

Lux stepped from the cottage and Morana followed after her, her chain falling to the forest floor. She scooped up the length with a loud oath.

"Are you trying to get us killed? You're doing a wonderful job of it so far."

Morana gripped the chain to her chest with both hands, spearing Lux with a ferocious glare. "And you're doing a wonderful job of annoying me. Though, as I remember it, you've never struggled."

"Shaw. That's the only reason you're doing this." And Lux continued to mumble to herself as she stepped amongst the trees, her boots silent in comparison to the ringing ones at her back. Her eyes stung in their refusal to cease staring into the shadows. At any moment, she felt sure yellowed eyes would appear. Followed shortly by very white teeth.

But they didn't come. Maybe the fates had decided to gift her a reprieve at last. She snorted, followed quickly by a huff of irritation as Morana's voice pierced the air between them.

"Stop! There's something in my boot. Don't sneer at me simply because I don't want an infection. Oh, it may be too late. I think it pierced the skin. Damn!"

Lux rolled her eyes, turning to find Morana swaying on one foot as she removed the boot from the other. She nearly toppled, and to steady herself, she reached for the tree.

"Morana! Don't—"

The soil shifted beneath their feet.

"What is this? Lux!" Panic-filled, Morana's voice rose to a shriek as she tried in vain to wrench her hand from the black trunk. However possible, the pitch heightened when the first vining root snaked up her leg.

Lux fell when the next shift occurred, the roots bursting from the moss-covered soil, coated with an oozing gore. It seeped through her skirt, staining her skin, but none of it was meant for her. Lux shoved the hair from her eyes at the blood-curdling scream ripping through the night.

The tree before her appeared as if ruptured from the inside out. It yawned wide, darkness spilling from its pit to dump ice crystals in Morana's hair and on her clothing. Morana's terror had finally petrified her into silence. When the roots pulled against her, she didn't even blink. Her body tipped forward.

But Lux refused to surrender anything to the wood, even a selfish creature like the mayor's daughter. Her dagger sliced through the empty space at Morana's wrist.

Black branches fell at their feet to writhe and twist like great snakes. Morana's voice returned, and she screamed again. Lux winced against it as she bent to hack at the roots too slow in their retreat. They, too, thrashed about as if in pain. Perhaps they were.

Lux gripped Morana's wrist so tight it'd likely bruise and wrenched her free.

Together, they tumbled sideways before Morana fell to her front, knocking Lux to the ground in the process.

"What the dev—"

Morana sobbed, scrabbling at the moss beneath her fingers, choking against the sludge spraying upward, dousing her open mouth. And for a moment, Lux laid there, unmoving, confused as to why, when slowly, Morana's body drew backward.

"*Lux.*"

Her name was a desperate plea on Morana's tongue, and Lux scrambled to her feet to see a faint glimmer of chain. The chain from the manacle drawn taut through the moss and pulled deep into the belly of the tree.

The steady motion was unyielding. More horrifying was that Lux couldn't see anything in which to sever. There were no roots. No branches. The tree itself was drawing her forward. And it'd swallow her whole.

"Help me, *please*. Oh, saints above, save me!"

Lux hacked at the chain. Aside from the barest indentations, it did nothing. "You hellish nightmare," she growled, spinning to the tree.

She could *feel* its triumph.

Shadow fell across Morana's ankles when Lux stepped over her, and the scream that shattered the forest wasn't Morana's this time but hers, as the trunk snapped around her arm, crushing the bone to the shoulder.

The branches bent, curling and twining toward her, welcoming...only to stop. To shudder. Leaves fell, slick as oil and darkest black.

And when the tree's expanse opened once more, it wasn't to draw Lux in further, but to spit her out.

She hurtled back with a silent cry against the pain, her dagger falling to the ground, her fingers unable to hold it any longer. She'd pierced the tree, and now it writhed in agony.

Morana, rather than lying petrified as she'd done prior, hauled the chain up from its depths as fast as she could. When the trunk snapped closed a second time, it was upon nothing. They were free. Morana continued to sob with great, heaping gasps, piling the metal into her arms. The final length sent the dagger skittering toward her, and she bent. Picking it up, Morana looked it over once; with tear-streaked cheeks, she held it from her.

Lux stood unmoving, simply attempting to breathe away the pain, but when Morana extended her arm, she reached for the blade. They'd have both been dead without it. She tucked it safely away as the mayor's daughter quieted at last.

"Is your arm broken?" The question almost felt woven with genuine concern, even amid the lingering hiccups.

Lux winced at an inadvertent movement. "Definitely." She released a controlled breath. "How is your ankle?"

"I'm sure it's hideously large, but it bears weight."

Branches continued to thrash above them. "Good. We shouldn't stay here any longer. I'm not sure what damage I've done, but I don't think this wood is the forgiving sort."

Lux braced her arm as best she could, though it didn't stop the hiss of pain from leaving her lips every couple steps. She could concentrate on nothing else. Instead, she counted on Morana to follow her, and to keep her eyes and ears open to any further threat around them.

"You've dropped something."

"What?" Lux didn't stop. The pain wouldn't let her.

"A page from a book. You know, we were taught never to tear apart our texts."

Lux did stop then, even as Morana's tone wasn't particularly vicious. She didn't want her reading it. "I'll take that back, thank you. And I didn't tear apart anything. It belongs to my aunt."

"You mean Riselda?"

Lux rolled her eyes, shoving the page deep into her pocket where it would hopefully stay put. "Yes, obviously. She's the only one I have."

A heavy silence fell for several heartbeats. One in which they avoided angry branches and furious roots. "I've always thought you knew. That this 'aunt' bit was built from a fondness between the two of you."

Blood rushed Lux's ears. "Knew what, Morana?"

"Riselda isn't your aunt, for one. How could she be? She's older even than I am. Than my *true* age. And she has no family."

The blunt force of those words sent the air fleeing from Lux's lungs. She gasped against it. "You're lying."

Morana walked ahead. "I'm sorry to be the bearer of bad news, but your family died that day. I'm not sure what Riselda's interest in you is, but it isn't due to familial duty. If anything, I'd be wary of her."

Even with the agony ripping through her shoulder, Lux almost choked out a laugh. Only her utter shock over Morana's words held it back. The mayor's daughter was as untrustworthy as they came, and Lux had been wary of *her* from their very first interaction.

She is lying.

Lux couldn't believe her.

"Your true age, is it? A glimpse of permanent death and now you admit to drinking lifeblood?"

Morana paused in her path, nearly causing Lux to collide with her. "I..."

"I already know, in case you're attempting at a lie right now."

Morana muttered a slew of unpleasantries. "Then why ask?"

Lux pushed them forward. "You, your father, Colden, the rest of your *lovely* family. Tell me how you've managed it. How have you managed to get away with immortality? Does not one old person recall finding you the same today as you were when they were a child?"

Lux saw Morana stiffen from the corner of her eye. She knew she risked hurting her by mentioning Colden, but these questions were too important in discovering what really went on inside Ghadra's only mansion. When they trekked on, Morana steadfastly silent, limping and no closer to answering, Lux felt what little empathy she'd built evaporate.

"We *deserve—*"

"I heard you, all right!" Morana huffed, and winced, stumbling on her injured foot. "I've had two names all my life. Morana when I was born, one hundred and ninety-six years ago. Giselle through the middle, as Morana's daughter. And Morana again, Giselle's daughter. My family's story is the same."

"That doesn't make sense to me. What dimwit wouldn't realize you wore the same face?" She felt near to abandoning Morana to the wood if she didn't tell the truth.

"We don't."

Lux stopped in her path, a new horror beginning to eat away at her. "You don't what?"

"Wear the same face, obviously."

Lux couldn't speak.

Morana spoke, instead. "I suppose I should say thank you for rescuing me. I'm sure it's only for the price my father has placed on my return, but nevertheless." She peered into the gloom surrounding them, ducking below a swiping bough. Lux, reeling yet, gripped her injured arm tighter against her abdomen. "I never imagined someone could live out here. What a horrifying place. How did you find me?"

Lux's mind stumbled away from all she'd learned and into what Morana asked now. But she would never tell her the truth. "One of the reapers mentioned a strange sighting in the forest. Rumor spread of a phantom, cloaked in grey. Your father is offering a reward, and I thought, perhaps, it may have been you, lost in mourning. When the figure vanished amongst the trees, I discovered you anyway."

"My kidnapper," Morana hissed. "When I return home, this entire forest will be combed to its edges."

"Do you have an idea of what it might be?"

"*Whom.* A woman." Morana glanced over her shoulder, eyes gleaming in the darkness. "A *dead* woman. She will pay for her crimes."

It can't be.

Lux needed something, anything, to disprove the theory unwillingly conjured within her head. Ever since she'd discovered a weathered page buried within a book in a cottage far from home.

She has no family.

Chapter Forty-Four

"Ms. Tamish!" The Shields' gazes roved between the pair of them, grime-spattered and wounded. "Inform the mayor!"

The shout directed toward the other man peering over their shoulder sent him bounding to obey.

Night teetered dangerously close to morning, and the beaming lampposts outside the mansion's doors gave Lux a splintering headache. The captain, for he must be, fixed a suspicious stare upon her. When she only glowered back, he relented. "We have been scouring the city for you, Miss. Top to bottom. Even braving the Dark, their plague and all."

Lux scoffed. Loudly.

Morana ignored her. "I expect nothing less from my father." She sauntered past him. "I must request the healer immediately. My ankle requires attention." The Shield moved to block Lux's path. "Oh, let her in. She's come to collect the reward."

The captain frowned. "What reward?"

Morana's eyes snapped to Lux's.

"My darling daughter! You're alive!" The mayor hurried as quickly down the wide staircase as was socially acceptable for his station, nightcap askew. Nearing Morana, he gripped her shoulders. "You're unhurt?"

"Only my ankle." She held the chain from her. "I've had the most horrific time."

The mayor *tsk*'d, his gaze seeking Lux's. "And the girl found you, did she?"

"She did."

A white-hot streak lightninged up Lux's arm, and she grimaced.

"You're so quiet, Necromancer. Injured?" The mayor's eyes penetrated the fabric of her shoulder.

"I'll live, Mayor. By all means, see to your returned daughter. I can wait. For a moment."

Her hidden meaning wasn't lost on Morana. "Yes, Lux mentioned a reward. Though the guard has no recollection of such a thing posted."

The mayor patted his daughter's cheek, lingering briefly over the bruise highlighting her cheekbone. "More a bargain than a reward, darling." He spun, his cap giving in and rippling to the floor. "Bring up the boy!"

The volume, as always, was unnecessary, and Lux released her throbbing arm to clutch her aching head.

"A boy?"

Morana's increasing interest in Lux's personal affairs could only amount to no good. "An innocent," said Lux, between her teeth.

The mayor's bellowing laugh reverberated throughout the chamber. "Hardly! But I'm a man of my word. The most generous of my kind. Especially when I receive something I want in exchange."

Lux's blood chilled even as a happy blush tinged Morana's grime-smeared skin. "I've missed you, too. Though where is that blasted healer? My foot feels as if it will burst!"

The mayor ceased his predatory stare to examine his daughter instead. "Gracious, let's get you settled. Then you must tell me everything. To think someone possessed the audacity to attack *this* family. This beautiful family!"

With the Shield supporting either side, Morana hobbled into the nearest and most lavish sitting room: quite unnecessary, Lux thought, considering how well she'd fared thus far on her own. Portraits of the Tamish family lined the walls; the greatest of all being Bartleby Tamish's. Little surprise. Everything had been decorated in a mixture of jewel tones so rich it made Lux uncomfortable to sit amongst the cushions. She hadn't seen this room in an awfully long time.

She picked a seat farthest from their party, nearly in the fireplace, and moaned as she sat, a mix of bliss and pain. When footsteps echoed from down the hall, her heart skittered.

It was only the sought-after healer, hair rumpled from sleep and in a cinched-tight robe. "Mayor. You've need of me?" His voice was a soothing baritone, and Lux relaxed in spite of her discomfort.

"Yes, yes. My daughter has sustained a significant injury. The ankle and the bruise on her face must be examined."

"As you wish. Where would you prefer the examination?"

Why did his voice do such a thing? Lux nestled deeper into the ruby pillow at her back. She wished him to continue.

"In my bedchamber. I don't believe any of these men, or the necromancer, need to see my exposed skin."

At the mention of her, Lux felt the full weight of the healer's gaze. "She's injured too if I'm not mistaken. Would you like her cared for as well?"

The mayor turned to Lux with a smile. "I would. It should only be fitting after all, being as she will soon live here. Reap the rewards of family, Lucena Thorn."

"Live here?" Morana's shrill voice broke the calm that had since blanketed the room upon the healer's arrival.

"*Ahem.* The prisoner. As requested."

All eyes swung to the captain in the doorway. His white uniform was spectacularly pristine, and his charge looked even more dreadful because of it.

Shaw stood beside him, dark gaze focused solely on the mayor. Despite his tattered clothing, his face purpled with bruises, and what looked to be various stages of dried blood across his skin, he still hadn't lost his spirit. Tears pricked Lux's eyes. She couldn't remember ever feeling so relieved.

They hadn't broken him. Not yet.

"Ah, and here is our *artist*." The mayor sneered. "Can't you have hosed him down? I'll never get the stink from this room." The captain gaped then stammered, unsure how to make amends for his blunder. The mayor ignored him. "No help for it now. Step in here, criminal."

Shaw was unbound; they'd obviously deemed him unthreatening. The captain moved to shove him forward, but Shaw expected as much, and when the hand glanced off the swift pivot of his body, he stepped into the room on his own.

"You wished to see me?"

Unlike the healer's, whose voice had calmed her into a relaxed stupor that had her wishing for bed, Shaw's voice sped her heart, her belly tight. When she sat up straight, her shoulder screamed at her. She'd forgotten.

"You may go." The mayor shooed Shaw away from where he sat beside Morana. At the younger man's bewildered expression, however, he added, "Home. You're free. So long as you remember one small warning."

Shaw's eyes couldn't have grown wider.

"If you mention anything, and I really do mean *anything*, of your unwelcome escapade within my home, I will personally eviscerate your entire family as you watch. And then, I will stand by as you feed their entrails to the trees. Or whatever else happens to get to them first. Do you understand?"

Shaw's warm skin had never looked so colorless. He nodded.

"Beautiful! Goodbye." With a dismissive wave, the mayor turned back to the patiently waiting healer.

Lux bolted to her feet. And then cried out against the pain it wreaked. Her knees buckled.

"Wait!" It came out much closer to a rasp than the shout she'd anticipated. Despite it, though, copper eyes sought her own. His lips parted. "Allow me to accompany him. I've to gather my things, make several arrangements. My business can't be so easily moved."

The mayor frowned. "I don't—"

"Riselda expects me."

Lux had moved to the center of the room, her hand fisted around the dagger at her back. The mayor studied her, searching.

He wasn't going to find anything.

"As you wish. My *last* favor to you." And louder, "Now, I'll kindly ask to be referred to as Magnanimous Mayor from this day henceforth." He laughed. The captain guffawed so loudly he choked. The healer smiled politely. Morana did not turn her scrutinizing gaze from Lux. "But mend that arm first. You're no good to me without the means to perform your skill."

Chapter Forty-Five

"You're alive."

"So are you."

The carriage continued on in silence once more. There was so much to say, Lux wasn't sure how to begin. A part of her remained in disbelief that her thrown together plan had even worked at all. That Shaw was beside her. Every dirty, tattered bit of him.

"How did you break bones this time?" His voice sounded less like his own now that they were alone, hoarse and broken.

As if he'd spent hours screaming.

She rolled the shoulder, sore but pain-free at last. The healer had examined it quickly, speaking in low tones all the while. Every muscle had gone slack in her body by the time he'd snapped the shoulder back into place.

She'd still screamed. And she'd cried out again after drinking the tonic he'd given her. One to mend the fracture hidden in the joint of her elbow.

I can't make it without pain. He had sounded almost sorry. Whether it was toward the agony he would inevitably cause her or toward his own shortcomings, she didn't know. What she had known was if Riselda had created it, she would have been whole without so much as a wince. Clearly, he dabbled in what he didn't understand, and his brilliance lay elsewhere. She had a feeling he knew it, too.

"Piercing a tree." She pulled the dagger into her lap, allowing morning light to caress its blade even as the coal-black wood of the handle absorbed all that remained. Shaw's eyes followed. "There's something strange about it. Branches don't break there. Leaves don't fall. But they do beneath this."

His fingers brushed across her hand and hers uncurled on instinct. He took the dagger, turning it over. "Has a tree ever been felled?"

"Of course n—"

An image. An axe, its handle coal black in Riselda's grip. And—maybe—an answer for a long-ago question:

What need for an axe could her aunt have had?

"I suppose I don't know," she finished.

He handed it back to her. "Why did he release me, Lux?"

She lied so often...but his eyes were on hers, and they weren't letting go. "Morana was kidnapped by the phantom. I levied her life with yours. And mine. I'm to move into the mayor's mansion."

One eyebrow raised. "Will you?"

"Never, of course." The dried blood on the torn cloth of his knee jostled as they traveled over cobblestones. "Shaw... What happened down there?" She steeled herself for his reply, unsure if she would be able to stomach it.

"They wanted answers. My accomplices, how I'd learned of the lifeblood stores, how I managed to get in to begin with... I wouldn't reveal anything, and so they resorted to their traditional methods of extracting them." He lifted his ruined shirt.

Bile rose in her throat. She sucked in a breath, so loud now in the heavy quiet. Her fingers quivered and still, she forced them to reach forward. To touch each bloodied bandage.

"The physician—" Her voice broke, and she cleared her burning throat. "The one that set my ankle. You have to go to him."

He lowered his shirt. "We'll see. I'm not particularly keen on him after listening to your screams."

"I refused his sedatives, and he did what needed to be done. If what they did to you didn't kill you, the infection that I'm sure is brewing in there will."

"What about Riselda?"

Lux swallowed. "Absolutely not."

THE CARRIAGE RIDE TO Shaw's home was some distance, made longer by the bustling bodies carousing in excitement for the Festival of Light. Lux woke, bleary-eyed and with her head nestled against the crook of Shaw's arm, her body flush against his.

Was this all it took? One sleepless night and a brief lull in conversation?

She pushed back, the blush in her cheeks transforming from one of sleep to deep mortification. She didn't want to, but she looked to Shaw anyway, ready to apologize.

A soft snore left his parted lips, his head laid back and turned toward her, eyes closed and relaxed in sleep. For the first time in many days, he appeared his age again, and Lux didn't feel the least bit ashamed as she watched him breathe. A soft smile pulled at her lips.

The carriage rolled to a stop.

Tawny eyes flicked open, narrowed and unfocused.

"You snore."

Shaw blinked his confusion away, glancing around the interior of the carriage with a furrowed brow. "I do not."

"I won't tell a soul."

He glowered at her until the door clicked beneath his fingers. "Are you coming in?"

"If you make me tea."

He huffed but gripped her hand, stepping down from the carriage.

Lux stumbled into him when he stilled at the alley's mouth. She choked on a breath when she realized why.

Shaw's door hung by one bent hinge; it threatened to give up its fight at any moment.

She knew how bad it would be.

For once, she begged to be wrong.

"Devil below," she breathed, feeding the fire flaring in her chest. But Shaw didn't hear her. He was already moving between the buildings, stepping through the doorway and into the narrow hall.

She came upon him as he knelt in the entryway, and Lux brought her fingers to her lips.

The paintings.

Please... Not his paintings.

They'd been mutilated, utterly destroyed. With precise strokes of a blade, the once-beautiful array of living color and light had fallen to shredded ribbons strewn about their feet, dangling from frames. The sight of them running through Shaw's fingers now made her eyes prick.

He stood, and without glancing toward her, continued into the kitchen.

The cupboards had been thrown wide, dishes pulled and tossed aside, food trampled across the floorboards, but her gaze landed and remained on a bird, painted in flight, shattered and unmoving upon the ground. Every teacup lay in ruin.

"What have you *done?*" Lux demanded of the mayor, his ears far away; if he weren't, he'd be dead. She picked up the bird, its edges biting into her fingertips, and Shaw returned from his bedroom.

"Tell me you still have the journal."

Flames leapt from his eyes.

They mirrored Lux's own.

"I have it."

He nodded, a curt jerk of his head. "This ends today."

"Shaw—"

He cut her off with a downward slash of his hand. "I won't live beneath the weight of his threats against me. Against my family. Against you. This ends *today.*"

"I only meant to agree with you, you know."

"You—" He paused, eyes clearing. "Right. Then I need to go to my family. Make sure they know I'm alive and discuss a plan from there. Will you meet me?"

She nodded.

"And you won't do anything reckless in the meantime?"

Chapter Forty-Six

WHEN THE 'YES' HAD left her lips, she'd meant it. Though now, as she stood outside the door to her home, she wasn't sure it hadn't, in fact, been a lie.

Lux gripped the handle, pulling it wide, and stepped inside.

It was a good day for the festival. Rare sunlight shone unobstructed through the windows and poured in at Lux's back. She let the door close, slow and noiseless, and with a fortifying breath, descended the stairs.

The first thing she noticed were the gloves.

She'd lost them. They had disappeared in the darkness. Abandoned in the shadow of a cottage, deep within the wood.

Now they were clean, dry, and laid upon the table side by side. They were meant as a warning. Or a threat. She brushed her fingers across them. *No.* They were meant as a test.

Riselda floated around the corner.

"Good morning, darling. You're late." Her face was off. It pulled tight in odd places while slackening in others, her eyes lit too bright. Riselda's smile tightened at Lux's perusal, feral and begging for her to say something. Thirsted for it.

She tipped her head, and long, slender fingers tapped against the table's surface. "What were you saying, Lucena?"

"I didn't say anything, Riselda." A thin sheen of sweat broke over Lux's body, and with a heavy stone coming to rest in the pit of her stomach, she swallowed.

The cackling laugh wasn't the deep, melodic one she'd become accustomed to. It was different. The high laugh of something, *someone*, else.

It was true, then.

"I know you didn't. I only expected you to. Some explanation, surely, for disregarding my advice and thwarting my plan of seeing you safe." Lux's hand fisted around the glove nearest her. "Yours?"

Lux studied those eyes for much too long. Every muscle quivered, pulled taut. "Yes. Did you find them?"

"Yes." And Riselda smiled, her teeth glistening. "How is Morana?"

"She'll live."

Riselda tutted. "I suspected it was you." Abruptly, Lux needed to sit down. She pulled out a stool. It screeched, and Riselda glared at her. "Your gasp as I struck that worthless girl gave it away."

Lux sneered. "And yet you still tried to kill me in the tunnels?"

"So dramatic. I only wanted to frighten you off. Of course, then you blinded me. What the devil was that contraption?"

"I don't know. I wasn't even sure what it would do when I activated it."

Riselda laughed. "I enjoy your honesty. It's a lovely change from that secretive little attitude." Pulling out a chair herself, she sat upon the stool opposite. "So, you've saved the mayor's daughter in exchange for your own life, was it?"

Lux been honest enough. "Something like that."

"I wasn't going to kill her, Lucena. I only wanted to make her experience all you had. Fear, darkness, hopelessness. A bruise upon her cheek." Riselda reached toward her, and Lux drew back. "Though, without lifeblood, she would have died in the forest eventually. Goodness, you should have heard her in the solarium, prattling on about her wastrel of a husband to the help. A solarium I solicited! None of it would have been so brilliant without my touch. Such a waste."

"When was this?"

"Last evening. When I happened to deposit a little tonic for sleep in her spiced chocolate. Her grief had been so *overwhelming*, after all." She winked.

It made Lux's insides boil. "Morana tells me you both have a long history. That you grew up together even. Does such a life-long acquaintance deserve your treatment, *Aunt?*"

Riselda blinked.

"I know Morana has lived long past her natural lifetime. Her family is selfish, scheming, and sordid, and so it didn't shock me to learn they harvested the lifeblood of Ghadra's poor as well. Very few would stoop to such an abomination. But you were there. A child as Morana once was." Lux gripped the dagger hidden against her waist. "Who are you, Riselda? Because you're certainly no family of mine."

The words hurt more than she thought they would. She was alone again.

"I'm your aunt. We *are* family."

Lux laughed, hollow and cold. "You're mad."

Riselda's face darkened. "Do *not* call me that." Her fingers twitched against the tabletop, as if they yearned for something between them. "I love you like my own daughter, Lucena. You're powerful and strong, and you hate this world as much as I do. I knew it from the moment I found you, wide-eyed with excitement in the Dark Market, that you would be different. And when your parents begged for my tutelage—you, a possible healer like me—it solidified our future."

"What future?" Lux wiped clammy palms down her skirt, the page of the book crumpling further within.

"To destroy the mayor. To devastate his family. And to devour this cursed city's walls to dust." Riselda leaned in, and Lux fought the panic. She didn't want to be in the presence of the demented gleam in Riselda's eyes any longer, but she felt frozen to the chair. "Your parents were so weak, you know. Not like us. Your mother idolized me from a young age herself, and I let it continue. Admiration, remember? She called me her sister as a child, to anyone who would listen to her incessant chatter, but it wasn't until she mooned over your father that I truly lost interest in her. She was too compulsive with her emotions. She *loved* everyone and everything. Unfortunately, I noticed those traits beginning to surface in you as well." Riselda's wolfish grin blinded. "And *that*, I could fix."

The wave of dizziness nearly sent Lux sliding to the floor. Riselda watched her closely, her head cocked and waiting.

"You killed them." Each word felt like a branding iron in her throat.

It wasn't a question. And Riselda didn't answer it as if it were.

"You were born to the Dark. Did you know that? Your early childhood was filled with crumbling walls and moth-eaten rugs. I gifted them the home you knew. The fools. They didn't even recognize the trap door for what it was. You should have seen your mother's face when I appeared that evening. *You've returned!*" Riselda rolled her eyes in memory. "She was blind to the true nature of the world, Lucena, and she wouldn't be convinced of what hid in wait. I'm sorry to have taken your parents from you, but it was necessary. It was the only way to show you that Ghadra does not care for you. The world does not care for you. Only I do, and I will never betray you."

Lux rose from her stool. "You have betrayed me beyond measure, Riselda."

The blade slipped between the bones of her chest like marsh clay.

Several silent seconds went by with Riselda perched there, mouth gaping in shock, hands encircling the embedded ebony handle. Lux drew away from the table. "I admired you once. I even loved you, long ago. But I am nothing like you. I may have darkness in my soul, but you have become eclipsed by yours. It is all you are."

Riselda pulled the dagger free, and it clattered to the floor, fallen from limp fingers. Blood pumped down the bodice of her dress, spreading across her skirt. When she made to stand, she collapsed, instead.

Lux turned away then frowned as an empty vial rolled past her feet, a drop of silver falling from its end as it came to rest.

"*No—*"

The blow to the back of her head thrust her into oblivion.

Chapter Forty-Seven

Grey walls shimmered and *shook as Lucena walked along the corridor.*

"Mama? Papa?" Her voice quivered. Knowing. Already, the feeling had taken root.

Curling vines pulsed up the walls, soiling the blue and gold flowers to black, and she staggered.

The bodies rested side by side upon the sofa with heads lolled forward. One dark. One light. Both stained crimson.

Lucena rushed forward, her slippers sliding in the puddle having formed upon the floor, soaking into the cushions, into the gold-tasseled rug. It splattered her sunshine-yellow dress. It had splattered the walls long before that.

She shook her father first, but when his head fell back, revealing the gaping wound, she screamed. Her mother's was a replica of his.

Lucena stumbled away.

She emptied her belly onto the floor.

The walls pressed upon her, vibrating in her vision even as she ran.

Into her bedroom, she gathered them all to her: The Risen, vials, decanters, and jars. Her hands trembled, and she nearly dropped them all.

Hovering over the lone clean space of the living room rug that remained, Lucena flung over page after page until she came to the Rise enchantment. She laid it upon the floor. She didn't know if they'd been dead long, but she didn't care. She'd enough for more than one try.

Their cold bodies were dragged to her, the mixture painted on, its ingredients measured precisely. She chanted the incantation—felt it take from her and give to them.

And she felt it fail in her very soul. Over and over, again and again.

Lucena's voice was raw, her body spent. But she swallowed her fear. She closed her eyes.

"Saints above, devil below. Allow me to know."

With the final remains, she let instinct guide her fingers. She sifted the wyvern claw. She stirred three times clockwise. She dipped the bat wings, sprinkled the moth powder, and stirred counterclockwise.

"Lucena, my love."

"Darling, we've missed you."

Lucena released a sob, hugging her parents tight. Their hands gripped her shoulders. Their fingertips dug into the fabric. Their nails punctured her skin.

She fell backward.

"Don't be frightened, my dear. It is only us."

Her parents rose. The walls rippled around them, their eyes murky and grey and clouded with shadow. This wasn't how it should be.

Her father bent, retrieving the small knife she'd used to cut through blood-dried clothing. Her mother smiled, her dimple deepening just as it used to.

"Shh, Lucena. Don't cry."

"It won't hurt."

The point pierced her skin at the same moment the broken vial sliced into her father's wrist. Blood spurted across her hand, and the knife clattered to the floor.

His teeth bared at her, Lucena didn't recognize him any longer. Her father wasn't here.

Her mother shoved her down, and the tacky moisture coating the floor seeped through her skirt.

"Close your eyes, Lucena."

She did.

And pierced her mother's heart.

"Pleasant dreams?"

Lux pushed onto her elbows in the now-familiar cottage, and the chain jangled. She felt for the lump that must be at the back of her head but found nothing.

"I applied a salve. And dropped a bit of tonic in your mouth as you slept. My apologies for the injury." Riselda smoothed back sweat-soaked strands from Lux's forehead, as gentle as a mother.

"Don't touch me," Lux growled.

"*You* stabbed *me*, if you'll kindly remember."

"Yes, and you conveniently had lifeblood on your person."

"I'm never without it, Lucena. Here, comb your hair. We must be magnificent for the festival tonight." Riselda tossed a brush onto her lap.

Lux stared down at it, at the fabric beneath it. She'd been washed and dressed in the sage gown.

Maybe it was the blow to the head. Maybe that was why she couldn't seem to understand what was happening. But what she did know was she couldn't lose control a second time. So, she brushed her hair and studied her chained ankle peeking from the silk skirt with a heart as heavy as it'd ever been.

When Riselda emerged again, it was in a resplendent indigo gown, the exact shade of her eyes. "Let me style it for you, my dear."

Lux's voice came out smoother than expected. "Do you mean for us to enjoy the party this evening, Riselda?"

The reply snaked around from her back. "We certainly will. The rest of Ghadra? I think not."

That maniacal laughter again. It sent a shiver up her spine.

Lux played into it. "What do you have in store for them?"

Riselda's face suddenly appeared before her, and Lux jolted. "Who gave you that dagger, Lucena?"

"I purchased it from a peddler." *True enough.*

Glittering eyes narrowed for a moment before Riselda spun. The cabinet along the far wall opened with the softest creak, and Lux gasped.

The shelves were filled to bursting. Hundreds of vials stoppered and shimmering silver.

Riselda gripped an axe from the topmost shelf, and she pulled forth Lux's blade from the bodice of her dress. She tossed them onto the bed. A matching set.

"These are mine. A very long time ago, I paid dearly for one axe, one dagger, and one seedling. I paid dearly for my plan of revenge. I've dreamt of this day for one hundred and fifty years." Her eyes rolled back into her skull as her body shuddered. "This dagger was stolen from me. So you can understand my interest in how it came to be in your possession. And thus, embedded in my chest." Riselda rubbed the smooth skin, pale and exposed, below her throat.

One hundred and fifty years. Lux pressed her eyes closed. "How old are you, Riselda?"

"Nearly two hundred I suppose." She pulled at a loose tendril of ebony hair having fallen over a flawless cheek.

"And whose face do you wear?"

Riselda scoffed, her words rushed and offended. "You think I would resort to prying off a cadaver's lips when I've my own methods? I am not the Tamishes with their uncivilized ways."

"But then—"

"Gracious me. Lucena, all you must learn to do is read what is in front of you and adjust your rhetoric accordingly. Most believe whatever you tell them, should you say it well enough."

Lux rubbed at the space above her heart. Staring down at the axe and knife, she felt sure she lived a nightmare. But her eyes were unable to stray from the cabinet for long. "Whose lifeblood is that?"

"Oh, I thought that'd be quite obvious. Perhaps I hit you too hard... Though you can't fault me, really. Your attack was unexpected." She reached back to run careful fingers across the rows. "These are the victims of my plague, of course."

Chapter Forty-Eight

Riselda unstopped a tiny vial of thickened, gold liquid. She inhaled, filling her lungs with a smile. "Ahh. Jasmine is one of my favorite scents." She held it from her.

The chain clanked loudly against the floor as Lux scrambled away. "Don't bring that stuff near me!"

"Relax. You'll ruin your disposition, and I don't have all the ingredients here to clear it. This requires more than just a sniff or touch of your fingertips to activate the disease." She replaced the stopper all the same. "My last vial. But it looks like it will go unused. Same for the rat. Though I suppose the howlers won't mind its unleashing."

"And here I thought they were some sort of pet."

Riselda laughed. Truer to herself, low and melodic. "Hardly. They ingest the vial's contents, I speak a carefully crafted incantation over it, and then release them into the streets. More so the alleys, if you're truly interested. From there, nature's way carries it on." A drawn pause. Riselda must have sensed her confusion. "Fleas, darling. They love rats. And they love the filthy beds of Ghadra's poor just as well."

"It's blood-borne?"

"At first. The boils, as I've told you, shouldn't be touched either."

"You harvested their lifeblood in the clearing. Before the trees claimed them." Lux spoke more to herself than Riselda as her mind whirled with what lengths this woman had gone to.

"Indeed. You've been spying on my whereabouts for some time, haven't you? I shouldn't be surprised." Riselda smiled, affectionately, despite the chain currently leading from Lux's ankle and Lux having nearly killed her hours ago. She sighed, content. "I'm sincerely delighted I don't have to argue with that doddering, old alchemist any longer. One well-placed knock to the head, and poof! Dead. Are you ready? We won't want to disappoint. The main act simply wouldn't be the same."

Lux rubbed her temples, still unsure whether any of this was reality. "And why is that?"

"Let me show you."

Beyond the cottage, the trunks of the trees were black as midnight, looming and petrifying in what they were capable of. Riselda caressed the bark, greeting an old friend, and it shuddered, its branches curling inward in welcome. It didn't wrap invisible claws upon her wrist. It didn't yawn wide, threatening to consume her.

"I was still very young when I transplanted that first seedling from my solarium. Can you believe Ghadra once had endless grasslands where this forest grew? It rose up quickly, that first tree, feeding off the buried dead and towering above the town within a year. And in another, a mate joined it. Well over a century later, and..." Riselda removed her hand, twirling in a slow circle, her face upturned. She paused, staring down her nose at Lux. "My sanctuary. I'm afraid they've become a little unhappy with me, though." She drew a vial from the masses contained in the satchel at her side. "They yearn for this. And I've been withholding it. Have you noticed that the more discontent a soul is, the louder it shouts? Soon, my darlings. Soon."

Crooning, Riselda stroked the black trunk again.

"You're responsible for the wood? Riselda, how could you?"

"I'm growing tired of your judgement! Do you not realize how much the mayor values beauty? Pretty people, pretty things. It's almost as much as he values power. You have both. I had both too. And when he forced me into a role I did not want nor understand, I *swore* I would be his end. Luckily for us both, I've endless patience, and tonight it will all come to fruition. Ghadra isn't simply dying, Lucena. Ghadra is already dead." Riselda unstopped the vial. "When the trees are content, they glow silver. Unfortunately for the mayor, and unfortunately for his dreadful town," the vial tipped, "this forest glows black."

Lifeblood splashed onto its surface, the shimmering substance stark against a dark backdrop. Then it melted away, revealing an inky festering wound, tendrils of grey twining forth. Lux felt sure her heart ceased to beat—until the soiled hand clawed forth.

She screamed, slipping in her haste to back away from the dirtied fingers, extending now out to the wrist, beckoning her forward. Her ankle caught, the chain held firm and clanking loudly as it pulled against the identical manacle around Riselda's.

Riselda didn't appear to notice, instead reaching with her own fingertips to brush those held within the belly of the tree. "It works. I can hardly believe it." She turned eyes giddy with excitement onto Lux's. "Did you know lifeblood can revive the dead, Necromancer? It is your opposite. You cannot revive those that have been drained." She stepped around the grotesque trunk and the hand trembling violently within, to unstop another vial with her teeth. "And lifeblood cannot revive those who have not. Every black trunk of this forest holds unanchored bodies." She emptied the vial's contents. "Now it's time to set them free."

THE SATCHEL WAS EMPTY. It'd been tossed onto the forest floor. And Lux and Riselda walked from the wood toward Ghadra's walls.

"Come, come dear ones! What you seek awaits!" Riselda's sing-song voice was followed by a high laugh, deranged and terrifying, and Lux shivered.

Blackened fingers had crawled forth from every trunk they met as they wandered through the heat-wrenching forest. Hundreds. It had taken hours. And though she hadn't witnessed more than dirtied hands and wrists emerge, she had once seen what happened when the twisted soul was freed.

Riselda's practice upon the crow was enough of an answer. Enough to fuse together the bits and pieces of the plan that she'd laid before Lux.

The revived would descend upon Ghadra, warped and hungry, and she was powerless to stop it. She hated the woman at her side and the chain at her ankle. She hated the carriage that waited outside their door, prepared to transport them to the Festival of Light and the unsuspecting victims. She hated that Shaw and his family were counted among them.

But what could she do? She'd already attempted to reason with Riselda in the wood, and when that had proven useless, to wrestle the collection of lifeblood from her grip. All it earned her was another thwack to the back of her head, leaving her dizzy and sick for long afterward. Riselda had threatened to knock her completely unconscious the next time. Lux knew she'd do it too and drag her body along for whatever length of time it took her to finish the job. Nothing, it seemed, would be allowed to thwart her plans.

She had met Riselda's smiling gaze and watched her undo the clasp at her throat, sending her grey cloak fluttering to the dew-soaked grass beneath them. She watched her square her shoulders and breathe deeply. She was so sure. Of her victory. Of Ghadra's collapse, the mayor's demise, and Lux at her side. For eternity.

Maybe Riselda hadn't always been a monster. But she was now.

Unfortunately for her, Lux was too.

"What will you do, Riselda, after the town falls?"

Her brow furrowed at the question. "When the mayor stole the knowledge of lifeblood and its harvest, how it could bring a body back from the brink of death, and sold that first crop to the outside world, I was furious. It was *my* knowledge. Gifted to *me*. And it is mine to wield." She looped her arm through Lux's, pulling her close as the carriage door opened. "We are going to travel all of Malgorm, my dear. Maybe even beyond. The Necromancer and the Healer.

You will revive the dead, and I will heal those nearly so. The secrets of lifeblood will never be uttered. They will die with our mayor. And the substance itself will never pass the lips of another, save you and me." She settled into the seat opposite, eyes glittering bright amongst the darkness.

"We will be the most powerful of this world."

"But first, the mayor will die?"

"Yes, the mayor will die."

Lux matched her, grin for grin. "Perfect."

And the manacles clattered to the floor.

Chapter Forty-Nine

The Light Market had swollen to bursting. Torches were lit, paper lanterns were hung and swinging above the square, and already, bodies swayed with drink. People sang, people laughed, and Ghadra had no idea what descended from the forest to destroy them.

The carriage rolled to a stop, and Riselda climbed down first, followed by Lux. Her green gown just brushed over the cobblestones, its edges only slightly marred from the lengthy hike through the forest. She glanced over the congregated mass and shoved the hopelessness down deep where it couldn't be reached. A subtle hint of too-old eggs wafted beneath the scent of food, drink and perfumes.

There were so many. Even if she could warn them, would they listen?

Riselda grasped her hand in an icy grip. "This way, Lucena. The stage awaits."

"The stage?" Lux pulled away her fingers. "What are you going to have me do?"

"What you do best. A demonstration of your brilliance. And I will do the same. The perfect distraction."

Except the perfect distraction had already woven through the crowd as they spoke. Purple shadows stained the space beneath his eyes, but even if Shaw wasn't yet healthy, he was at least whole. His brow furrowed as he neared them, sharp and suspicious. If Lux hadn't known him, she would have thought him furious. She did know him, however. Quite well by now, and she wondered how much he had already guessed by the concern darkening his face.

"Lux. Riselda." He nodded to them both as he stepped in their path.

Riselda's smile begged to transform into something else. "Ah, the young man who not only survived the plague, but the prison. How...convenient." She turned her severe smile upon Lux.

"It's nice to see you again. Is your family here?" Lux kept her face smooth of emotion. *Please, say no.*

"Yes. Enjoying the vendors. Have you been here long?"

She shook her head. "We just arrived. And I think the celebration will be over quickly for us."

Shaw's gaze narrowed further at the same moment Riselda latched onto her wrist. "Yes, so we must be going. Enjoy the festival."

Riselda didn't relax her grip until the stage rose up before them at the edge of the square. "What do you think you're doing?"

For the second time, Lux extracted herself. "I've done nothing."

"Your friend may possess all the survival instincts of a cockroach, but he will not survive this. No one will. I had thought you'd accepted that and embraced our future. Have you, Lucena? Have you embraced what you're meant to become?"

What Lux longed to embrace was a black-handled blade again. "Yes, Riselda. Ghadra is dead."

"Good girl." She patted her cheek. "Now take the stage."

But before she could, the mayor appeared instead, pushing aside thick, velvet curtains until he stood at the center, vying for the attention of the town. One by one, the masses turned toward him, with those too slow to do so helped along by the Shield.

"To the beautiful and fine townsfolk of Ghadra, I ask you, are you enjoying another flawless Festival of Light?" The most illustriously dressed clapped the loudest. The mayor's grin broadened, his face flushed. "Excellent, and you're welcome." He laughed, swallowing a healthy sip of wine. "Now, the time has arrived for the main event of the evening! Once upon a time, I discovered—and refined—two of the most powerful manipulators of the fates. One that can breathe health back into another so near death they've glimpsed the afterlife, and another who can drag a soul from beyond the veil to walk amongst the living once more. Thanks to my governance, together, they can cheat the cloaked beast known as Death. Ghadra's Healer and Ghadra's Necromancer!"

The shove at the small of her back propelled her up the steps and onto the stage.

Lux stared across the jumble of bodies, one as unrecognizable from the last. Painted and glittered, their faces upturned, they measured her, and they whispered. Her jaw clenched. *What is this game of Riselda's?*

"Thank you, Mayor Tamish. Both for another prosperous year and another spectacular celebration." Riselda pitched her rich voice, smooth and intoxicating, and Lux imagined the mayor melting into a wine-soaked puddle at her side.

He spoke instead from an ornate, high-backed chair, both gaudy and ridiculous. He rested into it like a throne upon a dais. She could just glimpse Morana behind him. "The pleasure is all my mine, my pets."

Those slurred words were for them, and them alone. Lux's fury rose, and she spun away from him lest she do something regrettable. "Fool."

Riselda pinched her arm.

"Citizens of Ghadra," Riselda's voice had lowered, eerie and mysterious, and bodies bent forward. "Fate would have you believe Death is inevitable. Death is permanent. But Death? While it may indeed be an unforgiving end, *we* and we *alone* can change the fates." Ice shot up Lux's arm as long fingers twined within hers. "Behold!"

Riselda threw her head back, her eyes upturned to the somber night sky. And for Lux's ears alone, she whispered, "Speak the enchantment with me."

"Back from death we beckon—"

Lux joined in a beat too late, catching over the words in her confusion. Riselda's grip tightened, and the words flowed over her in response, her instincts picking up where her mind could not. This was pointless, it would do nothing, and yet she spoke to them, and watched the people press closer, lapping it up hungrily.

"—a guide between life and fate. Mend what has been broken. Time. Mortality. Through the veil between realms, shall you follow this road. May your eyes become mine until you return home. Time of death, death in time—"

"Donte!" The name was a scream of disbelief over the crowd.

"Finish it." Riselda dug nails into her arm. Lux kept speaking, searching for the cause of the scream and the man responsible.

"From untimely death, we bid you Rise."

Another shout. "Masha! It can't be!"

"My Persephone!" This girl Lux could see, standing at the edge of the crowd in a tattered dress and dirtied fingers. She swayed on the tips of her toes, her eyes focused on the woman who'd cried out. Then, the girl smiled.

The ecstatic woman pitched forward, tripping in her haste to reach her long-dead daughter. She gripped her hands, brushed back her hair, and then her gaze sought Lux's. "You've brought her back to me."

The quiet words reverberated through the crowd, and the silence erupted.

"What have you done, Riselda." It wasn't a question, and panic rose in Lux's chest, a cold sweat breaking across her skin.

"The purge has begun." Riselda turned too-bright eyes to the mayor. "Welcome back your people, Bartleby."

The mayor's enjoyment over the crowd's delight in his choice of entertainment faded to confusion. He rose.

"Colden!" Morana's shriek was louder than any other. With a sweep of fuchsia skirts, she plummeted from the stage to the handsome man converging upon the market square. He wore a torn black suit, shredded bits hanging from his arms as he opened them wide.

She fell into them in a heap of tears.

"Is this some sort of trickery? His lifeblood was removed!" The mayor descended on Lux. She didn't pay him any mind, too focused now on the throng of once-dead bodies entering the Light Market.

"Yes, it was. I took it from him, and I put it back." Riselda shrugged, her grin unnaturally wide.

The mayor blubbered and blustered, for his words had abandoned him. Until finally, "But it has been too long."

The maniacal laugh jolted the few people still pressed close to the stage. "Precisely."

"Papa!"

Lux choked, her lungs frozen masses in her chest and incapable of movement. *Aline*. She recognized her voice as a man, an aged version of his son, entered the festival edge. He knelt, a crooked smile on his lips. The clouded eyes shown even in the dark.

"ALINE!"

"Lucena!" Riselda snapped from her power-mad daze. "Be—"

But Lux was already running. She jumped from the stage, jabbing into kidneys of those who didn't move quickly enough and sweeping ankles from those who wouldn't move at all.

"*Murderer.*"

Lux's heart skipped in recognition, and she twisted toward the voice, but the light of the lanterns proved untrustworthy. Any of the bodies around her could have whispered it, and yet...

"You don't see me? You didn't see me then, either." She glided around a collection of skirts: Ned's abandoned lover. Her formerly drab dress lay in rags against her skin, and as Lux replayed how angry her soul had been then, she didn't want to encounter it revived. Not like this. "How about now?"

"I see you fine. But if you don't mind, I'm needed elsewhere."

The woman cackled. "I don't think so." She withdrew a slender stick, no longer hidden behind her back, its tip sharp and glinting. "I found this. Probably some child's toy, but I think it'll do nicely, don't you?"

Much faster than anticipated, her hand shot forward, the metal tip leaving a bloodied gash along Lux's forearm.

Lux seethed. "I don't have time for this," she growled, finally catching the interest of those nearest them.

"How familiar. Little wench." The woman lashed out again.

But Lux expected it this time. When she pivoted, the ragged woman flew past her, unbalanced. Lux pushed further into the crowd, muttering all the while.

Of all people.

The flare of hot pain slicing down her back nearly sent her to her knees. To the right of Lux, a flamboyantly dressed woman bearing witness to the injury screamed. Though, instead of offering any sort of assistance, she whirled on her heels to flee the violence.

Lux reached for her, wrenching a hairpin free. It was sturdy, silver, with a pretty pearl decorating its end, and the woman cried out again, gripping wildly at her head, sure she was at risk for suffering a fate as terrible as Lux's own.

"Thank you!" Lux called out, a mere moment before she whirled, burying it in the eye of the assailant at her back.

Ned's lover tottered, her fingers twitching as if she longed to tear it away—that pearl encompassing her vision. When she fell backward, the masses collapsed with her, and they tumbled over one another in horror, their chaotic screams echoing against brick and mortar.

The bauble was a doll's eye, staring fixedly at the night sky. Stolen silver leaked from its edges. Lux spun before she could be tempted to feel any sort of emotion. The crowd parted easily for her now.

"Aline! Get away from him!"

Lux could just glimpse her: a sunshine-yellow dress, peppered with blood, and a knife protruding from her chest. She blinked again, and the image vanished.

In its stead, Aline knelt along with her father, tears streaming down her cheeks and dripping onto her violet skirt. She hadn't heard her. Or she'd ignored her.

"I've missed you so much."

"Me too, sweetheart, me too." His voice was honey-deep, like Shaw's. He cupped her cheek.

"What's wrong with your eyes, Papa?"

"Nothing, darling. I can see all."

Aline shrieked when Lux hauled her backward, only to quiet when she recognized who held her. "You brought him back to us. Thank you, Lux. Thank you."

"I didn't bring him back. He belongs to the trees. Don't go near him, Aline." Her throat ached with her screams.

"Come here, sweetheart."

Aline ripped from her grip, fresh tears pooling in her eyes. "How could you be so cruel?" She turned back to her father, watched him rise and prepare for her embrace, and she stepped forward.

The gut-wrenching scream tearing through the square didn't come from Aline. Quite the opposite, it came from a broad man who looked unnervingly similar to the one now standing above him. Brothers. Twins, even.

"Donte…" Blood bubbled from the corner of the man's mouth, a shard of glass buried deep in his neck.

"Thank you, Brother." Donte removed the shard with a spurt of crimson and sliced into the dead man's eyes. The crowd wailed, the bravest running now in every direction, but many—too many—still fell into the arms of those they had lost, oblivious.

The warped version of Donte cupped his hands beneath the trickle of silver liquid, and when it slowed to a drip, he drank. It dribbled down his chin as his head snapped up, and Lux grabbed for Aline again.

"Did...did he..." Aline paled. She sagged against Lux.

"We have to get out of here."

The girl's weight left her, suddenly swept up and into Shaw's arms. "I've got her. What's happening, Lux? Tell me quick." His eyes swept over the body, now lying in a pool of blood just feet away. The unanchored soul had fled, his brother disappearing along with it.

But Lux didn't get the chance to explain.

Shaw's father stepped beneath the glow of the lanterns suspended high above the market. The one who'd sacrificed all for him. Gone in his place.

"*Father...*"

"Son."

Lux gripped a fistful of Shaw's shirt. "Please, don't. His eyes. Look at his eyes." She cursed her lack of weapon, sure that even if Shaw and Aline hated her forever, she would kill their father to spare them.

Another scream ricocheted through the festival. Another life taken.

Shaw did as she bid, and his face paled, matching that of his sister. "Who revived him?"

His father dragged his hands from his pockets, fingers flexing.

"Riselda. She's responsible for the plague. She's been extracting lifeblood from the dead, bringing them back from the trees. All of Ghadra is meant to die tonight." Lux watched his father's hands clench and remained there. "They want more, Shaw. He craves lifeblood, and that is all he wants now."

Aline cried softly into Shaw's shirt, apparently still conscious. He shifted her weight in his arms, and with eyes glistening with unshed tears, he took one more step toward the aged image of himself. "I'm sorry, Father. For letting you take my place, for all you endured for me. Please forgive me."

"All will be well, Son. You can repay me easily enough."

Lux's kick to his knee sent him to the ground as he lunged toward his children, and when Shaw leapt out of the way, the barely held tears released, tracking down his cheek.

"I can't kill him," he breathed.

Lux's heart constricted, for she had thought the same thing, once. "If it's you or him—"

"No, Colden, please!"

Lux dragged her eyes from the man struggling up from the cobblestones to the one holding a blade to Morana's exposed flesh. But she was far away. Too far away to reach in time. Lux scanned around her feet. A stone, just small enough to rest comfortably in the palm of her hand. She scooped it up.

The rock flew true, striking Colden in the temple, sending him staggering back. But Morana, instead of fleeing, rushed to his aid.

"What are you doing, you imbecile!" Lux shouted.

A glint of murky-grey eyes swiveled toward her voice, recognition lighting his face, and with a smile, Colden drove the knife home. Morana screamed in agony, gripping her side with both hands as she fell away from him. Red droplets spilled over her fingertips.

Lux could see Shaw's father moving toward his children again from the corner of her eye. Same as she could see Colden striding toward her now with a feral grin. He hadn't even taken the time to drain Morana. Not yet. Lux searched frantically for another lucky stone but found none.

"Lux! We need to—"

"Leave me! Get Aline out of the market!"

She couldn't even spare Shaw a glance.

"Necromancer. Did you miss me?"

She planted her feet against Colden's height. "As one misses a parasite or a once-removed, prominent mole."

"I've missed you." He glanced down to his hand, momentarily confused by the lack of knife there.

Lux kicked him in the gut. He stumbled back from it and his mouth fell wide, parted in shock. Though, to be fair, Lux's did too.

Colden's hands encircled the blade protruding from his chest, his fingers cut and slipping against the point. Without another sound, he collapsed face-forward onto the stones, the knife buried to the hilt in his back.

Lux waited another moment to ensure he wasn't about to move again and sweep her legs from under her. When she glanced up, it was to find Morana, chest heaving and eyes bright.

"That bastard tried to kill me." Blood continued to trickle from the wound in her side, but it appeared to be slowing. She did a once-over of Lux before bending down and extracting the blade. "Are they all like this?"

Lux nodded, acutely aware of Shaw and Aline's absence. And that of their father. "All with eyes like his."

"That *witch*." Morana tossed the blade to her opposite hand and signed a cross with its dripping end. "Off to return the next to the afterlife, then." She swept away without waiting for any reply.

Lux pushed the loosened waves from her eyes, standing on her toes to view the stage. The Shield, the mayor, and Riselda—they were gone. The square's revelers were rapidly following suit, leaving more fresh blood than Lux wished to see in a lifetime.

He's fine. Death won't long for him again so soon. He is fine.

Except he wasn't. He was hurt and probably sick and hunted by a monster.

She forced herself to calm and think rationally. If she stood here much longer, she'd become just another source of lifeblood. She needed to move, but to where?

Where would most seek sanctuary from such an evil?

Lux smiled as she spun, dashing down the nearest alley. It was far from humorous. So many of the Light weren't greeted by those lost because they hadn't lost anyone in such a gruesome way. They were the first to abandon the market, and there was only one place they would turn to for refuge.

The mansion.

Chapter Fifty

Night cloaked Lux the moment she left the Light Market's many lanterns behind. Random shouts and muffled sobs seeped from alcoves and behind shadowed corners, and every few feet another dark outline materialized only to fade again. Ghadra had fallen into chaos.

She kept tight against the buildings' frames, not wanting to meet anyone lest they turn to her with clouded eyes and an insatiable hunger. Friends and loved ones were the most trusting targets, but that didn't mean Lux wasn't an easy one. Alone and weaponless, she was acutely aware of that fact.

She hurried down an open street, a cut-off shriek jolting her into a run. The revived could be killed like any other living being, marking the mansion as the safest place in the entire town with its large stone walls, unscalable wrought-iron gate, and the Shield. She would go there, demand admittance, and then demand the Shield be threatened into action. This was their *purpose*. So far, they'd done nothing.

The dark brick beneath her fingers gave way to smooth stone now, no longer crumbling but well-made and well-kept. The townhomes' few windows were high but large and impossible to reach. The doors were heavy with iron bars defending their length. How Shaw had managed any success in his thievery flew further beyond her comprehension.

Then again, he'd accomplished breaking into the mansion just fine.

At last, there it loomed, the darkest she'd ever seen it. The lampposts had been extinguished, leaving moonlight to highlight the pointed peaks that rose

"

to reach it, and it made the hairs stand on her arms and neck. Especially while listening to the wails of those trying unsuccessfully to breach the walls.

Lux crouched, eyeing the people pooling at the gate.

"Open the gate!"

"Help us! Save us!"

A young man scaled partway up a vine-covered pillar before crashing down to the stones with a shattering crack. He moaned once, only to have a ragged girl descend from the shadows. He didn't move again, and the shouts at the gate quickly transformed to horrified screams as the lifeblood trailed down her chin.

Lux stood, watching the girl braid long strands of dirtied hair back from her face. She was pretty with generous curves, full lips and wide eyes. But those lips were stained silver now, and those eyes were warped and unnatural. She grinned as another figure appeared from the street opposite.

The moon caught the deep blue of Riselda's skirts, and she smiled back at the girl even as Lux's dagger twirled in her hand. When the revived decided to take her chances against it, it was with one quick movement of Riselda's wrist that she fell to the cobblestones clutching a spurting throat.

Riselda wiped the blade clean against the body's ruined dress. Pulling forth an iron key from her bodice, she stepped over the widening circle of crimson to fit it into the gate. It turned easily, and the iron gave way without a sound beneath her fingers.

Lux moved from her hidden vantage.

"You have your own key? Or did you steal it?"

Riselda chuckled. It barely reached Lux's ears. "Of course, I have a key." Glancing over her shoulder, Riselda studied her. "Are you unhurt? It was foolish of you to bolt into the fray. The revived don't care who you are, and they don't care who I am either. You could be dead."

Lux gave the bloodied stones a wide berth, pausing at the gate. "I could be. Thanks to you."

Riselda's eyes narrowed. "Who is Aline?"

Lux ignored her. She had a feeling Riselda already planned to ensure Shaw's death, effectively severing all her ties to Ghadra. She didn't need to add Aline's to her list. "You created a plague, you murdered Colden, you kidnapped Morana, you released tortured souls upon the town. What is the next phase of your plan now, Riselda?"

Riselda tutted, spinning on her heel toward the mansion. "I harvested Colden's lifeblood; I didn't kill him. Sure, I deposited some very potent powder where he would inevitably find it, but he had his own will. As for my plan? The mayor has stowed himself away within his fortress, bolting at the first cry of death. If he won't come out...I will come in."

"What of the Shield?"

Riselda turned to stare off into the darkened city at their back. "Why do you think I've left the gate open?"

"COWARD." RISELDA LAUGHED, HIGH and amused. She shoved against the unlocked doors again. And again, they didn't give. "I can only imagine what he's found to bar them with. A family fortune's worth of heirlooms, no doubt. Come along, Lucena."

Riselda descended the steps.

"Where are you going?"

"You'd have your answer if you would simply follow me." She paused, glancing about. "A secret entrance."

They followed a winding gravel path across the dampened grounds. When the so-named secret entrance appeared before them, Lux scoffed. "The servants' entry?" The archway stood between two manicured hedges, the door hidden even from the moon.

"Mock away, my dear, but there are few things the mayor pays less mind to than the help. He won't have thought to bar this." She hauled at the ring bolted to its front. "Leave it open, won't you?"

Against every instinct, Lux indeed left it open, slipping after Riselda through the dark corridor until a low-burning fire greeted them, flickering from the grate of the kitchen. It was empty, most of the servants having left come nightfall to spend a few minutes at the festival before crawling into their beds. The remaining few were probably huddled in their allotted quarters too frightened to leave.

A sudden shuffle from the gloom of the opened doorway sent a shiver across Lux's skin.

"Wonderful. They've found it. This way." Riselda discovered the narrow steps leading upward with ease. When they branched off, she chose the center route. "To the ballroom," she answered Lux's unasked question.

The subsequent door didn't latch, swinging back and forth with the lightest pressure. Riselda swayed through, holding it wide for her to follow. "Ah, here we are. He's allowed in more than I expected."

Lux stood beside her within the inconspicuous alcove, regarding the richly dressed bodies currently sobbing and whispering and gesturing in anger. Many were drinking cider and wine beneath the dimmed lamplight, escalating emotions while simultaneously dulling the senses.

Half the ballroom had become filled with them—those from the Light. Lux scanned every face. Shaw wasn't among them.

The mayor swallowed the remains of his goblet with shaking fingers. The maroon of his jacket hid the drops spilled. He hovered amongst his favorites, pretending all was as it should be. "The Shield will protect us," he said.

The entirety of the Shield lined the room, several posted before each window and many stationed behind the towering front doors. Lux surveyed the pile of furniture stacked against it. No wonder it hadn't budged a fraction.

A creak on the steps echoed up from far below. Lux twitched. "Riselda—"

"Good evening, Mayor." Riselda stepped from the darkness.

The goblet landed with a ringing clatter and rolled away. "Riselda. How did you find me?" The mayor backed behind a wide man who'd gone pale.

"I will always find you." She cackled and the large man fainted, exposing the mayor in his entirety.

"Stay away from me, witch! You should have never returned; Malgorm has tainted you. I don't know what you've done, but with all these people as my witness, you'll die for it!" With the spittle having settled, and a snap of his fingers, the Shield moved in.

"Die? We will see who dies tonight." Scraping escaped the alcove at their backs. "We. Will. See." A woman with a cone of badly dyed hair shrieked first, though the others followed soon after. "Goodness," Riselda said. "How did they get in?"

Dirt and rags gave way to smiling faces and bared teeth. The poor of Ghadra, revived and thirsty, stepped into the ballroom after having followed the trail laid out for them. One after another, they lined the length. Riselda looped her arm through Lux's, pulling her close.

"Those of the Dark, behold your illustrious mayor in all his finery." Riselda gestured wide. "The entire lot of them have taken from you your right to prosper, leaving you crumbs instead." She clicked her tongue. "Despicable."

Lux wasn't paying attention to Riselda's anger-stoking speech. Instead, she searched for Shaw's father amongst the revived. She didn't find him.

When the gaunt woman Lux recognized as the Dark Market's purveyor of bat wings swung the fire iron she'd claimed from below stairs, the mayor blubbered. "Don't do this. What do you want, Riselda? What do you *want*?"

"Freedom—"

"You have it!"

"—and revenge."

The color abandoned his face, his red eyes meeting hers. "I've apologized."

"You apologized to a girl, long ago. Do you recognize her in me? Because I do not."

The mayor bolted.

And giant windows splintered, glass raining in. Dark and Light alike crouched against the onslaught, screams and cries reverberating against the high walls. Though, it wasn't until black branches wound through the gaping remains that true madness ensued.

"Riselda! What is this?" Lux staggered back from the snaking darkness slithering across the ceiling.

But Riselda had gone grey. "I don't know."

The whisper chilled Lux's blood until it trickled, slow as ice, in her veins. Never, in all her time of knowing Riselda, had she heard her sound *afraid*.

"Help!" The large man had woken from his fear-induced slumber only to have been caught up by a twisting branch gripping him about his middle. There wasn't anything invisible about the trees' embrace this time as the black limb squeezed harder, setting his eyes to bulging. "Help...me..."

His wheezing breaths were the last anyone heard before he was dragged from the wounded wall.

"Saints above, devil below... What have you *done*?"

But Riselda could only shake her head at Lux's question. "How are the trees *here*?"

She didn't seek an answer. Not from Lux anyway.

Lucenaaa.

Another scrabbling body was caught up only to be hauled through the shattered panes.

We have been cheated, Lucena.

Lux grabbed the black-handled dagger from a dumbstruck Riselda.

We do not forgive. We will take them all.

More glass splintered down the halls and in the foyer. Running would save no one, and yet they all tried. When the mayor's ankles were wrenched from beneath him, his shriek pierced Lux's ears.

"Necromancer! Morana! Riselda! Lucenaaa!" His fingers sought an invisible handhold. He slid across the floor, drawn toward the darkness beyond.

It wasn't a tree that held him as he thought, but a man. And not one of the revived, but of the Mayor's own elite. "Sweet, sweet revenge. Can you taste it, Mayor? Oh, I can."

The mayor cried aloud, "Oswald? A misunderstanding!" The man gritted his teeth against the mayor's flailing limbs. "She was willing! I swear it!"

"I—don't—care. She was promised—to—me!" With a last grunt of effort, he hauled the mayor upright, his arm encircling his throat.

Lux didn't move. Not a thought of saving the mayor entered her mind, though when Morana stood up amongst the melee, bloodied and angry, she wondered if she should attempt to warn this Oswald instead. Lux was fairly sure the drying red splotches adorning the expansive gown weren't all Morana's own.

The furious jab of a knife to the shoulder was all the encouragement the mayor's captor needed to release his grip. The mayor dropped like a stone, panting like a worn-out dog upon the tiles and clutching his sore neck as Morana circled the dumbfounded man. Oswald's distraction with her drew his attention from the branches hovering above him, and when a black limb encircled his throat, he didn't even gasp as he disappeared from the mansion.

"*What are you doing here?*"

Lux glanced to Riselda as she spoke to the trees. Though whether they gave an answer, she didn't hear. Half of the occupants were gone now, either dead or taken, and Lux started to wonder of her own fate when Morana cried out with rage, hacking at the nearest swaying boughs with her blade as they reached for her. A pointless endeavor, and her legs were soon swept from beneath her.

"Father!"

But the mayor took one last look at his daughter from the wide ballroom doors, and then he was gone.

Chapter Fifty-One

With a final, heaving slash of the black-handled blade, Lux freed Morana. The thick branch encircling her thighs faded and fell, while what remained of it swayed as if in pain. Lux lurched to the side, unwillingly bowing to the mayor's daughter climbing up her body until she stood on her own two feet once more.

"Much appreciated, Necromancer."

Lux rolled her eyes, ducking to avoid another claimed body being hauled through the air. When she glanced up again, it was to see Riselda's back vanishing in the same direction as the mayor. She pushed Morana's hands from her shoulder, sprinting after her.

The hall had no windows, and the further she ran, the further she left the reach of the trees behind. There was a peculiar groaning coming from the rooftop, but she couldn't think on that now. Lux squinted against the dimness, the lamps having been extinguished long ago, but when the first leering bust of the mayor rose up from its pedestal to ogle her, she grinned as she raised her hand.

"Excuse me!"

Lux reeled at the voice, the shards of the mayor's likeness littering the carpet at her feet. "Morana?"

"Clearly. And should you vandalize any more of my father's property, I'll stab you."

"Not if I stab you first."

A huff reached her as Morana's figure deepened the shadows. "Are you following them?"

"I was..."

"Good, I'll go with you."

Lux pressed her lips together. To believe she'd once thought Shaw an unlikely ally...

Morana moved past her. "Are you coming? I'd rather not find my father murdered by your *aunt*."

The barb sunk deeper for the person casting it. "Your *father* appeared quite content to give you over to the trees. I'd rethink my loyalties if I were you." Lux expected the palm swinging toward her this time, and she blocked it. "I've no loyalties to Riselda any longer, in case you were curious."

"I was curious." Morana rubbed her stinging hand. "She must be stopped, you know."

"Yes, I know." When Lux walked past Morana, the mayor's daughter fell into step beside her. "I'm just not sure how yet."

Another lengthy pause came and went. They reached the hall's end, the fork greeting them.

"My father needs to be stopped, too."

Lux picked her jaw back from the floor.

"Don't gawk at me. I've lived a long, fulfilling life, and I won't say I regret drinking lifeblood because I don't, but the terror I felt while Riselda's captive wasn't like anything I've ever known. And my father did that, repeatedly, to the people of this city. Kidnapped them for little crimes to throw in his prison." She shook her head. "He's two hundred and twenty-seven this year. Perhaps it's time for him to change his ways."

Those years were too long. He would never change. In Lux's short years, even she'd learned that, and Morana would too, if she only dragged the veil from her eyes.

"Will you stop drinking it?"

Morana hesitated. "I have another vial. Hidden in my vanity, ready to be unstopped and drank on my birthday, the same as every year as is tradition in my family. It's why this face doesn't age in the slightest." She caressed her cheeks. "I've thought—if I make it out of this night alive that is—that I'd gift it to you."

They were outside the mayor's study now, and it was eerily quiet within. "No, thank you."

"Why? It's already been harvested. Long ago. And it'd be a waste to simply pour it out. Your brilliance should live on, at least for one more lifetime. You might not even need to change your face if you don't wish to. Not many notice you as is."

Lux tried the handle. Locked. Morana pulled a key from a hidden pocket and slid it home.

"Oh yes. My brilliance. The only part of me worth saving."

"I didn't mean it like that, Lux." Morana huffed in her ear, irritated, but Lux ignored her, pushing the door inward.

The sight of Riselda and the mayor seated in corresponding armchairs took her aback. She'd expected a bit more shouting and a lot more blood. Rather, all she could discern was the mayor, sniveling between hiccupped gasps, as his gold buttons popped from his finery one by one.

"Morana!"

At the mayor's shout, the gleaming letter opener stilled in Riselda's hand, ceasing her torment for a moment.

Morana sidled in before Lux. "Surprised to see me, Father?"

The mayor's blanched grip on the armchair released one finger at a time, his face flushed. "No. No, I knew you'd escape. You're so strong. I've always known that...like your mother."

Morana smirked, moving around the desk to claim the mayor's seat. The one he'd abandoned to better converse with Riselda. Or the one she'd threatened him into. Lux rather believed the latter, judging by the mayor's furtive expression. His nose was in desperate want of wiping.

"Please. I've known for a century you had her killed. For her." Morana glowered at Riselda resting into the chair.

The mayor didn't bother replying. Instead, his watery eyes darted from his daughter to Lux to Riselda and back again.

"Were we interrupting something important?" Lux remained by the door. She wanted an exit at her back. "Because we have a fairly big problem out there right now."

Riselda's face was hidden from her. "Which is precisely what we were discussing. Bartleby tends to run from his troubles."

"My troubles! You started this mess—the both of you!" He clutched at his ruined shirt, monitoring the letter opener's movement.

"Don't lump me in with her," Lux fired back. "The Rise incantation is a useless chant on its own. It's lifeblood that caused this. You and Riselda, and your obsession with it. And you need to fix it! Rally the Shield. Send them out to dispatch the revived."

The groaning from the rooftop shook the very bones of the mansion. For a brief moment they each silenced as upturned faces studied the ceiling.

Lux finished with a whisper. "You planted this abomination of a forest, Riselda. Speak to them."

"*What*?" Morana and the mayor's voices unified in equal incredulity and horror.

"They won't listen. They won't stop. No one is safe... I can't keep you safe." Riselda finally turned toward her, eyes heavy with sorrow. "I'm sorry, Lucena."

The mad gleam had gone, and Lux didn't recognize what remained.

"They won't stop until what exactly?"

Riselda rested her head back, gaze unfocused above her. "Until they've taken every soul."

The mayor's face darkened, puce with rage. "You *monster!* You've doomed us all!"

The word was directed at Riselda who cackled, but Lux flinched all the same. "We are all monsters in our own right, Mayor. A man who preys on the weak and innocent counted among the worst of them all."

Lux almost missed Morana's penetrating stare, rotating between the three people before her, finally allowing herself to conclude what she'd refused for a long time.

The mayor only bristled further. "You were never going to uphold your end of the bargain."

"I'd sooner rot, to be quite honest."

With a shout of rage, the mayor flung back his chair, stretching to his full height. "No. You'll *live*. You'll live *forever*. I'll dump lifeblood down your conniving throat and force you to perform again and again so that I never miss seeing the day the fight leaves your soul. It will be my greatest achievement."

When he dodged around Riselda, straight toward her, Lux lunged at the bookcase in want of a weapon, even if that weapon was paper. But the mayor never reached her. He didn't make it past Riselda's hand. With shocked eyes, he studied the ax buried in his side before he slumped to his knees.

"Riselda..."

A final heaving groan and the ceiling ripped from above their heads.

The night sky opened, the moon full and bright, its light touching every part of Lux. For a moment, all she did was breathe. Then the moon disappeared, eclipsed by a soaring canopy of black boughs twining inward.

Give us what was promised. Give us what is owed, Lucena.

Lux shot from the shattering glass at her back to dive beneath the desk. The lights had blown out, but even in the shadows, she glimpsed the mayor free the axe from his side—only to scream as he was caught up. When his body lifted from the floor, leaving a trail of red, all she felt was relief.

The scream abruptly cut off only for Morana's to take its place. Hers was one of grief; the tree hadn't yet reached her, and still it tore at Lux's ears. For a similar cry had left her own throat once.

She couldn't stay here, hiding in wait for her fate. With a staggering breath for courage, Lux climbed from beneath the desk, her face upturned in search of their assailant.

Except, the trunk of the tree had stilled. Its branches curling inward. Inward and out again. Lux shook her head in refusal, thinking she'd made a mistake and perhaps she should simply wait out the rest of her life beneath the expensive furniture. Until she caught sight of Riselda.

Standing, a dark and regal statue, she faced the tree. The smile on her face was serene. Her eyes were closed. The tree didn't beckon to Lux. It beckoned to *her*.

The silence pulsed along with her heartbeat, and the boughs wound forth. Riselda allowed her head to rest back, ebony hair trailing long. When the first branch wrapped around their caretaker, it was gentle in its touch.

Riselda's brow furrowed with the next, tight about her waist, and as the third crept around her chest, her eyes snapped open. Her head turned, and her gaze found Lux's.

"I'm sorry, Lucena. For the past. For the future." Her eyes fell closed as the branches constricted, dragging her upward. "Remember me. Remember this: a necromancer can revive more than the dead."

Lux caught a flash of a coal-black handle and a glint of steel clutched within a pale grasp before the tree opened and closed around the body of the woman she'd long believed to be family. All without a sound. Lux felt the warmth of another who'd not long ago, only ever sent a chill across her skin. Morana moved beside her. They watched together, the boughs stilling, the silver twining up its length until it outlined every vein in every leaf.

Content, it spoke no more.

Chapter Fifty-Two

Dawn neared, and still Lux ran.

Shaw's childhood home was empty. His apartment was not. She dodged around a glowing tree root tunneling through its side, a trunk now towering above the alley with leaves that gleamed in the first kiss of sunlight. Glimmering leaves glinted everywhere, in fact. They stretched above rooftops for as far as she could see. The wood had destroyed Ghadra's walls, ransacked their buildings, and claimed their homes. They had taken back the revived and many more along with them.

Lux hurried past the Dark Market, past a massive tree extending from its middle, an empty stand propped and broken against a looping root. A dried raccoon paw still dangled from it.

Her eyes stung. The silence weighed, heavy. Had anyone survived?

Her home neared, and with every step, her heart beat louder. When she rounded that final corner, she didn't immediately see the tree blocking her door, or the branch extended upward through each floor until it pushed through the apothecary's open window, the main support of the building now. Her mind could only comprehend one thing: a mussed head bent low on hunched shoulders, rocking a body as murmured cries broke the quiet.

Blonde tendrils fell across the arm beneath it to caress the cobblestones.

Lux stopped moving. She stopped thinking. She stopped feeling. And then all three things crashed over her at once, propelling her around the tree, diving into her destroyed home.

The stairs were crooked, jagged and broken, but she managed down them. The workroom. She had to reach the workroom.

But it didn't exist anymore.

The jars, the vials, the decanters. The table, the loyal plants. *The Risen*. An entire portion of her home, the one place she felt alive even while encased by death, had been reduced to broken brick and smashed stone.

Lux fisted a hand to her mouth, blocking the sob, and she staggered away.

She ran to her bedroom.

She wasn't thinking properly. It couldn't bring back the dead. Not a body with lifeblood pooling still within it, and certainly not in the way she wanted. But it didn't stop her from sprinting, from heaving against the overturned wardrobe, and from crying aloud at the shattered vial, silver oozing through the cracks of the floorboards.

What would she say?

What could she say?

Tears pooled in her eyes, and she hurtled back up the steps. When she swung the door this time it clattered apart from its hinges. Shaw looked up, his eyes filled with such tormented *loss*, Lux couldn't draw her next breath.

"She's dying."

Lux followed his gaze back to Aline, resting with closed lids and the barest of breaths. Shaw's hand clutched a wad of once-white cloth to the wound in her chest. Every breath stained it darker.

Hot drops fell from her own lashes then. But Aline wasn't dead. She wasn't—

"All those vials we stole! Are there any left?"

Shaw shook his head; his hair brushed Aline's forehead. "None. My mother saved nineteen lives poised to fall to the plague."

Fine. That's fine. She would think of something else. "Everything is destroyed, but we have time. Just hold onto her. I can scour homes, the markets. I can trap a howler again. If you can just give me time, I can—"

"Lux..."

"I can do it, Shaw! You brought her here for a reason, didn't you? It's what I was made for. Please, just—Aline! Do you hear me, you stubborn, daft girl? Don't leave us. Don't give in."

"He stabbed her. He buried a blade in her chest, and I did the same to him. A tree took him. I killed my own father." His shoulders heaved; he gathered his sister closer. "And now I'm going to lose her, too. It's too late, Lux."

"Twelve hours is a long time!"

"Not enough. Not enough when there's nothing of this town left. There's no one left."

Already, Lux had compiled an impossible-to-obtain list in her head of every ingredient she needed. She gripped Shaw's hand, the one holding pressure until his fingers blanched, and she gasped. It wasn't warm.

He wasn't *warm*.

Shaw's gaze found hers, and the devastation in their depths stretched, endless and bleak. A frost made up of despair. Was this how her touch felt to others? How she looked? Her soul recognized the darkness settling in the other. It wasn't like the mayor's, Morana or his Shield. This darkness was different, but no less cold. No less an abyss.

Lux yearned for the light. She couldn't let Shaw know that agony.

If only—

"Lux!"

Shaw turned as she did, blinking against the unusual sight of Morana running, hair a tangled mass and skirt hiked to her knees. She held tight to the wound at her side.

"Morana."

"A woman," she sucked in a breath, "came. Searching—for a—healer. There's no one—left. Here." Morana thrust a vial of lifeblood into Lux's hands. The very last. "Take it."

Lux's entire body shook, and she clutched it to her chest. Without wasting precious seconds on more questions, she dropped to her knees. She unstopped the vial with quivering fingers, only made steady by Shaw's cool palms wrapped around them in support.

Together, they poured every last drop down Aline's throat.

To Death, she said, *You cannot have her.*

"Come back, Aline," Shaw whispered against his sister's hair.

"Your house—"

Lux ignored Morana, unable to breathe and refusing to blink.

The lung-filling gasp that followed next forced Aline into Shaw's crushed embrace. "*Saints,*" he breathed, ragged with relief, and Lux almost collapsed then, in hearing it.

Aline's arms came around her brother's neck in return. Her small shoulders began to shake. "What happened?"

Shaw's muffled reply could hardly be heard. "I should have known better. I almost lost you."

Several moments passed that way, with Shaw and Aline murmuring to one another, and Lux scrunching her eyes closed, hands stacked over her mouth as she attempted to swallow her emotion away. She opened them to see Aline pull back, then push. She stood and glanced down her blood-soaked front, and her mouth gaped wide for a moment before clamping closed, her gaze raising tentatively to meet Lux's. "I'm sorry I didn't listen."

Lux swiped at her eyes and willed her chin to cease its quivering. "I'm sorry I couldn't stop it before it began."

"You saved my brother. I shouldn't expect you to defeat a devil in the same day, though it would have been nice to have this dress for longer."

Lux's welling tears dried in an instant and she snorted.

Aline's voice dropped to a loud whisper. "What did you do to *her*?"

"Your devoted mother begged me to save you, so I did." Morana glowered, straightening her skirt. "And now I regret it."

Aline's mouth fell open for a moment before she burst into laughter. "Honest people are my favorite. Don't worry, you're still the most beautiful, even with a crow's nest on your head."

Morana blushed with gratitude, patting her mass of hair. "Thank you for saying so."

Lux sought Shaw from behind Aline. When he made to stand at last, she reached out a hand to help him. He took it.

It chilled her to the bone.

"Where's my mother now?" Aline asked Morana.

"I gave her the keys to the prison. I've met a few people as I ran here, but if there's going to be any number of survivors, I assumed it'd be there."

"Would you mind taking me to her?" Aline worked through her tangled blonde tresses with her fingers.

Morana smiled. A true one that creased the corners of her eyes. "Yes. And I have just the thing for your hair."

"*Our* hair." Aline fell into step beside the former mayor's daughter. "Are you coming?" She glanced back, her eyes meeting her brother's and Lux's in turn.

"We will meet you there," he said.

Lux watched them go, and then she glanced up to Shaw. He gazed back at her, his eyes filled with a shadow thicker than any fog. "You can tell me."

He stared down at his hands, dried a dull red. He shook his head. "Does it ever get easier?"

Lux stared at them, too, and opted for the truth. "It's been nine years since I killed my parents. Nine years of feeling cold and dark—and choosing to stay there. Because I thought I deserved to be broken. But I met you. And you were horrible to me, all warm and glowing like the sun, and it woke something... Something I thought I would never get back. Still, it's like an ember trying to burn away a midnight. Maybe I'll finally find my light in another nine years..." Her voice trailed off, thinking on how even if it took another decade for that ember to finally catch, it was still infinitely better than where she'd been. She lifted her head. "It is easier, I think, from then until now. I can finally swallow when I think of them. But you can't embrace that place like I did."

His eyes bore into hers, the copper and gold as faded and bleak as the crumbled wall behind them. Soon, it would build to an unscalable fortress to block out the world. "I don't know how to stop it. It's as if I've closed my eyes and stared into the dark too long, and I can't bear it."

When he would have turned away, she gripped his fingers. "What do you feel, Shaw?"

"What do I—"

"From my touch."

His brow creased. "Your touch calms me...and also...doesn't. It makes my heart constrict a little less, even if I know it will return."

Lux frowned. His did the same to her, and yet, this wasn't *him*. "The first time I touched you—the living you, that is—you were so *warm*. Your skin nearly burned me. Every time. Nobody has felt like that. Not even my parents. Riselda was cold, the mayor's like ice." She was losing him, confusion creeping across his face. "You're not warm anymore. Don't you understand? And I think I'm not either. I don't think I've been since the night I murdered them. There's something *clawing* about this darkness in me. I can feel its edges, can sense it like the dead. Like *death*. I can—" She choked, stumbling back.

"What? What's the matter?"

"I cannot forget. But I've got to... Do you think...?" She ran her hands over her face.

"Saints above, Lux. You're scaring me."

She grabbed for his bloodied hand.

"Can you help me dig?"

WHEN THE LAST BIT of stone was hauled away and the last remnant of dust blown from the cover of *The Risen*, Lux settled onto the righted stool.

She knew every margin of the book: the instructions, incantations and ingredients. And she knew she didn't need it anymore. She possessed more confidence in her brilliance, and in herself, now more than ever.

Once upon a time, a returned Riselda had turned to a final page and smiled over what she found there. Lux bared that same page now. She knew what it was, or at least what it appeared to be: some pretty writings, the print large and flourishing. But she never wondered at it more. She'd not needed to. *Untether*, it said. It didn't have instruction or a detailed list of powders and venom. No lore about its becoming or illustrations to hint at its purpose. And yet...

"Give me your hands?"

Shaw leaned into the table beside her, willingly lacing his fingers with hers. "What's this?"

Her mother's voice: *Shine bright, Lucena.*

"Shh. I will pry these claws from us." Lux shut her eyes. "Saints above, devil below—"

Allow me to know, she pleaded. Then she fell within.

She'd glimpsed it before.

But never like this.

Gnarled branches greeted her. Fingers bent and rigid. Unmoving.

Her soul was not only withered but barred, encased in a rib cage of poison. And pulsing behind it—inside it—yearning for freedom: the faintest glow. Lux trembled, twitching in her seat, breathing only when Shaw's hands tightened their grip. Intertwined, overgrown: she didn't know how she could ever peel herself free from its grasp.

Then she shifted her focus.

She saw his.

And it was impenetrable. Nothing but perfect, horrific darkness.

"*No.* You *monstrous*, wicked—"

"Lux—"

"Be *quiet*," she snarled and dug her sharpened nails inside.

Shaw jolted, and she did, too, but what was a little discomfort, a little pain, compared to years of feeling a shell instead of your humanity?

At last, when her fingers could dig no deeper, Lux fluttered open her eyes and read the words aloud:

> *"The weight of past lives, heavy and cold,*
> *Anchors that drag, roots that grow bold.*
> *Have courage to bloom in the darkest of nights.*
> *Untether your chains.*
> *Reclaim your light."*

She let the words choose their own pace, and some sentences stretched while others rushed, and with every syllable leaving her lips, Lux felt their energy bolster her instead of take. Just as they cracked her core, expunged the darkness, and polished what remained. Tears fell from her lashes, splashing onto her skirt long before she'd finished, but she could see it, glaring and brilliant ahead.

Light.

Lux gasped as Shaw did. With his next breath, he dragged her to him. Amongst the rubble of her and Riselda's home, he stole her seat and gathered her into his lap, and when he did release her hands, it was to wrap his arms around her, his head lowering to her shoulder.

Lux's heart pounded so hard, she knew he must hear it. "Did it work? Have I given you your ember?"

"You have given me more than that, Necromancer. I feel..."

"Warm?" His skin was hot on hers, so blissfully familiar, she wanted to cocoon within it. She wrapped her arms around his neck, and he lifted his head to press his brow to hers.

"The pain is there, but the guilt... I'm not drowning any longer." She had siphoned the frigid shadows from his eyes, and what awaited her made the heat of his hands sear upward and into her cheeks. His fingers traced the path of her blush. Up her neck, until his knuckle pressed to her chin, lifting it. "How do you feel?"

Lux's lashes lowered, and she breathed deep. Even in the darkness of her destroyed home, beneath the eerie glow of the tree, she still felt the sunlight on her skin.

An enchantment for forgiveness...

An untethering.

A release.

Finally.

"I feel light."

Chapter Fifty-Three

When Lux entered the mansion alongside Shaw, it was to find it entirely changed. The prison had emptied. Survivors, bedraggled and gaunt, stood in stunned silence over the gold-leaf walls, carved columns, and the destroyed panes of glass crunching beneath their feet. They stepped around the winding branches, silver-run and unmoving, with expressions more akin to terror even after all they'd experienced from below ground.

For the forest had claimed Ghadra as its own.

A smile tugged at the corner of Lux's mouth, watching Morana scowl over the bowl placed in her hands, given to her by Shaw's mother with eyes yet red from her reunion with Aline. More and more food appeared from the hidden doorway, carried up from the kitchen. A veritable feast for those of the Dark, even prior to their unfair incarceration.

The familiar head of the Brewing Bog's barkeep ran hunched down the hall, preceded by a rolling barrel of cider, as the smooth hands of the doctor that had once set Lux's ankle inspected those who had formed a line before him, even when he himself looked as if he may collapse with fatigue.

There weren't many—those survivors of the havoc wreaked by the mayor—and Riselda—but those that had made it out greeted one another with relieved smiles and kind gestures. It was a new beginning.

Aline waved from afar, directing the placement of platters upon a newly righted table. Perhaps her brush with death hadn't fully settled over her, or perhaps she was simply more resilient than most, but when a young servant girl with braided tresses, bent toward her in confidence, Lux observed Aline's responding grin. She could still find joy amongst the freshness of her sorrow, and Lux was thankful there did not appear to be rules in grief.

Shaw scanned the ballroom, his eyes settling on the gaping hole of the ceiling. Partially obstructed, a curving bough reached out. "What are we going to do now?"

Lux followed his gaze, sunlight glinting off the silver veins of the leaves. "Rebuild?" Shaw's side-eye left her chuckling. "The trees are content. You shouldn't have to worry about them any longer."

He turned toward her fully now. "You? Not *we*?"

Lux hesitated, and Shaw's eyes lost a little of their luster. "I can't stay here." She fought against avoiding his severe stare. "The incantation worked, I'm sure of it—the pain is more a wave now than a maelstrom. But it didn't erase my yearning to see what else is out there." She gestured upward. Toward the clear sky. Had it ever looked like that?

Not in her lifetime.

Silence brewed between them, thick with what he held back. Then, "Where will you go?"

"Anywhere. Everywhere. Morana will know how to get through the marshes; I thought I could journey with a group of merchants for a time." Shaw's gaze refused to relinquish her; she didn't know how much more she could take. "Remember your landscapes? I want to *feel* them for real. I want to touch the bark of a red tree. I want to climb a rugged mountain. I want waves of ocean lapping across my feet. I want to see all of Malgorm, whether there's truth to the rumors or not." She breathed in deep, her eyes fluttering closed. "And I want to feel the sun...always."

When warmth enveloped her next, it came from strong arms encircling her waist to clasp at her back. Lux buried her face in Shaw's chest, inhaling his scent. Her fingers tangled in the fabric at his back.

His words were a tattered whisper against her temple.

"Then I want that for you, too."

LUX WIPED THE SWEAT threatening to drip into her eyes, her bedroom finally righted at last. She stepped over the stain upon the floorboards, the lifeblood spilt there now a permanent fixture of the house, to settle onto her bed. In her hands, she held the missing page of Shaw's journal.

The mayor's latest favorite has settled in nicely. A gifted healer, we are told. She is young, not much older than his daughter, but with penetrating eyes aged before her time. I think he underestimates this one, as there is something unusual at work behind the placid mask.

I do not enjoy her presence.

Lux flipped over the page.

The young healer grew attached to one of the hounds kept on the grounds. It followed her everywhere, and its loyalty clearly left that of the mayor. He was not pleased. She's an odd way with such creatures.

The Shield dispatched the animal, and the feral screams of the girl still haunt me. She dragged the dead body away. To where, I do not know.

Lux shuddered, imaginings of a child Riselda attempting in vain to revive an animal without the brilliance to do so.

That was all. All that had been torn from the original, and the thought of it caused her to pull the old journal toward her. She flipped to the final entry. She'd read it before and chalked it up to an old man's disjointed musings. But now—

The weather has changed much in my lifetime. Ghadra's fog is inevitable come twilight, but the sun: it hides now. The mayor once commissioned his study to be window-less—to keep out the light, and now rain and clouds greet me every morning. What will become of this town? It grows dreary and bleak.

The mayor's birthday is unnaturally cold for high summer, and—alike his family—his favorite doesn't seem to age any longer. I confiscated a dagger she'd abandoned in the garden. Unnatural women should not have weapons, and this blade is exceptionally strange.

Then:

I discovered it.
The key to it all is beyond the eyes.

Lux shut the cover, resting it in her lap. She glanced out the window. Not a single cloud had crossed the summer sky, and now twilight neared. Would today be documented as a lucky accident with tomorrow unfolding in grey skies and drizzling rain once more?

She left her room.

An endless expanse of black greeted her when she paused at the bridge. Moss drying—dying—beneath its first taste of sunlight. The wood was gone. Only a fraction remained as a soaring silver grove far away, and she knew an empty cottage sat within, never to be graced with the grey-cloaked phantom's presence again. Belatedly, she wondered at the whereabouts of the howlers and whether they would find a new forest, a new home.

Lux glanced back at Ghadra. At its shattered stone walls tumbling with silver-run roots. Trees rose from within and amongst buildings. They surrounded the entire city's expanse like its life force resided within, and it had. Now they slumbered. They didn't speak to her as the fog rippled in from the marshes, less thick and no longer impenetrable. Content.

She understood why Riselda could hear them; her brilliance irrevocably connected with Life, the souls that make up everything that grows and the world at her fingertips. But Lux was not so tied to Life as she was to Death and dark things. And the trees, while certainly living, began as dark things. There were enough similarities between her and Riselda's brilliances; Lux wondered if Riselda felt the darkness as she could, too. That difference between a soul's warmth and cold. Perhaps with practice, she could even determine its cause. Guilt was not the only source with clawed fingers.

A task for another time. Her parents rested within the grove. Knowing their souls had traveled to the tranquil Beyond, unable to be dragged back and forced within a body once more, made her sigh with an unfolding inner peace. She tugged the black-handled dagger from her waist, turning it over once before dark waves cascaded into scattered piles about her feet.

Lux tucked the blade back within her corset, shaking out her shoulder-length tresses. She ran her fingers through them, and the weight of the world dropped away upon reaching each severed end.

Once upon a time, she'd made a terrible mistake.

But it was not unforgivable.

Lux lifted her face, and she smiled into the silence.

CHAPTER FIFTY-FOUR

"An election? How intriguing." Lux laughed at Shaw's animated explanations over the new politics reshaping the town. She shouldered her pack.

"A massive adjustment is what it will be. A real mayor for once over a tyrant." He smiled down at her. "Hopefully we'll have all the bumps smoothed over by the time you return."

"You'll have to learn to compromise first. Both you and Morana." Lux winced over the idea. "I may need to stay away longer than I thought."

He cut her a sardonic look. "Wait here. I've got you something."

Lux stared after him as he made his way down the ruined hall of his apartment. And as she waited, she thought over their relationship. From the first moment she'd met him, alive and warm, glaring at her over an armful of clothing, to the night she'd given in to his demands and abandoned him to his death. And to this moment. Their goodbye.

Her eyes stung.

Shaw reappeared before her with a grin that faltered. "What's wrong?"

"Who will I argue with while I'm away?"

His gaze softened, his eyes delving into hers. "You've never struggled in that before. I'm sure you'll find another to take my place."

A tear blinked from her lashes. He brushed it away with the pad of his thumb. "It couldn't be the same. The idea of losing you, of being alone again..."

"Try and lose me, love. See how well you do." She couldn't reply. If she did, a sob would escape instead. "Here." A smooth frame pushed into her hands.

Lux gasped. She traced the miniature painting with a reverent touch, the crow soaring in flight across a cloudless sky. It was so blue, the sunshine so bright. It almost hurt her eyes in the best of ways. The wind beneath the bird's wings whipped outward to rustle her hair, and not for the first time she wondered:

What could he do with a book like mine?

If it existed, she was determined to discover it. Lux hugged his gift to her chest, small and square and ideal for her journey. More tears followed the first's path. "It's perfect."

Shaw leaned in, pressing a slow kiss to her brow. His next inhale drew deep from against her skin. Lux shut her eyes, trembling. It couldn't be healthy for her breaths to be so uneven. She curled against him, but as his lips left her, she knew it would be awful, an absolute travesty, really, to not do more.

With only that thought, she grabbed hold of his neck and brought her mouth to his.

No wine this time, no whispering wood, and certainly no fear of death marked this kiss. And she gave him everything. Everything she felt, all she wished for. There was a hook in her heart, pulling her away from Ghadra. But she couldn't deny that a second had driven itself just as deep, pulled just as tight. Maybe it pulled even more.

Please. Stay, his kiss begged, honey-sweet.

But she couldn't, and *oh,* how she felt like breaking.

"When do you leave?"

"Hours yet," she whispered, threadbare. "Why?"

His answer was to kiss her again, agonizingly slow and terribly unfair. Her balance tipped and he swept her up. One arm at her back, another beneath her knees.

She supposed the world could wait awhile more.

SHE LEFT GHADRA'S WALLS that day with a promise shared between Morana, Shaw and herself. The knowledge of lifeblood's use that night would never leave their lips. Morana swore another drop would never coat her tongue. Shaw swore he wouldn't take justice into his own hands again, and Lux swore, if she happened to come across the mysterious buyers of the mayor's blasphemous wares, she would destroy all in their possession.

The dead deserved peace. Ghadra deserved peace. And so did she.

She had walked through the Dark Market one last time, a handful of stalls filled with goods having reappeared once more. The rats had died out, the potion weakening their bodies from the moment it had entered them, and the plague vanished along with them. The crone had hacked at her, surviving the descent of the forest against all odds.

"You still have that dagger, girl?" she had asked.

"I do. It's proved more useful than I'd thought."

The old woman had cackled before turning her unseeing eyes onto her face. "You look different."

Lux faltered. "I—"

"Not so dark around the edges, or there—in the middle. You finally decided to let it go then? About time is all I got to say. Grief, now, that's inevitable. You take it, endure it, and keep looking ahead. It's that poisonous guilt that'll wither you away to dead inside. That, and wickedness. Nasty stuff—can't be giving in to that." She had puffed on her cigar, staring off over Lux's shoulder. "You're free to be a great necromancer now rather than settling for just a mediocre one." Her cough was loud and deep. "Now, not many know my stories because they don't care to ask, and I don't have the time to sit here flapping my jaws when I could be selling, but I'll tell you a little something if you want? Yes? Well, my family didn't always live in this city. They were traveling merchants. For generations, first. You want to know a little secret?"

Lux had moved toward her without realizing.

"If you think we're unique here, just you wait until you see what's out there." One blind eye had winked then. "A little soul-devouring forest is nothing."

The navigator's empty wagon offered the perfect perch from which to view the marshes as they faded into the background. As they gave way to meadows with bright flowers that Lux had only ever seen crop up bravely once or twice in her lifetime. She leaned back, closing her eyes, smelling their sweet scent, and relishing the sunlight kissing her skin.

Her black boots crossed at the ankles, and her black skirt spread across the wagon bed. It gave way to a black corset with a wicked knife, and only the sunshine-yellow fabric beneath, soft against her skin, shimmered, new.

She would return. Someday. As she was sure she left a piece of her heart tethered behind. But as a butterfly, the first she'd ever seen outside of a book, flitted onto her palm, she opened her eyes and smiled.

The world awaited her first.

EPILOGUE

Shaw Roser didn't believe in ghosts, and he didn't believe in curses. But he did believe the devil existed, and that it currently rotted within the belly of a silver-run tree. Every twilight, he trekked to the mayor's mansion, walked through the wrought-iron gate, across the manicured grounds and through the rose garden. This day was no different.

The stone walls of the great house were nearly impossible to see. Trees grew together so closely, there were portions not even a rat could scurry through. He stepped over roots, brushed aside branches, and all the while his hand palmed the handle of a blade, tucked at his side. It didn't feel the same as his own. If he did choose to believe a curse, he would think this dagger carried one; it cast a sensation of wrongness through him wherever it brushed his skin. But she'd given it to him for safekeeping—though whether it was to keep him safe or keep the blade itself safe was unclear.

He came upon twin trees then. They were larger than any of the others, with overarching boughs so thick and high that they brought night upon him. He pushed the cap further from his brow—as the autumn rain could not reach him here—and frowned. The trunks were of a similar size, their leaves abundant and oil-slick, their roots gnarled and humped, but where both had glowed silver the twilight prior, only one did tonight.

Nobody knew for certain which one contained Bartleby Tamish and which consumed the conniving Riselda, but she'd told him in no uncertain terms that of all the trees laying waste to the mansion that night, it was these two that had desecrated the mayor's study and exacted their revenge. And so it was these two he ensured remained whole and unbothered, as he would risk nothing when it came to the devils being devoured within.

Twenty-seven days he'd come and verified all was as it should be. Tonight—four weeks to the day since the one whom made his heart feel like it was the only organ he should pay any mind to left him—things were *not*. Shaw stalked nearer, his boots light on the grass, his steps maneuvering around any blackened root. He didn't know what could cause a tree to become no longer contented with its meal, but he wasn't about to become its second.

He pulled the dagger free, careful and sure, and drew up short.

His teeth clenched, his grip tightening until he thought he might snap the blade he held. He began at the base and scanned his way higher, absorbing every layered cut.

A godforsaken *axe*.

The cuts were vertical, the trunk split, but without any source of light, he couldn't see for certain. Couldn't see for certain if those marks were made from the outside—or in.

A flutter caught at the edge of his vision, and he twisted to better view his shoulder. To the slick, black leaf rested there, curled at its edges.

He raised his chin and watched the rest fall.

Acknowledgements

It still doesn't feel real that a literal dream has become a book, and that book is now shared with the world. Cue the happy tears.

Thank you, Dad, for reading to us. Thank you for letting me read every Harry Potter book aloud to you in return. Through you, I gained by infinite love of all things fantasy, my obsession for LOTR, and the courage to finally make this childhood dream a reality. In exchange, I'll gift you a signed copy. I know, I know—just what you wanted!

To my mom: thank you for never turning down a bookstore trip. To my husband: thank you for never questioning said bookstore trips. I promise they've served a purpose other than fueling my love of reading and decorating my shelves—they've inspired and motivated me to get to this point.

To my sisters: thank you for being the people you are and believing in me from the start. To my early readers, my BCC girls: your encouragement is everything. It's been a long time since you read that first manuscript and look where we are now!

And finally, the biggest thank you to my readers! If you've picked up *Untethered*, I hope you enjoyed it. Your support makes all of this possible, and I am endlessly grateful.

ABOUT THE AUTHOR

GLORIA BOTTELMAN IS A fantasy writer and registered nurse. While living in the Midwest (and dreaming of the PNW), she spends her time trying to make sense of her many book ideas and walking in the woods—usually at the same time.

Untethered is Gloria's debut novel.

Connect with her at http://www.gloriabottelman.com or scan the QR code below!